BLACK CHERRY

BLACK CHERRY

Henrietta D. Elmore-Smith

ARCHWAY
PUBLISHING

Archway Publishing books may be ordered through booksellers or by contacting:

Archway Publishing
1663 Liberty Drive
Bloomington, IN 47403
www.archwaypublishing.com
1 (888) 242-5904

ISBN: 978-1-4808-2939-8 (sc)
ISBN: 978-1-4808-2940-4 (e)

Library of Congress Control Number: 2016904747

Print information available on the last page.

Archway Publishing rev. date: 04/15/2016

Friendship denotes love, loyalty, commitment, allegiance, trust, support, respect, admiration, dedication, poise, and patience.

....

This story was written for my cluster of friends.

Montages (1)

As they lay side by side he said, "Obviously there is no end to what we have. I care too much; so, is our love-secret inevitable?"

Once again, Mashé (Ma-shay) Boston had dozed off briefly until she was awakened by the subtle and salty spray of the seashore. For the past few days she has perched herself on her back terrace, reflecting on various lingering thoughts, and recently she has been having these reoccurring dreams of Chandler. Living alone is new to her, and Lou, her dog, whom she named after an old boyfriend, is somewhere around. After she feels fully awake, she checks the time, and it is a quarter past eight in the morning.

She rises and goes to her treasure chest, as she calls it, and once again, with a mix of high emotions, pulls out one of her favorite photo albums containing a precious collage of some colorful events of her past.

Routinely she opens it and gently smiles as her eyes rest fondly upon the first picture of the three of them. They were around seven years old though she recounts that Rhial (Ree-all) Curry was the oldest so she might have been eight. Theirs was a steady friendship intertwined with devotion, trust, promises, secrets, and fire.

It was summertime, 1979, and Mashé's family moved into their first new home. Her parents were high school art teachers. They liked Berkeley Hills, California;

so few Blacks lived there at the time and being from Kershaw, South Carolina, made Mashé feel unique. Eila Tulier Wynston lived across the street and how befitting her name—Miss Personality—so talkative and seemingly unafraid.

As Mashé focuses more on the picture, she notices that the background features the front of her house.

As close as they were, Eila usually went her own way. Mashé remembers on many a Saturday afternoon them telling their parents (Eila and her mother lived with her Aunt Lennie) they were going to spend the day at the library and it usually ended up just Mashé and Rhial and then upon their leaving for home Eila would show up with a glib explanation.

Rhial was the cheery and unassuming one and Mashé's nature was more or less virtuous. Usually ahead of their classes, Rhial wanted to be an executive, Mashé wanted to be a poet and a painter, and Eila always changed around—first, a lawyer, and then a New York dress designer or talk show host.

In high school, there were those contested moments, especially with the boys. Eila would cunningly try to sway whoever liked Mashé her way. Perplexing incidents, upside-down tiffs, and intermittent sought-after attention for notoriety; no matter what the case, there was this mysterious origin to them being "thick as thieves." They called themselves "The Best Girls." As she surveys other pictures, Mashé keenly recalls an amusing moment when they decided to go to the store after school. They were in the tenth grade and it was a Friday. This was a day they dressed alike. As they walked in, they spread out looking for snacks. Rhial usually went for the frozen push-ups, Mashé liked the sandwich cookies, and Eila wanted the cherry crème soda. At the counter was an elderly Asian woman; usually a younger man was there, perhaps her grandson. She spoke with a strong accent and sometimes it was difficult to understand her. Still, this was an opportunity for them to mimic her accent so when she asked what sounded like, "Will that be all?" They responded with a similar sounding accent and then they began speaking in a quasi-language as if they were foreigners too. They began to draw attention from customers who found them fascinating and more or less convincing. About ninety-nine percent of the patrons were Black and sometimes they would join in. On the serious side, they wondered why there were not more merchants on the block that looked like them. They would bring observations like this and others back to their families and were often told that Blacks and other people of color had different ventures or "When you grow up you can set an example."

As her eyes wander through each page, she comes to a photograph that recaps an experience never to wane.

It was 1989 and raining hard on a school day; in fact, it was the first day of senior week. Mashé was Senior Class President and she and her officers had planned the events for the entire week. Rhial was in the band, where she played the clarinet, and Eila was in the Senior Actors Society. Mashé brought the entire senior class to the auditorium, about 650 of them, and everyone was stirred. Mashé came to the podium to make a few announcements and Lou, her then beau, was backstage coordinating for the seniors' musical. Just as she was about to speak she felt a tap on her shoulder from behind.

Eila had gotten two other girls, Monette and Kedra, to dress up like the Supremes of Motown. It was a huge wonder where they got those "bouffant wigs." They wore neon colored windowpane stockings and matching short sequinned dresses. They were a sight. The next thing Mashé knew the soundtrack to "Baby Love" began and Eila asked her to announce them. All in all one had to admit they were good, their moves were on point, but they were not on the program. What Mashé had planned was the scenes with Theseus, Hermia, and Helena from Act One of Shakespeare's *A Midsummer Night's Dream*; immediately to follow was to be the entire cast singing the theme song, "Remember My Name," from the classic hit movie *Fame*, which would have included Eila. Mashé had orchestrated everything and somehow Lou was influenced by Eila to throw in this Supremes act and they had people dancing in the aisles—ultimately this was how Lou became her ex-boyfriend.

Eila's flair for spontaneity had gradually been wearing on Mashé over the years, but thinking back on it now she throws her head back and laughs.

The first turning point for "The Best Girls" was their early college years. All three managed to be accepted into the University of Miami; they longed to leave California in order to grow up. Mashé majored in English Literature with a minor in Art; Rhial chose Liberal Arts; and Eila did a double major, Pre-Law and Communications. They lived on campus in the same dormitory but in separate rooms. With the climate being relatively similar to California, they felt contented, except for those seasonal tropical storms.

There was this one night Mashé was in her dorm room preparing an illustrative essay for prose comparisons of William Shakespeare and Alexandre Dumas. She had been bolted down for nearly a day and a half with wide-ranging thoughts and without rest; eventually she managed to capture a heightened rhythm of theories and concepts. Her writing was beginning to flow fluidly from page to page when there was this sudden pounding at her door. It was way after midnight. She cautiously approached the door, asking who was there.

Eila: Mashé, it is me, let me in? Hurry!

Mashé, with her door ajar, questioned what the matter was.

Eila: I cannot let them find out I missed curfew again.

Mashé: (Stressed) Okay, then tell me because I have a lot of work going on here.

Eila: Yes,…I need to get busy with mine but last weekend I met this darling, he was at the Spring Party, and he asked me out. I think you missed him; that is right, you took off early.

Mashé: (Flustered, she motions Eila to leave) At this time of night you will not be noticed because the "sweep" has been done already.

Eila: Are you turning me away?!

Mashé: You made it sound like you were in danger, too much melodrama for me, Girl!

Eila: (Stumped) Mashé, we are like sisters.

Mashé: If you like, I will write you a note.

Eila was stunned and stood there for a few seconds stifled, which had to be a first.

Eila: Mashé, I would have your back—what is happening?

Mashé: Eila, you will he fine—but if you stand out here much longer, you will definitely draw attention to yourself.

Eila left in a huff and avoided any contact with Mashé for several weeks. This concerned Rhial, so she elected to be the mediator for them.

Customarily they celebrated their birthdays and this particular incident happened just before Rhial's birthday, which fell in December. Mashé's was in June and Eila's was in September. So obviously, the last birthday celebrated was Eila's. Rhial thought of her upcoming birthday as a way to reconcile their traditional threesome. For several weeks Rhial had to see Eila separately from Mashé and vice versa; it was quite taxing on her nerves and normally she was considered the docile one but she called Mashé when finals were about to start.

Rhial: Mashé, it is me. Are you real busy? I wanted to come up and talk about our situation. Oh yes, Mashé, it is my situation too! I really do not know what brought this all about but I want it to stop! And to be honest, you are more approachable. Good. I am on my way.

Mashé was surprised by Rhial's tone and had decided a few days earlier to contact Eila and end their rift, though she decided to let Rhial "speak her mind."

Rhial walked into her dorm practically pleading with Mashé to call Eila and apologize for whatever happened.

Mashé: (Defensive) It was not my fault…

Rhial: It does not matter whose fault it was. Tell me, was it over a guy?!

Mashé: Why did you cut me off? I was considering calling her and telling her that we should forget what happened and move on, but I would really like to know what you would have done. Mashé shared the main highlights of what took place that maniacal evening while impressed with Rhial's intuition on asking was a guy involved. Rhial said that it was Eila's nature to be impulsive and even though they have their own quirks, Eila "takes the cake." There was a bit of a lull, then afterwards Rhial gradually came to Mashé's defense.

Rhial: You know, I do see your point…but she obviously was not found out so "no harm no foul."

Mashé: She has always had this instinctive entitlement about her and seriously, why, should I tolerate it any longer? If I remember correctly, she has been written-up twice; and as you know the third time, the Manager can decide her fate and she could "get the boot."

Rhial: So since you plan on calling her anyway are you ready to do it now?

Mashé: Well, after talking with you it just occurred to me, why didn't she come to you first? Your floor is one flight below hers.

Rhial: (Ponders) She…probably felt I had gone to bed; it was after midnight like you said.

Mashé: No, Rhial, there is something to this. Why would she risk coming up four extra floors to my room?

Rhial: (Pausing) W…Why take this apart piece by piece? C'mon call her, my birthday celebration's coming up.

Mashé: (With levity) Right…I will call her later this evening, and stay calm, your birthday isn't until next month.

Later that evening Mashé did reach out to Eila. They both sat and talked in Elia's dorm room revisiting the incident and Eila admitted that she might have been "slightly inconsiderate" but she felt since they were friends, Mashé should have been more sympathetic, and she stressed this repeatedly. With her virtually endless rambling Mashé wondered was her friend a borderline neurotic. She asked Eila why she came to her instead of Rhial. Taken by surprise—her eyes looking away—Eila finally said it must have been her adrenaline in control, then paused and confessed, "Rhial is not you."

For Rhial's nineteenth birthday they celebrated at Julian's house. A senior and Florida native who boasted, "My parents conveniently work at night," Julian put it all together for Rhial. He was fairly nice looking though his key trait was his buff frame, and he had been a part of their social circle since the beginning. Rhial was hugging her girls repeatedly. Mashé, so amused by this, said she was glad it was a frivolous squabble. She found herself breaking away for something to drink. As she approached the punchbowl, she heard Eila yelp. She had just received a tempting message and excused herself from the party to meet her newfound friend. Rhial asked what friend but she scurried out the door without telling.

Rhial and Mashé were very disappointed with Eila's abrupt exit.

Rhial: It must have been that new guy; she could have invited him.

Mashé: (Impish) I could call her and find out.

Rhial: She'll be annoyed if you do that.

Mashé: Oh…so she cannot be annoyed. She takes off with little explanation. You are doing it again, giving her a pass.

Rhial: Well, did she talk about him when she barged in on you that night?

Mashé: She tried but I was not interested then. For some reason I believe she wants to keep him secluded from us. This is so like her.

Mashé remembers that Eila called shortly thereafter to say she would catch up with them later on but she did not. She also remembers Rhial taking it better than she expected and both concluding that he must not be a Miami Hurricane.

Everyone at the party pulled them back in so Rhial could blow out her candles.

For a time Mashé felt that the likelihood of finding romance on campus was virtually limited until on one fine Sunday afternoon near fraternity row she was trying to start her car. She had been with her study group and they wanted to break for lunch but she decided to return to her dorm. She was so irritated and she remembered leaving her roadside assistance card behind when she heard this melodic, alluring masculine voice resonate. He asked whether a beautiful woman could use his assistance. Her eyes glanced over and she intently noticed his mouth; it was an exquisite mouth and as she observed him longer she hoped the car would never start up. He had an even-toned light brown complexion and his glowing eyes momentarily constrained her from speaking. Slowly she collected herself and said this had never happened before. He gestured that she should be riding a bike like everyone else. He offered her free auto-mechanic services and then he added, provided they share a meal later in the evening, which would "make his heart sing."

While thinking back on it, just looking at him and listening to him had almost given her an orgasm; she heard someone mention this to be so—that a mere visual of an appealing person can make you…anyway she thought it unbelievable until the instant they met.

She had stepped out from that prude image which many considered her signature; since they met on a Sunday, Sundays would be their day because he attended school in Tampa, a four-hour drive away. On a couple of those Sundays, she drove to visit with him. His name was Chandler Tollare, and he was in his last year at the Law School at the University of Tampa. He also had a twin brother named Alton who was an officer in the Reserve and managed a medical facility in Pensacola. Chandler had the "art of persuasion" down—he was definitely suited for practicing law; and his audacious nature would tie in well too. Every time he spoke he seemingly lit up the sky, and Mashé struggled with becoming serious about him. He was a refined manner of person and every time they touched, Mashé could have melted. He appeared very attentive but sometimes there were moments where he left her in the dark; this was mysteriously appealing too.

She instantly remembers that they took a couple of pictures together back then and swiftly flips several pages and there they are—the two of them embracing on campus. He was looking better than fine. Whenever she thinks of him, a striking restless feeling comes over her and she finds herself clutching her album tightly.

Connection (2)

Mashé was well on her way to having her first collection of poems published. She wondered whether she or her publisher should be responsible for the publicity. She decided to play it safe with a small reputable company the first go-round. After graduation, she had returned home, stayed with her parents, earned an MFA, and became a junior college English Literature instructor, her main income. Rhial had met her fiancé, Halvan Sanders, in her senior year; they decided to attend graduate school and stay in Florida, move in together, and become entrepreneurs, having both majored in Commercial Marketing. Eila kept her promise to herself; she moved to New York City but did not find her dream job in dress designing or a similar field although she still wanted to study Law. Nonetheless, she did manage to find a position working for the state. She passed the entrance exam and immediately was called in for an interview.

Though situated in different parts of the country, the three of them stayed in touch. They predicted that Rhial would be first to marry and the first to have children. And since Eila decided New York City was her dream town, the next thing Mashé and Rhial knew she was mingling with those in high-end establishments as well as connecting with city politicians. Mashé was naturally curious about her friend. These dealings of hers sounded chancy and her Aunt Lennie had urged her niece numerous times to come home. She recalled one conversation with her aunt about Eila having much love for a man she met at Miami, that he seemed to be in and out of her life and this somehow may have been the reason for Eila's elusiveness. In the back of her mind Mashé was convinced that Eila could take care of herself even while living in New York City. Still to her Eila remained a big puzzle to solve.

🍒   🍒   🍒

Mashé was sitting in her room working on a poem she had kept stored for years in her heart. It was about Chandler; although his name would remain anonymous, she gave it a title clearly describing him. She hesitated to publish it because the fact that so few people knew of their relationship and the complications that surrounded them caused her to have second thoughts; she mused over it for so long. Later on she wrote a second poem about him called :Wizard of Love," which was published. The first one was her favorite.

My Clandestine Love-

Your eyes, your touch made my smile last-

Memories of your moods, your voice are now all a part of my past

Often I looked for you—to my left then to my right but you had gone instantly from my sight.

I am still living our carnal moments the few we knew wishing and hoping I could still feel you.

Are you doing the same trying to appreciate something untamed

Without shame sometimes, I just call out your name.

I cannot fault Love for this gift we missed

Something whimsical happened after we kissed.

"Obviously there is no end to what we have. I care too much; so, is our love-secret inevitable?"

Abruptly awakened again by that repeated dream, she brings a towel to her forehead. Mashé holds onto her album as it is about to slip onto the tile. She takes in a deep breath; her heart rate elevates so she reaches for a lukewarm glass of water. Wondering what the meaning for this reoccurring dream was—or could it perhaps bring an inconceivable revelation?

Since Eila's aunt was so concerned, Mashé decided to call Rhial and suggest they meet for a Best Girls weekend. Rhial was with it and they tried to reach Eila. After a few weeks she did respond saying she was working on a fundraiser with a few local officials and entrepreneurs; she had been in and out of town.

It was early February and they were on a three-way conversation:

Eila: Both of you are on my mind constantly. I have wanted to call you and as you could imagine something comes up. So where shall we meet?

Rhial: Let's meet at home. There are people asking about us and I want you to meet my "First Love."

Eila: "First Love," you always were old fashioned. So when is the big day?

Rhial: Sometime next summer. We have this nice place near Miami Beach. It's small but we like it that way.

Eila: Well of course…the closer the better. Mashé my girl, are you there? I hear you breathing. Oh and congratulations on your new collection of poems; gosh I hope you get a break.

Mashé: I was listening to the two of you, your infamous chattering, why cut in? And thank you, please spread the word around New York. I need my name out there.

Eila: I already have.

Mashé: We want you to come home for our get-together. I know that you are settled in the "Big City" but your aunt is really concerned about you. She has been trying to reach you too. She asked me to talk to you.

About fifteen seconds went by.

Eila: That will be quite a leap for three days.

Rhial: Your distance and mine are about the same.

Mashé: If the problem is expenses, I can…

Eila: I am just thinking out loud…I'll come home but I need to let you know when.

Mashé: What about your home address, you are in Brooklyn, right?

Rhial: (Cleverly) That's right if I had it I could drive up there to see you whenever.

Eila: Ladies, my address is 503 Clarkson Street, Number 2, in Brooklyn, New York.

Mashé: Since you are rubbing elbows with New York's finest, I was expecting your address to be in Upper Manhattan (they laugh).

Rhial: Do you live alone?

Eila: Well…I haven't found my fiancé like you, Rhee.

Mashé: (Impish) Eila, could you tell us what happened to your sweetheart, the one you met at the party?

Eila: (Reserved) Oh…he's around not as much as I would like but he's around. His job has him traveling from time to time.

Rhial: It has been a few years for you two since college; are you serious?

Eila: I always felt as though I was sharing him, I guess he was my first.

Rhial: Umm…I miss us so much! So, when!? We've got the where.

Another fifteen seconds went by.

Eila: Remember I need to square this first with "my people."

Mashé: (Insistent) Eila, don't keep us waiting—we are your people too. What is with this suspense?

Eila: (Subtle) Relax, Mashé, we are The Best Girls.

Mashé: Is there anything you want me to tell Aunt Lennie? She and your mother were right there for you. Eila, what happened?

Eila: Let's talk when I come home, okay? I will definitely let you know, but I need to go. I love you both…and tell Auntie I love her too and I intend to call her.

Mashé suspected Eila would take her time getting back. That is exactly what she did. March came and went, April came and went, and then in the middle of May Mashé and Rhial received a text from Eila that she would be home just before Mashé's birthday. Then Mashé had this brainstorm; she had a classmate at Miami named Tia Hightower who was from New York. She had heard that she became a psychologist and found her New York office online. A week or so later she called Tia. Tia was so glad to hear from Mashé. They brought one another up to date on each other and then Mashé shared a concern she had for her friend.

Tia: Yes, I remember Eila, very outgoing and might I emphasize "out."

Mashé: Why do you say that?

Tia: Oh you know…unpredictable though she was nice, I did not mean to offend you, I knew you were close. Is she all right?

Mashé: I have a favor to ask; it has been a while since we've seen one another; Eila lives in New York too and she has been elusive, slow on returning telephone calls.

Tia: So, you have been in touch with her?

Mashé: Yes, she supposed to be coming to California in a few weeks for a visit but I want to know what's happening with her. Yes, she is "outgoing" as you said…

Tia: It sounds like you are struggling with whether she's "acting out-of-character." What you have said sounds normal for someone like Eila. She is not missing or anything like that, but you feel a disconnection, still?

Mashé: Absolutely, Dr. Hightower. Do you know of a Private Investigator who is not too expensive?

Tia: (Laughing) Not in New York. Let me do this…I can find out what I can because in my field I can use my professional leverage without being in violation. I really don't feel the need to go that deep because she is not my client. I could just happen to bump into her; we knew each other in college so she wouldn't suspect anything. I could then in an indirect fashion find out about her activities and we could have an exchange of sorts. She needn't ever know we spoke about this. Her behavioral responses will be the key along with who she associates with. Personally, I concluded she was a loner early on, which is not considered abnormal behavior.

Mashé: I am so impressed, Tia. What a broad field Psychology is; you represent it well. I thought I would feel guilty calling you for this favor; you've made me feel more at ease.

Tia: It's what my colleagues and I call being sagacious-observers for the answers. Now, do you have an address, any contact information of hers?

Mashé gave Tia all the information she had while feeling slightly awkward doing so. Tia asked about Rhial, and Mashé told her she was staying in Miami working with her fiancé. Tia asked if Rhial knew of her plans to seek her help and Mashé said she had not mentioned this to anyone. Tia stressed that this be kept between the two of them. She said that initially they are searching for an unknown presence or situation and privacy is essential to all involved, especially Eila's.

Mashé: Of course and as I said Eila did say she was coming this way in a few weeks for a short visit. Tia, what if you do find something irregular in her activities? How long could this take? What I am really asking is when can you start?

Tia: First of all you have a suspicion; therefore we need to allow Eila to reveal that or if another person is the reason for her behavior in question. In my field it is not like a fishing expedition. If there is something abnormal, it will be uncovered. I have some calls coming in and I need to return to my real clientele. You will hear from me periodically, rest assured.

Mashé: I understand, Tia. Thank you.

Mashé remembers how she calmed down after speaking to Tia and made up her mind whatever was going on with her friend she had to let the Heavenly Father take charge. She remembers as a child her mother telling her that she, Rhial, and Eila were supposed to be different and then she added, "Some people are naturally difficult to read."

It was approaching Memorial Day weekend and Mashé had begun her umpteenth oil painting project. Working from her imagination she did a portrait of streams with rivers, and was applying distinct shades of blue, lilac and white throughout the canvas. She liked to characterize her paintings and wanted to emphasize through this one the forceful power of water. She exhibited with the strokes of her brush the moments in life that likened to the qualities of a stream, constantly moving with a delicate rhythm, uninterrupted, unhurried and steady. When concentrating on a river there is a faster pace, where life can bring on dips meeting up with big rocks, contending with deliberate swerving splashes due to the rushing currents as it blends in with other bodies of water, and as expected where there is a river there is a waterfall. In Mashé's depiction of a waterfall she applied broad dimensions of images representing rapid change displaying the effects of gravity: an illustration of the heights and depths of one's life where one could sense a kind of overflowing of outcomes or bringing on an abrupt impact of events. She later decided to name it "The Three of Us."

While taking a break she thought about the call she received from Chandler. His voice startled her. She asked where he was and he told her he was driving into her neighborhood. She remembered giving him her address before graduation and that was years ago and now all of a sudden he decided to make an unannounced visit.

Chandler: I have a civil case in Oakland and I wanted to see you but from the sound of your voice, it is nothing close to receptive.

Mashé: You'd think! You graduate from Law School and bid me farewell…

Chandler: Hold it, I never bid you farewell. You gave me an ultimatum.

Mashé: An ultimatum! All I said to you was I could not date an invisible man. I asked you was there someone else and you said you were breaking it off. Did that happen? And now you reappear!

Chandler: May I have permission to see you, Ms. Boston?

Mashé: Why do you want to see me?

Chandler: (Sighs) "Court is now in session." I did level with you, Mashé; when we first met I was involved and I admit we were getting serious, but there was not enough there for me; there may have been for her, still I broke it off. She became emotional and continuously called wanting an explanation. I never intended to continue seeing her but nevertheless we did off and on. Mashé, it was you I wanted in my life not her. And might I add that I saw your new book of poems online, I am so proud of you, Lady.

Mashé: Thank you…I would like to hear more about this woman, was she…

Chandler: Hold on, Mashé. (A lengthy wait) I didn't mean to take so long. My partner gave me updates on some new developments for our case. Now, may I see you?

Mashé: Chandler, it is really good to hear your voice. I do have plans later this evening. I didn't expect to ever hear from you.

Chandler: I beg for your forgiveness. I should have stayed in touch and you have every right to feel as you do. Ms. Boston, can't you fit me into your plans for this evening? Are you in a relationship?

Mashé: (Hesitant) I wouldn't call it that. How long are you here for?

Chandler: For the most part, it depends on you.

Mashé: Tomorrow I can meet you near the campus. There is a popular café called…

Chandler: I know it well. I cannot believe you are treating me like this.

Mashé: Call me when you are free from your case, if you change your mind…

Chandler: That won't happen. I need to see you and tell you what plans I have for us.

She arrived at the café before he did. She wore a white dress with a turquoise colored silk scarf.

She remembers him coming around the corner; he looked the same, fine. What was he going to tell her?

Long before she had decided to give up on him, but when their eyes met again the same wave of feelings held her attention. He basically lifted her from her seat as they embraced; his arms were strong, his smell was so fresh and as they stood before each other he asked her would she move back to Florida with him. At that moment, she had to take her seat. He spoke about the mistake of going into another relationship too hastily.

Chandler: You need to understand that it was more lust than anything, realizing the kind of person she was and being in school, it should have been casual.

Mashé: Should have been casual?!! My, my, so you enjoyed her company?

Chandler: (Recant) Yes I suppose I did—Mashé it was a physical relationship and this was before we met.

Mashé felt Chandler was like a wizard. His presence practically seized her senses, particularly the good sense to walk away. She desired a completeness with him. He stayed for about three weeks. She introduced him to her family; clearly the fire had been relit. During that period Chandler treated her like an empress. He took her to a resort in Santa Cruz and she was introduced to a different side of him. There she met his social circle, which encompassed only three people. Two attorneys, married, and one was a restaurateur who owned franchises on the west and east coasts. He rarely spoke of his twin brother, Alton, saying the family seemed to favor him (Chandler) more, which was not true. The same opportunities were afforded them; it was a matter of choice and while they were growing up he felt they had been close. Somehow after graduating from high school Alton sought the Armed Forces and he started college that fall.

She smiles broadly thinking about their last night in Santa Cruz; it was a Wednesday. The others had gone so after having dinner near the beach they went back to their suite. It was an unforgettable evening; he cradled her with a soothing and generous abundance of love.

The next day he took a plane back to Florida. She drove him to the airport. As he boarded he looked back at her as though he expected her to join him. Part of Mashé wanted to go with him, but she would need to find a job teaching or something. She told him that she loved him and to give her some time to consider his offer. That was one of the oddest days ever because early that afternoon Eila arrived and she had a message from Rhial and Halvan that they would be coming in that weekend. Still preoccupied with thoughts of Chandler, her reaction to seeing Eila sitting in her parents' living room was indifferent.

Eila: (Sarcastic) You are very happy to see me!

Mashé: After not hearing from you I concluded you were staying in New York.

Eila: I did say I was coming; I just had to decide when. There are a lot things happening. Did Rhial reach you?

Mashé: Y...Yes, she and Halvan are coming this weekend.

(While Mashé is looking for her parents Eila tells her that she can only stay for a week. She was invited to a political fundraiser and she needed to be there.)

Eila: Mashé… what's going on? Where were you?

Mashé: I was with a friend from out of town.

Eila: No…I mean where were you?! 'Cause you definitely are not here.

Mashé: (Focused) I am glad to see you, Eila. So you are politically inclined now?

Eila: What is his name?

Mashé: It does not matter. Does Aunt Lennie know you are here? I have to say I cannot believe the way you have treated her. Your mother's sister, Eila.

Eila: I am on my way to see her now. I wanted to see you first and besides from your cosmic behavior you seem fine.

Mashé: Have dinner with your aunt; spend some time with her and come by tomorrow so we can talk and catch up.

Eila: Fine…you do not want to talk about him?

Mashé: He's just a friend; seriously I am good and I am glad you made it in, finally!

Aunt Lennie's eyes were filled with tears as she gave her niece a big hug. She asked her how long she could stay. Eila told her she had to return to New York for a big event in a few days. Aunt Lennie asked if she could come back with her just to visit. Eila tried to sidestep this idea but her aunt was determined. She asked her again. Eila started muttering. Whenever this happened her aunt knew she was virtually undoing Eila's façade. They went into the den for a late dinner. They sat and began eating. Eila looked around and noticed some renovations had taken place; she liked the changes. Her aunt said it was time to make some improvements to an old house. Eila was not having very much eye contact so her aunt asked was there anything on her mind. She added that ever since she was a little girl she always felt her mind wandered a lot. Eila shrugged her shoulders and told her just the usual events of life.

Aunt Lennie: I would like to hear more about them. Have I ever treated you in a way you could not trust me?

Eila: No. Not ever. I just don't have any sizzling news to share like Mashé with her recently published poems and Rhial's imminent nuptials.

Aunt Lennie: This reminds me of those times when the three of you spent the night over here. You remember, you all would plan your futures as though you were having a contest with one another. You girls would go on and on trying to top each other's dreams. Now that I think about it, usually the contest was between you and Mashé. Jealousy is unbecoming, Eila; they are your best friends. (She paused for a few seconds.) Now that I think about it, best friends do tend to envy one another—Eila, is the contest still on?

Eila: (Blurts) Auntie, as usual your meals are delicious and I am full already. Let me help you clean up.

Aunt Lennie: (Curious) I see you have put on a few pounds; that New York lifestyle sparks your appetite to no end.

Eila: I…am trying to cook more like you and Mother. I have a schedule you would not believe so I find myself eating lots of sweets.

Aunt Lennie: That may explain the added pounds. Make sure you eat what is good for you and not just what's good to you. Now…tell me about this man you are seeing?

Eila: (Refrains) When did I mention a man?

Her aunt leaned her way with a staunch look on her face and asked the question again. Eila simply motioned her way to the cupboard with cleaned tableware. Aunt Lennie sensed her tenseness and said whenever she was ready she would like to hear about him, adding that she was excited about Rhial's engagement and suggested that they throw a bridal shower as the time neared.

Eila turned to her aunt, confessing that she had been seeing someone but lately they had become estranged. She admitted to caring very much for him but something happened or did not happen. She said they had not spoken in weeks.

Aunt Lennie: Did he withdraw or did you?

Eila: An interesting question; I did go by his home and he was not there.

Aunt Lennie: Did you leave him a message?

Eila: In a way.

Aunt Lennie: What way?

Eila: His landlord was approaching wondering who I was and I told him.

Aunt Lennie: This is very mysterious, Eila, and then it seems to play in well with your personality. I think you should try again. But wait! He's not in New York so that means you went out of town; to Florida? (Eila does not respond) Let's see, you said you met him while you were in college; my goodness something should have perked by now. You remember the percolator we had when you were a little girl? It had a system; you add the coffee grounds, the water and then just push the "on" button. I recall how patient we had to be with it. When the heat came on you could hear the hissing sound and in a matter of minutes, you had some nicely brewed coffee. Eila, you need a new percolator.

Eila: Maybe so but it was a peculiar kind of thing with him, like dealing with two people.

Aunt Lennie: It is odd that you seemed to do the pursuing and he is not responding. The next move is really up to him now.

Eila: (Uncertain) I agree, Auntie. Let's get off of this subject. I see you baked an apple cobbler.

Aunt Lennie: Go ahead—I know it's your favorite.

Later on that evening Aunt Lennie had decided to turn in before Eila and as she motioned to bid her goodnight Eila was standing in the den peering out the picture window looking into the night so she decided not to disturb her.

The next morning Rhial and Halvan arrived. They rushed from the airport to see her family. They were so happy. Halvan was strikingly good looking. Since their relationship had begun many questioned what he could have seen in Rhial. Though she looked better than ordinary, the question still surfaced from time to time.

Mashé was talking to Chandler. He said right after he landed he found out that he may need to return in the near future. He asked her had she thought more about his invitation to join him in Florida for the rest of her life. Mashé, trying to contain herself, told him she needed to know what "join him" meant, and after considering her teaching position here she asked him to relocate to California. He was surprised by her answer, and then went on telling her that he intended to mention he had an opportunity to become partner and wanted to weigh in on his chances. Mashé, still calm, told him that she knew his firm was also on the west coast and that if he made partner his job security would definitely allow him to relocate as well. There was a lull of silence and then he complimented her style of argument, saying he would never want to contend with her in a court room. Mashé wanted to say to this charming wizard that she could in no way risk her job and be able to leave her family at that point in time. Had the circumstances been different he would not have needed to ask twice because from the first time they spent the night together his moves encircled her intellect, her body, her all. This frightened her; she wondered was it ominous to be puzzled and in love at the same time. Chandler eased the conversation by suggesting that they revisit this topic upon his return and Mashé simply agreed.

As soon as she said good-bye, Rhial was at her front door.

Rhial: I called you and you did not answer.

Mashé: I know, I was having an interesting conversation. I saw your number appear.

Rhial: Is everything good with you? Why so serious?

Mashé: When time permits, I will give you the particulars. But Girl, I am so happy to see you. You look good and where is your man?

Rhial: He's at the house. I just spoke to Eila she seems cool and collected.

Mashé: We spoke briefly last night. She wanted to get into my business but I insisted that she visit with her aunt and we could start fresh today. So, what is our first move?

Rhial: I want us to go shopping and have lunch?

Mashé: Cool. I am ready, let's go to Aunt Lennie's house.

When they arrived, Eila walked out onto the front porch looking rather cute and yelling from the top of her voice. They hugged and told Aunt Lennie they would see her that evening. They met Halvan while he played cards with a few friends and members of the family. Mashé and Eila were impressed. He was mellow and strikingly handsome. They asked her why she was waiting until next summer to get married and she said they agreed that they would probably be better financially situated. When they arrived into town Rhial saw a suit displayed at this high-end designer's boutique and wanted to try it on so Mashé and Eila said they would browse in the meantime. Eila whispered to Mashé that it was amazing how Rhial managed to find someone like Halvan. She realized that looks should not be the only factor in a relationship but she wondered how Rhial did it. Mashé asked Eila if she was selling her friend short. She asked her to avoid making any insinuations, that Rhial was an attractive woman and "Looks were in the eye of the beholder." Eila lamented not in their case—even when it came to that cliché "opposites attract," there was no convincing her. She felt there was more to it and asked her did she notice her engagement ring. Mashé became prickly with Eila and told her who was she to challenge a person's choices. She told her to let it go. Though Mashé stood up for Rhial, she made the same covert observation. Rhial is a good person and very smart however, when you put the two of them together, you wondered how did they get together?

Eila: By the way, when will I receive my autographed copy of your collection of poems?

Mashé: I have a copy for you and I was intending to let you in on a secret… should all go well I will have a book signing this fall in your dream town; actually, it is a dream of my own.

Eila (Impressed) Well dream on lady—That is what I want to hear. You are going to the top. I just feel it: Rhial and I can walk around telling everyone that we knew you when.

Mashé: Do you mean that, Eila? Thank you! I am praying on this, Girl. And in time you will have some good news to share too…

Eila: That would be something. Why of course I mean it, you are an artist.

Rhial walks out styling in front of them.

Mashé: I like that Rhial. It was made for you. Are you buying it?

Eila: (Interjects) It is a sharp suit—you should have Halvan buy it.

Rhial: (Giggly) He would probably say wait until it goes on sale.

Eila: (Mystified) But, that may not happen for weeks and you two will have gone by then.

Mashé: Ladies, my birthday is just around the corner and since we will probably be apart on that great day let's celebrate before the end of the week!

Rhial: It is done. What would you like to do?

Eila: I think we should go to a popular restaurant in Belmont but it's your birthday so you tell us?

Mashé: First of all is Halvan cool with you leaving him with your family the entire visit? I would like him and a few others to join us. (Eila keenly observed her reaction).

Rhial: Mashé, he definitely wants to be included. We've talked about it.

Mashé: Fine. I will make reservations at that Cuban restaurant that opened recently; remember while in Florida how we could not eat enough of their Shrimp Asopao?

Eila: I am sure they will have dancing there too. This is going to be a night to remember.

Rhial: I am not claiming clairvoyance but I was reminiscing how we were planning our weddings and look at us, in no time you and Eila will be flashing your rings around too.

Mashé: Rhial, you more so than us. Though I am all for it, it just has to be a man that wants me as much as I want him.

Eila: Now that definitely sounds like a dream.

Mashé's eyes widened like two bright headlights and Rhial suddenly felt some blurry nuances dancing about but dared not pry and resumed with her pros and cons about the suit. In an instant Eila had walked away. Rhial, noticing this, told Mashé she would think about the suit and be out in a second to meet up with her and Eila.

Mashé found Eila, who had gone to the Aquarium. When they were children Eila was often found just standing before it. She seemed hypnotized by it. Mashé thought about the time when their school had taken their class on a field trip to the museum; during the tour, she noticed Eila was missing. Walking outside she looked down the way and noticed her friend staring into the Aquarium. She ran over to her asking her to come back with her. In an instant, she felt Eila was oddly becoming spacey. Eila with her glaring eyes asked her did she think those fish knew they were not going anywhere. It seemed to be a reasonable question if someone else had asked it; but this was Eila and with her you needed to spare a little more intrigue.

Mashé: Eila, you with your sarcasm just walked away; what's going on?

Eila: I guess I would rather not discuss weddings right now. I really would like that to happen for me some day. I hope you will forgive my behavior and this applies to Rhial and Halvan. I felt I could express my real self with you about their relationship.

Mashé: Eila, we are sisters and if those were your earnest feelings I want to hear them, though I would rather Rhial not hear them.

Eila: True. Did she buy the suit?

Mashé: She decided not to.

Eila: (Livid) There you have it, Girl! You saw how she shot into the boutique ready to buy it until I suggested he buy it for her. What does that say to you, Mashé?

Mashé did have a genuine curiosity about Rhial and that suit. She tried to ignore the points Eila made because it was not their place to pry; then she thought she would perhaps ask one tiny harmless question. What was their income? She did not ask directly. When they returned from their outing it was about 6:45 PM and Halvan and a couple of Rhial's cousins went with her father to a neighborhood sports bar. Since the three of them didn't eat out as planned they were ravenous. Mashé's mother and Eila's Aunt Lennie had prepared dinner and they walked in, going straight to the dining room. Aunt Lennie asked where the shopping bags were and they looked at one another and muttered that they didn't see any deals. Mashé's parents' home was spacious as well as eclectic; they were notable collectors of authentic antiques from around the world. Her father taught Art History and they had been to North Africa many times and brought back many treasured artifacts. Rhial had called Halvan letting him know that dinner was on the table; he responded that they were walking in the front door.

Mashé smiles revisiting this scene.

It was a gathering of friends like an extended family. When Halvan and Rhial's cousins walked in, Rhial literally jumped up from her seat to greet him. Mashé's mother, Aunt Lennie, Eila, and Mashé subtly observed this, glancing at one another.

After saying grace everyone eagerly selected various platters, filling their plates. As they settled in Eila, being Eila, began dinner-chat. First, she gave rave reviews over the spread and then marked her target.

Eila: (Brisk) Halvan, we haven't really talked. I was interested in the work you and Rhial are doing as entrepreneurs. Is it a nine to five schedule, or does Rhial do the mornings and you the evenings—how does it work?

Halvan: Yes, absolutely we focus on the retail buyers versus the wholesale buyers for the sake of commercializing as in goods and services. And be mindful that this could apply to practically any and all items out there. We, Rhial and I, make this information available to individual companies or partners. It gives them choices.

Eila: Please give us an example of the goods and services.

Halvan: Let's say, real estate, pharmaceuticals or...

Aunt Lennie: Pharmaceuticals, those are drugs!

Halvan: Aunt Lennie. Yes, legal drugs mind you, for private practice doctors and their patients. We provide the information on who is promoting the pharmaceuticals; it's a service, we are in no way selling drugs, although we provide access to those outlets that do; once again we allow our clients decide.

Rhial: Obtaining the best for their money. Think of us as a service bureau.

Mashé: So, may I ask how business is?

Rhial: We have definitely built up a clientele—and I was amazed with the competition.

Everett: (Rhial's cousin) I can imagine, but I am with Eila. How many hours do you put into this?

As they gave each other a glance Rhial and Halvan explained that sometimes he's online and sometimes she would be working the telephones; it depended on what day it was.

Eugene: (Mashé's father) You both earned Master's Degrees, right? Please help me understand the fulfillment you are gaining from this?

Rhial: It was Halvan's business plan to try it out. So far we are earning enough, it's not like we are struggling. Just like the airline tickets we bought to come here. We found the best price for us; many people are accustomed to traditional purchasing.

Trista: (Rhial's mother) I have no quarrel with tradition. As I said earlier, you might have better luck here in California. I was hoping you would land a good job with a future and if Halvan wants to continue as an entrepreneur, the impact would not be so great.

Tolson: (Rhial's father) To put it plainly—you would only have one opportunist, one hustler.

A mighty jolt seemed to resonate everyone's senses.

Rhial's eyes squinted as many others had a look of disbelief; Mashé and Eila focused on Halvan.

Halvan: Pardon me, Mr. Curry, but...we both are running a respectable operation; we have each other's back. True, there are moments when we evaluate our efforts and we see some promise in this. We're in a different era—there are many ways to make a living.

Mashé: (Interjects) Will this promise be long-term, as in years?

Once again, they gave one-another a glance then Halvan explained that this unsteady economy gave entrepreneurs like them an opportunity to blossom. He said he could not put a finger on or measure how far they would go, though he believed the experience had given them a lot of insight into where they were headed should they gain enough ground.

Mashé listened to him and watched Rhial intently. She was definitely in his corner, almost like a baby bird huddling with him.

Eila: When will you know you have gained enough ground?

Halvan: When we have earned enough credibility all around; when masses of clientele come our way repeatedly. (Rhial's parents shake their heads with skepticism).

Eugene: Don't laugh but I always thought entrepreneurs were ideally white folks. You two are the first and I don't want to discourage your dream or whatever it is you are calling it but even today Blacks need to establish a foundation within their fields…in my opinion the state of the economy is not our worry and never has been. Moreover, as far as the era we are currently living in we are still Black and the struggle continues for the majority of us.

Eila: Yes, Mr. Boston, a point well taken. Please understand that I work with entrepreneurs in New York from time to time and one of them is Puerto Rican— that's not white (some snicker). Halvan, I am still struggling with your point about the "unsteady economy." Have you two tried to obtain mainstream employment?

Rhial: (Sprightly) We could put some other "coals in the fire." As long as we are working together, we are learning together too.

Eila wrote a note on a napkin to Mashé which read, "Love is blind."

Aunt Lennie: I hope everyone has room for dessert; I made a sour cream cake.

They all quickly lifted their dessert plates.

As Mashé thinks more about that night she could not forget how Rhial behaved after dinner; she was fairly subdued. There was a baseball game still in progress so all but she, Eila, and Rhial went to the family room to watch it. Her parents as a routine went for their after-dinner evening stroll. Aunt Lennie bid good night to everyone and went home. The three of them rushed to the solarium and sat down with second helpings of the sour cream cake. For about ten minutes or more they politely glanced at one another, then Eila asked what was on the agenda for tomorrow. Mashé suggested a movie or to attempt shopping again. Rhial surprised them when she asked did they feel Halvan was too sophisticated for her. Right then Mashé felt challenged and Eila, who was more straightforward, said she thought so.

Mashé could not believe her ears. She watched Rhial put her plate down and then Eila asked Rhial how they met.

Rhial said it was their senior year at Miami. She went to a fraternity and sorority seniors celebration one Sunday. She had always wanted to join a sorority but she could not find the time to pledge. Eila said Rhial reminded her of a sorority girl and Rhial snapped back telling Eila that had she pledged, it might have done her some good. Eila seemed offended. Then Rhial told Eila she was too judgmental of her and a person who thought she was a prima donna was fooling herself. Mashé wanted to jump up and say "Amen." But Rhial had the floor with an elevated voice. She said Halvan believed in her and that she was jealous and telling them that she watched their reactions when they first saw him.

Eila came back assuring her that she was not jealous, she was very concerned and did not want her to be misled and reminded Rhial that she asked the question.

Then Mashé stepped in asking for them to calm down and said as friends we should be honest with each other, just use more tact. Then Eila sharply shifted to her saying why should she tippy-toe around the subject and reminded her that she felt the same way as she did. Mashé resented Eila's comment, boldly discounted her claim, and justified with Rhial that her interests in her relationship with Halvan were genuine and because she is sweet natured people tend to underappreciate that quality. Eila's eyes widened extolling how impressive her defense; she had buttered it up and mastered the English language so well then reiterated that they definitely felt the exact same way.

Rhial admitted that the going was rough for a time; there were some days they did not have much to eat just enough to pay the rent. They applied for government jobs one after another. Then one night she called her father and asked him for $10,000.00. She told him that she thought her tuition had been paid off but she received another fee bill. She asked Halvan to try for entry-level jobs and he staunchly refused, expressing how humiliated it would make him feel. She said she hoped they could pull this off because she didn't feel right lying to her parents. They worked so hard to put her through college and pleaded with her friends not to ever share her secret.

The same conversation intermittently continued with Tolson, Trista, Everett, and Halvan in the family room.

Trista strongly focused on the getting by theme of their story, putting emphasis on them planning to marry. Another concern that Tolson had was plan "B"; Halvan was cool and suave with his answers. He continued to assure them that he and Rhial knew there may be risks involved but they were in it together.

Tolson: How does your family feel about this?

Halvan: My parents are not together, though they are still cordial. I haven't spoken to my father about this. My mother feels as you do, what will happen if matters go south.

Tolson: Are your parents Floridians also?

Halvan: Yes they are. I am the first to graduate from college and the idea of pursuing this idea just felt so right. The others glance at one another then are quickly drawn to the TV broadcasting a grand slam.

Eila: So that I understand this, your father is basically your sponsor? Have you broken even in any way?

Mashé: Besides that I want to know what area you are living in?

Rhial: Bay County, roughly Panama City.

Eila: (Stunned) Oh...I remember some time ago you mentioned something about Miami Beach...

Rhial: I did but their leases were too high.

Mashé: Rhial, you have been dishonest with your family so...what about us? You said you weren't struggling. What about his family?

Eila: And how much of that $10,000.00 remains?

Rhial: I...really need to stop at this point. We are going to give this a few more months and then we'll have to come to a decision. I believe I can encourage him to listen. This was something he wanted to test out and I feel I should support him.

Rhial wanted them to know that they had come in contact with some really fine people of various backgrounds and it had been an eye-opening experience.

Eila: That is fine but he should support your dreams and ideas also, of which you have not expressed. Rhial, try to remove yourself from this situation for a minute. Would you be concerned if it were me or Mashé?

Rhial: That sounds rhetorical, Eila; so like you.

It seemed The Best Girls had reached a turning point. Over the years they had their differences and managed to move on but Mashé recalled Rhial's tone of voice and mannerisms; the room was filled with tension. Was their "thick as thieves" friendship about to teeter? Rhial was either oblivious to her dilemma or blatantly obstinate. How were they to continue? It was clear that Rhial was in love with the wrong man no matter how good he looked. Given these circumstances Eila and Mashé placed their hands on Rhial's shoulders, comforted her, and gave her their complete support then geared up to plan for Mashé's birthday dinner party.

They were celebrating to the max at the Cuban Fantasía (Fancy Cuban) in Belmont, California. Mashé contacted a couple of classmates the three of them knew from middle school—they had not seen them in years. The music made Mashé want to return to Florida. There was a combo catering to her hand and foot. Every song she requested they knew and the place was hot and grooving. Eila and Rhial no longer seemed to have an uneasiness between them and did the bolero together on a packed floor. The restaurant baked her a three-tiered birthday cake; it had three different flavors: chocolate, strawberry, and lemon. Halvan danced some but he preferred jazz and sat most of the time; naturally Rhial followed along to some degree. While Mashé was cutting a slice of her cake, a tall cute man grabbed her by the waist to dance with him. She had to make an effort to keep up—they covered the entire dance floor and made a nice couple, duly noted by many. Eila was preoccupied with a guy whom she managed to approach after his date went to the ladies' room; they noticed one another immediately once she arrived. He seemed to be of mixed background and average in height; earlier he walked by her a few times just to get a closer look. They conversed for a few minutes and then walked out to the patio; being so well acquainted with her antics, Mashé and Rhial looked at one another with suspicion. Halvan asked Rhial what was she staring at and her reply was she thought she saw someone she recognized. Mashé and partner were attracting a crowd and many shouted, "Musica, musica." They were in step with the beat—as with percussion music there is hardly any resistance. He swung her around, then he twirled, dipped, and she like other women appeared intoxicated by his lofty gyrations. The combo had finally come to a slow selection, giving them the opportunity to cool down. He was pleasing to watch on the floor and he was a man with busy hands; she had to insist a couple of times for him to control them.

Neil: Please pardon me; I am carried away by all I see. My name is Neil Rollins. I take it that you are the one celebrating your birthday? I hope you have many, many more.

Mashé: (Nonchalant) Thank you, Neil. I think I should return to my guests.

Neil: Well…before you go may I know your name? You know mine.

Mashé: Of course…Mashé Boston.

Neil: Mashé, that is stunning. What does it mean?

Mashé: Drawn from the water.

Neil (Curious) You mean like Moses?

Mashé: (Smiling) You are really free to interpret what you like, but that's a good assumption. My mother and grandmother named me.

Neil: They are spiritual people.

Mashé: Yes. There is a greater power without question.

Neil: Absolutely. Are you here with someone, Lady Mashé, husband, an escort?

Mashé: No and who are you escorting this evening?

Neil: Ms. Boston, I am a free agent. But answer me this? You must have had a relationship with someone recently.

Mashé: (Awed) How would you know?

Mashé: I sensed from your nostalgia or perhaps it's an imminent vacuum of some kind. As we danced your body language was tight—you could have been more agile with me. With Cuban dancing you need to be nimble and lively.

Mashé: (Impressed) How perceptive, though I believe I was tight because you suddenly grabbed me and whirled me onto the dance floor. I was taken by surprise. (Although she wondered if he was on to something—she did have Chandler on her mind a lot that day). I do love Cuban music.

Neil: Good. I...will be straight with you, Mashé. I am taken by you. Pardon my conduct, I should have asked your permission—I am definitely a gentleman, you seemed like the kind of person I would like to dance with and do other things with, respectfully.

Mashé was a little taken by him as well but did not want to reveal it; instead of going back to her guests she and Neil went to another table and became quite chummy, overtly.

In the meantime, Eila and her mystery gent went somewhere. The woman he came with returned and began wandering around looking for him. Rhial excused herself from Halvan and rushed over to Mashé.

Rhial: Mashé, pardon me but have you seen Eila? (Gesturing that a certain someone had re-appeared)

Mashé introduced Rhial to Neil, then calmly conveyed that Eila was no longer on the premises and she was not going to be consumed with worry about her escapades. With that retort, Rhial appeared baffled but considered the handsome company Mashé was keeping and decided to follow suit.

Novelties (3)

Mashé awoke to her alarm and rose quickly to dress. She decided she was going to teach during the summer and needed to consult with the administration to prepare. It had been about a week since the three of them parted from their visit. It would always be an unfinished week of events to her. She wanted to spend at least one more day revisiting. Mashé wondered was she the naïve one or maybe this was the normal state of affairs. She felt a change had come between them and their closeness. Her concern was for their roots to stay firmly planted no matter how far apart they lived from one another. Eila was the first to leave. She was asked about the guy she was with that night at the restaurant; once again it was another mystery to add to the pile. She said she had a great time and wanted them to come to New York. Rhial looked more relaxed and Halvan seemed to be a man of fewer words on their last day. When the taxi drove up she asked Halvan to go ahead and as she turned to speak, she was trying to force herself to smile. She seemed to have something heavy to say but instead she gave Mashé a strong hug and told her how proud she was of her and as time drew nearer she would send for her and Eila to come to their ceremony next year—it was to be a small, intimate, non-traditional "celebration of love," she called it. As the taxi sped away, Mashé said a prayer for her friend.

Later that evening Mashé's parents expressed how glad they were that she wasn't naive like Rhial and rambunctious as Eila. Then they asked a question she did not see coming, When was she moving? She was mystified—she was soon to be twenty-seven and just getting "her wheels to turning." Basically, it was their way of saying, find a husband.

The majority of the time while her friends were in town she had kept her cell phone off. Oddly, she started thinking about Chandler and Neil. Neil said he would call her during the week. She and Neil talked until the restaurant closed. He was an engineer by profession and worked in San José, where he also lived. They exchanged contact information and he asked her to join him for dinner in the coming week. With the cute expression on his face that night she could not resist but she wanted to know more about him before accepting his offer. That is when he said he would call her and talk about whatever she wanted. Without a moment's notice when she returned from her first day of teaching summer school she found Neil standing on the front porch talking with her father. They were acting as though they knew each other before—it turned out that his father knew her father from serving in the Navy during the Viet Nam War. Mashé was unprepared for his visit. Once again, he eased up on her and now her father seemed to like him. Normally he was so judgmental of her dates. Instantly she thought of Chandler. Her father did not seem to have an opinion of Chandler, probably because Chandler did not give her parents a chance to judge him. She greeted them and proceeded to go indoors when her father spoke.

Eugene: Darling daughter, what is the rush? You have a visitor; aren't you going to invite him in?

Mashé: I need to speak with Mom. Oh, pardon me, Neil, would you like to come in?

Neil (Smiling) I thought you would never ask.

Neil took a seat in the living room while Mashé walked through the house looking for her mother. She found her in her dressing room.

Clover: Hello there, I did not know you were home. It seems you had a gentleman caller. What a small world this is. His father and your father were in Viet Nam around the same period. They have not seen one another since. Something the matter?

Mashé: Nothing, I just wonder about things sometime. You seem to like him.

Clover: I just met him, Mashé. He said he crashed your birthday dinner party.

Mashé: He did in a way and now he is back again.

Clover: Do you like him?

Mashé: I don't know—he moves quickly; I am wondering about that.

Clover: His good looks meet my approval.

Mashé: (Flatly) Right.

Clover: Speak your mind, girl.

Mashé: Like I said. He pops up without calling me or checking in.

Clover: Where is he now?

Mashé: Downstairs waiting for me.

Clover: What! You are being rude. We'll talk later now go; entertain your guest.

When Mashé returned and noticed he was gone, she went outside looking for him and then her father came from the garage.

Eugene: What's going on?

Mashé: I don't know—he's not in the house. Did you see him leave?

Eugene; No, but you were not very receptive, agreed?

Mashé: (Anxious) Agreed. I had better call him or something.

Eugene: His father Clifford did well in the Navy and even though we faced a lot of trials he went from Senior Chief Petty Officer to Master Chief Petty Officer and then Flag Officer in the blink of an eye. I guess his son is "a chip off the old block." Nevertheless, he seems to be sincere. Does he make you feel uncomfortable?

Mashé: I am trying to put my finger on it. Like I told Mom, he just pops up and yes, I feel uncomfortable whenever he does that.

Eugene: As I suspected, the man doesn't want to waste any time. Understand something, I don't want you to feel obligated, though he seems like he's good people. You had better try to reach him and get things straightened out between you.

At that moment her cell phone lit up. It was Neil. He apologized for taking off without notice but his supervisor called about an operation at a technology site that was malfunctioning and they needed his input. Mashé felt fairly relieved because hurting his feelings was certainly not her intent. She too apologized for her behavior and asked him if he would like to try again tomorrow night—he quickly told her he would come by for her after work.

Later that evening Mashé went online looking for single-bedroom townhouses. She decided to bookmark a few for open house showings on Sunday. She knew at some point she would be looking for her own place. Her parents as usual were direct and honest, and even though her salary was commensurate with her education she wanted to do more and decided to begin another book of poems. She had already completed various works of oil paintings and often imagined her own gallery in the nearby village—that would be something she thought and started to pray.

While taking another sip of water Mashé reflects on a scene that brought effervescence to her quiet life.

It was an early morning; her class was about to begin when her cell phone caught her attention. She normally kept it turned off during class—it was Chandler. She had one of her leading students take over for a moment. She ran down the hall to a quiet corner.

Chandler: Hello, lady, did I disturb anything?

Mashé: I am teaching now, though it is nice to hear your voice.

Chandler: Wow, forgive me—I just called to tell you I am planning to come out that way in a couple of weeks so look out for me. I'll call you this evening—will it be okay?

Mashé: (Hesitant) What a question…yes.

After she returned to her classroom and resumed the lesson at hand, in the back of her mind Mashé pictured herself with Neil and then with Chandler; one was cool and the other aggressive. Both of these qualities she liked in a man. She was struck by Chandler in an instant; with Neil, he made more or less of a regular impression, though the more they saw of each other he began to grow on her. He was genuinely considerate of her and was interested in what she wanted to do. Chandler on the other hand, as her poem expressed was a mystery, a quality she also liked.

Later that night she called Neil and asked him if he would meet with her tomorrow to look at some townhouses. He was pleasantly surprised and asked her what time he should pick her up. She felt it would only be decent of her to tell him that she had a casual relationship with someone she met in college and it might become serious. She tried to practice in her mind how to tell him. One of the pluses about Neil was he had this boyish charm. He was usually upbeat, fun, and eager to please. At that very moment she received a call from Chandler. He apologized again for interrupting her class and asked had she thought more about coming back with him to Florida. He even spoke to some college instructors he knew and asked them to look into a teaching post in English Literature for her. Mashé asked him when did she give him a definitive answer, boldly stressed he was moving too fast, that she would be leaving her roots—her family, though she did have a fondness for Florida. Undaunted, Chandler stayed on course laying it thick about how he wanted to be able to reach for her at night's twilight and at dawn's peering instead of imagining it. As he went on with his attorney-style persuasiveness she closed her eyes and thought about the last night they were together. When his full lips pressed upon hers it was like she was covered with a warmth, an innermost passion that made her glide. Neil made romantic moves but she resisted feeling self-conscious. It was the very next day when Neil came to pick her up and made his move—as she recalled it was surely a pivotal moment for her.

Neil: Mashé, we haven't known each other long, and I guess we should define long—but I could save you a lot of money by you moving in with me. I'll be old-school about it, I dig you, Mashé, and I want you with me all the time. I don't mean shack up I mean…

Mashé: (Interjects) Neil…what you are saying is making me hyperventilate. I am old-school too so it may be better if we kept it at a gradual pace. I am very territorial so you might want to think twice…I am serious.

Neil looked directly into her eyes and said he was serious as well and liked territorial. He then pulled over and parked. He told her his salary was $95,000.00 a year and it was going to get better. He said that some things you felt right about, stressing that he felt right about her and asked for her hand in marriage; although if she would rather they get engaged and live separately, he could muster up some tolerance to do that. Mashé sat there gazing at him. This man just proposed marriage as though it were a done deal, and she could not bring herself to say one word. Then he reached for her and fervidly caressed her. He definitely knew how to kiss and she kissed back. Once again she was acting out of character; taking chances was not her forte, until now.

When they arrived to the first open house Mashé was nearly resigned to accepting his proposal, still dazed about actually getting married. In her mind the scene was different. Her man was to be her better-half, her divine mate. He was to be tall, well, Chandler was tall but Neil was taller. He was to be handsome, Neil and Chandler definitely fit the bill, though she wanted to be crazy in love with her man like she told Eila and Rhial when they were little girls, and honestly love seemed to be that missing ingredient. Unsure of her emotional stance she needed to search for courage on what to say—the choice of words, how this was to play out.

After they lookyloo-ed three properties Neil suggested that they go to his place in San José. As they drove up to the entrance Mashé was impressed with its appearance. The entry hall was wide and there were two bedrooms upstairs, very spacious and well furnished, and Mashé asked the question.

Mashé: Have you always lived alone?

(Neil had gone to the kitchen for some sodas. He walked back saying he did have a roommate at the beginning but it was not a good arrangement.)

Mashé: Why?

Neil: He had an unstable girlfriend that liked me and things got…all in all he moved out and I have not seem them since.

Mashé: (Curious) Had you known the two of them long?

Neil: I knew him from work and I met the crazy girlfriend through him.

Mashé noticed a distinct change in his demeanor as he spoke about this ordeal. Seeing him in a somber mood gave her a view of his sensitive side; though she did want to know more she decided to change the subject. She asked him if he was all right. He said he was fine and after that experience he preferred to live alone. Then he stepped back from his barstool stating he came home one night finding her waiting for him while her boyfriend went to a seminar. He admitted it was spooky but he handled it immediately.

Mashé: (Perky) Being tall like you are requires high ceilings—it must have been built in the 1970's.

Neil: How perceptive you are. It has handled a couple of serious earthquakes nicely due to its firm foundation.

Mashé: That is a definite plus.

Neil: (Smiling) So Ms. Boston, does this place appeal to you and once again this is just for dialogue; I don't want to apply unwanted pressure.

Mashé: Unwanted! That's comical. You have a lovely home and I have always dreamt of a two-story house with small manufactured waterfalls and streams.

Neil: Are there any children in that dream?

Mashé: (Pauses) After I have accomplished a few goals. yes, I see children in my future. And you? Or maybe I should ask, do you have children?

Neil: No Mashé—like I said I'm old school—there are set patterns already in place and sharing my life with a dynamic woman first is real. You are real, Mashé.

Mashé: When is your birthday Neil?

Neil: April 21st. Are you putting together some plans for me; if so the only gift I'll need is you.

Mashé felt as nervous as a cat. He stood before her and brought her closer. She tenderly responded and then they lay across his long sectional sofa. Having been with Chandler once again signaled an unyielding response. He paused and told her this reminded him of when they were dancing at the restaurant. She wanted to sit up and tried to assure him that he was a pleasure to be with and, true, his premonitions were on point. She did have someone else in her life but their relationship was unclear. She revealed that he was the only person she had been intimate with and even though she was raised to stay celibate until she married, they became serious just the same. Having been unprepared for his wedding proposal made her feel obliged to let him know it would be indecent to go any further. Neil, still caressing her, asked did she just now refuse his proposal. She twitched, giving him a stunned look.

Mashé: Neil…I gave you an explanation…

Neil: (Interjected) But why an explanation? Why didn't you come out and simply say, No!

Mashé: Because I presumed you would have asked me why, right?

Neil: So you are letting me down then? I am not trying to upset you Mashé—it appears that you might be unclear about him instead of being unclear about the relationship.

Mashé then rose from the sofa. She wondered was this so. Handling two men at a time seemed dishonest, though only one had asked her to marry him.

Neil: Mashé, you don't need to ponder on where I am coming from. Have I given you a reason to doubt?

Mashé: No, not ever. I have to know what I want.

Neil: Exactly! Seriously, I…would like for you to think more on this. Forgive me for rushing in on you. Just knowing that a woman like you exists gives me so much…you know if you'd rather I take you home…

Mashé: So much what, Neil?

Neil: As though my prayers have been answered is what I meant. Are you ready?

Mashé took him by the hand and they sat down. Her insides were churning, she told him to give her some time and added that she felt so lucky and hoped he believed her. Being face to face, he uttered think of us as love in progress.

As she entered, the hallway clock chimed 11:30 PM. Her mother appeared from the dining room and observing her facial expression asked her how her date went. Mashé with half a smile told her that Neil proposed. By further observing her behavior, Clover refrained from comment as her daughter slowly closed the door. They walked into the kitchen and took a seat. No words were exchanged for a few seconds, then Clover asked her daughter what was her response. She sat there looking through the curtains at a waning crescent moon—never had she felt so stifled. She told her mother the answer was pending. Neil was nice, she uttered, then her mother followed with but, there could be someone even nicer.

Clover: Girl…you are so brave, I admire you.

Mashé: (Surprised) Really? I need to be sure, besides Chandler called and he's coming back here in a couple of weeks and he's also looking for an answer from me.

Clover: I don't follow you.

Mashé: He wants me to join him in Florida.

Clover: Join?! As what?

Mashé: That's what we'll need to talk about.

Clover: You mean like Rhial and Halvan?

Mashé: I did not say that, mother.

Clover: (Sighs) You are working on thirty but hopefully not desperate. I want you to do what's best for you. Oh, did Neil have a ring for you?

Mashé: (Pauses) No he didn't though he took me to his home and suggested instead of buying a townhouse I could live with him as his wife. I believe he was being cautious when he proposed; buying a ring would have been too confident, and zealous.

Clover: Ump! You all are from a very strange generation. Did tradition go out the window? Then again, you may have a point, because you certainly have clearly shown that you are not that impressed with him yet he still pursues you. I believe you have a "hopeless romantic" on your hands, Ms. Boston. His fantasy has become a reality. Pardon my saying so but the hand you've been dealt is not as challenging as you think.

Mashé: Mother, as usual you are so perceptive.

Clover: One day you'll have a daughter and she'll say the same thing to you. Good night.

Mashé: Good night.

That following morning Mashé was in her classroom arranging quiz booklets before her students arrived when her cell lit up. It was Tia calling from New York with some information about Eila. Mashé took her seat immediately.

Mashé: Tia, it's good to hear from you. It seems like months ago when we spoke. How are things?

Tia: I'm doing well; Mashé, is this a good time for you?

Mashé: I have a few minutes—I'm listening.

Tia: I happened to run into Eila at a dinner party through a mutual friend of my husband's. I couldn't believe my eyes when she walked in with a group of either friends or colleagues. She recognized me instantly and we talked for quite some time. She mentioned recently going home for an overdue visit with you and Rhial. She gave me her business card—she works for the City as a Civic Consultant. She promised to call me so we could meet for lunch. I can understand your concerns. She is an exact replica of a social butterfly. I was amazed how she called numerous city officials by their first names. There were a few NBA players there also and she was well acquainted with them too. She was not to my observation making a spectacle of herself, but instead she was one of the primas in the room.

Mashé: Tia, how was she dressed?

Tia: Yes, she has filled out since college. I would say her suit was alluring and it worked for her. Now this is what I wanted to share with you. My husband and I stayed until the end of this social and she walked out with this fine-looking guy that happened to appear as she was leaving. I watched them go to the parking lot. She got in her car and he drove up behind her and they took off. I did not recognize him and he did not mingle with anyone—he seemed to have come alone specifically to meet her.

Mashé: Did you notice the make and model of his car?

Tia: It was a dark blueberry in color BMW with out-of-state license plates—top of the line too. I was not close enough to identify which state exactly, but definitely not New York. Another thing she did not let me get one word in edgewise and that is very unusual for me. Noticeably though she was stunned when she saw me and was curious as to how we connected. My husband is a CPA and handles the accounts of several of those attending. Mashé, the look on your friend's face.

Mashé: I am all the more convinced there is something going on by her reaction to seeing you there. Well, my class will begin shortly…Should I call you later this evening?

Tia: I am working late tonight but listen…as I told you I could only do this in a non-professional accord because she is not my client and then I could not supply you with any information as per legal reasons if she were. I need to gather something tangible first. There is nothing peculiar about meeting up with someone at a party; it is just that I believe he may be the mystery to the puzzle—by way of speaking.

Mashé: Understood…Tia, I agree there is a secret circling about—I do not want to violate her privacy but something is no doubt abnormal.

Tia: Tell me, how so?

Mashé: While she was here visiting I had a birthday dinner party at a restaurant and she met this man who clearly had the company of another woman and when this woman went to the ladies' room Eila and this man whom I did not recognize left together and did not return. Rhial and I asked her the next day about him and she said nothing—she refused to answer.

Tia: Thank you, Mashé—that is something I needed to know somewhat similar to what happened here. Without going into detail I am now inclined to take this to a different level. I had better go too; I'll be in touch. Take care.

Mashé stared out the window reflecting on her conversation with Tia. As a result of what she heard the idea appeared in her mind at some time to casually ask Aunt Lennie about any unexplained behavior patterns she noticed about Eila as a child.

🍒   🍒   🍒

Recently Rhial met with a group of skeptical realtors and a few members of the Panama City Beach Chamber of Commerce who had finally agreed to learn of a business proposal she designed for low-income neighborhoods. It was a collage of different ideas for making aesthetic improvements to parts of Panama City, for example. She impressed upon them to take baby steps by applying her version of different sources of marketing tools like consumer generated media to different prospects. For some time city officials were reporting that more funding was needed in order to carry this through. But Rhail's introduction on the use of new marketing technology put her on the threshold of a ground-breaking phenomenon. This brought her local media attention and already the Panama City Beach Chamber of Commerce was approached by many small businesses wanting to meet with her and some were surprised that she was only an entrepreneur.

The following day Rhial and Halvan were almost swamped with calls and texts wanting to pick her brain because they could see that the positive impact destined for those neighborhoods could bring other benefits that they wanted to be in on. Within a short period of time they both had booked their calendars for a consecutive three weeks, and those from Haines City, Florida, wanted to be included.

Rhial sent to Eila and Mashé a news video of her being interviewed in front of the Chamber of Commerce building on the same evening that they were on a three-way phone conversation for nearly an hour.

Mashé: You need to send it to your parents—I would love to see the look on their faces. You did it, Rhial.

Eila: Congratulations again! How is your man handling your success? Tell the truth! Well, from all indications you will probably end up putting him on your payroll.

Rhial: Eila, was that really necessary?! He and I are in this together; this is not a contest between us.

Mashé: (Interjects) Rhial, we have been on the phone for an hour at least. You two must be tired and you are three hours ahead of me. Where is Halvan, by the way? I want to congratulate him as well.

Rhial: (Modestly) He…had to step out for a minute; when he comes home I will give him your message.

Eila: (Prodding) It must be about 10:45 PM, right?

Mashé: (Clearing her throat) We'll say good night now; we are so proud of you. The next thing we know you'll be on the cover of *Forbes Magazine*.

Rhial: You think so?! Good night, my Best Girls.

As soon as Eila hung up her phone rang, it was Mashé.

Eila: Oh! Mashé, I beg your pardon? It was a simple question. Men are known for being jealous of their successful girlfriends or wives. I was just wondering, honestly there was no motive.

Mashé: I would like to believe you, Eila. She has been enduring a lot from this relationship and like you I would like to know more about him, seriously though, this was a moment to support her.

Eila: You know, Mashé, that is the difference between you and me. You "walk on eggshells" too much. Just come out with it. There have been times when you made me want to scream.

Mashé: Is that a fact?! You would not appreciate a friend of yours asking you how your man was handling your success?

Eila: In the first place I have a successful man on my agenda. Mashé, Rhial is carrying Halvan. She is, how do you say it? "Fronting." She asked her father for $10,000.00 to pay a phony college fee bill. I know she is the softest of the three of us; nonetheless she needs to place more expectations on him. I will just say this to you. I hope she does not marry him; he brings absolutely nothing to their relationship.

Mashé: You could be on point, Eila, but it's her choice, her life. Besides, you are not with them all day and all night…you don't know what he brings! (Mashé felt curious) So, Ms. Wynston, there is a successful man in your life?

Eila: I have been dating off and on a professional man. The one you missed at that party I mentioned.

Mashé: (Inquisitive) The same one from college? Do tell. What is his profession?

In that instant Eila told her, someone was calling her and she needed to take the call, so they said goodnight.

Emergence (4)

Berkeley Hills had been drenched by the marathon rainfall. Some main streets had been closed off and many had decided to forgo leaving their homes. It was Tuesday, about 9:30 AM. Mashé called the college and reported that she would be absent and would try again tomorrow. Her parents decided to take a trip to Los Angeles where an Arts Festival was taking place. She would have gone too had it not been for Chandler's expected return, and she wanted to prevent the possibility of Neil meeting him. Since their last visit she had politely declined two or three outings with him because she needed to complete some art work and basically wanted to delay discussing his proposal. His patience with her was considerate but her conscience bothered her more and more. When she went outside for the newspaper she had a call come in from Chandler. He unexpectedly told her he would be in on Sunday—his itinerary was moved up earlier. She had finally accepted a date with Neil on Saturday night so she had to call him.

Mashé: Neil, good morning. Are you up? Good. I wanted to know if we could change our date to Friday—I have an outline to prepare and I decided that this weekend would work best. I did not go into work today for obvious reasons.

Neil: You are at home?

Mashé: Y…yes. I decided to avoid those road blocks and work at home.

Neil wanted to stop by after work and offered to bring dinner. Mashé started to decline and instead told him she looked forward to seeing him. As she returned to her journal she felt the guilt cloud forming over her again. With her parents being away she could be more relaxed in saying what she should have said when they were together at his home.

Mashé had nicely set the kitchen table for two. The wet weather fiercely continued and then around 6:00 PM Neil came to the door with an aroma suited for a banquet. He had the Fantasía Restaurant prepare a delectable dinner for two.

Mashé: Neil, you drove all the way to Belmont?

Neil: Once I got to the overpass it was easy, not a problem. We haven't seen each other for a while—you look good, Mashé, on a wet August night.

Mashé: Thank you and you too. How was work?

Neil: Work is getting interesting. There are some political shenanigans going on with our unit. The two heads are bumping heads if you understand.

Mashé: Yes, I think so. How does that affect your role?

Neil: You know I will leave it to the powers that be, tonight I have a nice dinner planned with a beautiful woman so I am doing much better than they are. Allow me to serve you. By the way, where are your parents?

Mashé: In L.A. for a couple of days.

Neil tried to conceal the thoughts he was entertaining. So he displayed his genteel side and pulled the chair from the table to seat Mashé. There was enough food for four people. Mashé did not hold back; she had only eaten breakfast and nothing else. While eating she intently watched him. He looked different, which was a good thing. It prompted her to ask him besides working what else was going on. Neil said he and some college friends met up at a club in Burlingame to catch up. He said they had the best time and added they were all married and hounded him for what was holding him up.

Neil: I was cool, telling them that I had my future in the hands of an extraordinary woman.

Mashé felt like she was being pinned to the wall; noting his cleverness with the expensive dinner and telling his crew that it was about to happen gave her an idea.

Mashé: Neil, when you asked me to marry you it seemed impulsive. We should work on a friendship first. We need to know one another better, what do you think?

Neil looked puzzled, asking what did she think he was doing since they met. He asked her if she wanted anything else. Mashé uttered she was fine. Rising from his seat he came to her side, stooped down, and asked her to tell him what would she have him do. Mashé sat there speechless but thinking she should send him home. Neil asked for her hand, motioning her to rise and join him in the living room. They sat there together and he asked her to massage his temples, which meant reclining in her lap. Mashé was definitely unprepared for this and wondered what was to follow. With his eyes closed he spoke of her gentleness then suggested they listen to music. By chance the remote was nearby so she found a station playing by "luck of the draw" sounds from the 1970's. Her stimulating touch was becoming more rousing. She was frightened by sudden crackling sounds of thunder and Neil rose to comfort her. Holding her the way he was made her think of Chandler and she asked him to leave; she could not respond the way he wanted. Neil had an expression of disbelief; surprisingly he quickly stood up and spoke.

Neil: Maybe I should appreciate how you have tried to go along, Mashé. If you are not feeling what I'm feeling, maybe it's better to be friends except—I don't want another friend, I want a woman to want me—no one can tell me I have not been clear as a bell about that.

Then he pulled from his pants pocket a tiny black and gold jewelry box. Mashé held her breath for a moment.

Neil: I also went to the jewelry store in this weather and bought this ring for your left hand. It's one of a kind too. I guess it's obvious whatever he's got going on, it must really be potent; I give.

Then he rushed out the door. Mashé speechless again stood in the middle of the living room floor as she listened to him drive away.

It was Sunday afternoon and Chandler and Mashé had gone to the Berkeley Pier for an early seafood dinner. He was looking better than the last time she saw him. Their discussion ranged from music and politics to the best suspense movie released thus far. He shared the intricate details of his case and was happy to report that he prepared a brief that would bring all the allegations upon his client to a halt—complete exoneration. They had been together for almost a day and a half and there was no mentioning of his invitation to Florida. If she did move there she would be close to Rhial; though to her Florida and California were like comparing apples to oranges—anyway she decided to allow him the privilege to try her again. Oddly, her thoughts went to Neil. It had been three days since their incident. She wanted to call him to check on how he was doing. She told her mother just in spurts what happened and her reaction was to allow him some time. She added that love could not be forced on anyone—it's either there or it isn't. Once again she told her daughter that as nice a person as she was, he had to respect the fact of never being misled by her.

Chandler: Mashé, I asked you a question.

Mashé: Please forgive me—I have much on my mind. What did you say?

Chandler: What would you like to do now? My vote is to go back to our suite.

Mashé: Yes, but first take me to the mall for a moment—you and I have yet to go shopping together.

Chandler gave her a puzzled though willing look. When they arrived she remembered the fine jewelry boutique, the only one of its kind.

Chandler: My Lady, what do you have in mind? I remember now, I owe you a birthday gift. Please forgive me? All you had to do was say it.

Mashé: This is not about my birthday. We need to walk that heavy meal off, at least I do.

Chandler: Your frame is perfect; I have been longing to see it again.

Mashé peered at him as they clasped hands walking in. The first level was the food court and specialty stores so they casually took the escalator to the second level—she noticed the jewelry boutique immediately, then glanced at Chandler, who made no mention of it.

Mashé: There are some pricey items on this level.

Chandler: (Smiling) Oh, I see why we're here—all you had to do was ask me. I see that chic, as you would say, lingerie on display, yes very nice, I would love to buy that for you and love taking it off of you too. Mashé was taken aback; they walked right past the jewelry boutique.

It appeared that they were both set on two different planes so she slyly tiptoed over to the display window as he inquired about the lingerie. As she browsed, it occurs to her that maybe he did notice the boutique and by default jumped at the chance for the lingerie. With Neil there was no playing games; then she quickly thought, that is nonsense.

🍒   🍒   🍒

The taxi swiftly brought them to the hotel's entrance and they proceeded to their suite. Mashé was still in a bit of a fog and now more than ever wanted to speak her mind. As they walked in he presented a gorgeously wrapped gift box to her and wished her a belated Happy Birthday. While at the mall she had barely glanced at it. When she lifted the lid there was this stunning creamy blue colored piece that had to cost four figures at best. She made herself a bubble bath and sank in, still pondering on whether she should have spoken up. The bath water was luxurious—why not, they were staying at a five star hotel downtown. Chandler was on the other end showering and singing as well. As she soaked she wondered did he think he was that clever; well, it certainly looked that way. She did not want two men walking out on her, but how could "silence be golden" in this instance?

Chandler called out to her with his salacious self. She remembered how his eyes bucked when she walked out doing a catwalk version. Mashé gradually felt more disenchanted though she still wanted to submit to him. In those few moments they spent together all they did seemed to be on his terms; again, she was obliging. As she sashayed around for him her immediate thoughts became more tangled. Right then she stopped and plopped herself onto the opposite end of the Italian leather couch with legs crossed, pouting. Chandler walked over asking what happened to his show. With no response, he started stroking her right cheek—he was wearing only his briefs and asked her to remove them. Mashé sat in silence. Unfazed his arms tightly wrapped around her, then he planted his infamous kiss which kindled the moment; the thoughts of the jewelry boutique and all else vanished. Routinely he enjoyed clutching her hair, as his hands pulled her head gently back they landed onto the mattress. Chandler began loosening her snaps and straps. He turned her around and with one tug it was off. With her body still moist Chandler entered her in a fashion having her succumb to the limber style he desired. Mashé was his sensual ballerina for the evening.

Chandler was the first to awake, whispering to her that he needed to be in court in a couple of hours. Mashé rose and as she got her bearings wished him all the luck. It was going to take some effort but she was going in to work. He ordered room service and when she took a swallow of some strong brewed coffee it seemed to have given her a lift. Chandler went to the shower and lathered up with a song. Mashé began packing, rushed to take a quick shower, and asked the front desk to call her a taxi. After she dressed she crammed a Spanish omelet and bran muffin in her mouth and finished with a gulp of orange juice.

Chandler walked out drying off, suggesting that tonight they should meet up with his friends to celebrate but he was amazed at Mashé as she opened the door and walked out.

Mashé: Can't make it—I have other plans. (Chandler runs out after her.)

Chandler: May I come by tonight? Let's talk about whatever is bothering you, that good?

Mashé: Fine. See you tonight. (Mashé really wanted to say, don't bother.)

When she arrived to work her class was there waiting for her; she apologized and proceeded with the course outline. During lunch she didn't join the other faculty as usual; she went straight to her cloak room for a snooze.

That evening when she arrived home she could hear her landline ringing and rushed in to answer it. Chandler was calling to say he was on his way there. She said fine and went to the kitchen to start her dinner. She was feeling a little underappreciated and this was not the first time she had felt this way with him. Now, in thinking about Neil it would have been the exact opposite but her feelings were completely different. She goes upstairs to change into her silk caftan. It was a bit suggestive but the only action on the menu tonight would be conversation. When she returned she cut a couple slices of sourdough bread and decided to pan-fry her fish to make a fish sandwich with coleslaw. As she was about to take a bite Chandler appeared at her door with a solid hard knock. When he walked in she was presented with a long-stemmed red rose.

Mashé: Thank you very much. Come in and have a seat. So you realized why I took off this morning?

Chandler: Not really! We had a sensational evening, you seemed pleased with your belated birthday gift, so I am here to have you fill me in. Also, I have good news my lady. The judge ruled in my favor—all charges have been dropped. With that behind me I can now return to my home office—this one was grueling.

Mashé: (Suspicious) Congratulations! So, what time is your flight home?

Chandler: (Glancing over) Why so formal? So let's talk about it?

Mashé: It! Chandler, for a lawyer you appear clueless about what you should be doing about us. Our visits are few and they are usually revolving around your needs. Not once have you asked me what I would like to do. I suggested the Mall and you went straight to that intimacy boutique. Sex was on your mind and that, Mr. Attorney, is not criminal except you asked me to relocate to Florida with you. Do you feel where I am going with this?

Chandler listened attentively and walked over to sit beside her.

Chandler: Mashé, the ball is in your court. You said you were concerned about your teaching post here, that you liked the college and I respect that. I told you I put in a good word for you to a friend of mine in the community college system. There is no need to be concerned. True, you would be away from your family and familiar surroundings, but you can visit them and they can come and visit.

Now, what is the matter with making new friends? Ah, the clueless part I don't understand—I thought you liked what I bought you until this morning when I noticed it was still on the floor.

For a few moments they sat there gazing into one another's eyes. Mashé was struggling with his unwavering, egotistical behavior. He then rose telling her he needed to get back to the hotel. He told her how disappointed the others would be for not joining the celebration and he also wanted to leave with her the sexy item he bought. She said she was just expecting something else. He brought her to him, saying you are a wildly mysterious female, then enfolded her with his charming affection. As he turned for the door he asked her where her parents were. Surprised, she told him they were out and would be home later. That was strange because he rarely spoke of them or even acknowledged their existence.

That fish sandwich was so delicious, she wished she had made two. Then she heard the front door open; her parents were back. She greeted them saying that they just missed Chandler. Her mother's interest was piqued. Her father said he had a full day and wanted to turn in. Clover joined her at the kitchen table to hear all of the particulars. Mashé only intended to give her a few highlights and then turn in herself, but Clover wanted a complete rundown. Mashé assumed her mother knew they were intimate. She spoke of how Chandler wanted her to come to Florida with him and that she really loved him, but instead of an engagement ring he bought something for her to sleep with him in. Wondering how he could be so clueless.

Clover: Sweetheart, you need to ask yourself that.

Mashé: (Sensitive) What do you mean?! I asked him what I meant to him.

Clover: Mashé, you are grown and intelligent but you are dancing around this man like a little girl. He is an attorney—a good profession and you need to be smart, not childish and mushy. He appears to be rather self-serving and you have been serving him generously, right? I wanted to mention this earlier but I wanted to see how you would handle things. Do you think I am on point?

Mashé: So I'm the one who has to speak plain English? I am sure he doesn't expect me to live with him.

Clover: The last thing I want you to do is feel apprehensive. Women need to stay a step ahead, especially with the very intelligent kind. Look at the irony of this; one of them actually buys an engagement ring, you snub him; the other one does not and you call "foul." My dear daughter, how did you manage to send two men away in two weeks' time?

Mashé didn't want to respond to that one though she thought, "How could this land in her lap? It looked like she needed to do some self-analysis—just then she thought of Tia's and Eila's activities. She and Clover ultimately said good night and proceeded upstairs to bed. While she was sitting on the foot of her bed and not sleepy, again Neil came to mind so she wanted to call him.

It was getting chilly; dusk would come soon as Mashé sat on the terrace looking out over the ocean. She was looking forward to the moonbeams that seemed to skip over the water.

She did call Neil that night. She remembered how hesitant she was when she heard his phone ringing; he didn't answer but a woman did. Mashé asked to speak with Neil as she gave her name. Instantly Neil came on the line.

Neil: Miss Boston. Could you hold on a minute?

Mashé waited longer than she wanted and then he came on again.

Neil: I had to come upstairs to my landline. So what is going on with you?

Mashé: I have thought a lot about what happened the other night. I could not allow another day to pass without speaking with you. I hoped you would be receptive.

Neil: Mashé, I did not like the way I took off, but you know I have taken a good look at us and I know I did nothing wrong. You made your choice and I need to respect it. Friendship is for friends and love is lovers.

Mashé: (Awed) How poetic…I am in total agreement. It seems you have company so I had better say good night.

Neil: Mashé, you are not interrupting anything. Hearing your voice again affirms what I still feel for you. Our love is not finished.

That last statement made her feel somewhat unsettled—it haunted her for some time. Right then her phone lit up. It was Chandler.

Chandler: Did I awaken you?

Mashé: No way…what's on your mind?

Chandler: We are at my friend's restaurant, I am sitting alone at a booth so I can talk with you privately, also, I went ahead and changed my flight for tomorrow, a noon departure just in case you might want to see me. After I spoke with you earlier I decided I needed to share some important information with you. I have held off long enough.

Chandler told Mashé that he had to confess something to her. He was trying to squash it on his own hoping it would eventually be forgotten, admitting once in a blue moon he should listen to his conscience. He spoke of the woman he had the casual affair with, the one from Miami. He began speaking very softly and Mashé was listening attentively. He passionately reinforced how he cared for Mashé and worked himself up to say that the woman came to him over three months ago saying she was one month pregnant and assured him he was the father. Chandler tried to encourage her to have an abortion but she refused. He then asked her to provide results of her pregnancy test and she stated she no longer had them. Later that evening he consulted with a Law School classmate of his, Tristan, who practiced family law, and was told that he needed to be tested to confirm her claim. His classmate stressed how he would not want to be declared the *de facto father* due to a lapse of time, that some jurisdictions in the state of Florida were strict with regards to those matters. Chandler said he concluded that this meant he should marry her and then wait to annul the marriage in a few months.

Mashé: (Riled) Chandler! You are married?! If you are really the father would you still get an annulment?

Chandler: Hold on! We did get married, but we never lived as man and wife. After the ceremony, she said she needed to leave town for a few days—for some time she has been living up north—this happened back in May I believe. So, I just went on about my business working, and so forth. For weeks I tried to reach her, she was nowhere to be found, and this made me very suspicious. Then a couple of weeks ago when I had just returned from California she appeared at my front door saying she was no longer pregnant. I insisted on knowing what actually happened—and she spoke in riddles; right then and there I decided to annul our marriage. As I said earlier I never intended to stay married to her. I contacted my classmate Tristan again and gave him the news.

That very next day, Chandler said, he and his classmate went to the County Administration Building to file for an annulment on the grounds of marital fraud.

Chandler: Mashé, you were on my mind during this entire ordeal. My parents don't even know of this. It's true I was attracted to her, but not in a romantic way…

Mashé: (Monotone voice) Okay, so when was the last time you saw her or spoke to her?

Chandler: Just before I came here to complete my case and above all to see you.

Mashé: Why?

Chandler: She acknowledged the receipt of the annulment documents and was rather miffed that I had not discussed it with her—she is one audacious woman.

(Moments of silence)

Mashé: That is probably one of the qualities you found attractive about her. Oh yes, and that means you bought her an engagement ring.

Chandler: Pardon me?!

Mashé: Yes, Chandler, pardon you. This woman whoever she is has a hold on you; this explains your non-commitment. I must admit that was some charade.

Chandler: No doubt. What! Non-commitment, Mashé, I handled everything appropriately and you are a sophisticated woman who knows that this man, me, wants you with him all of the time. Mashé, I took care of the problem. The ring was nothing—very simple. Wait a second, you think that I would marry only under pressure?

Mashé: Is this female out of your system? She doesn't appear to be.

Chandler: (Defensive) She was not in my system—not the way you are implying.

Mashé: Chandler, it is late and I need to let all of what I just heard settle in. Anyway, you met her before you met me.

Chandler: Mashé, what does that mean?

Mashé: (Vexed) I never took you for a person who wanted "to have his cake and eat it too." And the louche behavior of this woman—why are men so attracted to women who...men of so-called good sense allow something like this to ruin their families. Chandler, I need to go to sleep and you probably do too. Fine, you took care of it but is the problem really solved—is it really over?

Mashé remembers the weighty silence that crept in before they said good night.

Reflections (5)

Mashé jumps when Lou scurries underneath her chair, making her photo album fall to the deck with a few pictures sprawling. She feels so guilty. Here she is revisiting some flashbacks of her life and she has not even fed him. She finds his dish and fills it with some leftovers from last night. He detests dog food. She grabs her glass and refills it with water. When she returns she quickly collects her fallen pictures before the wind could blow them away. There are about seven of them and they are of Rhial's bridal shower. What a day that was. Sitting back in her chair she recollects that Rhial and Halvan came back to Berkeley Hills because it made the most sense with most of her family and friends there ready to celebrate and they planned to wed in Florida.

Her parents had a smorgasbord; they went "all out" and why not, she was their only child. Halvan's divorced parents were there too. About fifty people came and brought a multitude of gifts. Eila was her unusual, generous self. She supplied a unique array of games and prizes and Mashé took the pictures. The real "oomph" of the day, though, ignited after the shower ended.

To Mashé it feels like it happened yesterday.

After most of the guests had gone, Mashé and Eila were helping pack away the gifts; Halvan and the other members of the family had moved to the family room when Mashé noticed Rhial standing alone in the backyard. She motioned to Eila to follow her. Rhial looked like a zombie. Her friends asked her why she was outside alone. Rhial seemed to be holding back tears. She got her bearings and asked that what she was about to tell them be kept a secret. Eila and Mashé listened as their friend told them Halvan was going to be a father but she was not the intended.

Eila: (Livid) See! I told you he was not the man for her. I knew he was wrong...

Mashé: Rhial, what do you know?

Rhial: Halvan said he met her a few months ago at one of the meetings we held for our clients. He kept late hours sometimes, I assumed it was related to our work. I am not sure who she is. He said he was going to take care of it.

Eila: It?! How so?

Rhial: She was supposed to be getting an abortion. Halvan said they met at the clinic but as soon as she was called in by the nurse, she backed out and ran out. (This story resonated all too well for Mashé regarding Chandler's circumstance.)

Mashé: When did you learn of this, Rhial?

Rhial: When we boarded the plane coming here.

These three stirred up yet kindred spirited friends held hands and said a silent prayer. Mashé wanted to share her situation about Chandler but could not bring herself to do it; besides, they were not engaged to be married. And while standing there it occurred to her that she had made love with a married man; at least part of the time. Whose circumstance seemed worse? That was really not the point—the point was, one of her best friends was in a pickle and needed her support. Eila was so upset. Mashé and Rhial had to calm her down because she was insistent on confronting Halvan in front of everyone. The unwavering fact about Eila was she was willing to come to a friend's defense. When they were in the seventh grade Rhial was being bullied by a girl named Lenora who supposedly ran with a gang. Lenora told everyone around school that she was going to snatch Rhial after sixth period. Well, she was the one who got snatched. In fact, she missed about a week of school. Eila somehow knew these thugs who wanted to help, but she told them to just brush up on the girl—Mashé had come to realize then that Eila was capable of doing some outlandish things.

Eila: Ladies…I will be fine. Rhial, what is your next move? Are you going through with this?

Mashé looked upon Rhial's face with her usual expression of countenance. She always seemed to hold things together; even when they were children she seemed to be a person beyond her years—she would always try to reason with her and Eila whenever they bickered.

Rhial: Many people marry those with outside families. I am really not convinced that he is the father.

Eila: Well, I hope you are convinced that they slept together—he could not deny that. You know what I am going to call him, Mr. Pop-up behind his back—every time you look around something he's into just pops up. Rhial, please think this over?

Mashé: Rhial, I agree with her you have a blossoming career. You're on the right track. We can return the gifts for you with a suitable explanation.

Rhial: No!!!

Just then Aunt Lennie came to the window, motioning for them to come in.

Aunt Lennie: Rhial, Halvan's parents are leaving and it would be impolite not to see them to the door. Rhial, are you feeling all right? Eila, Mashé, what happened?

Rhial: (Pretending) I am fine, we were revisiting the plans we made as children and it appears that one of them is on point. I am the first to marry—we were just being sentimental.

Mashé and Eila glanced at one another.

Later that evening Mashé broke her solemn oath to Rhial and told her mother the crux of her friend's plight. Clover had pity for Rhial; like Eila and Mashé, she wondered what he saw in Rhial. Though Rhial had many good qualities she quietly contemplated their relationship; was Halvan really in love with her?

Clover: I see her as too plain for him and then again it is unfair to pre-judge. This is just you and I talking.

Mashé: Of course. I love Rhial and I just could not bring myself to tell her my honest thoughts. Eila and I agreed that she should re-think this situation, but she seems to be going on with it. Bottom line I thinks she feels Halvan is her last chance.

Clover processed what Mashé said and followed with.

Clover: She is the bride. She holds the cards and it is her call. I advise you to say nothing further; just be there for her whenever possible. She has caring parents and I will just pray that all goes well over this. Mashé, this is why I am so proud of you. You have a pretty good sense of character. I so want to see you married, though not for my sake or your father's but for yours. So, I want you to take your time.

After hearing this Mashé decided to postpone sharing Chandler's escapade. She and her mother were able to talk about most anything; nonetheless, this subject was too sensitive and she still loved him, which had her tangled all up inside.

For nearly a month, Mashé had not spoken to her Best Girls or even Chandler. She went to work, did routine shopping, and stayed caught up with the latest news, amusements and looked forward to the change in season now that autumn was approaching. Her parents were on another trip this time a little closer, Napa Valley. She admired their relationship. Mother was her father's second wife. There were no children from the first marriage. The way he explained it, he was in the Service more than at home. Oddly, she pondered on how life would be if she stayed single for the rest of her life. Rhial's situation caused her to think over and over again about Chandler and her. She was teetering on calling him to say that she would not come to Florida to be with him, that her feelings for him probably would never change. All things considered, it was probably best to avoid listening to her heart in order to keep it from breaking.

More than a week later on a Saturday afternoon Mashé got a call from Jasmine, an old acquaintance, inviting her to a patio party. It was to start at 4:00 PM and go into the evening. Mashé remembered how timely this was for she had not been out for a while and she would probably meet up with some familiar faces. This was just what she needed. It being an autumn evening she decided to dress a bit upscale but brought a wrap in case the temperature cooled. While going through her wardrobe closet she came across two items; either one would do—then a box fell right in front of her; it was the birthday gift from Chandler. She probably threw it up on the shelf in haste. She paused to open it. The workmanship on that garment was exquisite. While thinking back on that day she felt her reaction to it was on-target. She wanted to forget about their last evening together, though how could she do that? He was her match so she decided to give it time, the best way to handle it. They had not talked in a while and she was definitely not going to call him, though she hoped he was doing well. She promised herself that she would hold her chin up even though her love-life was lopsided.

It was approaching 4:00 PM so to avoid being the first to show up she sat in the den and turned on the television then instantly, the phone rang, and it was Tia.

Tia told her she was on her way to a political fundraiser on Long Island coordinated by Eila. She was supporting one of the local city officials there for an upcoming primary election.

Tia: Mashé, I wanted to call you earlier but things just caught up with me. Eila was out of town for a while. Did you know this?

Mashé: Well, about a month ago she was here to attend Rhial's bridal shower. She was only here for a few days not a week even.

Tia: She was gone longer than that. Whatever it is has led me to a dead end. She seems to be conducting herself in her usual way. I will be seeing her tonight so I will call you tomorrow night—are you going to be in?

Mashé: (Giggling) I will need to check with my social secretary—I am on my way out now. But what about the guy you saw her with before—he could be there tonight.

Tia: You have a point, though like I said he was driving a car with an out-of-state license plate and then again it may have only been a New Jersey license plate. Glad you brought that up. Don't let me keep you—we'll talk tomorrow.

One could hear the music a block away. Swarms of people were flowing in and Mashé was surprised that there was valet parking. This was not Jasmine's place but her boyfriend's. He had a mid-management post with the Golden State Warriors franchise. Mashé had met him and Jasmine at a Christmas party three years ago. She was so glad she chose the appropriate outfit. Normally, she did not attend functions like this unescorted but she had changed a few of her values—the caliber of people she associated with would not change but she reached a new level of maturity—she did not care what others may think. She planned on having a great time. When she entered it looked like the party had moved indoors. She looked around for Jasmine and tried to see anyone else who looked familiar; then she had a tap on her left shoulder—it was Jasmine, who looked gorgeous.

Jasmine: I am so glad you could make it on short notice. I love what you are wearing. Give me your secret for that small waistline?

Mashé: (Laughs) Glad you invited me. You are the one with style. We must stay in touch more often. Did the party move indoors?

Jasmine: Gordon (her boyfriend) decided to invite more people—now the party is indoors and outdoors. In fact I am looking for him. Wait, did you come alone?

Mashé: A rare occasion.

Jasmine: Well, we'll need to fix that. Would you like to meet a Baller? I mean, the NBA and NFL are here, lady.

Mashé: (Modest) Oh no. I want a mature man. Besides, I am a college instructor; they wouldn't be interested in me.

Jasmine: (Amused) Looking the way you look, quit with those excuses.

Mashé: Seriously, Jasmine, I can mingle but I am not looking right now. I was sort of in a relationship, bi-coastal, there were some unique circumstances, I'd better…

Jasmine: (Insistent) Mashé, this is a party, now come with me.

When they found Gordon he was mixing and serving drinks to a few guys he worked with and Mashé was introduced to them. She had a few admirers approach wanting to nuzzle up but she played them all off. About an hour had gone when the music selection changed from slow jazz to disco. People got busy. Wellington, one of the guys who did business with Gordon, asked Mashé for a dance. Wellington was cute and tall too. He and she had gotten into a mild conversation about sports, social issues, and relationships earlier. He was definitely a worldly person and very well dressed. He seemed to show interest in her but Mashé stayed neutral. Then the Disc Jockey played a classic slow jam, "Betcha By Golly Wow," by the Stylistics, one of her favorite groups as a child, and Wellington noticed her reaction; now, they were dancing. It was happening again, this man's touch reminded her of Chandler. She later believed this to be the case because she missed him. Then a voice that she had not expected to hear "rang true"—it was Neil's. He and Gordon knew one another they were just a few feet away from Mashé and Wellington, and they were talking loudly. Mashé turned her head the other way. She quickly imagined exiting through the patio before he saw her. When she looked in his direction, again, she noticed a fair-skinned woman standing next to him and they were holding hands. Mashé tensed up and didn't know why—she probably would have reacted differently had she come with someone.

Wellington held her closer and she did not resist this opportune moment. She decided to close her eyes, the lights had dimmed, and she was feeling the moment when to her surprise that familiar voice grew closer.

Neil: Hello, Ms. Boston, Wellington, it's been a while—how are you, Man?

Wellington: Doing quite well. Good to see you, so you know Mashé? What a small world!

Mashé: (Cordial) It's good to see you, Neil.

Neil: Oh, please pardon my manners. I would like you to meet Lara Nastle. Lara, this is Mashé Boston and Wellington???

Pleasantries were exchanged and as the song ended Mashé quickly excused herself.

Wellington asked her where she was going and she told him she was thirsty so he followed her. Neil watched them intently until they were out of his sight. Lara touched his face asking was he all right and he just muttered, fine.

Wellington: Mashé, I hope you are not trying to get away from me. What happened back there? Did I say something wrong?

Mashé: No you didn't. It's just that I have not eaten anything and Jasmine told me earlier to try the hors d'oeuvres made by this world-class caterer Gordon hired.

Wellington: You know, Mashé, we could go for some real food. There's a nice restaurant just down the way. How about dinner with a stranger?

Mashé wanted to decline but having run into Neil and his date, she decided to accept as long as they went Dutch.

They went to this charming restaurant that only seated couples. Mashé thought that she should bypass this scene but Wellington was so interesting to talk to. They were seated upstairs in a cute moonlit loft. Wellington told her the party would soon go bust because of her absence.

Mashé: I hardly think so. Parties of that nature rarely run short of women.

Wellington: You sound like an expert. Believe it or not and with all due respect, I got lucky…lucky enough to dine with you, I mean. Mashé, a woman of your caliber, how did you manage to come to a party unescorted?

Mashé: (Sighs) I am in an unresolved bi-coastal relationship. And I am not the desperate kind to look up escort services. I know Jasmine so I was rather comfortable coming alone.

Wellington: Until he walked in.

Mashé: Pardon me?!

Wellington: How long have you known Neil?

Mashé: (Hesitant) Just…a few months. How about you?

Wellington: For a while. You both seemed to have some billowing nuances going on—his girl picked up on it too. (Mashé thought: So what!) Well, I feel sorry for him. I know we just met this evening, however, what are my chances of seeing you Mashé?

Mashé: It might be best not to. I have a lot on my mind and it would not be fair to you. Ah, why do you feel sorry for him?

Wellington: Pardon my sarcasm. He looked bewildered, maybe even whipped.

Mashé: (Concerned) He did?!!

Wellington: May I pry? Is he the one?

Mashé: He? Oh my bi-coastal boyfriend, I would like to think so. There are some areas that need to be discussed and men generally speaking, not all dance around the subject of commitment or just expressing their real feelings. But tell me something about you?

Wellington: I had a wife but she didn't want to be married anymore. I have been a free man for two years running.

Mashé: You seem to be at peace with it.

Wellington: It was an arranged marriage—we were betrothed as children.

Mashé: Is that still going on? Pardon my asking; weren't you two miserable?

Wellington: Not always. Well, it's no secret any more. We had a trust fund in our names set up by my father and her father.

Wellington explained that he came from a well-to-do family. He said his parents were domineering but he knew they loved him and he loved them though he said he wished he had challenged them more as he was growing up. He explained that they were to remain married for a given amount of years and to have children in order to benefit from the trust fund and even though she was an attractive woman, he did not love her and was tired of pretending. Mashé was impressed when he told her that he shared with her some portions of the trust fund upon the final divorce decree.

Mashé: You handled that like a gentleman.

Wellington: Yes, I felt I did too. Ah, this person you have the bi-coastal relationship with, does he come your way more or do you both even out the visits?

Mashé: He is the one who has been coming here to the west coast. I am a junior college instructor; my time away on a repeated basis would not work for me. He has more freedom of movement due to his profession.

Wellington: And that is?

Mashé: He's an attorney, corporate attorney.

Wellington: That's admirable. I am an Investment Banker; I inherited my father's and grandfather's bank. Back to a more interesting subject, which is you, Mashé. What are some qualities you want in a mate? You said earlier that men in general seem slow to commitment or something like that.

Mashé: Yes, it depends on the person, right? I need to know that I am not wasting my time. Companionship is important but if I am to spend the rest of my life looking for it, then so be it. Your past marriage, if I may say, is a perfect example; you were not happy.

Wellington: True and I am free of it. But, she w as not my choice and I was not hers.

Mashé: Wellington, you did say that she wanted out. It sounds like you were willing to go long term. And I don't know you well enough to give you all of the qualities I would like to see in a man.

Wellington: It's true she did want out; what I didn't tell you was I had stopped trying. And why don't we work on that? Let's get to know one another? Starting now.

Mashé: (Placid) As I stated earlier, I am in a relationship and I would rather avoid complications. You are a pleasant and intelligent person to talk with; actually, I could only see us as acquaintances.

Wellington: (Genteel) Well, that's definitely an unexpected answer. Though I will say this, you are a lovely woman, Mashé, back at the party I noticed you immediately and forgive me, but this attorney could be more scrupulous on your behalf..

Mashé: (Smiling) Yes, I am inclined to agree.

Wellington: I would like to tread lightly on another topic.

Mashé: (Bracing) And…that topic is?

Wellington: Neil Rollins. Would I be out of line….by….

Mashé: So far you are not. Neil is a caring and upstanding person. We did date for a while and then parted ways—though we are still friends.

Wellington: Neil and I were classmates at Bayhill High School. You are right, he is a good person. It is just obvious to me that there may be some feelings that still need attending to. As you can see I am inquisitive by nature, and I am interested in you.

Mashé: Being attracted to someone can be a gamble. You have no guarantee those feelings will be reciprocated. As you said about your marriage—there you two were thrust into a relationship that was supposed to be sacred; instead it was all for money. Life is too short to gamble with your feelings. Sincerity has to count for something.

Wellington: I respect your sentiments, Mashé. Though I think you need to live a little. We all gamble every time we wake up in the morning, get into our cars, or board a plane. I believe it depends on how far we are willing to go in this world. You are right, it was not for love that I married, yet I have to say that my intentions were sincere at the onset. I prefer to decide on my destiny in the romance department and that could take some time. What I am grateful for is, I won't have to wonder what it was like because I have had a taste of it. You said earlier that you would not mind spending the rest of your life looking for companionship. Seriously Mashé, I don't think you really meant that. Being lonesome is not living.

Mashé: (Roused) Well put, but loneliness is altogether different—I realize there are no building blocks—and as my father has said to me many times, "A ship was not built to stay in the harbor."

Wellington sat back in his chair smiling.

Wellington and Mashé talked for over an hour before ordering their dinner. They talked about nearly anything and everything. Wellington tried intermittent ploys of flirting, which she managed to derail. As Mashé recalls she could have talked with him until morning; instead they were the last to leave at closing. He tried to woo her into meeting with him the next day, Sunday; again she resisted though they did exchange phone numbers.

As dusk approaches Mashé rises from her seat, feet firmly planted on the deck, leaning on her rail, wondering whatever became of him; they never spoke again.

🍒 🍒 🍒

The next morning Mashé awoke around 11:00 AM with thoughts of Rhial. She decided to go downstairs, make breakfast and call her. Since her birthday was coming up she thought she would check on her, see how the wedding plans were coming along. Then a forethought came, she decided to just wish her Happy Birthday and avoid the topic of wedding plans. Her call went directly to voicemail so she gave her name and asked her to call her back. She needed to call Jasmine too. Then out of nowhere Neil came to mind. She was irked by her behavior. She didn't need to pretend, she could have stayed by socializing in another room; Gordon's house was spacious, and that would have been best. However, the time she spent with Wellington was practically invaluable. And even when she fussed over paying her own check he insisted on paying for both meals. That restaurant was expensive. Oddly, she thought it would be a charming place for her and Chandler to dine, if they could ever come to terms. Well, maybe not. While she was beating her eggs her parents strolled in. They found Napa Valley to be their best get-away spot thus far. They asked her to "put them in the pot." She quickly grabbed more eggs and decided to make cinnamon toast, West Indian omelets, and coconut lime with mint cocktails. A favorite of her paternal grandmother. What a mood she was in—perhaps some credit went toward Wellington and some to Neil. It felt nice getting out last night. It had been a while since she had danced and been admired by young ballers, even though none of them measured up to Chandler. Clover came down first saying her father had to take a call, just keep his plate warm.

Clover: This all looks delicious. Anything exciting happen while we were away?

Mashé: I went to a party last night—it was definitely the place to be.

Clover: Did you meet anyone interesting? Hold on, did you go stag?

Mashé: (Smiling) Stag, Mother? Yes, I did. But I mingled and had a great time. It was like one would say, "the cat's meow."

Clover: So, a man was in there somewhere?

Mashé: Yes, just socializing, that's all, Mother.

Clover: If you don't mind my saying, you seem to be saving yourself for this man who lives in Florida? And when did you last talk with him?

Mashé: I supposed it looks that way. You are referring to Chandler. We haven't spoken in weeks. Anyone else who approaches me does not spark my interest. Well, Neil was a possibility.

Clover: I was about to say, you two seemed chummy for a short while. Did you two ever…?

Mashé: No, Mother, we did not. He was at the party last night too.

Clover: Please, tell me more?!

Mashé: There is nothing really to tell. We spoke, he introduced me to his date and that's the long and short of it.

Clover: How weird was that? Running into him with a date and you unescorted?

Mashé: To be honest, he did not know I came alone because I was in the company of a good looking investment banker. We talked, danced, and enjoyed one another's company.

Clover: Conveniently serendipitous. I must hand it to you, your grandmother would applaud this breakfast of yours. (Eugene came down to join them, at which time a courier knocked at the door.) Presented was a small envelope addressed to Ms. Mashé Boston. She signed for it and tore it open. Just a small index card with a one-way first-class plane ticket attached.

There was a message: "Miss Mashé Boston, please marry me? I have your ring here waiting for you."

One would have thought Mashé was having spasms. Her mother ran over to read her proposal then shared it with her father. Her parents watched closely as she turned to face them.

Crossover (6)

Tampa Bay was having unusually fine weather and Mashé was settling into her new condo. Her eyes were fixed on her engagement ring practically every other minute. It was a shimmering cushion cut white diamond. She preferred to live as a single woman until they married. Chandler accepted this much to his chagrin, However, one would have thought he moved in as often as he visited. Also, as he promised, a teaching post was available for her in the English Department at Tampa Bay Community College. Fortunately, she was able to obtain a Leave of Absence status instead of a Resignation in California. The semester was just about to start when she arrived. It has been two weeks so far and Rhial was too happy to have one of her Best Girls close to her again. Interestingly enough they were all living on the east coast again. She and Mashé planned to have lunch at her condominium when she and Halvan returned from a conference in Pensacola. Upon settling in she also planned to call Eila. She would love to see the expression on her face when she tells her she moved to Florida and that she was engaged—she made Rhial promise not to tell her.

Before Mashé moved to Florida she called Tia to let her know she was going to be slightly closer to New York City. Tia was excited and said she meant to call her that morning but had a client with an emergency. Tia said she had more information to share and would call her soon. Mashé gathered the news must not have been that significant because it had been two weeks and Tia still had not called.

It was a Friday evening close to 6:00 and Chandler and Mashé were planning to go out to dinner. Also on Saturday night they were to see a musical in Miami Beach. She was looking forward to this because they had not been out socially and she wanted to become familiarized with her new surroundings.

She had just stepped out of the bathtub, eyes squinting from the suds, when to her surprise there stood Chandler waiting to wrap a bath towel around her.

Chandler: (Schmoozing) Would it be all right if we do dinner out tomorrow just before going to see the musical? I brought dinner home for us, it's in the oven keeping warm, and I was hoping you would do the same for me.

Chandler once again was having his way—before she could answer, his enticing wizardry amorously seized her. She was so set on going out and wanted to resist; still she consented as expected though this time they frolicked on her rose-colored, lattice style posh Italian carpet. She relished their first time together. It was magnificent; clearly, he knew he was her first. And since then, she has felt like she's been making love with an acrobat—like having a bustling rendezvous. She yields to his ramming thrusts, causing her groans to become louder; to his liking. His large, strong hands kneaded her backside when unpredictably she was heaved onto the bed. Despite the few moments of rest, their loving stretched beyond twilight.

Poised to believe that she could rise without incidence, Mashé put on her robe and went downstairs to search for her dinner or early breakfast. There it was in the oven. A Creole seafood stew, one of her favorites he discovered when they began dating. Thinking back about her mother's comments on dealing with a smart man like Chandler convinced her that she needed to be more assertive, not in a way that would turn him off. She had been from time to time, which she is now convinced is why he asked her to marry him in the indirect manner that he did. She knew he was not the subtle, apologetic type. Sometimes she adored his affectionate style, but she did not want to be undermined by him. It's apparent, he planned this whole situation (premeditated); he knew walking in with a regular fried fish dinner was not going to fly.

Something else was nudging her. He had not mentioned his first wife and even though there were no indications of her presence, she still wondered. As she took the first spoonful she closed her eyes savoring it all. Yet another reason to be glad she returned to Florida. She heard heavy footsteps and it was him walking in with just his briefs. She thought, If he was thinking about going at it again, Oh no!

Chandler: Good morning, my sultry queen. You are giving me that look I don't understand. I have loved you well and fed you well. What's up?

Mashé avoided eye contact, stressing how much she was counting on an evening out instead of an evening in. It was becoming disconcerting, nearly sputtering she was not his concubine. She asked him to please leave his lawyering at the office and just be the man she intends to marry, genuinely catering to her as she has been to him.

Chandler walked over to the kitchen nook and sat across from her. With a composed expression he said that ever since her arrival he had been feeling complete, that finally he had the right one in his life. He felt like he had been celibate more like forever and he was honestly wanting to share his love for her and along with that, he liked her cooking. He assured her that they would do the dinner plans and the musical like she wanted and also meant to add that his parents wanted to meet her so she would need to be ready around 3:00 PM on Sunday to go to South Beach.

Mashé found the Sunday visit plan somewhat impromptu but instead of mentioning this she asked him had he been in touch with his former wife and was still wondering whether his parents ever met her?

Chandler gave her a sharp and poignant look and reiterated that he kept his relationship with her quiet—there were no introductions because he never was serious about her. She was the one with an agenda and it failed. As for being in touch with her, he recapped that the last time they spoke was when she appeared at his door fussing about the annulment decree. His voice tone changed giving her the impression that she had touched a sensitive nerve. He went on to explain that with an annulment it is treated as though the marriage did not take place and in essence was legally erased. He added that he wanted her to trust him because he would never consciously expose or subject her to a precarious situation.

Mashé replied that it was not about trusting him but more about not trusting her, and that her impressions of her could be she might be unbalanced; she felt he might be hiding this woman from her.

Chandler quickly scoffed, "hiding you, Mashé, are you serious?" He said in his line of work he was unquestionably familiar with, "unbalanced." He said she was persistent and he should have been more resistant. He went on to say that his parents were great folks but they would not have taken kindly to the likes of her—it would not have been pretty. In his eagerness he noticed that Mashé was just about done with her meal.

Chandler: It appears that you are not wearing anything underneath that lovely pink robe. Later on I need to go into the office for a couple of meetings, but I will definitely be back here in time for us. You know you and I could enjoy each other right here on the kitchen table with a quick one?

Mashé: (Placid) I think that would be uncomfortable and like you I have some work to do, I need to grade some essays and since you have my Sunday calendar filled in I had better attend to them very soon, you understand.

Chandler: (Coy) I just knew you would want this as much as I do.

Mashé: I will make it up to you tonight two-fold; in the meantime let me make a hearty breakfast for my man.

Just as she was about to rise Chandler took her tenderly by the shoulders, sat her down, and began fussing with the buttons of her robe. He struggled with undoing them. They were the magnetic kind that latched around. Mashé did nothing, she enjoyed watching this brilliant man friskily tugging away to undo her buttons. He then instantly lodged his face into her bosom. As she braced for what was to follow her robe was brought over her head then dropped onto the seat. She tried to move but he had her in a tight snug. He rushed back to her cleavage, his hands began traveling up and down her back. Then came his infamous roaming tongue; at that moment she broke free telling him to remember where he left off, it was time for his fried eggs.

The Miami Theater was sold out and when Intermission came Mashé and Chandler went into the lobby. Mashé was enjoying it so far; Chandler seemed indifferent and was thinking about the Miami Heat game that was about to begin.

Mashé: So from your silence I am wondering, are you enjoying it?

Chandler: It has been so long since I have attended anything to do with the Fine Arts. It's different—what makes it exceptionally pleasant is you are here.

Mashé: (Curious) Chandler, I realize you did this for me but I would never want you to be bored. You think you can handle the second half?

(Chandler thought, sure if it were an NBA game.)

Chandler: Of course. Look, the lights are flickering; we had better get back to our seats.

After the musical Mashé and Chandler took a stroll near the pier. There was a mild wind blowing as they walked hand in hand. For about twenty minutes or so they said nothing then Chandler noticed the Oceanfront Hotel just ahead and suggested that they stay the night.

As Mashé recalls, it was a romantic kind of evening. The clouds were at their floating cirrus stage and it was pitch black with a few noticeable stars. She had not packed anything and she always felt he had pre-arranged it.

Mashé: I want to go home. Why stay here?

Chandler: Lady Mashé. Look at the shoreline, the waves. We can have a room on the second story and enjoy that splendid view from the balcony. We are both romantics and as I recall you promised me a "Night to Remember," to coin a phrase.

Mashé: Yes, back at my place though. You do not play fair.

Chandler: (Irked) Look, never mind. Let's go to the car and go home. I was just trying to be a little adventurous. You always seemed like the type to try different things. I did not think you would resist an enticing temptation.

Mashé: I can be adventurous, just not tonight. Anyway, I need to go to a supermarket and buy some personal items. What about your parents?! I can imagine how funny we are going to look walking in dressed the way we are.

Chandler: We can tell them we just came from church service.

Mashé: That's the first time I have heard you mention the word church. By the way, we are going to be married in one if that is all right with you?

Chandler: Someone is being very sarcastic. Yes that is fine with me, what a question?

Mashé: You know, we are closer to South Beach then we would be back in Tampa, so it does make sense to stay over. See this is what I have been talking about. I could have packed and felt more at ease about this.

Chandler: Listen to my plan. After we have a good breakfast we'll go to the nearby mall and buy whatever suits you. It will be our secret. Cool?

Mashé: Fine. I hope there is a vacancy.

Chandler: There should be.

Mashé: (Curious) Have you been here before? Tell me?!

Chandler took her face and planted a walloping kiss on her lips lasting for a few moments.

When they entered the foyer there was a nice popping fireplace going. For beach property it looked better than Mashé had imagined. As he said they got a room with a balcony and a beautiful scene of majestic dark water and sky. Mashé was warming up to this idea. Then again his slyness still needed to be reckon with. As soon as the door shut Chandler undressed down to his briefs and turned on the Ultra-HD television. He asked was she hungry and she said she could eat something light only if he joined her. It was close to eleven o'clock when he called the front desk and placed an order of assorted sandwiches. They had a service that would go into town and bring back late night orders up to a certain hour. Mashé got an answer to her earlier question. She took a guest robe from the closet and sat on the sofa and watched the show with him. When the sandwiches arrived they looked scrumptious and she helped herself. He didn't eat.

Chandler: So, you were hungry.

Mashé: Walking along the promenade and taking in that sea breeze made me hungry I suppose.

Within thirty minutes he looked over at her and she had fallen asleep. She looked so cute all curled up and peaceful but a promise is a promise. He whispered her name a few times with no response and adored her purr-like snore. She was startled by a succulent kiss on her shoulder, now fully awake and smiling. With her robe removed like that morning, his roaming tongue resumed. She arched her back giving him leeway, this privilege was given throughout the night; she yielded to every one of his positions. Around 10:45 AM Mashé got into the bathtub. She ached and wondered would she be ready in time to meet her in-laws-to-be. She stood up and looked into the full length mirror—her hair was a sight and it was all Chandler's fault. He always had to play with it; she was a bit unnerved, she needed her hair oil and flat-iron. She sat back down and almost dozed off when Chandler walked in with a small plastic shopping bag. In it were a high-end electric flat-iron and other hair essentials.

Mashé: (Uplifted) You think of everything.

Chandler: Absolutely. Hurry up, Lady Mashé, so we can eat and shop. Then sometime later, I can play with your hair again.

En route to his parents' home Chandler shared some family history. His father served in Viet Nam and was now a retired Realtor, his Mother a retired Nursing Director. He tried to reach his brother as well to stop by to meet her.

Mashé: Do you think he will come?

Chandler: He has my voice message and whenever there is something major happening he'll come to family events. Mostly though it's birthdays and the holidays at best.

Mashé: He has the qualities of a loner.

Chandler: Yes, we all have concluded that; maybe when he sees you he'll perk up. One thing about the men in my family, lovely women become a distraction. And I mean that in a positive sense.

Mashé: So, we need to be clear about our wedding plans. We are going to have two ceremonies; I cannot believe any of this. First here and then back at Berkeley Hills.

Chandler: Looks like we are going to say "I do" twice, Like I said whatever you want.

Mashé: Actually, one ceremony would be more practical.

Chandler: True but…

Mashé: Would you object to the ceremony taking place in California, since I have relocated here? That's what Rhial and Halvan have decided. I do not want to piggy-back, but it would be less stress on the bride and groom.

Chandler: Hmm.

She was getting the sense that Chandler was on the fence. Fine (to herself), they will marry in California; like he said, whatever I want. Besides, she has relocated to Florida. She had been thinking about her parents lately. They had mixed feelings about Chandler. They had yet to have a decent conversation with him. She had an idea, she would throw a small engagement party—but where should it be—here or in California?

Chandler: Oh yes, I am scheduled to be away for a few days. There is a corporate client that has retained my services to defend them in a Conflict of Interest case. It is a major food franchise. They cover southern Florida and parts of South Carolina.

Mashé: Interesting. My family is from Kershaw, South Carolina.

Chandler: You are a southerner from California. Here we are. There, the house sits on a hill. My father had it built from the ground up.

Mashé: (Astonished) I was not expecting this. Chandler, you are rich.

Chandler: Nope! My parents are. Good returns in real estate investments for certain. That Florida and California have in common.

Mashé was more than nervous; she was perspiring at the temples. Then she told herself that all would be fine, though he could have given her a hint of some kind. The housekeeper, Merla, answered and suggested they go to the dining room. Mashé looked around and was struck by the fine paintings of what appeared to be family members from years past. Then two people approached, Chandler's parents, DeAnn and Garrett. Mashé immediately understood what Chandler meant about his parents, they had a distinction about them, like a King and Queen, though she was not intimidated. Introductions were made and DeAnn asked if they were hungry; she had some food prepared for them.

Mashé: Mrs. Tollare, we did have brunch earlier (Chandler sharply glances at her). But…

Chandler: Mother, we'd love to see what you've prepared.

He went over to his parents and gave them a generous hug. Mashé just stood there unsure of what to do.

Garret: Mashé, so my son got you to come to Florida and you are a college instructor. Did you find employment yet?

Mashé: Yes, Mr. Tollare. I teach at Tampa Community College. Chandler was instrumental with this. I was very lucky.

Garrett: (Leans over to her) My son has the power of persuasion. Have you met his brother, Alton? He's on his way here.

Chandler: What! It will be good to see him. I've been trying to reach him.

Mashé: It would be nice to finally meet your twin brother.

DeAnn seemed to be studying Mashé, as to whether she would measure up to her son.

DeAnn: Mashé, I understand you write poetry and are published.

Mashé: Yes, that's right.

DeAnn: Chandler, it seems you have found an amazing woman. Mashé, why don't you join me at the table? Seldom do I have female company and it's a nice change having another woman to visit with. You are a stunning looking young lady. May I see your engagement ring? (Holding her hand to the light) Son, it's nice but you hardly did her justice. Is there another band to go with it?

Chandler: Well, if she wants another ring band; I am new at this Mother. (He winks at Mashé)

Mashé: Mrs. Tollare, I love the design, I am very pleased with it.

DeAnn: I don't mean to impose, when I married Garrett I wore a modest setting too but in time I was able to reach the next tier so to speak and finally it happened. (DeAnn displayed her wedding ring with multiple gems)

Mashé: (Struck) Mrs. Tollare your ring is very exquisite. I think it's going to be a while for me to get...

Chandler: We'll wait and see. Mother you are always showing off your wedding ring; now I've been put on the spot. Maybe I should find another job.

DeAnn: Before you do that tell us, when is the wedding and where—you have said very little about it, Chandler. You were always such a secretive child. (Mashé was impressed with that point, him being a secretive man also).

Chandler: The bride to be is in charge. I have told her whatever she wants.

Mashé: We decided to marry in California, Berkeley Hills to be exact. That's where I am from (Chandler cocked his head in amazement and his parents noticed this). Since I relocated here, it is probably best to have the ceremony there; my parents want to be in on the planning. As far as the date is concerned, I realize the commitments Chandler has with his upcoming cases and we need to be sure. However, we'll be married before the holidays approach.

DeAnn: I…see. Well like Chandler said, you are in command.

DeAnn told Garrett that they had better clear their engagements planned for the next two months.

DeAnn: Mashé, what a unique name. What does it mean?

Mashé: Drawn from the water.

Garrett: Fascinating, like relative to a ritual or spiritual reference.

Chandler: You know in essence you are drawn from the water at birth.

Mashé: That's correct. Some think of the baby Moses too.

Mashé smiles recalling that visit at Chandler's parents' house and when his Mother inquired about her name, Neil's image popped up right before her.

The pace of the visit picked up when Alton arrived—-he and Chandler were indeed identical in more ways than one.

Alton came in with an unusually pleasant demeanor, his family surmised. He and Chandler had similar build and carriage. He walked in and went directly to his mother, giving her a hug and shaking his father's hand. He and Chandler embraced like brothers do and conversed a bit before Mashé was introduced. Alton asked her did she have a twin sister that he could meet and they all laughed. DeAnn asked Merla to serve them lunch.

As they ate Mashé was observant of the enduring silence. She wanted to start up a conversation, then concluded that this was normal for them. Just at that moment, Alton had a question for his brother.

Alton: So, who will be your Best Man?

Chandler: I was hoping you would be.

Alton: (Impressed) For real, well I'm in.

Garrett: That was easy. Son, how is the job going for you, any new developments?

Alton: (Avid) Dad by the end of the year Rogier's Medical Group is going to have a new name: The Tollare Medical Group.

DeAnn: Oh my goodness, Am I hearing correctly, you are buying them out?!

Garrett: It seems we have two celebrations going on here. Both of my sons are at the top of their game. We will celebrate tonight at dinner. (Mashé was puzzled—why did he say both his sons? Chandler looked over at her and whispered I know what you are thinking—I will explain.)

Chandler: Dad, Mashé and I go to work tomorrow.

Alton: Me too. But let's wait until after the wedding—the ink won't be dry until the New Year anyway.

DeAnn: In that case I want Merla to bring out the sparkling wine so we all can make a toast. You know I will need to contact my Charity Guild and have both stories placed in our next newsletter—I think I had better call our president right now. You all please continue—Merla remember to bring out the sparkling wine!

Mashé pauses, picturing her and Chandler leaving from his parents' home that night.

Chandler explained that his father would sometimes put both of them in squeamish positions, especially Alton.

Whenever he (Chandler) excelled at something it was always, Good for Chandler. When Alton would achieve at something he would congratulate them both. He stressed how much he detested it and how badly he felt for his brother other than that—they were both encouraged to pursue their dreams and they always got the exact same gifts for Christmas and their birthdays. He gave his mother credit for those instances. He did say that when they entered adulthood that practice stopped. Chandler knew his brother must still feel alienated but he apparently knew his capabilities and moved forward.

Mashé refrained from comment and presumed that some fault of his parents was justified. She recalled hearing some odd stories about twins and triplets and what they endured; how they tried to establish their own individuality and somewhere along the way that fair measure of attention and love from family for some was unequaled.

Mashé flips through more pages and comes across a picture of the three of them taken after Chandler took off for a legal conference in Las Vegas, Nevada, for a week.

She and Rhial had flown back home for a few days to finalize all of the particulars for the wedding. And Eila just happened to show up unannounced. Only she and Rhial had planned to meet.

She remembers setting the wedding date for the second Saturday in November, and Halloween was approaching. She snaps her fingers as she pauses, recalling that Rhial and Halvan decided to forego a big wedding and eloped instead, causing "quite a stir." She also realizes that was the same week Tia called her to bring her up to date about Eila.

She had just finished a long telephone conversation with her mother about her wedding dress, wedding cake, and who would and would not receive a wedding invitation. With Eila showing up impromptu Mashé and Rhial were amused because she originally said she was too busy, but to keep her updated. If ever there was a time when friendship could reach its "Turning Point," this was it. Now, about the conversation with Tia, when Mashé's cell phone rang the Best Girls were on their way out to dinner, so she told Eila and Rhial to go ahead; she would meet them at the car.

Tia: Mashé, it has been a roller coaster month for me, how about you? How are your wedding plans coming along?

Mashé: Yeah, all seems to be coming together, actually I am back in California now visiting with my parents. And guess what, Rhial and Eila are here too

Tia: Oh no!!! I hope they are not there with you, Eila especially?

Mashé: Of course not—I sent them away. We have privacy, trust me.

Tia began by reminding her of the political affair she and Eila attended given by a mutual friend. She said this was in mid-September at a social affairs center in Lower Manhattan. Tia said she and her husband arrived before Eila. She spoke of many dignitaries present and how well attended it was. Tia said Eila walked in with the same guy she saw her with whose license plate she could not determine. Tia indicated that by the looks of this man he worked out and how well he was dressed. She asked a colleague of hers who he was and was told, an attorney from out of town, and that he and Eila met at U Miami. The moment Mashé heard that last piece she felt a twinge in the back of her neck. She remembered Eila speaking of this guy she met at a party while at school, but she thought they had drifted apart. Mashé interrupted her asking if she remembered seeing this man while attending U Miami. Tia said, she didn't. Then she told Mashé there was more, but Mashé interrupted her again. She asked her to describe his overall appearance. When she finished Mashé told her that she needed to cut their call short; she had to go see someone. Tia sensed the tension in her voice and wondered why the sudden change. Mashé started to hyperventilate and with the phone still to her ear Tia said, he had a twin brother.

Mashé told Tia she had to hang up. She had locked herself in the second bathroom; her parents were not home. She let herself out and began pacing back and forth. Thoughts of betrayal and stupidity ran through her mind. To her this was surreal; Chandler and Eila. She repeatedly said, "Oh goodness me!" She then heard knocking at the front door. Eila and Rhial were telling her they were hungry, to hurry up with the phone call. Mashé tried to collect herself. How could she marry Chandler now? She could not eat anything now and went to the door to let her friends in. They walked in giggling about the time when Rhial disguised her voice on the phone telling Eila she had just won a new sports car and it was parked outside her front door.

They both looked puzzled, as Mashé plopped herself on the couch. They both ran over to her asking who she was talking to—what happened. Mashé inhaled deeply and then sternly looked over at Eila asking her had she ever been married. Eila froze for a second or two and then asked her what made her ask that question. Mashé with an elevated voice looking toward her asked her again, had she ever been married. Eila said while backing up that she was but it was annulled. Mashé slowly rose from her seat and asked her was her former husband's name Chandler Tollare, the lawyer, the one she met at the party at U Miami? Eila, totally stumped, with eyes bulging, placed her hands on her hips.

Eila: How do you know about him? Yes, we dated off and on; in fact I just saw him before I boarded the plane to come here.

Mashé was fuming, she asked Eila to leave immediately; she needed to clear her head and she asked Rhial to leave too. Rhial said she would not leave until she knew who Chandler was and why she was upset with Eila.

Mashé snapped, saying that Chandler was her fiancé and he has a twin brother named Alton. Eila almost lost her balance as she held onto the pillar behind her.

Eila: Mashé, I did not know you knew him. You have to believe me. I met his twin brother once when we bumped into him at the mall. Wait a minute, when and how did you meet Chandler?

Mashé was shaking and Rhial asked her repeatedly to calm down because her face was changing colors. In a monotone voice she said she met him on the U Miami campus also after a study group session. She said she felt he was out of her league, with her straightlaced image she could not see herself seeing him, but he was so genteel, charming, and affectionate—almost like being under a spell.

Eila: So true.

Mashé: What do you mean, "so true"; you don't play hard to get Eila—now that I think about it, it makes perfect sense. I am the one who got fooled. Were you really pregnant with his child?

Rhial: Eila! What's going on with you—you kept your pregnancy from us? What's with all of these secrets we are keeping from each other?!

Eila was stifled, a rarity.

Mashé: Eila, since I have known you, you have slipped around going places doing who knows what. When we were teenagers you tried to slyly encourage guys who liked me to like you too. And all the while for some strange reason I admired your spunk, I did not understand it but I must admit, we should have never been friends—friends are loyal and true to each other. There is not going to be a wedding and I have to tell my parents to cancel everything. You know what? My wedding gown is ready; they called to tell me to come and pay the balance, my Mother had it flown in from New York, a very expensive process. Oh Lord, this is a mess. Could you two please just leave, I'll be all right somehow.

Rhial: (Solemn) Fine, Mashé but I should go back to Florida with you.

Mashé: Oh right. Yes, I will use the same ticket to return...I need to move my belongings back here and my job at the community college, I need to look into that too before I go.

Rhial: Let me help you Mashé, please. I can make some calls, you are too upset.

With Mashé's back facing her, Eila approached her cautiously.

Eila: (Humbled)) Mashé, there are things I have done I suppose I felt inclined to do without thinking. No one got hurt; what I mean is you are my girl and you have to believe me. He came to me using his charms and swagger too and like you said, in essence I am prone to make it easy. Mashé, I have admired you since the day we met. I may have been envious but I don't do foul. And that stuff you mentioned back when we were kids; Mashé, that's not me at all now. And after this experience my ways are changing.

Mashé: You did not answer my question.

Eila: Umm…no I was not pregnant but I really thought I was. I was just late. Mashé, I fell in love with him like you did. He said our relationship was done. But you know, each time I called him he was receptive and, well, we behaved as though nothing happened; I suppose you should not hear this from me, Mashé. And you know, I don't believe he knows we're friends—how could he? I never mentioned you and strangely he never mentioned you either. Did you ever once mention me or Rhial?

Mashé: He knew of Rhial once I moved to Florida to be with him. Eila, you two deserve each other; forgive me, but I need to be alone now.

Rhial: (Skippy) I have an idea, let's have a slumber party. (Mashé and Eila look perplexed) Seriously, we can go to my parents' house; they won't be back until tomorrow night; they're at a couples retreat.

Mashé: How sweet is that? You two go on.

Rhial: I will supply the food and wine.

Mashé and Eila in unison: Wine!

Rhial: I know nothing of this Chandler and how often does it happen when best friends want the same person. He has unconscionably made my two best friends nearly fall out…I cannot let that happen. We must always be sisters. Please don't let this split us up (she becomes emotional).

Mashé: (Sighs) Good idea, Rhial, I will join you but…I will not be much company.

Rhial: Great. Eila you come with me; give her some space. Mashé; meet us at my house in one hour. Oh yeah and bring your CDs too, you have the best collection of oldies I know.

Finally, she was alone. She went upstairs to lie down. Lying on her back, she looked up at the ceiling wanting to call him, so she did.

Chandler was still in Las Vegas at the conference. He had been asked to present a paper to a body of attendees, most of whom were third year law students, on the current distinctions of civil action lawsuits versus criminal lawsuits.

Chandler: Chandler here, baby you have been on my mind, I have been going over this presentation and you are the English scholar, listen, and tell me what you think:

In the United States, civil suits are brought to both the state and federal level courts. A civil case within a state court could be when a corporation is suing another corporation for not living up to a contractual agreement .This is my area of expertise.

Now, with many criminal cases, there may not be a distinct victim. For example, state governments arrest and prosecute people accused of violating laws against driving while drunk by reason that our society proclaims this as a serious violation that may result in a menace to the general public.

How am I doing so far? Mashé, are you there? Hello. What's going on?

Mashé: So far what you have sounds interesting and studious. (Thinking to herself he obviously feels confident about it)

Chandler: (Curious) Why did you call, Mashé? Talk to me.

Mashé asked Chandler did he meet a woman by the name of Eila Wynston at U Miami. At first Mashé thought the phone went mute, then a moment later he said Yes and put his paperwork down, coming to his feet to ask her, Why?

Mashé: She and I grew up together here in Berkeley Hills.

Chandler: Mashé, can you get on the next jet and come here to be with me? I need to speak with you in person. Baby, I did not know you were friends, how could I?

Mashé: Chandler she said she was with you today before coming this way. Is that true? What happened to your resistance?!

Chandler: Ahh...yes she was. She called me and wanted to talk. I told her this was the last time, that I was engaged to marry a woman that I truly love. She did not take that news very well. Mashé, I will come there, forget about coming here because if she is there now I need to be there with you so she can witness where my true feelings are.

Mashé: You know, I was devastated when I found out. Eila did not tell me. I promised not to reveal their identity but this person has seen the two of you in New York City acting like the "adorable couple."

Chandler: That was during her escapade that I explained to you. I was only up there with her twice.

Mashé: Wait...if you are in Las Vegas then where did you two meet prior to her coming here?

Chandler: (Riled) She came to Las Vegas—I did not invite her. I told you she was a piece of work!!!

Mashé: (Sighs) I just told her that you two were made for each other—that you and I are not of the same fabric, if you will. She told me she loves you, Chandler. Isn't that crazy? Because I love you too. I am calling the wedding off. This is a royal mess, way over the top as far as I am concerned. I am moving back to California. I'll be leaving for Florida to pack up my belongings and I will give you your diamond ring back. I know some folks will ask me why, but I don't care about what they think!

Chandler was so insistent using his speaking prowess to sway her to listen. But this time it was not working; she told him, good bye. Mashé asked herself the question in her mind over and over again why she barely mentioned Chandler to her friends. Eila was obviously secretive with her love life, so she decided to give credit to her subconscious. She cried some, then went to the bathroom took a long shower, which she sorely needed.

When she arrived the slumber party was in progress. They were so glad to see her. Eila seemed to have had one drink too many. And she was telling Rhial about this new guy she met in New York and how infatuated he was with her. She said he worked for the New York Stock Exchange and was very successful. He had a nice studio apartment and they spent a lot of time indoors. At this comment, Mashé and Rhial glanced at one another, cutting their eyes. She said occasionally they did meet up after work for dinner and talked for hours on the phone and he had this fanatical attraction for her breasts, as though they were a couple of hero sandwiches. Rhial and Mashé looked at each other, then rolled on the floor laughing.

The next morning it was close to noon when the Best Girls were just waking up. Mashé was still in a fog, like a trance, but better than yesterday. Once again Rhial stepped up and helped them keep an even footing. Mashé wanted to inquire about Halvan's situation but was too consumed about her own. As she thought about yesterday's talk with Tia and all that followed, it was apparent that Eila and Chandler were being honest so now the ball was basically in her court. Ironic how all of this turned out. Here she was secretively having Tia tap in on Eila's every move to learn about her obscure behavior and it turned into a snafu.

She could have been like Rhial, but she was not Rhial and bottom line, her fiancé slept with one of her best friends and married her too—no way could she stomach this. How could she ever face him again? She told Rhial she was moving up her departure date—she was boarding a plane today for Florida. Luckily, she moved into a partially furnished condo that she had lived in for only six weeks so she should be able to have some return on her deposit. The lowest point of this would be telling her parents; however, she knew she had their support either way. And there was a little voice inside saying, her mother would probably be so relieved. The other lowest point was missing Eila as she took an early taxi to the airport.

Unbreakable (7)

It was the middle of November and Mashé was in her classroom making preparations for her final examinations. Fortunately, she had been able to return to work and reclaim her post. She realized she had been blessed on many levels. Each day was her day of reckoning and as her father told her, she managed to avoid an avalanche, and that the next time was going to be perfect.

Mashé's eyes were closed while going over in her mind her return to Tampa Bay basically to clean up! Rhial insisted on coming with her to help. Mashé was so appreciative; she was able to pack her belongings in half the time. Her plan was to get in and get out, avoiding an inopportune moment of Chandler showing up. She couldn't deny it; she was hurting for a good while and the worst part was none of this was intended or deliberate—it was like an unfortunate coincidence. As she and Rhial walked out of the front door for the last time her phone lit up; it was him but she did not answer. On the plane back to California she and Rhial spoke on many topics and she found herself feeling more at ease—but she had her moments. She confessed to Rhial that Halvan was, "A Walk on the Wild Side" type of guy in her opinion and she wanted to apologize for all of the prejudgments. Rhial told her that she felt her undertones though appreciated her support at her bridal shower even though it was irksome to her and noticeably more so with Eila. It was interesting to know that Halvan mentioned that he thought she (Mashé) was the classiest one. Rhial said she and Halvan loved each other and if this woman is to have his baby then it would not break them up—they had to show strength. He knew he was wrong stepping out on her but she forgave him. Mashé gained a new level of respect for her friend particularly when she asked her about her debacle with Chandler, of how she would have reacted. It would stay with her forever.

Rhial: I feel your situation has some obscene and extenuating circumstances. You found out that he slept with your best girl and then they married followed by an annulment too. I honestly believe the weight falls more on Eila because he obviously did not want to marry her; he wanted you for his bride. Eila has a quality that I don't admire—you faced her and told her 'bout herself. She is erratic and has this boundless familiarity with men. I am sorry to say this, Mashé, but Chandler was tempted, he is probably one of many. My Halvan was tempted by someone who is not my best girl. What would I have done? Probably the same thing you did, regrettably so, even though you still have love for him.

Christmas was around the corner. Mashé had pulled off from the campus to do some Christmas shopping, not for gifts but for a new place to live. She did not mind staying in Berkeley Hills, although she did not want to spend most her salary paying off a mortgage either. She wanted to find a place with a lease option to buy type of arrangement. The condo she leased in Tampa was close to perfect. Her parents didn't even know she was looking. She visited about three locations and smiled as she thought how Neil offered his place of residence to be hers as well. She had been thinking about him off and on. While driving home she noticed a Grand Opening banner of a new spa treatment business and thought that a spa treatment would be better than drinking a bottle of wine every day. When she had the dress returned and cancelled all of the orders with the vendors she decided that should she ever have another chance to be a bride, they would do like Rhial and Halvan, elope. On a serious note Mashé wanted to get married someday, imagining life spent with a man who wanted just her; perhaps she needed to wake up. She had not spoken to Eila since the slumber party—this was probably best. She drove in and parked and sat there wondering about the amount of money she could spend—surely it was not going to be anywhere near what her wedding would have cost. When she walked through the crystal glass like French doors she was greeted by two women with a thick accent. She was offered red wine, iced filtered water, other drinks; she declined and asked for a consultant. The kinds of services offered seemed endless. She spent about an hour or more taking a tour and meeting many of the trained personnel who looked as though they couldn't wait to get their hands on her. She would like a massage and organic facial to start—though would rather come with a friend. She thanked them and promised to make an appointment soon. As she was leaving they gave her a discount certificate on any three spa services. Just having that brief interaction with strangers lifted her spirits some. She repeated in her mind what her mother advised, "Now is not a good time for you to be alone. Go and circulate with your peers." She opened the car door and was taken aback when she saw a handsome man walking toward her—it was Neil. Her heart seemed to have jumped to her throat. She just stood there; he had changed somehow. He had that appealing look about him as he did at the party. She said to herself to relax: it is only Neil.

Neil: Ms. Boston, or is it Mrs. Something—what are you doing on this side of town? You look nice by the way.

Mashé: Thank you, Neil. You look so different; in a good way, I mean. This is a surprise. I was just looking into this new Spa Treatment service before going home. I am also looking for a new place.

Neil: I have heard that brides get to be taken to these places and spend mega-money. Your skin is perfect—you really don't need it. Did you say you are looking at property—grammatically speaking, in first person? I heard you were moving back east somewhere.

Mashé: Thank you. I, am not a "bride to be" anymore, Neil. I am still Miss Boston, I am in California to stay, and yes, I was speaking in first person.

Neil: (Inquisitive) The grapevine needs to catch up, so give me the latest. In fact, it was Jasmine who told me. I felt a little cheated not hearing about this from you—I still thought we were... friends?

Mashé: I admit I thought about you, Neil, and wanted to share the news but in the back of my mind, I sensed you might be somewhat hostile toward me.

Neil: Hostile! Toward you, never. Do...you have some time? I believe this to be a heavenly plan, us bumping into each other like this. What do you think, Miss Boston?

Mashé: It is possible.

They just stood silently before one another for a moment. Mashé was feeling nervous. She wanted to open her car door, take a seat, and drive away quickly—why was she once again wanting to get away? Neil opened his arms for a hug and she responded willingly. This time he did not feel like Chandler; he felt like Neil. She tried to conceal her tears. Neil stepped back, dried her eyes, and this time embraced her affectionately, asking her to follow him to a restaurant he recently discovered that would be just perfect for them; curious, she agreed. They wound up at the same restaurant where she and Wellington had dined. She yelped.

Neil: Something funny?

Mashé: I dined here not long ago with someone you know—it was just a friendly dinner, mind you.

Neil: Someone I know, who?

Mashé: Wellington, he was at Gordon's party.

Neil: I see...which brings me to ask, is he still in the picture?

Mashé: He… never was.

Neil: (Curious) How did you come to know each other?

Mashé: Umm, a mutual friend. What about Lara Nastle?

Neil: A closed chapter in my book.

Mashé: (Awed) Seriously?! That sounds definite.

Neil: She was a fine person, just not my type. And it appears that you and I were destined to meet at this point in time with similar circumstances.

Mashé: Similar circumstances?

Neil: (Smiling) We are free agents. Well, I know I am.

Mashé: (Clearing her throat) Yes at the present time we are single people about to enjoy a delectable meal together.

He took her by the hand and told her that Lara was too attentive and very fussy. He told Mashé she was on his mind constantly and even though he had resolved that he might not ever see her again, he knew he wanted her in his life and that his attitude was not to give up. He asked her what he was lacking that she wanted or needed.

Mashé was struck by his words. She could not bring herself to say she was not attracted to him because that evening when they first met she was. But she had Chandler in her life (seemingly) and she felt uncomfortable seeing two men at the same time. Just then she thought about Eila—how it would not have been difficult for her; maybe that's what she admired about Eila: not her capriciousness but by going for what she wanted. But anyway she had told Neil that it would not have been fair to him or her when she was trying to figure out the behavior of a man she fell in love with. And as she sat across from him he was becoming more appealing by the minute—by noticing this, what was there to stop her now? Still distracted by the mishap of her wedding plans she wanted to decline her dinner with Neil and go home and sulk, however, she had to move forward so maybe this very moment was a good start. She assured him that he lacked nothing and she asked that he be patient with her.

Neil: I'm going to try my very best to make you forget all about him. May we start from the beginning?

Mashé: Why not?

Neil: Mashé, I know you said you were coming from the Grand Opening of that new Spa but you mentioned you were house hunting—that's a pricey location, how nice for you.

Mashé: You are the sharp one—I was looking for a place with access to several popular locations. My parents have been so wonderful after my recent hiccough and I love their house but I need to have my own place now.

Neil: Now this is an all too familiar scene. Have you found what you are looking for?

Mashé: I did see one that I liked. It would be a lease agreement though; I want to be sure.

Neil: May I join you, again? I think you have inspired me—I need to find a larger place.

Mashé: Your townhouse has many rooms and is in a prime location.

Neil: You like it that much—would you like to move in? I couldn't resist.

Mashé: No harm done—I thought it was cute. It will probably be this coming Sunday; are you free around 2:00 PM?

Neil: I have cleared my calendar just for you.

As closing time approached, they walked to their cars and Neil asked to follow her home she agreed. When they arrived at her doorstep Mashé felt like a teenager, she grappled with what to say. It felt very weird being in his company again but welcoming all the same. Neil sensed her teetering and kissed her left cheek then asked if he could go further. She gave him a leery look. He smiled and kissed her mouth. Mashé was embarrassed, then put her arms around him and kissed him back; prolonged ones resulted. Mashé stepped back saying she would see him on Sunday. Like in a classic romance movie, they wanted to stay in each other's embrace. When they finally said good night Mashé went to her room to lay across her bed. She felt revived somehow.

Being with Neil again felt so déjà vu, like they rediscovered each other. She noticed that her land phone had a message. It was from her publisher. Her recent book of romance poems was gaining notable momentum in sales. A huge book fair would take place in New York City in February and she had been formally invited to participate, with airfare and accommodations included. Mashé was ecstatic and accidentally woke up her parents; they ran in and she shared the good news. Their household was surely in need of some well-deserved joy.

Early that following morning Mashé was awakened by Neil. He had this unusual cool quality in his voice asking did she sleep well. She said she could hardly sleep and told him why. He congratulated her and said they should go out and celebrate. Mashé liked that idea, then that feeling of hesitation resurfaced. He sensed it and said that only what she wanted to happen would happen.

Mashé: You are perceptive as usual. It's my thoughts of adjustment, they still need untangling. I really feel this opportunity came at the right time. This will be my first time going to New York City. (Eila came to mind)

Neil: Well, Lady Poet, are you free to dine with me this evening? Your choice of restaurant.

Mashé: Certainly. A nice simple dinner. I know, we should go where we met.

Neil: You are the romantic. I shall come for you around 7:00 PM?

Mashé: That's fine.

Neil: Before I let you go, you stated you had some thoughts still untangling; if there is anything you want to share or vent about, you will have my undivided attention. I hope you know this.

Mashé: Yes, Neil, I do and I appreciate it. Please know it goes both ways.

Neil: I like that. I look forward to this evening.

After his call Mashé decided to contact Tia; they had not spoken since that unfortunate revelation that was shared. She wanted to apologize and let her know she would be in New York City in February.

Mashé: Tia it's me, Mashé, you have a moment? First of all I am calling to apologize for my behavior. It's so peculiar when you vigorously venture out to learn about something or someone and in the process it blows up in your face. However, I am not regretting calling you for assistance. I found out what I needed to know about a supposedly good friend of mine. I was to marry the man you saw her with and oddly enough he did not know we were friends. But I did not want to spill all of the drama. I also called to tell you that I will be in New York City in February and I wanted us to meet up. Yes, I have published a book of romance poems and there is going to be a book fair and I have been invited to participate. Thank you, Tia. Yes I am very excited, it's what I need—something inspiring to look forward to. No, I have not seen or spoken to Eila for quite some time. How about you? That a fact? Well…I trust she is doing fine at whatever she's doing.

Tia told Mashé she needed to put on her professional cap because she sensed in Mashé's voice possible uncertainty that the debacle she recently experienced would impair the long-standing relationship she had with Eila. She spoke of the Human Condition, the uncertain impacts or events of life. Some will be pleasant and some will be unpleasant. People are subject to get along and not get along depending on the circumstances. Tia wanted Mashé to understand that we all will have some inevitable experiences in this world and to have a valuable friendship is priceless, uncommon. and requires constant attentiveness. She empathized with Mashé's sudden change of behavior over the telephone that somehow they had something in common with the same man. She told Mashé how lucky matters turned out the way they had for her as well as for Chandler and Eila, stressing that while the news was unsettling, she and Eila needed to let it pass. She wanted to take the blame because she could have declined to help Mashé's unusual or perhaps unorthodox request but she had aroused her curiosity due to Eila's long-standing reputation. In her profession as well as for personal reasons, this took precedence.

Their conversation lasted for some time. They delved into discussing the highs and lows within relationships—those challenges between men and women too and the many contrasts and variations that interplay in emotional encounters.

Looking back, Mashé is glad she had that talk with Tia and for many years they stayed in touch. She actually remembers a parable her mother shared with her when she was small, *"Good friends are like gems precious and rare; Bad friends are like autumn leaves found everywhere. Have many friends but only trust two. Learn to paddle your own canoe."* As her thoughts return to the dinner she had with Neil, she remembers telling her parents that Neil would be by.

They were pleased to hear this, especially her father. When Neil arrived they brought him into the living room and began asking him why he disappeared. Mashé was so embarrassed but Neil was sucking in all of the attention. Finally, they were free to leave for dinner.

Neil: (As they drive off) I really like your folks. They remind me of my parents; if only you could show the same enthusiasm for me as they do.

Mashé: (Wincing) Obviously it is your winning personality. And that sounded sarcastic—didn't you tell me that Lara was too attentive or fussy over you?

Neil: I supposed I did. But, coming from you now that would be a different story. Seriously, I am feeling special tonight because a bestselling author is riding in my hoopty.

Mashé: Hoopty…this is hardly a hoopty I was about to ask when did you get it? This is quality. (Neil is driving a Jaguar XF)

Neil: (He lets the top down) I drove it off the lot last week. I'm leasing it. I recently got a raise and things are going pretty well at the office, finally.

Mashé: I remember you said a while ago your boss and another department head were at odds with each other.

Neil: True, now they are both gone.

Mashé: So, engineers are politicians too.

Neil: Oh definitely. We are approaching the restaurant. I can smell their fish stew from here.

Mashé and Neil are warmly received by the maitre d' as though he were expecting them. They are seated outside near the water's edge. They both ordered the famous Ropa Vieja. It were as though time flew as they talked about nearly everything under the sun.

Neil: Miss Boston, you have quite an appetite— that explains your perfect figure. Meaning, it all settles in the right places.

Mashé: (Modest) Thank you. The last time we were here we could have talked all night.

Mashé noticed that Neil's temperament did a slight shift. He was studying her thoroughly as though she were a fine painting or better yet a mosaic. The combo began a nice and slow jazz selection, which prompted them to dance. He held her close and by his being tall she felt so tranquil. Gradually the ambiance seemed to encourage a warm sensation; Mashé felt a solid message coming from his moves. She imagined that they were the only ones on the dance floor. She rehearsed in her mind how she would react to Neil wanting to take her home—if she refused him again what kind of impressions would unfold? When the song ended they looked into one another's eyes; without question for her to decline again would be amiss.

It was quiet in the car as they drove away. He reached for her hand, bringing it to his lips for a peck. When they reached his place he parked alongside his front door. As he led her to the door he asked her was she as excited as he was? She looked at him smiling, telling him this was probably inevitable. Her response seemed to have made his ears ring. Mashé had figured Neil to be a confident person, skilled at his profession, highly intelligent, and rather laid back. With Chandler, he was confident, highly intelligent, duly professional and successful, very persuasive and sensual maybe more overt in that area to say the least; both worked out and both were good looking, but with Neil, he had to grow on her. Her gradual attraction to his appearance was not to ignore the fact that any woman would find him attractive. There she went again making comparisons. She wondered if he had been comparing her to Lara or other women in his life. The non-dialogue between them made her feel a little antsy.

Mashé: (Entering his townhouse) Neil, do you think or rather how do you feel about comparing people? People you date I mean.

Neil: I really haven't. I just know what I find more appealing about a person. People should be different. I know for certain there is only one Mashé. Have you been comparing me to your ex-fiancé?

Mashé: (Modest) Yes, I have—past tense of course. (Observing that he had rearranged his furniture and may have added a little paint) I see you have made some improvements.

Neil: The work of Lara Nastle. So you like it? Well you did say improvements. Like I said, I am ready to make a move. Once again, we share "a common thread."

He approached her from behind and whispered, "What else do we have in common?"

Mashé: I can think of several things.

Mashé acted as though a covering had been lifted from her uncertainties. She turned to face him. He went for his back pocket and brought out the little box he wanted to present to her at her parents' home the night he stormed out. It popped open; her eyes absorbed the sight of a brilliant heart-shaped diamond. She was speechless. Neil continued to watch her reaction. She worried that it might appear as though she were accepting the ring out of obligation. She sheepishly looked up at Neil and he looked back. He took it out and placed it on her ring finger and no words were exchanged. They went up the staircase to his master bedroom. They hurriedly undressed each other. They started out subtle as his body enshrined hers. Into the evening, Neil got a little wild and Mashé released herself entirely. Her response to him was bold and relishing. As they rested, Neil idolized her repeatedly with his touch, telling her once again that she was unquestionably his black cherry: her perfect form, her skin, she had mellowed to his taste; he said, "You are just ripe for me." Mashé lay there quietly, appreciating his corny romanticism . These two lovers unfazed by the new dawn enjoyed a timeless time together.

At about 5:00 PM Mashé wanted to take a bath, as did Neil. Up to their necks in bubbles, Neil told Mashé he was going to keep her captive in a nice way. Mashé reminded him of their agreement on Sunday—only one day away. He said he did not forget, then brought her to him and with a passionate zeal, Neil had Mashé holding on.

🍒   🍒   🍒

Mashé turned the key to the front door and tiptoed in as though she had returned from prom night. It was nearly 8:30 PM. She concluded that her parents must have gone to a movie or out to dinner. She went upstairs and found a note on her bed stand from her mother, it read: *Chandler came by.* That was all and instantly Mashé took a seat. She repeated again and again in her head that she was over him. She could not wait until her mother returned. She was feeling sleepy so she took a nap and with it came a dream. It started out with her walking alone on a lengthy narrow road, somewhat curvy, not knowing where it was leading to. It was sunny and she was in good spirits. Suddenly the weather pattern changed. This great gust of wind hurled behind her and lifted her up from the ground then spun her around; seconds later it was calm again but when she touched the ground the road split in two, now what was she to do? When she awoke she sat up hoping not to have another dream like that. Apparently, she has had too much man stuff going on.

Later that evening when her parents returned they told her that Chandler had come to the house around 11:00 that morning. They said he seemed so disappointed that she was not there. He was in town on business and wanted to speak to you. They said he expressed deep regret over what happened. He mentioned his parents wanting them to know how much they admired Mashé. He also wanted to know the expenses involved so he could compensate them;

they were touched but refused, letting him know they were not upset with him and then her father emphasized to him that Mashé had moved on and that he had better do the same. After that comment, Clover said he seemed curious but bid them a good day in so many words. Mashé was struck by her father's comment and right then she showed them her engagement ring. They looked at it and then looked at her. Mashé told them this could be a long engagement because she and Neil had some significant plans in mind.

Eugene: It looks like you've landed on your feet and this time you will bear fruit.

Mashé gave him an odd look.

Clover: He means grandchildren.

Mashé kept it to herself but she was slightly sorry she missed Chandler. To her Neil was the one without question and she knew it must be reinforced. She guessed that Chandler decided to show his face rather than try again to reach her by telephone. She thought of calling him just to say that her parents appreciated his gesture though her father with his own unique brio finished it well. Deep down she knew the chapter on Chandler was still open. Perhaps some of life's chapters are endless, she pondered.

Neil and Mashé went looking for a very special Christmas tree for her new house. She was about two miles away from her parents. It was a two bedroom with a small backyard and she loved it. Neil wanted to move in and of course she said to wait until they said, "I do."

The wind was cutting so they hurried and decided on a cute Whiteberry. They had fun bringing it in her house. They were so tired but not too tired to eat. Neil set the tree up in the living room and Mashé made meatloaf sandwiches. About thirty minutes went by and she asked him from the kitchen did he want to eat in the kitchen or in there. When she walked in with their dinner, he had dozed off on her couch. He looked very peaceful lying there so she went to the closet and got a blanket for him. As she was about to rise and return to the kitchen, she felt a tug on her arm. She turned around; Neil was awake and motioned for her to join him under the blanket. There they stayed for the night.

The next morning she awoke first and since it was a Saturday there was no need to rush to any particular place. Mashé had not talked to her mother for a couple of weeks so she called her.

Clover: Good morning there, how are you? Have you put up your decorations? Your dad is here. How is Neil? Great, when you see him again tell him hello for me. What do you think I should buy him for Christmas? True, a gift card could work—but they are so impersonal. Pardon my asking but will your ceremony take place this year or next? I just wanted to get an idea. Is it because of the book fair? I understand, I'm just so excited for you, Girl. Fine, I will tell your father. Love you too.

When Mashé returned to the front, Neil was still asleep so she went to the kitchen and started breakfast. Now her mother had her thinking about an actual date for their wedding. The more she thought about it the more she was considering eloping. She resolved that time would clear all of the recent developments from her head. Most of the time she hadn't been thinking of Chandler, then something was said or a song was heard, and there he was again in the forefront. The kitchen doors swung open and a tall sleepy man walked in and said he is hungry.

Mashé: Look who's up. Here you are, have a seat.

Neil: All of this for me? I couldn't help but hear your conversation with your mother about us setting a date. My mother asked me about that too—by the way would this be a good day to spend some time with my folks?

Mashé: I was wondering when I would finally meet them; what time?

Neil: I casually mentioned to them that we would be over tonight.

Mashé: I…see. Then tonight it is.

Neil: May I move in? I love the food here.

Mashé: Neil, why don't we elope? Seriously.

Neil: You mean before we go to see my parents?

Mashé: (Laughing) No. We could do it on New Year's Eve?

Neil: Well…then are we buying a new house before then or am I moving in this nice little house?

Mashé: We'll have about a month to decide. I rather like the idea.

Neil: Whatever works for us, Mashé? I kinda feel that our folks will be disappointed if we elope. I am just hoping it is not connected to your recent situation. This is me…Neil.

Mashé: I wanted to avoid starting that process all over again. We could go for a smaller version, simpler, less flamboyant. Please, Neil, I need you to understand why.

Neil: That could work. I just want you to look forward and prevent the remnants of your first engagement from diminishing our plans. Think of it as a, "Trial and Error" experience.

Mashé: (Sarcastic) Could you have been just a little more candid? Really, Neil, I want you to keep in mind that my family and I need to rewind our energies, our thought process. I intend to see our marriage through to old age.

With Lou chewing on her house slipper Mashé wipes a tear away.

Another pivotal point in her life when she was determined to rebound on what she felt she lost. She thought more about the feelings of her parents than her own. She realized she reacted hastily to Chandler's proposal, perhaps as a result of all the many impressions that danced in her mind whenever they were together. They never pushed her into marriage though they did long to see her happy. She fell in love with two distinctly different men and it took the rare happenstance of a best friend's role to help her see more clearly. It had nothing to do with what she'd lost but actually what she'd gained.

She scurries, looking for the picture of her with Neil and his parents the first day they met. There, she finds it.

Mashé was impressed with Neil's mother—she was beautiful and his father was highly spirited.

He asked about her father and was almost in disbelief when Neil mentioned they met and now their children are getting married. His parents' home was in San Pablo, her first time visiting that part of the Bay Area. Their house had the architecture of a mission, as did many. It was a split-level structure and Zora took Mashé on a tour. A soft-spoken woman though one could not be mistaken about her character; she carried herself with lots of pomp. Donovan, Neil's father, was an engineer also. The G.I. Bill had paid for his college education. Zora was a homemaker and very creative at it. She had wondered for a while whether her son would ever find someone special enough. She admitted to him being fairly insistent and imposing, but those were qualities his mate would need to adapt to. It amused Mashé when she said that Neil had not brought many girls home and figured she had the wherewithal. As they entered the family's gazebo, she then asked Mashé did she know how the mind of an engineer worked. Before she could answer, Zora surged into her rendition. An engineer has the ability to assemble thoughts and ideas, which creates substantial results. They have the unique quality of deciphering and interpreting the how and the what of different mechanisms; and they can usually preempt a situation or condition to avoid an issue. Zora said she knew when Neil was in middle school that he was going to take on the same profession as his father. She added that what was also interesting, engineers tend to use the same concept with people and she ended with saying that was why she concluded Mashé had the wherewithal—Engineers know what to look for and then they perform.

Zora: This almost completes the tour, I have a favor to ask?

Mashé: (Braced) What is that, Mrs. Rollins?

Zora: Please sign my book? Call me Zora.

Mashé saw that she had a copy of her latest work. She believed Neil knew but didn't want to spoil the surprise. She and Zora became well acquainted. Zora said she had always wanted to write. Somehow, she could not muster up the courage.

Mashé: From my point of view it is not about courage, the key to me is taking pause from your everyday life, your usual surroundings and creating one of your own; you are an artist who takes possession of her time and events.

Zora: So well put.

Mashé: Do you have any thing that you have written or started? I'll take a look at it if you like?

Zora: Would you really, Mashé? There is a box of drafts around here somewhere—I will take you up on it. Let's have our dinner now.

Evidently Neil had watched the two of them intently because when they returned to the dining room he was standing there waiting to ask what they talked about. His mother was quick to respond, "Girl talk."

On their way home Mashé persuaded Neil to allow them to live separately as engaged people should. She did not want their commitment to the tradition to seem like a farce—one of many beneficial insights she reaped from her first experience. They pulled up into her driveway and Mashé gave him a generous kiss and bid him good night.

Neil: You are cutting our night short? Why? And what did you and my mother talk about anyway?

Mashé: You come from a very wholesome and loving family, which explains the way you are.

Neil: (Suspicious) Sweetheart. What did the lady tell you?

Mashé: She wants only the best for you, and she and I realized that we shared similar points of view. I am not going to reveal the details, just know that we discussed other topics, not just you, Mr. Engineer.

Neil: Okay, I think I have an idea now.

Mashé: Good. I need to get some sleep, Neil.

Neil: I could help with that.

Mashé: More specifically, uninterrupted sleep, Mr. Rollins. How about you and I getting together in the middle of the week? I'll prepare dinner for you.

Neil: Until then. I am in love with you.

Mashé: And I am in love with you too. Good night

Trimmings (8)

It was mid Christmas morning and Mashé and Neil were still in slumber. There had been a late shower on Christmas Eve, providing a divine morning that was clear and fresh. Neil wasn't supposed to stay over but when Mashé invited her parents and his over for Christmas dinner, he insisted on staying to the likes of Santa's helper, he claimed. Luckily, she was able to prepare the casseroles and desserts before matters became ultra-romantic. Neil charmed her right wrist with an early Christmas gift: an elegant pearl and diamond channel bracelet. Once she opened the box, all of her maybes and noes rolled to yeses. He put his feet on hers complaining that his were cold, and that was the signal for her to rise and get busy.

Neil: Where are you going? Aren't we set for tonight's dinner?

Mashé: Ahh…"We" need to be sure everything is just perfect. My future in-laws are coming here and the place needs to be spotless. (As she dressed, Neil asks if they should announce that the wedding is planned for February 14th next year)

Mashé: Only if the subject comes up. I prefer sharing this later because then it would be too late for them to try and talk us out of it. My mother was swamped with many tasks because I was still in Florida. If I had been here to help things would have been different, though she never complained and I know she stayed up late calling different dressmakers, caterers, and what have you. Doing it this way prevents us from being stressed. I appreciate your understanding and I was so touched when I saw the wedding suit you ordered for me—it is chic. Who ever heard of the groom ordering his bride's wedding apparel? I must shower you again with luscious kisses.

Neil: (Impish) Now is as good a time as any. You know Mashé my spending the night with you occasionally is cool. Don't forget the wedding suit I bought is white.

Mashé: Ump! I will let you have that one. You know it is Christmas time, so work on your tact.

Neil stayed in bed while Mashé looked around once more. She was really proud of her little house. The holiday decorations and her dining room table made a majestic impression. It was definitely time saving to have Neil over to help. She heard her cell phone and remembered that she had it on the kitchen table.

What a surprise call it was. since they were little girls the three of them would call and wish each other a Merry Christmas. Of course, Rhial had the lead—she knew Mashé or Eila would not initiate the call; she was like our "Bridge over Troubled Waters." She can still recall verbatim exactly what they talked about.

Rhial: Hey we got a three-way going on here. Well, I'll go first. Merry Christmas to my Best Girls!!! I love you!!!

Mashé: Love you too. Yes, Merry Christmas to you, my girls!!!

Eila: Do you mean that, Mashé? Seriously, Merry Christmas?

Mashé: Eila are you okay?!

Eila: Yes. I often wanted to call you and just chill and talk like before. I felt paralyzed, I am still shaken over it.

Mashé: Eila I have something to tell you: I am engaged again.

Eila was hushed.

Mashé: Relax, his name is Neil Rollins. We're doing it in two months…Eila are you there?

Eila: That's just like you to land on your feet. I am happy for you—when!

Mashé: February 14th and guess what else? I have been invited to a Book Fair in New York the same month; it will take place that first weekend.

Eila: What! I am giving you a big hug through the phone right now. Rhial, did you know?

Rhial: Well yeah.

Eila: See, you two are foul.

Rhial: You are hard to reach and besides I don't like to text—anyway more news to be shared.

Eila and Mashé braced themselves.

Rhial: (Excited) I'm pregnant.

Eila dropped her phone and Mashé momentarily stood still and speechless at first.

Mashé: Rhial, congratulations…I supposed Halvan is excited? How is the situation with the other woman, if I may ask?

Rhial: That's the other good news I have to share, she is not carrying his child… it's not his! (Rhial started crying)

Eila: We should be there together for Rhee. I can understand how emotional this must be. Congratulations, twice!

Mashé: Definitely. Wait a minute, were you pregnant when we had our sleepover? Also, you were lifting boxes and what have you when you helped me move out in Florida.

Rhial: I suspected I was then but I just confirmed it last night, my doctor's office gave me a call.

Mashé: Oh my goodness, you should not have done all of that lifting! And what about the wine?!

Rhial: Listen, I have been examined, baby and I are fine.

Eila: Seriously though, you need to take care and slow down. Wow, you have been busier than I thought. (They laugh out loud)

Mashé: When are you due?

Rhial: Late June or early July.

Mashé: Well, I hope the baby comes in June.

Eila: You would. (Humbly) May I give the Baby Shower?

Rhial: Of course. Though I just want to do it simple, not like the Bridal. Let's talk about you, Eila. Who are you seeing? The same guy?

Mashé: Right, Mr. Hero Sandwich.

Eila: Yep he's still around and he is a gentleman I should not have told you that. My drinking has always done the talking for me.

Rhial and Mashé responded with a resounding AMEN!!!

Mashé: Eila, have you spoken to Aunt Lennie?

Eila: I am calling her after we speak. I may be out that way New Year's Eve and then I can meet your intended; with your permission?

Mashé: Fine.

Eila: And Mashé, you did believe me when I said I didn't know about you two?

Mashé: Yes, Eila. Let's leave that in the past where it belongs. True, it has been a sore spot for a while but luckily nothing really happened, like my father said.

Even trying to camouflage her feelings was a challenge—it seemed that no matter how she tried to move forward Chandler would be like a backdrop in her life.

Neil came into the foyer asking Mashé who she was talking to.

Mashé: Ahh…it looks like I have a visitor; I need to go. Congratulations again, Rhial.

Eila: Mashé, is your "Santa Baby" there with you?!

All three released a gusty laugh.

The Christmas dinner brought satisfaction to everyone's palate. Donovan and Gordon continued to enjoy reminiscing about their Navy days while they both added more bourbon to their homemade eggnog. Zora and Clover fussed over Mashé and wanted to talk about the upcoming wedding plans. Mashé politely tried to change the subject while Neil glanced over at her as if to say, See, I told you. Mashé admired her mother's receptiveness to going into the particulars again—she was truly a woman of stamina, without question. Mashé was feeling some well-deserved security observing how Neil's father and hers were well acquainted, their families basically shared similar value systems and life styles; and she appreciated the real family bonding that was happening.

Zora: Mashé, Donovan and I would like to open our home for your bridal party dinner. Give me the date again for the wedding; I will need to get in touch with the caterer at our church. He trained in Europe; you will be so impressed with…

Clover: (Interjects) And I will sponsor your bridal shower. Just to confirm your colors again, did you say violet and crème or lilac and crème? Let me know when you want to meet with the florist because…

As they rambled, Mashé stood before them as though she were in a hypnotic trance. Neil walked over to her and asked if she was feeling all right.

Mashé: Mother, Mrs. Rollins, forgive me I had not planned on discussing our wedding plans tonight; in fact I was looking forward to singing Christmas songs and Mother baked her legendary coconut yellow cake that has been sliced for everyone. Neil and I agreed to February 14th as our special day (Eugene and Donovan pause to listen). The ceremony should be intimate and simply elegant. Oh yes, Mother my chosen colors are lilac and crème as you said. (Thinking that before they were violet and crème)

Eugene looked poignantly at Clover.

Clover: Mashé, there I go again…I only wanted to be sure of what you told me. Now that the date has been settled, we have more than enough time.

Mashé: (Modest) Could we all meet in the living room? I have something to share with you, especially to Mr. and Mrs. Rollins.

As they all sat Neil took Mashé by the hand.

Mashé: First, I want to say that the dinner was, "Through the front and out the back door good," as my grandmother would say. Mother, your lamb shanks and jambalaya as always just perfect, and Mrs. Rollins, your Waldorf salad, please share the recipe with me? Some time ago Neil asked me to marry him and I shunned his proposal, but it had nothing to do with him, it was me and another man whom I met in college. Mother, please don't feel self-conscious about asking about my color choices. It's true, had I married him my chosen colors would have been violet and crème. Mr. and Mrs. Rollins, when I broke off the wedding just a few weeks ago I had gone into an emotional spiral. I would have preferred to have dreamt it, but it wasn't and I faced up to it. He and I had a peaceful parting and I am so indebted to my parents. They held up for me so well as if nothing happened. You see the wedding was to be exceptional, like I imagined with my friends as a little girl. I had the design of my bridal dress in place, a towering wedding cake, who my bridesmaids would be and the colors they were to wear. Should I ever have a little girl I will probably advise her to avoid letting her imagination run away with her.

Eugene: And Baby, we are so proud of you.

Clover: Hallelujah!

Zora and Donovan were looking puzzled.

Zora: I wanted to have a daughter after I had Neil. It did not happen until now. Donovan and I appreciate your explanation of things. I gathered something went awry because the night you two met, I believe it was at your birthday party; all Neil talked about was you and then one day he stopped. I did not ask why and besides him being grown, I decided not to be a prying mother as I am capable of being (Donovan nods in agreement). I am sorry for your mishap, the reasons are probably complex, though please know that now you have proven yourself to be with the right man and I am glad Neil is that man. (Neil was in the Amen corner, saying in their case, Opportunity knocks more than once)

Clover: So, by downsizing your second endeavor you are trying to spare my feelings and your father's. Mashé that is commendable, but whatever you desire you deserve it. I am sure Neil agrees with me.

Neil: Mrs. Boston. Thank you. My sentiments exactly.

Eugene: Stop fretting over all the money and time we spent.

Clover: And should you have a little girl or a boy as well. Let their imaginations soar.

Mashé was blooming inside again as a bride should and preferred to keep the plan for the intimate wedding ceremony as it was, and make a huge invitation list for their reception instead, which would be at the Berkeley Hills Country Club as before. Clover, Zora, Eugene, and Donovan all professed that their big day would be "The Talk of the Town" in a positive light. And of course, her father added, "Think of the first time as a dry-run."

Mashé is holding Lou in her lap with tears of joy trickling down her face. Another pivotal moment to treasure. Every time she cruises through her photo album a new eerie revelation surfaces; sometimes she felt as though she were involuntarily solving a mystery. Now she is more touched by the effects of all that took place on that extraordinary Christmas night than on their actual wedding day itself.

Her mother was the supreme Wedding Coordinator. At first, she wasn't sold on the wedding suit Neil purchased because it had a slight slit in the back that popped as she walked. Mashé thought it was adorable. The design and fabric were impeccable. It was made of moire taffeta organza, ivory in color. Neil had a local popular seamstress order the fabric from Egypt, shared her measurements, and chose a designer's version to make it from. The back was lacy and delicate and it was hemmed at the knee. Her Mother had the florist design a corsage made of lilac buds and white Sedona tea roses, aromatically intense.

Eila did come home to spend New Year's Eve with Aunt Lennie. Mashé brought Neil by to meet both of them. Mashé watched Eila's reaction when she saw Neil for the first time; she behaved very nicely, displaying her ladylike manners. Aunt Lennie kept on and on about how fortunate Mashé was and then took her to the side to ask her would she please help Eila find a good man. While Neil and Eila were visiting in the front, Mashé reminded herself to talk with Aunt Lennie about Eila's suspicious behavior. Aunt Lennie told her that as bright a person as Eila was, growing up minus a father and then without a mother as well may have been the reason. When Eila's mother passed on, she tried to fill her shoes to no avail. Aunt Lennie said that was when Eila seemed to have produced a second personality. Her goings and comings were a mystery, yet she never seemed to miss a day of school and she tried to encourage her to continue to attend Sunday school and church like Mashé and Rhial. Mashé thought for a minute and did recall that within that time Eila did attend Sunday school but she did not see her seated in the usual church pew during worship services. Mashé was so touched by Aunt Lennie's concern over her wedding debacle. Apparently, Eila did not give her the full story, and Mashé definitely was not going to; she concluded that if it had not been for Aunt Lennie things might have been inconceivably worse for Eila.

Trailblazer (9)

New York City, a bustling town and Mashé was on her way to the Hilton in Upper Manhattan. Her agent was there waiting for her. The publisher ordered about 1500 copies of her book. She had these anticipating thoughts of meeting several of New York's bestselling authors and she needed to conduct herself with self-assurance. She had done a few local book signings but like the cliché, "It doesn't get better than this." Neil wanted to come to support her but his workload needed him there; besides if any concerns arose about their upcoming wedding, he could handle them. She had not spoken to Eila since that Christmas morning and anxiously hoped to see her. Rhial said she was on her way up. Halvan had to stay in Florida for a few back-to-back meetings.

As she entered the hotel lobby her agent, Von, rushed up to her.

Von: Mashé that was a long flight; did you stop anywhere? I thought it was non-stop.

Mashé: It was, you are just excited. We are here, Von, this is the deal, and so what's next?

Von: You need to check in. I understand your suite is ready.

Mashé: My suite? Sweet!

After checking in they went to her hotel suite; it was on the twenty-first floor. They had a seat in the living room. The Book Fair Coordinator gave Von the agenda displaying the site, the Javits Center. He told Mashé that her book booth would be ready at 8:00 AM tomorrow and that they should be there by 7:00 AM. They were expecting over 100,000 people.

Mashé: Whoa! 100,000 people are expected and you had the publisher order only 1,500 copies?!

Von: Relax. Yes, Mashé, the hardcopies are your visual—just remember the e-book version will be your, "claim to fame," let's pray.

Mashé: Yes I believe we should pray. Von, I hope you know what you are doing.

Von: This is your month, your year. After this big affair, you are going to be a Mrs. oh… I just thought of something. We'll need a small press party at your wedding reception.

Mashé: (Angst) That cannot happen!!! Seriously, Von, definitely off limits. Put in a photo of me with a caption in the local newspapers or something.

Von: (Defensive) Mashé, that was thoughtless, I forgot about your previous situation, please forgive me. However, it could be good publicity for you since you have become a notable poet—I can see our readers coming from all sides of the globe.

Mashé: Von, I am excited too. Please! I would like to keep my personal life personal. I only want my work to be publicized.

Von: I need to share this truism with you, Ms. Boston; you are in New York City, prepare yourself for anything and everything.

Mashé and Von covered a few more details and then they said goodnight. Mashé gazed at the panoramic view. She could see the sparkling lights from the Hudson River and the cars and trucks on the George Washington Bridge looked like tiny beams of light. She felt like she had reached a pinnacle of sorts. She had not set any particular goal when she became a poet so this certainly brought her a sense of fulfilment and that extra money would be an added plus. She knew the royalties depended on the percentage she sold. All those involved must get their share and that is a very significant unsavory fact she had learned as an author, and realized this applied to other artisans as well.

Mashé was surprised by her phone chiming she thought she had turned it off she notices an unrecognizable number.

Eila: Mashé, pardon my late call I know tomorrow is your big day where is it taking place? The Javits Center. Of course I have been there. Amazing, I am really proud of you. I want you to know that I plan on being there and we are going to take lots of pictures. Have you heard from Rhial? Exactly...I told her the same thing, in her condition she should stay at home, I guess the train ride up should be okay. By the way, give me the name of your book again? *Loving Rhymes*, that's catchy. Mashé, I am really glad for you and I am also glad we are still friends, I mean real friends. Right, you need your rest. I will see you tomorrow and good luck. Bye.

Mashé started to unpack when her phone chimed again, and she quickly answered.

Mashé: Eila, did you forget something?

Chandler: This is not Eila, it's me. How are you?

Mashé clumsily took a seat.

Mashé: Chandler. My goodness it's been a while. How are things?

Chandler: Things are good. I am right outside your door, may I come in for a quick minute?

Mashé: What are you doing in New York? Oh, wow what a question.

Chandler: Mashé, don't cut me down at the knees. I came here to see you and only you. Please let me in for a moment. Mashé, you know me.

Mashé slowly approached the door and peeped through the security portal, recognizing the man she almost married. She decided to allow him in. Chandler was looking better than before, and Mashé was displaying indifference, perhaps this was a test; she needed to prove her strength and fidelity. He seemed overjoyed to see her and gradually she had to admit seeing him again was stirring and reviving.

Chandler: I want us to sit down for a few minutes and go over some things and then I will leave. First of all, congratulations, Ms. Boston, you are blowing up, big time.

Mashé: Thank you. All the same I'll need to give it time.

Chandler dwelled on how good it was to have her in his life for a short while and he replayed over and over again in his mind how he could have saved their relationship. He said all of his life he had been able to achieve and pursue what he wanted. His family had the means for him and his brother to have many advantages—he said that Eila was not in his league of people to associate with, that her behavior was over the top and he could not see himself married to her for any given length of time. He stressed that she knew that using pregnancy would get his attention—he pressed on the fact that she tested his value system. He looked at her left hand.

Chandler: Congratulations are in order for you again. It would be insincere of me to say I…wish it were us, nonetheless, I want you and him to be happy; by the way, who is he?

Mashé: Thank you, Chandler. His name is Neil Rollins. I appreciate your explanation and I have spoken to Eila, we were very frank with one another and I am fine with all of it. I learned a few things about myself, like the need to do what is best for me and in spite of whatever happens in life to move forward. I believe you are going to find happiness soon, unless you already have.

Chandler: The truth will be revealed. May I have the last hug before you marry?

Mashé wanted to resist, here they were inches from one another, and he was fine all over. They seemed to be sharing mutual sensations. Instantly, Chandler reached out to hold her firmly, absorbed in his arms with dubious thoughts, they then reclined across her bed. They lay there silent for twenty, maybe thirty minutes, when he says, "Obviously there is no end to what we have. I care too much; so, is our love-secret inevitable?" All she could say was, "Chandler, please leave." So he did.

It took a while before she fell asleep and when she did it took Housekeeping to wake her up. The front desk had called her earlier to no avail. She looked around wondering was it a dream or had he really been there? Anyway, she ran to the shower with suds abounding telling herself to wake up. Leaving the shower she ran around looking for her electric rollers and there they were, where she put them on her nightstand. Her hotel phone rang and she put it on speaker.

Mashé: Good morning, Von. I am good. Who could sleep? Though I am hungry. What! No way, I am going to be more that fifteen minutes, because I have to do my hair. Why do you say Unbelievable? You told me your wife was Black, well, I don't have a wig to throw on. Give me twenty minutes? Please?! We won't be late. See you in the lobby.

Mashé dressed in her sienna colored two-piece tube skirt and cross-over jacket. It had the look she needed for a place like New York City. Leaving the elevator she noticed Von pacing but when he saw her he paused and they dash to a waiting taxi holding up traffic.

Von: Well, I have to hand it to you—you did say 20 minutes. And I must say, you have out-dressed yourself. You definitely came prepared, I wish you luck—I wish us luck.

Mashé: Am I expected to do a reading or talk? You were to provide a schedule.

Von: I expected an e-mailed attachment, don't worry I am sure you'll be updated when we get to the park.

When they arrived at the Javits Center there were book booths stationed everywhere and a stage was assembled for live entertainment. Mashé had lit up like Times Square. She eagerly stepped onto the convention center floor searching for her book booth, very anxious to see if all her books had arrived. Von managed to find the coordinator, whose name was Sinji Mays. Mashé's booth was grouped with the Fiction Genre Section aligned with Suspense and Drama. The local press had already formed a huge huddle near the Fiction section and Mashé gave Von the look of "keep them at bay." Mashé's watch read five minutes to eight, as she walked into her booth there was an enlarged picture of herself.

Mashé is wondering whatever happened to the picture.

Right then and there the Book Fair announcer approached the microphone welcoming all participants to their twenty-fifth annual Book Fair—the largest ever held on the East Coast. He gave the signal to security personnel to remove the barricades and with that, people began flowing in.

It appeared that Science Fiction was the popular topic. Von had the job to lure folks in Mashé's direction. It took a while but enough people gravitated to her to have her first reading. Some authors had video presentations although she was comfortable answering questions and talking with different people on what inspired her to be a poet. She shared this scenario:

The words we communicate are from our thought process, for example, the mind of a child is considered to be freer than that of an adult. They have yet to be trained to think like adults and perhaps that's how my journey to becoming a poet started. Attending church and listening to my favorite songs formulated imaginative scenes. Or riddles I heard repeatedly stayed with me over the years and by considering myself a romantic I visualized lovers portraying their affection not necessarily through physical contact but through using provocative words, because words are powerful and usually eternal.

The Book Fair was moving well. There were some people showing genuine interest and others merely wanting to talk; Mashé had perfected her diplomacy to a point that no matter what the motives of these people, she was going to be the star attraction. It had been a while since Mashé had seen Von when he appeared with their lunches.

Mashé: Food. How did you know? It looks like New York is showing off today.

Von: As promised. You have some friends looking for you. Mashé looked up and saw Eila and Rhial; she runs over to meet them. Rhial was beginning to show and Eila, dressed to impress, brought two male companions.

Eila: Mashé, I would like you to meet Ashon and Jonnell Montgomery. Guys, please meet the renowned poet, Mashé Boston.

What struck Mashé immediately was that Ashon and Jonnnell were twins. For a second she glanced at Rhial, who was already wearing a look of restraint on her face.

Mashé: Ashon and Jonnell, what a pleasure, and I appreciate your interest in poetry.

Jonnell: Yes, but we are interested in *your* poetry. We would like to celebrate your success in a big way.

Mashé glanced at Rhial and Eila.

Ashon: My pleasure as well. Very nice to see you here, Mashé. My brother and I would like to treat you and your friends to dinner tonight?

Mashé: (Reserved) Let me be sure I am free. I will let you know.

Mashé rushed back to her station and Eila was right on her heels.

Eila: Girl, I love what you're wearing. I know what you are thinking. It's a coincidence; how could I plan this?

Mashé: Eila, I am happy you came, leave it to you. They seem nice, but I probably will be relaxing tonight. They are definitely men of means—where did you meet them?

Eila: They are bankers and we met at one of my fundraisers.

Mashé: Do tell. By the way, where is Mr. Wall Street?

Eila: (Beaming) Lowell, he is working right now but we are getting together later tonight. He wants to buy your book online—but I told him you cannot sign an e-book.

Mashé: Thank you, Eila!

Eila: So, how are the sales?

Mashé: It is too early to say, but I appreciate the stream of people—I feel so fortunate. At this point I'm not concerned about the number sold. I am loving this experience and the timing could not have been better.

Rhial joined them.

Rhial: Did you two forget about me? Eila, the twins are charming as well as a little fresh. What is the probability of you knowing two pairs of twins, men mind you, in a given lifetime? I don't know. (They laugh out loud)

Mashé: You seemed like you were enjoying yourself. How are you feeling these days?

Rhial: There has been no morning sickness so far; I am feeling great. I will cut back my hours when I reach six months. And ladies, big announcement, I want to move back to California.

Mashé: That a fact. Have you mentioned this to Halvan?

Rhial: No, I will bring it up as I approach my due date, which is as you know late June or early July.

Eila: Is this a strategy that you have come up with? Like at your point of delivery he will be more considerate, agreeable to whatever you want?

Rhial: Yes and no. I want us both to agree that since my parents are there they could help me with the baby and I will probably take a break from working, but not for long.

Eila: But his parents live in Florida, and his argument could be the same as yours.

Rhial: Believe me, Halvan and his parents are not close. Don't get me wrong, they made themselves available when we decided to move from Panama City to where we are now. His mother cooked dinner for us once and the father put some of our furniture in storage. Now, bear in mind that his parents are divorced, so having them in the same place at once, slim to none. Our bridal shower was an exception and they traveled separately.

It was announced that two hours remained for the Book Fair. Von called Mashé over to meet with some prospects, and Rhial and Eila came as well to watch the goings on. Mashé's stack of books was getting lower and lower and she was tingling all over. Von whispered to her that they were definitely making a profit and after this event there should be others to follow. Mashé was very surprised with the show of supporters, and maybe after this Book Fair was done she might consider changing her flight to a flight this evening—she missed her man and wanted to be with him.

Mashé was suddenly approached by at least fifteen college girls saying their homework assignment from their English Literature class was to come to the Book Fair and interview a famous poet and would she be their subject? Mashé agreed. They asked her all kinds of savvy questions like, Who was her most favorite poet that ever lived? Mashé pondered, then said she could offer two very prolific ones: Langston Hughes and e.e. cummings without a doubt. One student said their syllabus listed their works as required reading. Mashé said so did hers. This "struck a chord" when she told them that. Another one asked about a well-recognized female poet she admired. Mashé thought of Rita Dove, a Black woman who won the Pulitzer Prize in Poetry. These students were sharp, they kept Mashé on her toes and she met each question head on. When they finished with their myriad of questions, pictures were taken and many more of her books were signed.

It was plain to see that her Best Girls, Eila and Rhial, were relishing these moments with her. With the Book Fair now winding down, the twins asked Mashé had she decided on their invitation to dinner. (Mashé wanted to bypass their offer because she really wanted to change her flight plans and they were friends of Eila's).

Mashé: Ashon, Jonnell, I have had a full day and I really feel….

Jonnell: Just dinner, Mashé. By the way your name is so unusual, it sounds spiritual.

Eila: (Interjects) Mashé, listen, don't disappoint them. Bring Von with us. They have made reservations at this high class private club on Park Avenue. It will be my first time there. Mashé, we haven't been out together for who knows how long. I have heard wonderful things about its atmosphere, the clientele, the food, c'mon, Girl! This is your night and since you're getting married in less than a week's time…

Jonnell: Oh no, you are breaking my heart already!

Mashé: I was about to ask you two bachelors where your dates are tonight?

Ashon and Jonnell said Eila assured them that she and Eila were available Then Rhial shouted: So, does that mean I'm your chaperone?

Eila: No disrespect, Rhial, but in your condition I was wondering if you were going to hang with us throughout the evening.

At that moment Mashé heard her name being called from a distance. Mashé turned around and could not believe her eyes and then she turned to look at Eila.

Tia: I bet you thought I wasn't coming. Mashé, I am so proud of you, this is fantastic. Oh…Eila, it's good to see you, and Rhial, you look great. (She called out for her husband to rush over). Langley, we're over here, everyone this is my husband Langley; these are classmates of mine from college.

The wind is picking up again and Mashé is so tickled about that scene at the New York Book Fair. It was a true highlight of her life for a long time.

The expression Tia gave her when she noticed Eila was unforgettable; still she handled herself well, in fact, Eila was behaving a little peculiarly. Nevertheless, there was no way she could have ever linked the two of them (she and Tia) to revealing her connection with Chandler. Later that evening she recalled the comment Eila made saying she didn't know she and Tia kept in touch after college and Mashé casually replied that they corresponded from time to time.

Oddly enough she somehow feels Chandler's presence there. Combing through her album she does come across a picture of them at that private club, a definite keepsake.

Eila: So this is the Secret Rose. Ashon, Jonnell; this place is beyond what I expected. How long have you two been members?

Jonnell: It's been quite a while, our father is one of the shareholders.

Eila: Mashé, what do you think?

Mashé: It is a stylish place for sure. Tia, how about you and Langley?

Tia, I have heard of it of course, but I never thought I would set foot in here. There is a reason why it is called private.

Langley: (Facetious) If my wife were understanding, I could become a regular here.

Tia: Oh really?!

Rhial: A word of advice, people, don't give others the impression that you are unaccustomed to these kinds of surroundings. Act cool, where is your swag.

Mashé: (Walking over to her) I see you learned a few things as a Floridian Entrepreneur.

Rhial: (Whispers) Seriously, Girl, how long are we going to stay? I have heard about the activities that take place in clubs like this. We need to talk to Eila too.

Mashé: Well, Eila is a "tough cookie"—I can see how uncomfortable you are. Let's ease into it. I'll pretend to get a call and then you follow my lead.

Rhial: A good plan…but now I need to go to the ladies' room. This pregnancy has me going twice as often. I will be right back.

Ashon called for all in his party to join him in a room reserved just for them. It was deep blue in color and the ceiling had shimmering lights to emulate stars in the sky. There were a couple of women there waiting, dressed in what could best be described as a mini- tutu and stilettos. Of course, Eila led the way. As soon as everyone was seated the women gave menus to them all. Mashé's jaw nearly dropped to the floor. Rhial returned, took a seat, and glanced at Mashé. Jonnell waved his hand to signal a server to pour the champagne and not just any champagne, it was the Dom Perignon White Gold Jeroboam.

Mashé was sitting between Tia and Eila. She leaned towards Eila.

Mashé: Did you see the brand of champagne? One drop of it must be worth $5,000.00.

Eila: (Amused) Well, you sure know your champagnes.

Mashé: Seriously, how did you meet these twins?! And by the way, I noticed their time pieces; a Cartier or Rolex, they are good at banking.

Eila: All right…I went to a reception for one of the fundraising coordinators I work with and they approached me, introducing themselves. They seemed very pleasant so we exchanged phone numbers. What is the problem? This is a legitimate operation. We're in New York City, not Kansas City!

Mashé: What!! Look Eila Wynston, my work is headed for a major upswing and I am not going to gamble with it. Now, I need a direct answer—I am not going to be steered into another snafu, especially with you involved.

Eila: (Spunky) Snafu! Getting fancy on me again. I thought you said you were moving on. You are still blaming me for your wedding blunder with Chandler. Blunder, how is that for my vocabulary?

Mashé: (Resentful) So, you had to come out with it. I'll say it again, you two deserve each other—listen, you don't have to trick people into getting what you want. Think about it.

Eila: (Livid) Mashé, what are you saying? Where do you get the gall…

Mashé: (Sarcastic) You mean temerity… don't you? (Gradually drawing attention to themselves)

Tia: Shhhh…you two. Don't do this in here. (Tia was careful not to say too much so as not to give herself away)

Rhial: (Hinting) Mashé, do you have my phone? (Mashé ignored her)

Mashé: (Riled) I am so tired of your entitlement issues. You don't need to use me to get yourself into a place like this. Pardon me, gentlemen, something has come up and I need to go. Please forgive me?

Rhial: Yes, Mashé, I am coming with you.

Jonnell: Before you leave, Mashé—take a look at this? (He shows her an order for her e-book, *Loving Rhymes*. (He ordered 1000 of them) Mashé, darling I have sent them all over the globe as gifts. What do you think about that? (One could hear a pin drop)

Mashé: (Modest) Jonnell and Ashon, I am so appreciative of your support. You actually know 1000 people around the world? Nonetheless, you two don't know the history of our relationship. Eila and I from time to time find ourselves at opposite ends of the poles, in a way, so forgive me for my part in this small rift. I must say, that it is probably because of you two that my agent referenced a significant profit in my e-book sales today. I am so humbled and Eila, I…must thank you mostly for it is because of your networking and our friendship this happened. (Many onlookers seemed to admire how she handled it and watched the two share a forgiveness hug, though Rhial and Tia were looking unsure)

Ashon: I guess that means we can continue? People, I am ravenous.

Mashé sat there feeling like "Silly Putty." Eila seemed to have gotten the advantage, with her helping involuntarily. How could she allow herself to be drawn into this? She still wanted to leave. She looked at Rhial, who was wearing a look of "What now?" Mashé started to smile because in her heart she cared for Eila, but in her mind she was rather peeved over this situation. Maybe Eila was sincere in a weird kind of way—it was just this whole scene seemed questionable. Tia leaned over and asked her how long she was to stay in New York and Mashé said she planned to leave tomorrow on a noon flight. Tia asked to meet and talk before she left—about tonight. Mashé told her to come to her hotel suite later on. The dinner was close to obscene, meaning there was New England Fried Haddock, Seared Halibut in white wine sauce, Smoked Pork Shoulder, lobster bisque, Spanish Soufflé, and Creole Dumplings with assorted cakes and pies. Mashé ate morsels from a few dishes and so did Rhial. About an hour had passed and people were deeply engrossed in conversation with the live music, which meant it was Mashé's and Rhial's cue to exit inconspicuously.

Mashé and Tia made eye contact for a second; then Mashé spotted a server and called him over. She wrote a note and instructed him to give it to Eila after they left, he was tipped a twenty. Tia watched Mashé and Rhial as they made their way to the elevators. Her husband Langley wanted to stay but he followed her as she motioned past an unaware Eila and others.

The elevator door opened and Mashé and Rhial walked briskly to the revolving doors. Rhial mentioned how strange she thought it was for there not to be any visible security, but Mashé pointed out the surveillance cameras throughout. When they hopped into a taxi, Mashé asked Rhial whether she had a place to stay and Rhial said she had planned to take a late train back home. They both laughed, and Mashé asked how long the trip was. Rhial replied, no more than a day. Mashé told Rhial she was staying with her at the hotel.

Rhial: What did your note say?

Mashé: "I need to get back to the hotel it's getting late. Thanks for everything, you, Ashon and Jonnell." I had to keep it simple. You see how I was put on the spot back there? What is it with her, Rhial? I mean you two knew each other before I came to California.

Rhial: Now that I think about it until you came, she seemed fine. Being little girls was different then. We played well together and bottom-line, Mashé, you are special and she is envious, I refuse to say jealous; friends are not supposed to be jealous of each other.

Mashé: I believe that too. But in her case I wonder. You are special too, Rhial.

Rhial: We are a special threesome. You bring creativity. What do I bring?

Mashé: Backbone, and Ms. Wynston brings combustion. (They giggle) On the serious side, I spoke to Aunt Lennie about her behavior and she believes not having a mother might be the reason.

Rhial: That could be one of the reasons. Her mother was a considerate person, very pretty; she reminds me of Aunt Lennie somewhat. I don't really remember her father that much. I think something happened, Mashé, and we do not know what, that's my sense of it.

Mashé: Now, you are on to something. For the most part to me Aunt Lennie has had this docile impression about her. I don't think Eila received that much discipline. Maybe Eila's been given a pass most of her life. But you know, she is so smart, and quick.

Rhial: Mashé, in that case I'm convinced New York City is the town for her. I like what I have seen of it so far, with the exception of the club, but look it's non-stop, more or less restless here, how about you?

Mashé: (Smiling) New York City? Only to do business and maybe a little shopping. And tomorrow, I'm going to be doing a little of that before my flight home. Are you in?

Rhial: You have to ask? And what about Eila?

Mashé: Now, that is so you. I will let you do the honors—why not, make it a threesome. You know I heard Jonnell mention an after party. Let's wait and call her when we reach the hotel? (Instantaneously) Rhial, I want to see Times Square.

Rhial: I'm ready.

Mashé and Rhial had the driver cruise them around Times Square for a period of time. At one point, they were let out in front of a couple of active cafés and novelty shops. They took pictures with their phones and Mashé introduced herself to a few people who liked poetry, encouraging them to look up her book online. Given Rhial's condition, they returned to the taxi. When they arrived at the hotel Mashé had a call from Tia. As the elevator stopped on the twenty-first floor, they enter her suite and Rhial slipped out of her shoes to feel the posh deep carpet. As Mashé closed the door, she did a call-back to Tia.

Tia: Good, I tried to reach you earlier. Have you spoken to Eila any more tonight?

Mashé: No I haven't, why?

Tia: They spoke of this after party, did you know about it?

Mashé: Jonnell mentioned something about it; I was not interested. Did Eila go and where is it anyway?

Tia: The Bahamas! And I believe she plans to go.

Mashé: Seriously! That is unbelievable! That's crazy!

Rhial came rushing in from the living room.

Tia: I saw this helicopter stationed on the landing pad atop of the building next to us.

Mashé: Has it taken off yet?

Tia: Langley and I are in the car. I think it's still there. Langley said it was supposed to take them to a Learjet, which can hold up to ten passengers. Eila said she was going. Mashé, most of the people going are men, including those questionable twins.

Mashé: The Learjet probably belongs to them. Tia, thank you for telling me this. I'll call her now. Yes, I will let know what I find out.

Rhial: The party is in the Bahamas?! I can just imagine what's waiting for them there.

Mashé: Rhial, c'mon, let's not speculate, Eila is adventurous, but not stupid. Gosh, I hope she hasn't gotten on that little bitty plane.

She called and her call went to voicemail. Since it would probably be too late to go back to that private club, Mashé decided to call the New York Police Department.

Mashé: Good evening, there is a possible kidnapping about to take place, Officer. All I know is a Learjet with several men and a couple of young women are about to take off for the Bahamas. No, please I would like to remain anonymous. Yes, I did hear someone talking about an emergency departure. It must have been about thirty minutes ago. Yes, I will wait for your call back. Thank you very much, Officer.

Rhial told Mashé she hoped she didn't over-extend herself, though she had a hard time thinking of an alternative. Mashé and Rhial agreed to keep this a secret. They imagined how irate Eila would be to find out that one of her Best Girls blocked her travel plans. They both wondered why they weren't invited and was Eila even aware until the very last minute? And Mashé wondered, did she ever read her note?

Mashé: Let's keep in mind that a Learjet normally carries up to ten people according to Tia's husband. There were about twenty-five people in that private dining room.

Rhial: Knowing Eila she has probably done this before. Oh, Girl! I hope we didn't over-react.

Mashé: Ump! Over-react?! Rhial, this is Eila Wynston we're talking about. It's getting late; we should go to sleep, it may be hours before we know anything.

As they prepared for bed Mashé's mind wandered to Neil. She wanted to call him so much, though he might be asleep, and if she told him all of what happened with the private club situation and her friend hooking up with two strangers to go to the Bahamas and then her calling NYPD to report a kidnapping, it would surely upset him. She really wanted to be in his arms right now. She was so glad Rhial was with her. Rhial had prepared her bath and Mashé turned on the flat screen TV. The local news was on; suddenly Mashé was hollering for Rhial to come where she was.

It was reported that the NYPD received an anonymous tip earlier in the evening of a possible kidnapping attempt. They were showing four men handcuffed with their heads bowed entering the back seat of a patrol car. Mashé and Rhial were frantically looking for Eila. The reporter conveyed that the police had interrupted a private jet destined for the Bahamas and carrying several kilos of illegal substances. Mashé and Rhial did a victory dance.

Mashé's phone received a call. It was Tia and Langley, who were blown away and asking had she ever reached Eila.

Mashé: Not a word. I tried calling her cell, it went to voicemail. (She thanked Tia over and over again for calling her about what was obviously scandalous, and Tia, like she and Rhial, said she hoped and prayed Eila was unaware of it all. There was a call waiting on Mashé's cell.)

Eila: Mashé, it's me, I'm at the police station. No, no charges against me, but they have to check the background of everyone who was there. I am so glad you weren't there, Mashé, you and the others. Seriously, I did not know about that jet going to the Bahamas. I thought the after party was going to be at one of the high rises down the street. I wasn't the only one misled. There were two other women, the ones that served us. Yes, I did get your note and at first I had wished you had come to me but then I know how you are when your mind is made up. Mashé, this was your big day and it could have been a fiasco. Please forgive me for speaking to you the way I did earlier? I should have listened to you. You were right about me; I am such a show-off. We cannot let this get back home. I called Lowell; he's on his way here. If you could have heard the tone of his voice when I told him where I was.

Mashé: Rhial and I would never reveal this to anyone. (Cautiously) Do you want Tia's phone number—she is concerned about you too.

Eila: (Long pause) Tia is? If…you would call her for me and let her know I am fine. They are going to release me soon, I hope. I have to get back now.

Mashé: Wait, Eila, Rhial wants to talk to you.

She fell across her bed thinking, That was a close one. She needed to give Eila some space. A "fiasco," that was putting it mildly. Her friend plowed right into overkill. She and Rhial were burdened with another big secret. Then again, as her mother would say, "this too shall pass away."

Precedence (10)

The sanctuary for Mashé's and Neil's wedding was adorned with lilac and crème decorations. Her mother had her assistants add gold appliques to the drapes and floral designs on display throughout. This added a glitzy appeal to the entire room; now it had a majestic presence.

Mashé was seated at the vanity table having her hair arranged in a fashion she never thought of. She watched as her hair was cascaded, frizzed, and straightened, and when finished she looked distinctive, yet trendy as though she were a star. Rhial, standing nearby, looked elegant in her own right. They could hear the chattering of Eila and Jasmine in the next room recommending to each other what brand of make-up to use.

When Mashé returned from New York, she behaved as though all went famously, because in a sense it did. She, Rhial, Tia, and her husband Langley agreed a few days following the incident that nothing out of the ordinary happened. The news of the seized Learjet destined for the Bahamas made national news and when Neil picked her up from the airport he asked did she see any police activity around her way. She nonchalantly mentioned that she saw it on the news like everyone else. It bothered her lying to Neil because she believed if matters were reversed, he would have told her everything.

Clover entered and received a round of applause for all of her efforts. She was dressed to impress with a white speckled fox stole draping her shoulders. She came to Mashé and asked her to join her in a vacant dressing room. Clover shut the door and presented her one and only daughter with a golden South Seas single pearl necklace representing "something new." One tear after another streamed down Mashé's face. She could not imagine how much her mother spent on this piece; she put it on and posed in the mirror.

Mashé still wears the necklace and found the picture taken of her and her mother on that unforgettable day.

There was a voice on the other side of the door telling Mashé and Clover that the time had come. Clover took her daughter by the arm, asking why Eila was acting somewhat removed. Mashé quickly replied that it was a sentimental time for her because she and Rhial beat her to the altar. Clover said she did not think that was it. She missed her outgoing and whimsical manners. She said that even Aunt Lennie was concerned. Saying that she seemed less talkative and more aloof.

Mashé: Maybe Aunt Lennie should come out and ask, "What's going on with you?"

Clover: You two are so close, if you find out anything at all, let her know?

Mashé: Mother, you know what day this is? Now you need to be escorted to your seat. I'm sure Dad is looking for you.

Mashé hugged her mother; then Clover joined the wedding party. Mashé was so close to excusing Eila as one of her maids of honor; she felt stuck, imagining the high level of attention that event would have brought. With regard to forgiveness, she was working on it. Day by day she released a little more animosity (similar to that of a hot air balloon). At the bridal shower thrown by Rhial and her mother, Eila gave her a complete set of her long stemmed crystal goblets from her bridal registry. Nearly everyone at the shower wondered if she had spent her entire house note. Mashé appreciated her gift, playing it off graciously; Rhial was not fooled and later told the bride-to-be to give it time. Tia was unable to attend but sent her and Neil authentic Portuguese porcelain tableware.

As Mashé stood in the vestibule with her father awaiting their cue, he affirmed how happy he was that Neil was the one. Speaking frankly, he said Neil should be her husband since he proposed to her twice. When the doors opened Mashé saw at the altar a man waiting for her who loved her from day one, and as she came closer the thought of Chandler crept in and she quickly looked over to Eila; there she was with a broad smile on her face—for some odd reason it comforted her.

Pastor Sandamore officiated the ceremony. He had baptized Mashé, Rhial, and Eila together on Palm Sunday when they were ten years old. In his delivery he mentioned to the small room of guests that Neil and Mashé had experienced some trials while courting and that Mashé almost got away. He expressed, "The credit goes to spiritual intervention, love and patience, which has joined them together this day."

As they faced each other, Mashé was awed by Neil's magnificent face. They exchanged the traditional vows, then Neil spoke to Mashé in this fashion, "It is my honor to be your husband and each day from now on it will be my purpose to please you." Then he lifted her veil and laid a lengthy kiss, indicating to all what was in store for her.

The ushers led all wedding guests to the Country Club across from the courtyard. Several reception guests were there waiting to be led in. Some complained that they were invited to the first one, which included both events, and this time they were only invited to the reception. The Boston family did have an insert in the wedding invitations explaining their changes and asked that the wishes of the bride and groom be respected. It appeared that over four hundred guests joined the happy couple, and a huge buffet was in place. Neil and Mashé were the first to enter. Mashé walked over to have a gander at their six-foot-tall wedding cake.

It brought all the impressions of a Saint Valentine's Day theme. Patterns of lilac hearts were on every tier. Neil wiped a tear from her cheek, asking was she all right? She told him she was so blessed to be Mrs. Neil Rollins.

As the guests were led in, a live band appeared and began playing a rendition of "All This Love" by El DeBarge, held in confidence by Neil. The bride and groom glided across the dance floor as though they were alone. Neil whispered in her ear that he had an even bigger surprise.

Neil: Because we are in the off season I have chartered a jet, well my parents did, to fly you and me to Saint Thomas, US Virgin Islands, tomorrow and your parents have put us up for the night at the Ritz Carlton. Now, is that cool?

Mashé: It's...a cool way to start a marriage. However, when we get back home from our honeymoon, I won't know how to act. Our parents are golden and I am so in love with you, Neil. (She repeated in her mind "a chartered jet" to the U.S. Virgin Islands)

Neil: I love you so, Lady. You know what? We can leave now, we're official. Our life together is going to be an adventure, I promise you.

Mashé: (Cunning) Seriously?! We need to be receptive to all of these people. Just for a little while...and then we'll sneak out.

Neil: That's a plan. "Partners in crime."

The photographers asked Neil and Mashé to be seated at the head table with their family members for a series of pictures. So many testimonials were expressed, shortly thereafter the bride was asked by the Best Man, Neil's cousin named Clifton, to dance with her father and Neil to dance with his mother. Mashé was touched by all of the effort put in by her family and friends. Having entered a new year, she still tangled occasionally with trying to remove herself from her sensitive experiences with Chandler. Marrying Neil was her translation into a relationship filled with anticipated resolution and need for genuine bliss; however, she wondered if she would ever reach genuine closure.

Rhial, Mashé's Matron of Honor, called all bachelorettes to the floor. Eila sprang to her feet and stood a few inches directly behind the bride. A count of fifty-five eager women approached. Eila heard a few sharp comments from behind her insinuating she was bull guarding and to step back; of course they were ignored. Rhial and Mashé were telepathic on dreading an outcome that could be embarrassing; however, everyone else found this to be entertaining. One thing Eila did not need was a cheer on. And Lowell was there cajoling and then proceeded to stand up. Mashé had the idea to throw the bouquet upward toward the ceiling and then it would look like fair game because she remembered that when they were in the tenth grade she and Eila promised one another that whoever married first, the bridal bouquet was hers. The bouquet was doing a drift mode going from side to side until it landed right into Eila's awaiting hands. She was so excited and shortly thereafter heard some grumbling as she walked by Mashé whispering, Thank you.

Now it was the groom's turn to throw the bride's lilac and crème colored garter. Neil positioned himself and closed his eyes, tossed it, and it reached the hands of Lowell. Eila is ecstatic she twirls around then ran to Lowell. She took the garter and glided it up her right leg and Mashé had the photographer take a few pictures of them. She then felt the warm touch of her husband's hand in hers coaxing that their moment had come. Mashé barely had the opportunity to speak with most of the guests, so she tiptoed over to her parents and told them they were sneaking out. Interestingly before the side door closed behind them, Mashé turned to look for her two Best Girls who were laughing and line dancing with some classmates from high school.

A limousine pulls up. It had a crème exterior and a lilac colored interior. Neil told his new wife it was hard to locate but he finally found one. They sped away to the Ritz Carlton. When they arrived, Mr. and Mrs. Rollins were taken to the wedding suite. She wondered what her parents paid; it was extraordinary, better yet "off the chain." When she walked on the carpet, it was so soft she told Neil she wanted to roll in it. Neil told her he would love to roll in it with her. He then found the remote for the sound system, searched for some classic pop jazz; the acoustics were perfect. The phone rang and it was room service letting them knows they were right outside their door. Mashé had gone for a tour; there were eight rooms in all. Neil called her back to the foyer. When she returned there before them was a champagne basket surrounded by hors d'oeuvres that they could hardly make out. They were seated at the table, and Mashé was asked what she would like to drink. She wanted a Peach Bellini and Neil wanted a Kir Royale. While enjoying their drinks Neil whispered to Mashé, "When is he leaving?" In a matter of moments, the server did depart and Mr. and Mrs. Rollins had eased into a very warm bubble bath. Feeling mildly tipsy, they cleaved onto one another with their arms and legs. The next thing Mashé knew she was being lifted and carried onto the bed. They were now face to face and then it happened again, a vision of Chandler, she quickly shut her eyes. Neil did not seem to sense anything. Somehow, Neil did bring her back and center for within minutes she was hollering his name. On and off until noon Mrs. Rollins was rocked by the vigorous agility of her amoureux.

The clock read 3:00 PM and the newlyweds were up and dressed. The luggage for their honeymoon had been brought in last night. She was feeling so hearty, like she had been restored, though she was concerned. Was her subconscious playing tricks on her? She hadn't been thinking about Chandler, then, maybe there were remnants floating around. Nevertheless, the outcome was right here and now. She walked over to admire the beautiful Japanese garden through a portal window. Neil called out to her.

Neil: It's time. I got a call, the plane is ready.

Mashé: Let's go. But I'm hungry.

Neil: C'mon, lunch is on the plane. Hey. Let's make love on the plane?

Mashé: You know, your mother was right.

Neil: Really, how so?

Mashé: "Engineers know what to look for and then they perform."

Essence (11)

The charter private jet was a Falcon 2000 and had been cleared for takeoff. Mashé and Neil were strapped in but Neil wanted to take his wife to the rear lounge cabin. Mashé had a mild phobia for small planes and wished someone had consulted with her about this arrangement way in advance. The takeoff was smooth and as they climbed, Neil whispered to follow him to the rear. She urged him to obey the pilot's orders, to stay strapped in until further notice. "At the drop of a hat," Neil was reminding her of Chandler, pressing her for carnal contact. After they reached the appropriate altitude, the pilot stated they were free to move about. Neil was ready but she told him she was still hungry. Neil paused and sent for the steward to serve his wife whatever she wanted. When the steward asked him for his order as well, Neil declined and uttered "later on." Neil asked whether Mashé had a fear of flying and she admitted she did when it came to small private jets. Neil assured her that his father's friend, who managed his own charter service, was reputable and stood by his product. Neil bragged how as a child he used to fly locally with his father and co-workers who engineered small aircraft—he boasted of the intoxicating-like feeling every time he got into one of them. Mashé's comeback was that it would have been considerate to ask her. She appreciated the generosity that went into this but she was more stunned than surprised. Neil turned to her and said it was his fault because he wanted it to be a surprise; his parents did advise him to tell her. Serendipitously Mashé no longer felt remorse for not sharing the episode that she barely missed in New York City and told her husband she was calmer now than before. Finally, she was served a delectable meal. While she was enjoying it, her husband told her he would be in the cockpit talking with the crew about events taking place in Saint Thomas. She detected an attitude; she meant no offense, though how can she convince him? She finished her meal and now she was sleepy as she peeked out the window she saw beautiful mountain tops and soft billowy clouds; now she was enjoying this flight. She recalled that the pilot said their flight would take about seven to eight hours. Neil seemed to be having a good conversation in that cockpit, so she decided to take a nap. It then occurred to her that Neil must have made love on a plane like this; he was so insistent. She changed her mind about the nap and called the steward over to beckon her husband for her. Looking concerned, Neil asked if everything was all right. With a look of desire she asked him if he was ready. Neil reacted without hesitation. They went to the rear cabin, Mashé did not expect such a tiny room, obviously making for a tight frolic. Neil wondered what had come over her, He asked her what she ate for lunch, and she said raw oysters.

Neil and Mashé were having a rest period. He was unprepared for her taking command; still he was fulfilled in every respect. They are awakened by the pilot's announcement that there was an hour and one half remaining in flight time.

Neil: (Facetious) Do you like this kind of flying now?

Mashé: Only when you're on board. (Impish) You…like making love on a jet better?

Neil: I believe I do because the jet's in flight, bringing sensational enhancement.

Mashé was impressed with that wild concept and she would stay prepared; there was more to learn about Mr. Neil Rollins.

They cleaned up and dressed to return to their seats. When they were close to arriving, another succulent meal was prepared for them. Mashé noticed some of the islands as the jet was descending. She was so excited. Her parents had been the globetrotters in the family and now it was her turn. The pilot announced that they were about to hover over Saint Croix.

They were instructed to buckle in as the jet was about to touch down. It wasn't the smoothest of landings but a blessing for all to make it in one piece. Mashé had another jaw-dropping moment when she noticed a stretch limousine awaiting them. The wind was blowing profusely as they rushed over to get in.

Saint Thomas was a lush green island country. Neil chose The US Virgin Islands because the weather was reportedly perfect for honeymooners during February and March. In the latter part of the summer was when the weather warmed up, and the added attraction now would be Mardi gras. Mashé was still struck by the fact that ever since she said "I do," she had been traveling like a starlet, and she reminded Neil that it was dangerous to spoil her; she might not want to go back to her old ordinary life style. He told her that they could notify their employers to allow them an extra month. She knew he was teasing her.

There were many hills in Saint Thomas and the driver has taken them to a secluded villa resort atop one of them; the word paradise would be an understatement. Multitudes of slender coconut trees and flower gardens surrounded this charming place of solitude. Once again a jaw-dropping experience for Mrs. Rollins. Neil enjoyed watching her reactions. They both couldn't wait until they reached the entrance.

Mashé looks up at the sun; she doesn't have a watch near her but she guesses that it could be around three o'clock in the afternoon.

Neil put everything into that experience in Saint Thomas; he was trying not to miss a beat when it came to her happiness and she gave her all as well. There were only a few pictures taken on their honeymoon; that was odd—she had thought there were more; anyway, the few she found showed them at a pool party where they met an enchanting couple, then she questioned what was the extreme term for enchanting?

Mashé and Neil were greeted by a cluster of women dressed in their exotic native attire. They were particularly drawn to Neil; he reacted like a human sponge, and Mashé took notice. Instantly a tall brown-skinned man took her by the hand and offered her a fruit and rum drink. This was their welcoming party. There were huge straw hats placed on their heads, then loud Reggae music was heard as Mashé was escorted into the foyer. She looked back at Neil and he was totally engaged; some of the women were noticeably good looking. Her mother was right. "When you marry a good looking man, rich or poor expect the unexpected." She stood there watching them as her other escort was trying to encourage some dance moves. Her first thought was to go and retrieve her husband; then she had a change of heart—this is a good experience, so she decided to let it flow and pulled out her cell to record it. Bastian, her dancing escort, then twirled her around. She knew he was doing his job so they both bounced to the beat and Bastian was just too glad. They seemed to attract some onlookers and there was no doubt this man's behind had rhythm. In a matter of seconds, she heard a familiar voice.

Neil: Excuse me…Mrs. Rollins our room is ready. Sir, I would like to have my wife back. (Mashé was wearing a smirk) You know I want to visit Cuba one day; I can imagine my wife taking off dancing without me.

Mashé: (Teasing) My partner's name was Bastian; he was welcoming me to this luxurious place. You have good taste, Neil. I am going to bask in all of its splendor too.

Neil: Mashé, none of those women compare to you.

Mashé: They saw a fine Black American man and got excited, I took a video, it is a keeper for sure. We could call it your belated bachelor party (Neil stood before her awestruck by her sarcasm)

The newlyweds had two attendants, one for him and one for her. They were taken through a passage of more tropical foliage and Mashé took her husband by the hand. She was convinced there was no better place on earth. En route they walked into a pool party in progress.

The music was bumping, people were splashing, blending, and dancing. Neil and Mashé seemed to be taken in by it—they asked the attendants to allow them a moment; they were struck by a life-size ice carving of a voluptuous mermaid. Neil alluded that she had to be a sister. Then they heard this voice from behind them.

Cyril: I wish she were real too, my Man. Pardon me, my name is Cyril and my wife's name is Florina; we're from Chicago. (Neil introduced himself and Mashé. Cyril had to be about 6'6"tall, maybe an inch taller than Neil. They both were into fine jewelry. Florina invited Mashé over to their patio table)

Florina: So you just arrived? We try to come down here at least once a year. That is a fabulous wedding ring you are flaunting there. How do you like mine? (Florina flashed what appeared to be a three-carat diamond mounted in platinum wedding ring. Instantly, much to her chagrin, Mashé thought of Chandler's mother displaying her setting.) You two look like newlyweds, how sweet.

Cyril and Neil joined them. Mashé and Neil were picking up some strange vibrations. Cyril ran over and got drinks for all of them.

Neil: No, really, you shouldn't; my wife and I need to settle in.

Mashé: Yes, it is a little early for me anyway. But thank you.

Cyril: So Mashé, I guess my wife has told you we try to make it down here about once a year. It's better than practicing at home.

Neil: Practicing?!

Florina: Yes, we're Swingers. You two just missed the group we had here on Saint Valentine's Day. Seriously, it is so much better when you travel. This is how we fine tune our marriage…

Neil reached for his wife's hand. Mashé was trying to restrain herself from laughing.

Mashé: Florina, there is no one on earth better than my husband.

They take off.

Neil: (Smiling) Baby…I appreciate the compliment but now that woman is going to come looking for me.

Mashé: (Bold) She wouldn't dare. Here is our humble abode.

One of the attendants opened the French doors. Looking into the entry hall they saw sprawled, excessively enhanced bronze figurines. The only one they seemed to recognize is Cupid. Neil made a good analogy—palatial dwellings like this needed to remain in seclusion. The attendants gave them a schedule of activities for each day of the week, and brought to their attention the grand festival, and Mardi gras, which are celebrated before the Lenten season is recognized, would take place in a local town later in the evening. They said they lived on the premises and would be available for assistance at any hour. The schedule of meals reflected that lunch would be prepared in less than an hour and that their meals could be brought to their room if they preferred.

They covered several more details and then said they would return later in the evening to turn down their bed. Neil assuring them he would do it. They smiled and quickly excused themselves. Neil turned to face his wife and discovered that she had walked onto the terrace. She seemed deep in thought. Mashé appreciated how their wedding went. Everyone was supportive and Neil was her hero but did she deserve all of this? She definitely wanted this marriage to work because when they go home, that's when the tests and trials would come. She loved Neil but there must be another kind of love out there. The kind that distracts, and lingers—she wondered if she has the symptoms of "first love syndrome." She could not fool herself and knew she didn't marry a fool. Maybe when they return she would call Tia. Neil joins her.

Neil: Mrs. Rollins, is everything to your liking? What's happening?

Mashé: (Sentimental) You are what's happening. I think you went beyond the "call of duty." Neil…you'll need to be patient with me.

Neil: Okay, what does that all mean? Mashé, you are my black cherry, I picked you and I'm the luckiest man on earth. Fact! It was apparent when we met you were preoccupied with someone else; now your mind is on us. It's a miracle when you can go out into this world and find what you want.

Mashé stands up again slowly walking along her deck. She cherishes the memory of that very moment on their first night there in Saint Thomas.

As they stood on that terrace as far as their eyes could see was sea and sky with the sounds of the tropics and the tall palm trees swaying in rhythm with the waves. That very moment, adoring that very scene, spawned her desire to paint landscapes. She had done still life and human subjects but her best works were with nature.

Lou, her cute and frisky companion, wants to go for a walk. They have not done so in a while, but every mid-afternoon he's on his hind legs to remind her, it's time. Instead, she goes to her cupboard and finds the snacks and toys he likes in hopes they will suffice. Looking back on that night, the Mardi gras festival, she shakes her head, recalling what a time they had.

After their lunch they were surprisingly approached by their attendants asking them to follow them to a special room. When the doors opened they saw a multitude of elaborate costumes in red, purple, green, gold, blue, and all in between. They looked at each other questioning whether they should do this, especially Mashé. Neil made everyone laugh when he said he was not too fond of wearing tights. Their attendants said it was Carnival time and the experience would be like none other; that's what concerned Mashé. Still, they were curious; Neil said he could imagine how the feathers would look flowing and swinging from his wife's hips. Mashé called him a Naughty Neil. Mashé only wanted to be a spectator from a distance; there was no real need to dress up. They were assured that practically everyone on the island would be celebrating and when they were ready to come home, a transport would bring them back to the villa. Neil cleverly said it was his wife's decision, promising never to leave her side, tights and all. Mashé stood there pondering; then a ritzy outfit caught her eye. It was a rich shade of maroon with bouncy ruffles; the matching head piece and mask were stylishly handmade. She told them to allow her to first put on this particular costume, mask and all; she wanted to take a picture and send it to her family and a couple of friends and then she would decide whether to go further. She told Neil he had to do the same: select one that he liked and take a picture with her. They both stepped into their dressing chambers, as they were called. Neil was first to come out. He selected a boldly decorated blue and black ensemble and his healthy athletic legs looked good in tights. The curtain opened and out stepped Mashé, she looked as though she had a part from a period movie, perhaps *Black Orpheus*. Everyone's eyes applauded her.

Neil: If we go you must stay by my side all night. I think I would like to buy this item for you. (Whispering) We could have our own private carnival.

Mashé: You are a vision yourself.

Pictures were taken with their cells. They changed and guardedly decided to partake of the festivities. Neil assured her it should be fine and he understood her concerns. Mashé felt being in a strange country though beautiful required them to play a low profile. It would be hours before Carnival so they decided to browse in the nearby shops. They noticed a bird sanctuary and tried to memorize the names of each one. There was the Yellow Warbler, the Pearly Eyed Thrasher, the Bull Finch, and several species of parrots. There had to have been at least two hundred birds; being in their presence produced a calming effect. Mashé looked out of the window and saw an art gallery; she rushed over, Neil didn't notice. When she entered, she saw paintings worth thousands of dollars on display. The proprietor offered her a tour. She quickly called Neil telling him where she was. So many of them were three-dimensional, magnificent art works, and she entertained the idea of having a gallery of her own. Neil joined her.

Neil: This is right up your alley. You don't mind if I check out the leather store right next door, do you?

Mashé: Of course not. See you soon.

Mashé was introduced to the fine works of some local artists. Many were lithographs; still she was in heaven in a sense. By happenstance, she observed one that she must possess. It was an oil painting, a stately depiction of a mermaid. Mashé's eyes perused every line. The artist captured true human qualities from a mythical character. She was lifelike—skillfully a genius work of art. She had full, shiny black hair and tanned skin with eyes that resembled emeralds. The backdrop was violet with hues of amber. She was perched on a rock glistening probably from the splashing water.

Mashé: Please! Tell me how much for this one?

Proprietor: Would you like to guess?

Mashé: (Puzzled) That sounds like a trick question.

Proprietor: No not at all. It was brought in from a local art school—somehow left behind.

Mashé: Really?! That's unbelievable. What would you sell it for?

Proprietor: I have been asked that so many times.

Mashé: It will be a wedding gift for my husband—I cannot leave here without this painting. Tell me what you want for it? I am nowhere near wealthy, but I need to have it...for him.

Proprietor: I am sensing that. Does $700.00 sound reasonable to you?

Mashé: (Closes her eyes) Yes!!! Please send it to this address in the States?

She was so proud of herself. With all of the plans she was making for their wedding there seemed to be no time until now to give him a gift. She really hoped he would love it and it might have a remarkable effect similar to the ice carving he admired. Walking into the leather store she found him sporting a classy dark brown leather jacket.

Neil: So what do you think?

Mashé: It's you, real nice.

Neil: You must have enjoyed your time in there? That artwork was obviously very expensive, how did you do? I can't believe you walked out empty handed.

Mashé: I'll have to give it time—but thus far it's the highlight of my day next to you obviously.

Neil: Good. You had me nervous for a second. I have decided to buy this.

Mashé: Excellent choice. You know we need to hurry back, it's almost carnival time.

Neil: I love the way your costume takes to your curves. Makes me want to skip it altogether. You do know that tonight is our official wedding night?

Mashé: (Facetious) I suppose you are right. We had better charter a jet then.

Neil: The lady has jokes. My sweetheart, when we come back it will seem like we are still up there.

Mashé: Naughty Neil.

They returned to their room and found their costumes freshly pressed and waiting for them. They heard a knock at their door. Their attendants were dressed for carnival and had come to offer assistance. Mashé was getting excited; she picked up her elaborate head dress. She also brought out her makeup bag and her attendant went to work. After she was done Mashé was so impressed, she was definitely ready for Mardi gras.

Mashé: The finishing touches are our masks. (Admiring her husband) Neil, you look like a cavalier, better yet, a mystic. Seriously, we may have found your alter ego.

Neil: Then, what shall we call him?

Mashé: Umm, Aeru?

Neil: Now that sounds like a warrior. Good one. Now I need to pick one for you. How about, Mayale.

Mashé: That means powerful woman, I think.

Neil: Or a woman who's married to a powerful man. You know, this suit is not half bad.

Mashé: Look who else has jokes. Are we ready people? Aeru?!

On their way to the foyer they saw many others dressed for carnival. And many women were wearing provocative costumes. Neil's eyes stayed fixed on a few of them but Mashé kept her composure; she anticipated there was more amusement to come. She was imagining what it must be like in Brazil.

Neil and Mashé with others climbed into a transport and the driver announced that he will take them to Sugar Bay where the festivities are already under way. Neil and Mashé were gradually feeling the happenings and Neil told her to remember he did this for her; confounded, she came back with she has not been staring at those with little clothing. He sharply looked at his wife telling her he would be looking at her later on with absolutely no clothing.

Neil: Mrs. Rollins, a look doesn't mean anything. And what about Mr. Bastian, you know you liked his bouncing. The human body is a phenomenal creation, particularly yours. And besides I'm wearing this mask, how do you know where my eyes go?

Mashé: (Amused) Your neck, silly. It turns. Why are we discussing this?

Many transports, including the one Neil and Mashé were riding, reached Sugar Bay. The Caribbean music resonated and the aroma of food was tempting. They all headed for the main boulevard, where the stompers were performing. This was considered a traditional event so Mashé and Neil rushed over. There were about fifteen men in radiant costumes entertaining the crowds with their vigor and arousing routines. Many of them flirted with those in the crowd; basically they were considered a star attraction. After they passed came the Ritual Dancers; these graceful women were extravagantly dressed and everyone seemed dazzled by their nimbleness. But what Mashé wanted to see and hear were the steel drum bands. There must have been about twenty or more of them. The melodious quality of their playing sounded as if one hundred men were performing. She recalled reading when she was small about the history of the steel drum, which formed from African culture. She was struck by the fact that a beautiful instrument such as the steel drum evolved from slavery. The parade was a long one and Mashé and Neil wanted something to eat and drink, so they maneuvered their way through the masses and found two cute elderly ladies selling limeade and vegan sandwiches. It started to get hot so they located a nearby shaded area. Everywhere they looked people were celebrating and partying. A local came by to tell them that it was time to join in the parade. Mashé declined immediately but the woman said her brother knew her and said she was a good dancer. Mashé asked who was her brother and the girl pointed a couple of yards away. She recognized him; it was Bastian. Neil said it was a strange coincidence. Mashé still declined, saying she wanted to finish eating her meal. Then the girl moved to Neil and asked him to join in the parade. He too declined, so she said she would be back later. Neil asked Mashé did she want to walk along the Bay because it was cooler over there. Mashé felt she was fine as long as the shaded areas were available. Clamor, including the music, was constant, and Mashé and Neil were in the mist of abundant joy. They both loved to dance and as a group of percussionists streamed by they fervently responded with their version of calypso swing. Now many others were with it and the clamor elevated; as a result a passerby plopped himself between Mashé and Neil, showing off his animated dance style; then came another and another. Neil told them to hold on, to wait; he called for Mashé to take his hand—she tried but more dancers with their heavy gyrations abounded. It looked as though many of them teamed up to take over the entire block. Mashé looked for Neil and Neil looked for Mashé. She managed to free herself from this sea of people and found a wooden table to stand on. Looking out over everyone, she called out to Neil. This was so bizarre: how could this happen? She tried to identify some police officers whom she noticed when they first arrived; now they were nowhere in sight. She then heard her husband calling her; she frantically looked around, where was he? Then his voice faded. She was beginning to feel pensive. She didn't know a soul out there and now must decide was it better to stay above the crowd or try to muster her way through to find him.

The sun was setting and this only means the same clamor continued into the night. Thinking this cannot be happening she was determined more than ever to find the police to help her find her husband. She jumped down and two men came upon her and she staunchly told them to step off; unfazed they moved on. She got an idea—maybe Neil went back to the transport and would be waiting for her there. She started to trot and now she was going faster. She saw two transports that were almost full. She leapt onto the first one looking for Neil; he was not on it. She asked the driver had he seen a man of her husband's description; he said he had not so far. She went to the other transport and climbed on calling for Neil; again he was not on board. She asked the driver to help her find the police—her husband is missing.

The driver sent a text to the police station and was awaiting a response. The driver could see that she was distressed and asked her to take a seat. He asked her was she from the United States and she said yes. He shared a few facts about carnival, saying anything can happen, especially when it came to tourists. He told her to be calm, that the island was not that big, she would see him again. He received a police response, they wanted to speak with her. Mashé took the phone and answered every question. She was advised to go back to the villa. It was getting dark and they wanted her to be safe. She asked could she search with them; she told them they were on their honeymoon. Mashé was feeling so guilty. Neil had asked her if she wanted to walk along the Bay; it now registered that he wanted to be romantic, what she was thinking?

The driver stressed he had to leave now—his shift would end soon. He said the police told him to tell her that they had circulated a communique about her husband and to understand that tourists are affected by some wild antics during carnival, not to insinuate that he was in any danger but to rest assured that they would contact her the moment they find him. Mashé reluctantly rode back to the villa, sending prayer after prayer after prayer to have her husband brought back to her in one piece. She resolved that whatever was going on, she believed that by now they realized they picked the wrong tourist. Then again she was trying so hard not to think the worst. When the transport came to a stop Mashé was the first to step out and dashed to the front desk. Her fancy make-up was ruined. She asked the clerk if any reports had come in about her husband and she asked for her attendant. The clerk was confused and didn't understand what was going on, though she did send for Mashé's attendant, who ran in.

Mashé related to her the story of herself and her husband getting separated during carnival. Her attendant assured Mashé that her husband was fine. She said this occasionally happened to tourists because they appear to be easy targets. She said she should have warned her and her husband that even though carnival is a spiritual event and people enjoy the masquerading, a small few can interfere with the merriment. The clerk called Mashé's attention to the police car driving up; they had Neil.

The door swung open and Neil stepped out looking flustered. When he saw his wife he went straight to her and Mashé ran to him. There were two other men in the police car who were also brought back. One was from Italy and one from the United States as well. It turned out as suspected they wound up in a whirlpool. Neil and the others somehow were blindfolded by women and led into a small building a few yards from the parade. They were tied up and when the blindfolds were removed these women entertained them with song and dance—nothing exotic. Mashé was furious and wanted to speak with the police chief.

Neil: Mashé, rest assured, I have already done that. The police broke in on that party or whatever it was and hauled us all to the police station. I told them to let me go I was the one restrained; they pushed me and as a result, I punched one of the officers in the mouth, he's in the infirmary. At the police station we were told that they needed to make a report; the other tourists and I were cleared of any wrongdoing once they realized we were essentially the victims and so far I have not been charged with "assaulting an officer." Listen to me, Mashé, I told him to take his hands off of me. Any way sweetheart, I am so glad you are all right. I worried that the same thing had happened to you.

Mashé was so proud of her husband; as she predicted, they chose the wrong tourist, and she prayed that the officer's jaw would be all right. The Italian, Carlo Gianni, and his wife, Gabriella, came over to introduce themselves. They were highly upset and wanted them to know that of all the times they have come to the Virgin Islands, nothing like this "terribile cosa" (awful thing) had ever happened to them. The unique thing about this couple was they were well-to-do. Carlo was in textile shipping and asked Neil and Mashé to have dinner with them on their yacht the next night. They both hesitated. Carlo said his yacht was anchored at Bolongo Bay Beach Resort. Neil said he would think it over; they had been through a lot today and it was their honeymoon.

Carlo: (Excited) Really! Gabriella could plan a great party for us. In your honor. I know how you feel—we are going to write a letter to the Governor of the Virgin Islands about our experiences.

Gabriella handed them her husband's business card, adding that they are staying at the villa further up the hill from them.

Neil: I don't want to make waves. This is our first time here and I have already punched an officer—in self-defense of course. Don't misunderstand, we appreciate your invitation; we just need to collect ourselves.

Carlo: Absolutely, take your time; we will wait for your call. Mashé, you should have seen your heroic husband—he gave that officer a splendid punch while he was still blindfolded.

As Mashé and Neil said good night to Carlo and Gabriella, Mashé put her arms around her husband telling him she was going to prepare a nice bath for him and then put him to bed. Neil came back with, "as long as you join me." Suddenly Neil's attendant appeared and offered help. Neil told him to come back tomorrow.

Their bath was fragrant with all of the emollients sprinkled in. They had removed their masquerade apparel and sunk in. Neil apologized to his wife, saying he should have heeded her suspicions and Mashé apologized because when he mentioned taking a walk along the Bay, she should have agreed to it. She said she would have loved to have slapped the woman who blindfolded him. Neil told her they were some pretty hefty women.

Mashé: And you are saying all of that to mean?

Neil: I mean, let's try to enjoy ourselves tonight; you know, I'm not tired anymore. What did you put in this bath water?

Mashé: A lady never tells. You know it just occurred to me…our attendants were the ones who encouraged our participation in Mardi gras, right? So, I am just wondering do you think…

Neil: Please don't go there.

Mashé: And what about Carlo and Gabriella? Do you think they're Swingers?

Neil: Mashé, remember Italians are Catholic.

🍒   🍒   🍒

As they reviewed the events of their first day it occurred to them that neither one brought their cell phones to carnival. Neil confided in her that he wanted to punch out one of the women during all of the commotion. While washing his back she told him his secret would stay with her and the best part of all was that it's over. Neil felt he made a bad choice in coming to the Islands. Mashé told him not so and that they should focus on their honeymoon and she wanted something to eat too. Neil saw that it was past midnight; nonetheless, he suggested they wake up their attendants and make them earn their gratuity. She agreed. Within an hour chicken marsala, fish cakes, arugula salad, stewed conch, and fried bananas were brought to them. They enjoyed a picnic in bed. Later, they had each other for dessert.

The sunlight boldly shone through their window blinds and they both heard a tapping sound at their window, a hummingbird busily trying to reach a flower pressing against the window. As Mashé stretched, she nearly falls out of bed but Neil reached for her in time. They had worked their way to the foot of the bed.

Mashé: I love making love with you; it is a little dangerous. So, what is for breakfast?

Neil: I see you don't quit. Whatever you want, Mrs. Rollins.

Mashé: How about a mini-tour today, something unhurried?

Neil: Our first full day on this Island. You know what, we could fly to Saint Croix and go for a ride in a glass bottom boat. I have always wanted to do that.

Mashé: And afterwards we come back and have that ultra-spa treatment I've been hearing about.

Neil: Mashé, I am not too fond of the idea of someone, a stranger, putting their hands on you—all over your body?!

Mashé: A masseuse, it's a fine profession.

Neil: Whatever they do, I can do better.

Mashé: No argument.

She reached for the pamphlets to read on other available amenities. Neil called the front desk and booked a small plane for them to Saint Croix.

Neil: I promise this day is going to our day. Before you know it, the week will be over.

Mashé: There is so much to do while we're here. If there is no going to a masseuse, then shopping is next.

Full from breakfast, Neil and Mashé were boarding a plane for Saint Croix. The two islands were about forty miles apart. Before they knew it they were landing on the Island. Like Saint Thomas, there was beauty everywhere. A transport came by to take them to the port near Salt River for their glass bottom boat cruise.

Mashé: I've been meaning to ask you, can you swim?

Neil: I am one of the best. And you?

Mashé: (Smiling) Like a mermaid.

Neil: That a fact! We must put it to the test. Let's make plans to go to the pool before we leave paradise?

Mashé: Honestly, I cannot wait. What if we see sharks while we're in the boat?

Neil: Let's hope they don't see us. Seriously, it's possible baby sharks would be seen and you'll think like a lady and say, "They are so cute." You will enjoy it, trust me.

Mashé: (Inquisitive) "Think like a Lady." In that case, how many times have you made love on a charter jet?

Neil: (Reserved) Do you think you married a jetsetter, Mrs. Rollins? I have always imagined doing it only with the ideal woman. Therefore, that means you.

Mashé tried to process his answer, and was about to pose the question again differently, then decided not to.

The transport brought them to port and the boat was waiting. It appeared they were the only ones scheduled to board. It was the way Neil planned it. They were given life jackets and then they stepped down into the cabin. There before them was the glass bottom of the boat. Thus far all they could see was kelp, live seaweed, pebbles, and rocks. The owner of this vessel was Javeer Sams, a native of Saint Croix and their tour guide for the afternoon. He welcomed the newlyweds, pointed out the safety features of his boat, and promised an adventure was about to happen beneath their feet. Javeer explained that the Caribbean Sea had wondrous marine life. He seemed passionate about his job and keenly interested in the newlyweds and where they were from in America, expressing seldom did he see people of color do much sailing. Neil and Mashé found that to be almost laughable and unbelievable; being natives of California they invited him to come to the States so he could broaden his scope on the nautical activities and achievements of the Black community. Being modest, he confessed he had only traveled to one place and that was Venezuela, where he met the love of his life, or so he thought until on the eve of their wedding day when she told him her husband wanted her back. He spoke of how devastated he was at the time. Then her maid of honor, Simona, stepped up to him and convinced him that she was the better woman. He married her that very next day and she is still his better woman, going on twenty years with two sons. Neil and Mashé were moved by this story and it seemed they were slightly telepathic when later that evening they both thought of his tale.

Javeer had carried them out about one hundred feet from shore when Mashé noticed some tropical fish called French Angelfish and then as they went further out they saw a school of Squirrel Fish. Neil was getting it all with his camcorder. Neil told Javeer that his wife wanted to see baby sharks and Javeer said this very region was where they congregate, pointing out that they are small by nature and called Rainbow Shark Fish.

Mashé: Their size is so tiny but multicolored.

Neil: Go ahead, say it. "They are so cute."

Mashé: Well they are, but what about the not-so-cute sharks? Where are they?

Javeer: (Grinning) Well, this is a great big body of wartah—they could be anywhere ya' kno'.

Fixated on his words Mashé then felt something crawling on her lap and she jumped up.

Javeer: Pardon me Missy, that's me pet Gillis. He's a Dwarf Gecko. He's harmless.

Neil teased her saying he has it all on tape. Especially the sudden shift in her facial expressions with Javeer's response, "Well this is a great big body of wartah—they could be anywhere ya' kno'." Mashé gave Neil a piercing look to tell him to record the marine life and not her. She found his playfulness attractive and compared him to Chandler's self-centered and proud disposition; would he even get into a glass bottom boat? She closed her eyes, "There I go again. What is it with these justifications?"

Javeer gave highlights on the US Virgin Islands, telling how they were once British Virgin Islands and although they cannot participate in the US National Presidential Elections they did have elections to vote for a delegate to the US Congress.

Javeer: Did you know Saint Croix is the largest island of the other two, Saint Thomas and Saint John?

Neil and Mashé said they knew. He proudly spoke about the original people of Saint Croix, the Arawak Indians, then later came the Carib Indians, originally from South America. Neil asked when African slaves were brought to the Virgin Islands. Javeer said they were brought over by Europeans around 1717 in the hundreds but, he added, before the end of the eighteenth century the African peoples were the predominant race.

Neil: As they still are today.

Javeer: You are right. And remember we are a mixed-race population too.

Javeer shared many more fascinating points about his home. The ride was to last for only ninety minutes but they were given an extra hour because they had become very comfortable with their conversations and the historical and cultural facts captivated the newlyweds so much that when they returned to port Javeer extended to them a meal at home so they could continue their talks. They had to decline but they extended an invitation to him and his wife to come to Northern California to visit with them. Javeer told them they had to see one more eye-catching spectacle. He had their attention. He said to count to ten and then look down. They did so and what they saw was the splendor of the Coral Reef. Javeer said recently the US Government had expanded the *Marine Protected Areas*, which meant this great delicate marvel of ours would continue to flourish.

It was near mid-afternoon when they boarded the plane back to Saint Thomas; Neil thought of reconsidering Carlo's invitation.

Neil: Should we accept Carlo's invitation?

Mashé: It would be another adventure, positive I would hope. They seemed sincere; I really want the rest of our time here to be memorable, in a good light. The glass bottom boat trip was a great rebounder from Carnival and Javeer was so full of knowledge. I only want things to continue, smoothly from now on.

Neil: We are of the same mind, my Queen. I have his business card here when we get back I will call him and find out what he has in mind.

When they returned to the villa, Mashé pulled a fast one and ran to the bathroom. Neil followed her asking her what she was doing. She reappeared wearing a sleek looking flesh tone bikini and told him she will race him to the pool, just outside. Having been caught off guard he scurried to find his luggage containing his swim trunks. He found them, jumped in them, and ran outside. Mashé had already dipped in and was getting acquainted with other guests.

Neil went to the deep end side and dived in. He made a clean entrance—very little splash. Mashé and everyone else applauded. She was now swimming face up and Neil decided to swim underneath her; he gently took her by the waist and upper back and lifted her up as in a water ballet routine, and Mashé froze.

Neil: Relax, Lady, I have you in the palm of my hands, right?

Mashé was up above the water being rotated and the others were watching, cheering, and telling Mashé to hold on.

Mashé: Neil, please put me down?

Neil said okay, and let her go and she yelled, No! Embarrassed she swam to the opposite side where it was slightly shallower and treaded water. Neil slowly approached.

Neil: Wow woman, you made a big splash—we are going to need more water in the pool.

Mashé: (Smiling) Some people just do not play fair. You swim well, not as well as I do, but with a little more practice…

Neil: Shall I lift you up again, Lady Mermaid?

Mashé: That will not be necessary, Mr. Merman.

Neil: Neptune was one—who was the other?

Mashé: Poseidon of course, but there are others somewhere. Do you still want to call Carlo?

Neil: I do. I would like to get a whiff of a rich man's lifestyle.

It was their first time on a luxury motor yacht. Carlo and Gabriella over-extended their hospitality. Both lovers of Italian food, Mashé and Neil ate like royalty.

Carlo: Gabriela and I are glad you accepted; at first, we thought you did not take us seriously. Neil, I have good news for you. You will remember that I said I would write the Governor of the Virgin Islands a formal letter of complaint. I also mentioned about your self-defense with that police officer at Carnival and you can relax, he will have a swollen jaw for some time but nothing was broken and it is believed his teeth are still intact.

Neil: Much appreciation. You know, Carlo, it was just impulse, I felt I had to do something. and the weirdest thing about it I was not that I was concerned about myself, I was concerned for Mashé. I am not saying she cannot handle herself but when you are blindfolded and all, I did not know what to expect.

Mashé: You are my true Aeru, my protective warrior.

Neil: Yes…I'm your Man.

Gabriela: Tell us, Mashé, how you two met. You are a remarkable couple.

Mashé and Neil looked at one another; then Neil elected to tell the story.

Neil: On this particularly June night, I had a taste for some Cuban food. I was tired but when you step into the Cuba Fantasía restaurant, the aroma and the music stimulates you. Little did I know there was more stimulation to come my way. I saw several people celebrating someone's birthday and they were having a really good time. Then they brought out this three-tiered birthday cake and I saw this gorgeous woman holding a knife about to cut a slice when without thinking I pulled her onto the dance floor. (Neil purposefully skipped some major parts and just finished with their wedding ceremony)

Gabriella: Magnifico! Carlo and I had an arranged marriage. We were betrothed to each other at birth. Also, be mindful he is older than me (They laugh). Our marriage has been, I believe you Americans say, "one of a kind."

Mashé was keenly interested in this, with thoughts of Wellington.

Mashé: It also sounds like "A match made in Heaven." If you don't mind, how old were you when you met for the first time?

Carlo: I was ten and she was eight. It was not until my senior year in high school that a ceremony had been planned for us by our families to make it official. We married on her twenty-first birthday.

Mashé: Any children?

Gabriela: We have one handsome son.

Mashé: Is he betrothed to a certain someone?

Carlo: No. We decided to allow him to choose.

Neil, Mashé, Carlo, and Gabriella continued to converse on several topics while cruising and enjoying the view of a red setting sun. Mashé told Neil that it looked like they have gone out too far. Neil sensed her concern and said it was time to go home so he told Carlo his wife was tired. Carlo obliged and directed the crew to return to port. Gabriella asked Mashé would she join her for lunch on land tomorrow? Mashé gave her an inquisitive look then accepted. Carlo asked Neil if he would like to go snorkeling with him in the morning just off the shore. Neil, having more or less impressed upon his wife how good a swimmer he was, pondered then expressed an interest. As the four paired off Mashé wondered if Neil should go snorkeling in those waters because it was the Caribbean and it could be very unsafe.

Mashé: I could postpone my lunch with Gabriella and we could go swimming in the pool, like you suggested.

Neil: It's just snorkeling, not scuba diving. And we are going to be out just a few feet.

Mashé: I don't have a good feeling about it Neil; I want you to call him and cancel.

Neil brought her to him and hugged her snugly for a while.

Neil: There is no one luckier than me; I have all your love for myself. You know what, come out and watch us before you have your lunch? You and Gabriella. I promise to bring back a baby shark.

Mashé: You think that is funny? It would make me feel slightly better. Yeah, I'll come with you and Gabriella will probably be there too.

Neil: I know what will relax you. The casino. Let's test our luck tonight and then when we come back you can give me a scented oil massage.

Mashé: Good idea. We've had a full day of it and I still feel like there is more to do with you.

Neil: There will always be more to do with me.

They went to their room, cleaned up and then took a ride to the Saint Thonas Island Casino. Neil and Mashé looked for an inviting slot machine. They finally saw one that might work so they played it together. Time had taken off and so had their money—this one-armed bandit was trying their patience, but Mashé had that stick-to-it-tiveness.

Mashé: Now that it's full it should pay off at any moment.

Neil: Sweetheart, I'm playing it because you wanted to. I am into craps. Slot machines are rigged to win for the house; it's a ploy for suckers, all by design.

Mashé: I like craps too and roulette. C'mon, stay with this a little while longer?

Neil: (Sighs) As you wish.

As soon as he said, "wish," the display showed three crowns and a treasure chest of golden coins. This paid $25,000.00. If they had gotten four crowns across they would have won, $50,000.00. Mashé was beside herself. She wrapped her arms around Neil's neck and kissed him multiple times. An attendant came over and checked the machine because it was one of the older versions; it paid real coins and the newlyweds were filling up one gambling cup after another.

Neil: What a blessing, we need this money too. You are my lucky charm, Mrs. Rollins.

Mashé: We can put it toward a new condo?

Neil: (Excited) Or just do an add-on, like for a nursery.

Mashé paused.

Mashé: Nursery?

Neil: Don't you want me to fill you up with beautiful babies?

Mashé: Yes, in the distant future but not in the near future.

Neil paused.

Neil: (Intent) Mrs. Rollins, why don't we order room service and talk about this over a nice late night dinner?

Mashé: Fine, but first we need to convert all of these coins into soft-money.

She finds a photograph of the two of them when they hit that jackpot. They were so fortunate; she remembers how they both were hoping for a hit and she was glad they took off after that because those slot machines have a knack for taking the winnings all back.

They had a good dinner that night. They talked about bringing babies into the world and for the first time Mashé observed a very sentimental mood coming from Neil; he was determined to be a father and shared a deliberate plan.

Neil: I did not think I would like goat chops but they were tender and delicious.

Mashé: I thought if I like lamb chops I would probably like goat chops.

Neil: As usual your logic is priceless. Now, I see we have papaya custard for dessert.

Mashé: I love it too. Now shall we discuss the nursery again?

Neil: By all means. I would like three children at least. Boys or girls, no preference.

Mashé: I would like two or maybe three. We'll need a huge house and lots of money or enough money that is. Neil, I have plans professionally and I would say maybe five or so years from now makes the most sense for you and me. We need time for just us, Neil. We have started a new life together; we need intimacy and to become more aware of each other's habits and interests. We have a healthy start, just keep in mind my body will be the incubator.

Neil: Mashé, five years is a long time. Share what you plan to accomplish in five years?

Mashé: Becoming an established poet. I want to do some ground breaking in this area. I need to take some postgraduate courses and do more traveling. I really have not been anywhere. Our honeymoon has taken me out of the States for the first time. We are healthy, we're ambitious, and we share similar goals. Umm, are you saying you want me to get pregnant on our honeymoon?

Neil: (Teasing) You mean you have to ask? I was thinking about three years. I appreciate the personal goals you have set for yourself. Why would I stand in your way? Anyway you will be in your thirties; are you sure about waiting that long?

Mashé: "Waiting that long." Listen to yourself, listen to us. This discussion is too premature. I think I'll just go to bed and since we have been here it's been a little peculiar off and on. But my darling, we are $25,000.00 richer. (Mashé would like to take a portion of that money and pay her parents back for their lost wedding expenses)

Neil: Now what are you thinking?

Mashé: Maybe we should split our winnings. I mean essentially we won this money together. It was your idea to gamble and it was my idea to play the slot machine for suckers.

Neil: All right, now you are getting sensitive on me. Think about it, if we had won one million dollars, what would you like to do with it?

Mashé: I would give some to charity. Also, pay for all of those bills waiting for us when we return home. How about you?

Neil: I respect the charity part, but I would focus on buying a house and if this were the case, would you still want to wait five years to start a family?

Mashé: In that case No. We could work with your three-year plan.

Neil: (Intrigued) I asked the question about the one million dollars because people are usually motivated by money and having more of it could make meeting their routine expenses in life more manageable and comfortable as in raising children for example.

Mashé: I am definitely motivated by money and because of that recent awkward experience in my life I have learned to consciously have more patience, like avoid rushing to judgment. Now, where does my husband see himself in five years?

Neil: Your husband would like to become the head of his own unit. I have some ideas that would broaden the technological platforms we currently have in operation; and this could require travel time, domestic and overseas. Be mindful though, I desire a family first; these plans of mine will require very careful planning through the course of time. I could handle either, or, however, my field could go in many directions; it all depends on certain factors.

Neil continued to emphasize his personal plans. Mashé found him to be so appealing when he was serious. Actually, she concluded that he was a serious person by nature. He would definitely make a great father and she knew she was capable of being a wonderful mother. She could only remember holding a baby once, when her cousin, Joelle, had a little girl and she named her after herself, which she thought was an ideal thing to do should she ever have a daughter. Neil was trying to get her attention.

Neil: Lady Mashé, you are in deep thought; come back to me?

Mashé: (Affirms) Right now, I believe you and I should get in deep with each other. Do you still want to talk babies or do you want my famous scented oil massage? Please note there is no pressure.

Neil: I will say it again, you are priceless.

They rose and went into their bedroom. Neil undressed and stretched across the bed and Mashé went for her oil treatment system. Neil's cell rang.

Neil: Carlo, yes what's happening? Absolutely, just tell me what time again? That a fact, well for me I have to have something in the morning before I go out. I have snorkeled before; it will be cool. Take care.

Mashé: (Curious) So, what is the plan?

Neil: Carlo wants me to meet him at Northside Beach tomorrow morning around eight o'clock. He advised that I not eat anything, and of course I told him I need something to get me started. He will be going ahead of me.

Mashé: I can get you started.

Neil: (Looking up) No question there. You are my masseuse and I am ready for you.

Mashé brought in the heated oil mixture and began applying it to his upper back and working her way down to his waist. To her this was nice and she enjoys canvassing his physique, this man had a solid build. Having babies with him would be divine. It really mattered that he supported her intentions though. She liked his hypothetical concept of having one million dollars; yet that amount of money could vanish very quickly. With their winnings of $25,000.00, they needed to treat it as though it was one million dollars because it was unexpected. Thoughts about her book royalties arose. She would need to check with Von when they returned. She paused and decides to call him early in the morning before they take off. It would probably be early in the evening where he was; hopefully she could reach him.

Apparently Mashé had a soothing touch because Neil was asleep. How funny was that; he was supposed to do the same for her. Somehow she persuaded him to move over so she could climb in. She concluded that the food, the drink, in fact the whole adventure of the day with her magical touch relaxed him so, he was possibly out for the night. As she looked at him he was even more handsome as he slept. Mashé had just fallen asleep when she felt a sweeping motion across the contours of her body. Neil was awake and in dire need of some loving. Instantly, he had her in a splay style, and with an earnest pull he had her underneath. His mouth journeyed and prowled repeatedly from her neck down. He whispered to her to be loose and within a second she was twirled on her face. Neil was bringing tremendous momentum and wanted her to be more limber. For a while they rested, then resumed into the night as his extensive springy and buoyant acts led them onto the floor. Luckily, he was underneath this tine. They stayed there until they were awakened at nine o'clock in the morning by a frantic call coming through on Mashé's cell.

Mashé: (Drowsy) Hello, hello who is this? Yes, Gabriella. What happened?! How is that possible?! Stay calm okay?! You called the police?! I see…and the ambulance too?! We are on our way there.

While snorkeling Carlo had come across a Lion's Mane Jellyfish, the largest of its kind. He had only been in the water for about ten minutes according to his wife when she noticed he had been pulled under. When the paramedics arrived they had to pull him from the water. Carlo told them that when he was attacked he felt an intense burning sensation and felt paralyzed. Neil and Mashé tried to comfort Gabriella. She said she had pleaded with him not to go snorkeling, she just had this queer feeling, but she was relieved to know that this particular jellyfish's sting was not life threatening. Neil looked over at Mashé in disbelief. Gabriella rode with her husband in the ambulance and the four of them planned to talk again when he was released.

Neil: Mrs. Rollins, I have been married to you for 72 hours at best, and again I am feeling like the luckiest man alive. This was worse than Carnival. Tell me, are we in the wrong place?

Mashé: Are you serious?! These are unplanned events, Neil, but I believe in following your own premonitions.

Neil: Mashé, I apologize for challenging you, do you know what the odds are for a jellyfish of that size to show up here? I heard one of the fishermen say that they normally congregate in the Atlantic Ocean and Baltic Sea regions. You know this climate change scenario has me wondering.

Mashé: Of course, there could be other threatening marine life out there coming close to shore. It's like guesswork and I am so thankful my man made mad love to me last night that kept us sleeping in.

Neil: You know I have some more for you. And wait, your massage, I bet you thought you had me. You have talented hands, actually; with all your skills you make a nice, complete little package.

Mashé: Really, Neil!

Neil: (Suavely) Mrs. Rollins, may I treat you to lunch at the Ritz Carlton?

Mashé: Please do and afterwards take me shopping.

🍒   🍒   🍒

Neil and Mashé went back to the villa to change. When they arrived at the Ritz Carlton they were seated outside with the ambiance of the tropics surrounding them, and unbeknownst to her he arranged for some musicians to serenade them while they ate.

Neil: I have been meaning to ask you, tell me about you and your best friends. How unique it is to keep friendships since childhood, especially for women.

Mashé: Are you saying that men do not bring drama to their friendships?

Neil: Bar none, women invented the drama.

Mashé: (Sarcastic) I must remind myself that I am on my honeymoon. My Best Girls, Rhial and Eila; we have known one another since the second grade. On our block we were the only three Black families at the time. Don't misunderstand me: it's not just because of our race and age. We knew from the beginning we were meant to be lifelong friends because we are very different. Another reason being the only child, no siblings. Now, it would have been cool for you to have had some lengthy conversations with them to hear their versions. The bottom line is, I love them as though they were my sisters—I often said when we were growing up that we were sisters with different parents. I promised to buy them some duty-free souvenirs, maybe that orchid perfume to start with.

Neil: I think the three of you holding up this long is admirable. There were quite a few friends and kids I knew on my block but, I just really have one friend that I have known since the third grade and that's Corin.

Mashé: Corin, yes he was sought after by quite a few single ladies at our wedding. Does he have an intended?

Neil: Corin swears he will never get married. He did bring a date with him but I believe they are merely friends. He just got a new job, he's a graphics designer and teacher.

Mashé: My father told me once that to have one good friend for a lifetime is a treasure.

Neil: Then in that case, you hit the jackpot. By the way, what did we decide to do about our 25 grand?

Mashé: I suggest we split it. You can still plan for your add-on and I can still pursue my goals, which in part is to pay bills.

Neil: So $12,500.00 each, that is not half bad for a night's work. You encouraged me to keep going; I am so glad I did.

Mashé: I remember hearing my mother and other relatives say that a man who listens to his wife lives a long life.

Neil (Stumped) You made that up.

Mashé: (Smiling) Why not put it to the test. The Lion's Mane Jellyfish, well actually you still planned on snorkeling, but you overslept, now had you gone out into the water with Carlo…

Neil: (Interjects) That's an "old wives' tale" spoken by some old wives. Let's get back to the 25 grand. I have just a couple of days remaining after we return home so we can go to the bank together, deal?

Mashé: That's fine. I have a week remaining so, I think I will sleep the majority of the time. In my waking hours I will need to send out thank-you notes to our guests.

Neil: Getting your rest, a good idea; we have been going non-stop. My mother can help with those notes. I just remembered what I wanted to ask you. In all of the years you, Rhial, and Eila have been tight friends, there has never been a falling out, ever?

Mashé was about to take a sip of her iced tea, then paused and looked at her husband. She could tell him that there were some incidences when she and Eila could have split up as friends, that Eila was the Drama Queen of the three of them, that she was partly to blame for the cancellation of her first wedding and so on. But, they vowed that no matter what, they were bonded for life.

Mashé: Why do you ask?

Neil: Curiosity. As I said it is so unusual. I guess I can look it up in the Guinness Book of Records. On a serious note, I watched your friend Eila at our reception, the one you said lives in New York. She was determined to catch that bridal bouquet and then when my Man caught the bridal garter, she slipped it on and posed with him for a picture. Myself and a few others were wondering about her.

Mashé: Your wondering is justified. She is the eccentric one to put it mildly; still she's my girl. Now Rhial is the more demure one and she's expecting her first baby.

Neil: Yes I spoke to her husband, Halvan; he said he was going to be a father twice. If I'm not mistaken, his first one is due by the end of this month, am I right? So Rhial is his second wife?

Mashé: (Taken aback) You are more up to date than I am. I knew of another woman suspected of being pregnant with his child, though I was under the impression there was a misunderstanding.

Neil: (Concerned) So, did I say something wrong? Maybe you should ignore what I said, those were his exact words.

Mashé: No sweetheart, these are grown-up situations…Rhial has so much character, I have a comfortable feeling inside of me that all will go well with her and Halvan. (Mashé decided that after she called Von she would call Rhial)

They went to the famous Havensight Mall in Saint Thomas. There were jewelry stores everywhere and Mashé was keen on one particular pearl and diamond ring that she saw the moment she entered. Vowing to herself that she would not use her portion of their gambling winnings, she told her husband that she would be browsing and to plan on meeting up in a half an hour. He agreed and went to a sporting goods store. Her head turned around to look at that ring again. This time she walked in to be closer to it. She looked for the price and there on a tiny sticker was printed the amount of $25,000.00. She started to laugh. What a coincidence; as she turned to walk out Neil showed up telling her there were some fitness wares she might want to see, and then he noticed her facial expression.

Neil: What happened in here?

Mashé: There is a ring in here that caught my eye and it only costs $25,000.00.

Neil: Are you for real?! Let's take a look at it!

Mashé: (Gasps) Oh I have seen it.

Neil: But I havem't .

Mashé: Well if you insist. Here it is.

Neil: It looks like you too. Do you want it, Mrs. Rollins?

Mashé: Yes and no. C'mon, Neil, take me to the sporting goods store?

Neil: (Stern) Mashé, I made you a promise at the altar that I was going to try in every way I knew how to make you happy. Do you want the ring? We are still keeping our deal to split our winnings; I will buy it for you, Baby.

Mashé: I have a ring and I am wearing it and I have you, whom I cherish the most. It's just a thing us girls go through—it will pass.

Mashé gets up to put on another wrap and her little Lou is taking a nap, at last.

Neil was so entranced with buying that ring. The Jellyfish incident made an impact; he was serious and it seemed like he wanted to reward her somehow. After an hour went by she had convinced him that there would be other rings, maybe not like that one, but she could move on and they finally moved on to visit other shops. That whole honeymoon experience changed their perspective about many things.

Intricacies (12)

The newlyweds were glad to be on American soil again. As soon as they drove up in front of their house (formerly Mashé's) they stooped down to kiss the ground. Mashé called Von and inquired about her royalties. He explained that it was too early to provide any specifics. He wanted her to understand that the organizers of functions like the one they attended in New York City were high profile and it could be more than a month before they saw any dollar signs, but he assured her, they had a bona fide contract and a check would come. They spoke on other matters like book promotions and future book events. While the luggage and packages were brought inside Mashé called Rhial again; she had called her before their plane took off but it went to her voice mail and she preferred not to leave a message. Again, it went to voicemail; this time she did.

Mashé: Rhial, I guess it must be about 3:00 in the afternoon there. Neil and I had a very eventful honeymoon, perhaps I should say dramatic. Anyway, we are home and I want you to call me as soon as you can, bye. (Then she decided to call Eila)

Eila: Mashé, I have missed you. How was Saint Thomas? Girl, you missed the latest. Let me bring you up to date. Yes, I spoke to her last night. Now listen. The day after your wedding Rhial told me that Halvan received a call from the other woman telling him she was going into labor and she wanted him to come to the hospital. Okay wait! Halvan tells Rhial that they need to take a red-eye so he can go see about her. Rhial is confused; she said she asked him why he had to go; the real father should be there, not him. Halvan said he might be the father after all because even though he told her a while ago that he wasn't, he only said that to keep her from worrying. I mean, really! So, they took a red-eye flight back to Florida and when they landed he goes straight to the hospital. She ended up having a cesarean section. She had a little girl named Kristan. Oh, I do not know if she has his last name or not. I told her I would come down there if she wanted me to. Being Rhial, she would rather handle this solo. At this point, she is probably wondering about her future with him. No, her parents don't know about this. I was the only one up until I told you.

Mashé: I am glad you offered to be with her. This is a situation no married woman would want to be in, especially when she is expecting a child as well. I hope she calls me back soon. Well, what is going on with you?

Eila: I have been working almost non-stop. We have this state senator race coming up, so I am working with that. I am still seeing Lowell; he is my darling. We are going out tomorrow night.

Mashé: How nice, so you two do manage to get out in public once in a while!

Eila: Funny. We are actually a couple now…I think.

Mashé: Have you talked about it? Right now, you don't sound like yourself. You like to be direct, it's not like you are demanding, is it? He must be the bashful one.

Eila: Quite frankly, I have been the shy one, with him, that is. Mashé, I'm a different person with the opposite sex. Perhaps shy would be too light a term with the others. He seems to be interested in me—I can relate to him. It's like I have always had this attitude to be "the one," to be in front. That's the way I have been with men for years. So we do what we do without questioning or reasoning. I imagine you are probably thinking I have been "selling myself short." I know you and I have never talked about it. And I know I have not made it easy for you and Rhial over the years.

Eila spoke to Mashé in a lucid fashion; it was refreshing, as if she had matured. She mentioned feeling the need to be a step ahead. She spoke of having little respect for her mother and Aunt Lennie. She remembered her father having a lot of gumption, though he was not around very long, so maybe she was a "chip off the old block."

Mashé: What I am gathering is you like Lowell, it's more than casual; you want him to like you, or how about, love you? I appreciate you sharing this, Eila. It is unfortunate about your parents and your Aunt Lennie. You know without a doubt, Aunt Lennie cares for you, it is true she is unsophisticated, but she has been your main source of support. Also, my parents and Rhial's parents treated you well. I am not a social worker but whatever the reasons are for your behavior, you can fix it and it sounds like you want to.

Eila: It felt good telling you too, Mashé, I surprised myself. I remember this one particular July fourth picnic, you saw me get into a car with these two guys, let's see, their names were Nathan and Collins. You tried to stop me, and I remember exactly what you said, "You've got a lot of nerve." It looks like I will need a lot of nerve to impress upon Lowell what I want.

A call waiting came in on Mashé's cell; it was Rhial. Mashé told Eila that she needed to talk to their friend.

Rhial: You made it back. A surprise for me?! I cannot wait to see it. I supposed I am well considering the circumstances. Have you spoken with Eila, I see, what did she tell you? That is about right. No, I did not go to the hospital with him; he dropped me off at home first. Soon, I will enter my second trimester and I am supposed to go for an ultrasound next month. Mashé…I am on the fence about what to do. I have thought a lot about my future and my baby's future. I guess I was blind as a bat when I married Halvan. I am aware that you and Eila weren't the only ones feeling that he was too good for me. And when this other woman came into the picture I was so determined to look the other way, to adjust to it. But at first, he actually looked in my face and told me it turned out the child is not his. I am beginning to wonder does this woman know who the father really is? We have not met but yes, I know who she is.

Yes, Halvan said a paternity test will be done. Also, I insisted that he leave the house until all of this is settled, either way. I need some room to breathe, to think. Now, I kinda know how you felt, I'm referring to your first incident. I need to be strong like you, Mashé. We speak at least once a day. He said he is living with his father. His father offered to meet with us and be our mediator. He told Halvan that he did not want to see him experience a failed marriage like him and his mother. I have considered moving back to California because in my condition I should not have all of this stress, and the irony of it all, I have a contract with the city of Miami Beach; it is for an urban planning project. This happened about a month ago. I meant to tell you and Eila about it, but your wedding plans were under way. Yes, I am very excited. No, Halvan had no part in preparing the proposal, only me, thank goodness. From what I understand, the City Council will oversee all the operations, which makes sense. It will take from six months to a year to complete.

Mashé reasoned while listening to Rhial it was looking more and more like a contentious situation. She listened a little more and then felt compelled to interject a little clarification.

Mashé: Rhial, I never implied that Halvan was too good for you. To take this further, Rhial, you yourself had reservations about him, maybe you could not pinpoint them but you became self-conscious. He is a very nice looking man and he knows it. It could be that women have made things easy for him, meaning there's no real effort on his part to take the first step. Now, here you come, a sincere person with talent and the ability to succeed, with no hidden agenda, just being you. I believe he saw an opportunity to be with someone unique. He became a new Halvan and it appears he is now in battle with the old Halvan.

Rhial: How insightful you are, my friend. Who was I fooling?

Mashé: Rhial, please think more about coming home? I remember you said yourself that you were going to forge ahead even if the baby were his. I have no crystal ball, none of us do. If you have not told your parents, you should. I recall the situation with the $10,000.00 you asked your father for—in this case you will need to be straight up. Whatever your decision is, you have my total support and I speak for Eila too.

Rhial: Mashé, forgive me for asking but do you still love Chandler?

Mashé: Interesting that you would ask. That is a chapter in my life that may never be finished. The answer is subject to flipping—I guess it depends on my mood. People who marry for love are exceptional to me; they will probably surpass every test that comes their way. I married for love like you, Rhial, and you know it just occurred to me that you should take your father-in-law up on his offer—there could be a rude awakening waiting to be revealed.

Rhial: There could be. My goodness! I love this time we're having together, Mashé; nonetheless, where is your husband?

Mashé: A good question. I love talking with you and Eila, it's our therapy in a way. I had better look for Mr. Rollins. I meant to ask, did you receive a cell phone picture from me?

Rhial: Yes, I did; you looked so exotic in that outfit, so how was Mardi-Gras?

Mashé: It was over the top, seriously. I will go into detail when we talk again. There were some bizarre antics going on.

After their conversation, Mashé went to the den, noticed that all the packages were in, and found her husband at the computer. He looked up and saw her, then gestured for her to sit on his lap and in so doing, she looked at the screen then looked back at him.

Mashé: Neil, are you still bugging over that jellyfish incident. Sweetheart, you never went into the water. Have you heard any more from Carlo and Gabriella?

Neil: I have a short message from him that he sent yesterday. They are flying home tomorrow. He is going to visit his doctor to be on the safe side, though he feels good. Mashé, look at the size of that thing?

Mashé: I am so glad to know that he's feeling better and we must stay in touch with them. I have something to show you, would you follow me please?

Mashé noticed that the painting she bought for her husband from the gallery has arrived. She asked him to open it. He looked at her smiling and was very interested in what was inside. Neil took one look at the oil painting of the mermaid and just stood there in amazement.

Neil: Mashé. What did you pay for this?

Mashé: A lady never tells. I was offered a good price for it, really, what do you think?

Neil: Her beauty pales to you, but if she were real—I would have to do some...

Mashé: I see, so you find her to be that enticing.

Neil: I love this and it is three-dimensional too. Who is the artist?

Mashé: I was told that the artist is unknown. It is a mystery and that adds even more character as well as value to it.

Neil: Let me thank you by picking up some dinner for us—anything you want. What would you like?

Mashé: We can put in an order where we first met, you can surprise me.

Neil: Yeah they should still be open. I will call them. Wait, I have a call coming in from my boss; this must be urgent—he knows I have two more days before I return to work. Hello, this is Neil; you have great timing, this is our first day back. You want me to mentor? That's fine, who is he? Pardon me, who is she? Amber Vale, what is her background? That school has an outstanding Engineering Program, so she comes highly qualified, I would think. Right, that conference is coming up too, yes I understand. Good. I will see you in two days. I will tell her. Thank you. Good night.

Mashé: They miss you already; we were only gone for a week.

Neil: Truth be told, engineers rarely vacation for the benefit of job security. Like I was telling you, we have new department heads and one of them is over my unit. He and his wife came to our wedding, Jamison Leigh, he asked me to give you his regards.

Mashé: I see…so what was urgent? I heard the word mentor.

Neil: There was no urgency, though he did want me to be prepared to meet the newest member of our team. We had an opening for a Systems Engineer Internship for quite some time and just a couple of days ago he filled it. The person holding this internship position could be hired on a permanent basis.

Mashé: And?

Neil: I have been selected to take this person "under my wing," to coin a phrase. I am to introduce and familiarize this new person with all of our operations. Look, sweetheart, it is time to eat so let me call Cuba Fantasía. By the way, I brought you something back from our wild honeymoon too; there is the box, open it?

Mashé picked up a cute little red gift box. She popped the lid and there was a designer necklace of eighteen-carat gold. She put it on immediately. Before Neil opened the front door, she draped herself around him.

Mashé: You are spoiling me. I love this necklace. It looks like it came from the same store as that $25,000.00 ring I was admiring; the whole store's interior was practically all red.

Neil: You are very observant. Your necklace is nowhere near the price of that ring but all I will say is it is good to be working. Our dinner should be ready now. I'll hurry back so you can continue with your showering of appreciation.

Mashé decided to call her mother.

Clover: Hello, Married Lady. How was it?

Mashé: Mother, I need to see you in person. We had the time of our lives and I mean that literally. How are you and Dad?

Clover: We are fine. We were wondering when we were going to hear from you. Did you do a lot of shopping?

Mashé: Yes, and I have something for the two of you—it is a very charming work of art by a popular local artisan.

Clover: I cannot wait to see it. You sound tired—there must have been lots to do while you were there? Listen, all of your wedding gifts are in our cellar, no rush. You should get some rest tonight and let's visit tomorrow. I will tell your father that you two are home. Sleep well, my Mashé.

Mashé is in their bedroom unpacking; she had made some good selections while there. She hoped her in-laws would like the hand carved birch wood figurine she bought; they were the most challenging to shop for. Since they came to mind, she decided to call them as well to let them know they are home.

Zora: Mashé, where are you two lovebirds? Great. Thank you for thinking of us. When do you go back to work? Good, you have some time to relax. You need help with your thank you notices, of course, we'll set a date. I would love to help—it gives me an excuse to see all of your gifts. Where is Neil? Have him call us when he comes home?

Mashé pulled out her camera hoping that before she returned to work she should have the prints made, and including extra copies. It occurred to her that since they were home now she had better upgrade her cooking skills—there were so many things to think about. It might not be a bad idea to think about taking a sabbatical; then again, she may need to put the brakes on that tempting idea. Neil walked in with a huge bag.

Neil: Mashé, the manager said he remembered your birthday party and since his restaurant brought us together, the meal is free—his wedding gift.

Mashé: That is unbelievable. What did you order?

Neil: It is from a menu for newlyweds, his idea.

When Mashé looked inside, there were fresh oysters, which she enjoyed on the charter jet; they really enhanced her libido. Fried bananas, a honey glazed baked chicken, garlic spinach, and chocolate covered strawberries, several of them.

Neil: Here is a pitcher of mango rum punch.

Mashé: (Facetious) This was very thoughtful but you go to work in a couple of days so you had better eat light.

Neil: Mrs. Rollins, what are you insinuating? None of this is for me; it's for you.

Mashé: Seriously! The table is set so let's eat. Before I forget, I called your parents and spoke with your mother; she's going to help me with those notes like you suggested, and she wants you to call her.

Neil: Glad you called them; I had better call her right now.

Neil went to the den.

Mashé did not like to eavesdrop on phone conversations but she felt the need to listen to her husband speaking with his mother.

Neil: Hello, it is your son. I am good. What is happening your way? I would like to hear more about that. Yes, Saint Thomas was an adventure. There were some moments of suspense, which I will share with you later. No, not too serious. Where is Dad? Yes, Mom, see you soon. Dad, that charter jet was the supreme experience, just as you said. (Mashé gasped, wondering did Neil get the love-making idea on the jet from his father?) Please extend our appreciation to him. It was beyond our imagination. (Mashé scoffs) I will probably be by next week because I go back to work on Wednesday, that is soon. I got a call from my boss earlier; he has a unique assignment for me. They have hired a new systems engineer, a woman (Mashé thinks, Is that so!). Yes she is assigned to me and of course there is our annual conference coming up, this time it is in Las Vegas… it should be interesting. And guess what? My wife won $25,000.00 at the casino there, absolutely. Yes, I will tell her. (Mashé scurried back to the kitchen table)

Neil: Here I am. I thought you would be eating. My father said he wants to know your secret on charming one-armed bandits.

Mashé: All it takes is luck. I wanted us to eat together; it's still warm. There is so much food here. This should last us for two or three days. This was very generous of him. You know our wedding gifts are in the cellar at my parents' house. Maybe we can transport them over here this weekend?

Neil: Why not. We can do it on Saturday; I have a couple of friends in mind to help me.

Mashé: (Solemn) I spoke to Rhial this afternoon, Halvan's wife. It seems like what he told you is true. The day after our wedding the other woman called him and told him she had gone into labor, so they took a red-eye back to Florida. Rhial said she had a baby girl, and he promised her he would take a DNA paternity test.

Neil: This must be very upsetting for your friend and the drama behind this is his quick response to her call, meaning he may or may not be the father but they obviously slept together. His actions were questionable, but I will not pass judgment, I only met him once; though it has been said that the first impression you have of someone is most likely a shoo-in.

Mashé: She said she may come back here given her condition and stay with her parents. She asked him to leave so now she is there alone, pregnant, and trying to keep her chin up. At this time, she needs Eila and me with her, but she will not admit it.

Neil (Inquisitive) As her friend, where are you with her situation? You seem to feel you have a role or obligation.

Mashé: Neil, it has always been that way with us. My thoughts and prayers are with her, I want to know she's going to be okay. Eila, as you know lives in Brooklyn, New York, and has asked Rhial to let her come down, to be with her, but she said, no. There are some underlying factors too, but overall she has to meet this quandary head on. Neil, she told Eila and me months ago when we first learned about this that many people marry those who already have families and they manage to move forward. Maybe I don't feel as comfortable about Rhial handling this situation as I thought.

Neil: That was then, Mashé. He has confused her with his latest behavior. It is obvious she is trying to be strong.

Mashé: So true and at the time she found out about this woman she herself was not pregnant then. How perceptive of you.

Neil: May we switch the channel to us now?

Mashé: Certainly. Neil, I want us to always be on an extended honeymoon. This is a first and only marriage for you and me.

Neil: Amen.

Kindling (13)

Since their return from Saint Thomas, Neil and Mashé had been settling into a happily married couple routine. Along with teaching, she has been cooking and baking and making their home an endearing residence. They split the $25,000.00 winnings. Mashé shared a generous portion with her parents from the non-refunded expenses of her first wedding and paid bills with the remaining, including the credit card statement holding the $700.00 for the oil painting she bought for Neil. Working later at night has become more frequent with Neil. Sometimes they would not see one another until the next morning. Her schedule was basically the same; she put in a seven-hour day and any work she needed to complete she brought home. For Neil, there were distinct details that required his presence on the job. His new boss, Jamison, was a man of precision in every respect, and all who reported to him needed to follow through accordingly. Amber was at Neil's side almost every hour on site. As a woman engineer, she had been driven to know all she can and she appreciated Neil's style of instruction and guidance. Recently, Neil and Amber had stayed beyond normal working hours and she insisted on treating him to dinner and each time he refused her offer. He often tried to encourage her to leave around 6:00 PM like many of the other entry-level employees did; still she preferred to stay and observe his applications. On this one particular afternoon, Neil and Amber were viewing a video on flight control productions for commercial aircraft and Jamison walked in to learn the progress Amber had been making.

Jamison: I see you have our new video on flight control productions. (He wanted Amber to tell him about her impressions with their operations. She expressed a comfort level that she liked and that Neil was very knowledgeable and very patient with her.)

Neil was sharing these particulars with his wife while she was massaging his temples as she cradled his head in her lap.

Mashé: Do you like your new assignment, working with interns, that is?

Neil: I would say yes, sometimes, and then other times I would like to be totally focused on my projects; I feel as though I now have two jobs in one. She is a very bright person and wants to prove to us all that she can keep up. That is a concept she brought about. I don't think anyone there has made her feel incapable of performing at the level expected. She was hired because she is qualified, not because she is a woman.

Mashé: I can understand how she feels though. She is the first female systems engineer hired there and this is probably a carryover from her college days. Women and particularly women of color who look like me must be very assertive working in a man's world. I am the only Black English Literature Instructor in my department, though we have many people of color, men and women well represented in the other disciplines, and remember this is at the community college level.

Neil: What is the predominant race of people in your classes?

Mashé: There is a mixture. My morning sessions are half-and-half, meaning Black and White. In the afternoon sessions, there are a mixture of Latin Americans and Black.

Neil: Okay, so the majority of your students are Black.

Mashé: Yes, this semester, it will change next semester, mind you. When I taught for a brief time in Florida, the majority there were White. Demographics are a contributing factor.

Neil: I can imagine even more fluctuation in the four-year colleges as well as universities. While I was in college, there were a few of us and a few women majoring in Engineering.

Mashé: Of course. They have those stiff academic criteria to meet. We must remember however, that Affirmative Action is still an enforced Federal Law and has made a great difference for people of color and women—it must stay intact. So, when is this big conference coming up?

Neil: In a couple of weeks. Oh yes, we have a reception this coming Friday night and we are to bring our spouses.

Mashé: That is an event to look forward to. Your colleagues viewing the better half and asking questions that are none of their business.

Neil: Careful, Mrs. Rollins, it will be a pleasant evening. Our department heads want to show unity and comradery are still in effect since those recent changeovers I mentioned. We must look happy.

Mashé: What does Amber look like?

Neil: (Mischievous) She is tall and fairly attractive, she reminds me of my mermaid, you know the one in the oil painting? But, you can see for yourself Friday night.

Mashé: (Sassy) I think it is time for you to lift your head from my lap. (She quickly rose)

Neil: A man cannot joke around with his wife?

Mashé: That's not it. Your heavy head was making my thighs go to sleep. I am ready for bed, Good night, Neil.

Neil: (Leery) Oh. Good night, I will join you soon. (As Mashé entered the hallway, she heard her husband's cell ring; Neil answered and she eavesdropped)

Neil: This is Neil. Yes, how are you? Something the matter? We can go over that again tomorrow, absolutely, not a problem. You are doing fine—this is your first job. I have a task for you that will encompass what we have covered since you started. I will assign it to you next week. No, as a matter of fact, I am really not that tired. We will talk tomorrow. Take care. (Mashé continued down the hallway, changed into her pink negligee, and went to sleep)

At 6:30 AM the alarm sounded, waking them up. Neil had locked his arms around Mashé as she began to squirm.

Mashé: Don't make me late. It is time for mid-term exams. We'll play later, Lover man

She went to the shower and Neil rose and waltzed in, joining her. He took her shower gelée from her and applied a generous amount to her back. Mashé would have liked to be receptive to his hearty massage though she remembered that the last time this happened she just did make it in before class started. She gently took his hands into hers, telling him to meet her back here tonight, she would have a gift for him. This apparently worked. As she drove onto the campus, she parked and sat for a minute or two and wondered what her surprise gift could be. She snapped her fingers and remembered that she bought a cute deep blue lingerie ensemble while on their honeymoon and he is unaware of it. So, she would rush home before him, have dinner ready, and serve him an appetizing three-course meal wearing her new lingerie. It was fun using him as her human guinea pig. All of those famed recipe books she kept stored over the years were now giving her an upgrade in the kitchen. Instantly she pondered over this new intern of his. She refused to be suspicious; still she had this haunting feeling going on in her subconscious. Amber appeared to be the aggressor—wanting to treat her husband to dinner, calling him on his cell after hours. She wondered if Neil had told her he was married? Ump, maybe she was married. This was a subject she wanted to take up with her mother and maybe his mother. For now, her stance would be to let it run its course).

Mashé had asked her students to begin their English Literature mid-term examination, indicating they had 75 minutes. As she sorted through her mail, she found a letter without a return address. She opened it and discovers it was from Chandler. Instantly she begins rustling with various pieces of paperwork on her desk, which attracted the attention of a few of her students. As she settled down, she slowly began reading.

Dear Mashé:

Please do not toss my letter until after you have read it all. It was so nice to hold you in my arms that one last while in New York City. You looked very irresistible, and you are on my mind constantly. I am doing very well, my clientele has increased somewhat, so business is good. I understand you are officially a married lady. The best to you and the man who took my spot. Mashé if you can find it in your heart to forgive me, I still feel as though you are holding me responsible for the situation involving your friend. Anyway, aside from that I want us to move forward with healthy memories of each other, I mean before that unplanned misfortune you and I were devoutly in love, am I right?

Nevertheless, this is just to let you know, you were always first, Mashé.

Your Love-Secret.

Chandler

P.S. You can toss this letter now.

Mashé placed the letter back in the envelope and sat at her desk in a daze for a couple of seconds, then thought about the man she was going to romance tonight and went back to work.

The day went by smoothly and then Mashé looked at her mound of mid-term examinations to grade. She called in her teaching assistant, Elliot, to begin the process. She divided them evenly between him and herself. Since he began work in the afternoon, she instructed him to grade as many as possible. There was one student who raced in explaining that he had a family emergency and wanted to see if she would schedule him for another day. She granted his request and directed him to the Testing Center, where he could take it online from the school's Intranet using a test code she formulated specifically for him. She glanced at the time and it was 4:30 PM. She bid Elliot a good evening and took off.

She made a stop by the grocery store and as she was beginning to approach home, her cell rang; it was her husband.

Neil: How are you? How was your day? We are busy here back to back. I am going into a meeting it should take about an hour. Is that so! It sounds like you have everything figured out for us. Believe me; I do not want to miss out, but as the saying goes. I need this job; I will be home as soon as I can. Love you.

Mashé, carrying satchel and groceries, made it indoors and shut the door with her foot. Now that Neil was going to be later than she expected, she need not hurry. Her planned menu was Seafood Shish Kabob of lobster and shrimp, sautéed Swiss chard with risotto joined by sparkling white wine. For dessert, she was serving a double-chocolate mousse. She set the table with a beautiful white linen tablecloth and matching table napkins given to her by her mother at her bridal shower. She took a sudsy shower and afterwards splashed on a fragrance blend of exotic flowers and spices. Now for the grand finale: her deep blue lingerie. Spring had not arrived yet so she turned on the furnace. In rethinking her observation of Neil's new intern, she decided to have a chat with her mother.

Clover listened attentively to her daughter's brief description of Neil's newly assigned intern, in terms of the cell phone calls after work, offering to take him to dinner, and him coming home later than usual. Clover asked Mashé did she trust her husband.

Mashé: Yes I do. However, I ponder on trusting his intern. I would like my husband to be aware if need be.

Clover: Fine. When I asked about trusting him, there may well be other situations similar to this and I am curious as to how you will react. From personal experience it is not about trusting the other person, the spotlight is on your husband. At this point in time, I would not stress it, why, because your husband loves you. Have you seen or met her yet?

Mashé: Neil's operations are having a social tomorrow night; all employees are expected to be there and to bring their spouse or guest, so I will see her tomorrow.

Clover: Company's want their employees to feel like family. So look forward to meeting this young lady at this affair with a happy face. Have you questioned your husband about her or brought her up for discussion in any way?

Mashé: No, however…

Clover: Good. I am proud of you. If anything is sizzling it will be in her skillet, not his, rest assured. Now, I heard you mention you might call this to the attention of your mother-in-law. I suggest you put that idea on hold and I am not really sure why, I just have a feeling. Girl, you have been married a little over a month; try to keep peace in your household, because basically, that's where it matters most.

Mashé heard Neil driving up, thanked her mother, then hurried to the front to display her "welcome home" pose. The key clicked and the door opened; Neil was humming along when he took sudden notice of his wife.

Neil: I am so sorry, Ma'am, I must be in the wrong house, Oh! Mashé, is that you?

Mashé: Really! Anyway, your dinner is ready.

She twirled around, heading for the bedroom. He followed her, picked her up, and they landed on the bed. They spent a considerable amount of time there, when Mashé eventually encouraged him to eat the dinner she secretly planned for him. Neil said his appetite was for his wife, but he said he would meet her in the kitchen after he changed clothes.

Mashé changed from her lingerie to a chemise fleece. When she entered the kitchen, she heard a call coming in on Neil's cell. She walks over to see who, it read: "Amby." She looked down the hall to be sure he was still in the bedroom and then wrote Amby's cell phone number on her notepad. Since so much time was spent in their bedroom, she would need to reheat the entire meal; she smiled thinking maybe she should have put on a regular pair of jeans and a T-shirt. She realized that because of their work schedules the opportunity for genuine intimacy was almost coming to a halt. She felt a little self-conscious when she refused him in the morning or late at night; she read an article some time ago that the woman should be flexible no matter what their schedules—it might be because generally the male's thoughts are mainly to succeed in the act. The point registered that there was more pressure placed on the wife to be more accommodating; she thought that maybe she was on the right track. She heard Neil coming down the hallway.

Neil: It definitely smells good in this house. Mrs. Rollins what prompted you to greet me at the door in such a manner. You know, you have curves I didn't know about and I thank you.

Mashé: We are husband and wife and I want our time together to be extraordinary, beyond measure and…

Neil: And all of the above. This is a fine meal. Now for tomorrow, the reception and dinner starts around 7:00 PM. I will come home, change, and we will leave immediately.

Mashé: Are you expecting something from this event? It sounds like a requirement to be attending—I hope people are going to enjoy themselves.

Neil: Functions like these are to tap into what I call your hidden life, which some people want to peer into. I only invited certain people to our wedding, even though you decided to reduce the invitation list. None of my staff or department heads know that you are a successful published poet; if they find out, fine, but I prefer to keep that on the low.

Mashé: I completely agree with you. But we must be charming and receptive just the same and act like normal people.

Neil: Lady, you are making fun of me.

Mashé: Sweetheart, it will be fine and I will follow your lead.

Neil: I want another shish kabob.

His cell phone rang. He looked over to see who was calling, then resumed eating. Because of its angle on the opposite end of the dinner table, Mashé couldn't see who was calling that time, but she had a pretty good hunch. After careful thought, she knew exactly what she was going to wear tomorrow night; if there was competition out there for her man, she would need to be fully prepared.

Amber Vale was a tall, shapely, lovely woman. Her skin was flawless and her mannerisms were refined. She had an alluring look about her. When Neil and Mashé entered the banquet hall, Amber's eyes seemed to beam toward him. She was wearing a stylish beige fitted after-five dress, which no one could deny accented her physical frame, and matching shoes with the popular stiletto heel. Mashé wore a black and white strapless yoke tiered after-five dress with matching two-toned high heel shoes. The moment Neil looked at her he said he wanted to treat her to an evening flight destined for the Isle of Capri. Neil seemed to notice Amber immediately, though he and Mashé headed straight to his boss and his wife. They conversed for quite some time when it was announced that "dinner is now being served." Everyone proceeded to the dining room; Neil and Mashé found their table and were about to be seated when Mashé heard her name called from behind.

Amber: Pardon me; you are Mashé Boston, the poet. (A few people's heads turned and one of them was Neil's) I am a fan, honestly. My favorites are "The Muse of Love," "The Dancing Magician," and of course, "My Romantic Trials"; I am truly excited to see you in person…

Neil: (Interjects) Amber Vale, meet my wife, Mrs. Neil Rollins, also known as Mashé Boston.

Amber (Undaunted) Then let me start all over. Mrs. Rollins, it is a pleasure, I just joined your husband's team; he has been so wonderful to me. I just had no idea I would see you this evening, I mean you, the poet.

Mashé: Ms. Vale, I am quite pleased that you like my poetry. How fortunate for you to have a mentor like my husband, he is one of the finest in Systems Engineering, which you have probably realized. I trust you will have a marvelous dining experience this evening.

Amber: (Smiling) Indeed, I will… and it has been a pleasure. Neil, you have a good evening too. You both look great.

Neil: (Formal) Thank you, Amber.

Mashé could see Neil glancing at her through her peripheral vision, and she wondered what he was thinking. The dinner was a gala of every dimension. There must have been nearly 700 people there. During the course of the meals, several of Neil's colleagues passed by striking up brief conversations, talking shop, and then to everyone's surprise came a disc jockey, playing the latest jams and oldies.

Neil: Are you up for dancing?

Mashé: You don't mind dancing around people you work with?

Neil: I do but this is a nice slow one—harmless, right?

Mashé: Ah…right.

They joined many others on the dance floor and here came Amber again, this time with her date, whose name was Joshua Castille. She felt Neil take her to the other end of the dance floor as if to distance him and herself from Amber and her date. She did not want to think anything of it; still she had to admit this woman was not a powder puff. Mashé resolved that a woman like her probably believed she had something to prove; therefore, she was the ambitious type. Mashé liked that kind of character, to succeed one needs to aim high, with the exception of aiming for a man who is already taken; this last point was pivotal in her mind. It was nearly midnight and several people started to leave; Mashé and Neil wished some of his colleagues a good evening. As they went to claim her wrap, Jamison rushed up to remind Neil that the Conference was next Wednesday, but he wanted them to be there by Tuesday morning for a special presentation.

Neil: I am looking forward to it; I signed for my tickets on Thursday. I am ready to go. See you next week, Jamison.

Looking at Mashé, Neil told her the man always seemed to be on pins and needles.

Mashé: Don't be concerned about him. You were the "man about town" this evening. I think that is how it goes.

Neil: That is because I was your escort. This dress you are wearing, it is arousing, was this your plan?

Mashé: Is it working?

Neil: What a question. I know a place we should go before we head home.

Mashé: As I said, I am following your lead.

🍒   🍒   🍒

Neil and Mashé drove to a classy supper club in Emeryville. It was practically filled to capacity; they barely found two seats and there was live entertainment too—it was pop-jazz night.

Mashé: What made you think of this place? It is obviously happening.

Neil: The first night we met I wanted to bring you here. You notice that the majority of the people here came in pairs. I wanted to be in a secluded location in a way; of course the most secluded is our home. I enjoy the setting here. This may be premature but I want us to buy a house. With the $12,500.00 of my half I have paid a few bills. I now have about $8,000.00 remaining.

Mashé: Neil, I wish you had spoken sooner. I paid off some old bills and reimbursed my parents from their expenses of my first wedding. I only have a few hundred in my savings.

Neil: I am good with that. This is only dialog for the time being. I want us to be in a neighborhood that suits us. Where we live is nice, the people are pleasant; however, I want better for us. I am saying all of this because I have a gut feeling I am being groomed for one of the top spots at one of the connecting operations; this would still be in San José but it will require more time away, like occasionally out of town.

Mashé: (Pauses) How much time in the "occasionally" are we speaking of? Neil, did you bring me here to prepare me for something? And all the while I thought it was this dress.

Neil: Calm down. Do you want to stay where we live now? Like for years to come or would you like an upgrade?

Mashé: How dare you make fun of my little house? I have the option to buy. What happened to the add-on project you spoke about in Saint Thomas? Seriously, I think it best that we build up our ability to buy elsewhere. Why not try two or three more years from now? Oh I know, we can buy the house where we are and then sell it for a different price or maybe even sublet?

Neil: Mashé, I admire your real-estate savvy. I am glad you are being open-minded with me. You asked what I am preparing you for. I am preparing you for an above grade lifestyle, Mrs. Rollins, and that does not only refer to property—I mean across the board.

Mashé: Is this why you want us to have children so soon because of your possible frequent absenteeism?

Neil: Is that a rhetorical question?

Mashé: Would you have preferred keeping that $25,000.00 that we won in a vault?

Neil: Mashé, I had spoken to you about my plans, but it was not until I went back to work and had a meeting with my boss and his boss, Ulrich Evans, on the expansions that are taking place. Therefore, what I was envisioning for myself, for us, was slightly less ambitious. I was playing it safe.

Mashé: There is nothing wrong with playing it safe, Neil. I would rather have you all of the time and live in a shack as long as there is running water.

Neil: I love you, Mashé, and I want you to trust my judgment.

Mashé: I love you too. Trust is what it's about. Does any of this have to do with Amber Vale?

Neil: (Pauses) How did she pop up in this conversation?

Mashé: Well, isn't she going to the conference in Las Vegas?

Neil: Yes, I believe she is.

Mashé: Will you be mentoring her in Las Vegas?

Neil: Sweetheart, this is a business trip. You have obviously made an observation that she is spunky.

Mashé: Yes, well she is not as spunky as I am. It seems that you will be working closely together for a long time and as I told her, there is no finer person to learn from than you.

Neil: I appreciated that compliment, it reminded me a little of a similar comment you made while at the pool when we first arrived in Saint Thomas—the Swingers, "there is no one on earth better than my husband." Yeah, you have spunk all right.

Mashé: Neil, I was totally taken by surprise, what nerve, we barely knew them and we were being recruited. As we agreed, trust is a major component, and as you know, I may be traveling myself on behalf of my literary work. I just returned from New York City, it was an unforgettable experience, and I believe this is just the beginning. No matter what is going on, we are an item.

Neil: You said a mouthful. Therefore, now that we have a picture of what could be ahead, we are of the same mindset and as for your question about Ms. Vale, she is just another employee, no more no less. (Mashé would have preferred not to bring up the name Amber Vale, and she was pretty satisfied with his behavior towards Amber while at the banquet and she believed Amber got a sense of her persona as well. Once again, Tia came to mind and it looked like it is time for another chat and not just about Chandler. They stayed and enjoyed the ambiance and music until closing.

She had started cooking breakfast when Neil brushed by, kissed her "so long," then sped away to a waiting taxi headed for the airport. They barely said two words to each other and she was trying to get a breakfast sandwich ready for him. She heard her landline phone, the ID read, J. Leigh.

Jamison: Good morning, Mashé, pardon me but I need to speak to Neil, is he still there?

Mashé: No, he has been gone for about five minutes. Did you try his cell?

Jamison: It went straight to voicemail. Amber just called saying she is having car trouble and needed a ride to the airport. I am already here. No problem, she can take the next plane out; I will call her back.

Mashé: Certainly Jamison, have a good flight.

Mashé thought how interesting, and she wondered if Amber tried to reach Neil before calling Jamison. She looked at the time, it is 7:45 AM, which meant it is close to 11:00 AM in New York. She called Tia.

Mashé: Tia, good morning.

Tia: Good morning, Mashé, what a surprise. How was Saint Thomas?

Mashé: It was fabulous, and there are a few other adjectives I could give you. I am on my way in to work and I wanted to make an appointment by phone with you for later today. I have a couple of questions for you, not too serious but to me worth mentioning; afterwards you can send me the bill.

Tia: That's funny, Mashé. No bill. When do you take your lunch?

Mashé: Around 12:30 or so. It will be 3:30 for you.

Tia: That will work for me; my sessions should be done. I will call you then.

Mashé arrived a few minutes before her first class. While assembling her materials she came across Chandler's letter. She decided to read it again. She believed what he was doing was on purpose. She always believed his ego complemented any and all he did. So in writing this short letter to her, it was intended to kindle her attraction for him once again. She remembered the few times he got under her skin; she even found that stimulating. She checked the time, she still had a few minutes so she called him.

Chandler: Mashé, you read my letter. I was hoping you would. But to receive a call from you is more than...

Mashé: Please, Chandler, you were expecting my call, I know you were. So, how are you? In your letter you made it sound like you are a high roller. I am pleased for you.

Chandler: Yes, business has picked up significantly. How did your book sales go at the Book Fair?

Mashé: I have not seen my royalties yet. On the surface, it went famously.

Chandler: Famously! I like that and I am pleased for you as well.

Mashé: Actually if I had only sold one book it was worth the trip. I met some fascinating people. A college English Literature class cane to interview me and I was so humbled.

Chandler: I know, I sent them.

Mashé: What?!

Chandler: Hear me out first. I know a member of the faculty there. I simply expressed that it would be an event that they should not miss and to make a point of meeting you. Whatever way you were approached was not my idea. Mashé I know how awkward it felt to have me in your hotel room. I wanted to stay, and I am not ashamed of anything and neither should you.

Mashé: Do you travel to New York often?

Chandler: Lately I have been. Why do you ask?

Mashé: Mere curiosity.

Chandler: No, Mashé, I have not seen your friend Eila.

Mashé: Chandler, my class is about to start. It is good to hear your voice again, believe it or not. Please avoid writing me again though?

Chandler: Whatever you say, Mashé. Take care.

Mashé welcomed her students and passed out the results of their mid-term examinations. She congratulated them on doing well with both the Eighteenth and Nineteenth Century selected readings though she expressed her discontent with the results showing only half the class knew who Phillis Wheatley was, emphasizing she was a Black woman poet of the eighteenth century who was a slave and was the first Black woman to be published in America. Her slave owners allowed her to learn to read and write; Wheatley was her slave name and maintained as her published name. She instructed her class to obtain *Phillis Wheatley's Poetics of Liberation* by John Shields and prepare a two-page summary of their impressions for next week. She pointed out that the final was going to cover more details relevant to the nineteenth and twentieth centuries and less on the twenty-first century and encouraged them to review their syllabi.

While savoring her homemade sandwich Mashé received a call from Tia. She told her of her reoccurring thoughts of Chandler, and that she recently received a short letter from him. Tia asked how her relationship was with her husband, to describe it. Mashé said they were in love. They were very attentive to each other, though their work schedules sometimes put intimacy on the back burner. Tia asked did Chandler remind her of her husband, in any way? Mashé confessed that at the beginning he did because when they met she was still seeing Chandler and refused to go out with Neil at first. Tia asked had she ever mistakenly called her husband Chandler, Mashé gave an emphatic, No. Tia said she had to ask to give her a complete resolution. Tia put her on hold for a moment, then came back with her perspective on what she had heard. Tia said this reasoning was separate from her clinical training. She explained that there was an emotional tug of war going on. She said experiencing a suddenness that involved finding out about her very close girlfriend and the man she loved, or still loves, and intended to marry in a relationship, caused a slight impairment to cope. Tia analyzed that

Mashé being attracted to Neil gave her refuge, personally and publicly, almost like having a cushion to fall back on. While in her effort to move forward her subconscious has kept what she wanted or needed to release; therefore she had some moral issues and inhibitions overlapping.

Mashé: All of what you have said sounds on point except for my feelings for Chandler.

Tia: You think so? With your permission, I would like to know what his letter expressed.

Mashé read the entire letter to Tia.

Tia: Mashé, do you think you can let him go completely?

Mashé: Tia, that's what I have been trying to do.

Tia: Why haven't you thrown out his letter as he mentioned? I believe I know and Chandler knows too. You are not ready to let him go. True, you are moving forward in your new marriage but you have some old baggage moving forward with you.

Mashé: Well, I have something else to add.

Tia: Please!

Mashé: Earlier we spoke, I called him after I read his letter; toward the end of the conversation I asked him not to write me anymore.

Tia: Very well, but you were passive, you made a request. I think you should be insistent that he not ever write to you again. We're speaking off the record here. What you are experiencing could all go away. Let me ask you this, if Chandler had died suddenly, would it have made a difference?

Mashé: I don't want to think that way...I would be grieving over him of course...

Tia: I am asking you to use your imagination just for a moment.

Mashé: Yes, Tia, I suppose it would make a difference, knowing I would never see him again and then realizing I would have to live without him.

Mashé stood up for a moment.

Tia: Mashé, listen to yourself, the decision rests with you. You need to release that baggage you are holding onto. You may never fall out of love with Chandler, but you married Neil. You could have still married Chandler, but you chose Neil because...

Mashé: (Interjects) He married my best friend, which was later annulled, and because of my friend's questionable behavior, I would be reminded of it forever.

Tia: Now, if he had married a woman you did not know, with the same conditions applying, would you have married him?

Mashé: (Ponders) That's a good question.

Tia: I will leave you with that to consider. I have some meetings to lead.

Mashé: And I have classes to lead. Tia, this was very thought provoking—I admire the spirit you have with your profession.

Tia: I remember you did say there was another concern.

Mashé: Yes, as you know my husband is an engineer; when we returned from our honeymoon his boss called and said he recently hired a new intern for him to mentor. The new person is a she, a very bright and attractive woman. He has been staying late at work from time to time and he told me she had offered to treat him to a meal and he refused. There are a few other details but for the sake of time...

Tia: Mashé, this is unreal, it sounds déjà vu to me. That is what struck me while I listened. As you said for the "sake of time." This is not your concern; as long as your husband is handling it appropriately, meaning, he should not in any way give her an inch of encouragement. The word trust is what you must focus on. And this time this woman, the intern, is not your best friend. A very interesting scenario.

Mashé and Tia agreed to keep in touch whether it was a concern to unravel or just to visit.

Coming home to an empty house for the next three nights had Mashé pondering what she should do with her time. This particular day was eye opening and she felt much better, though she could not find it within herself to throw away Chandler's letter. She wondered what it was like to be an impulsive shopper, just once. Then she looked in her glove compartment and found the discount certificate from the new Spa. Instead of shopping incessantly, she thought it best to go to the Spa. She drove around for a while before she found a place to park. When she walked in she was told she had a thirty-minute wait. While perusing the décor, she happened to see a hummingbird whiz by. She walked over to the window to have a closer look, which compelled her to sit down with her pad and pen to write a poem.

The Song of a Hummingbird

The Hummingbird sings each time it flaps
Its wings—
Some are yellow and brown and some are
green with red
What makes them move so swiftly is the desire
for nectar so sweet and when they are done they find a
branch to perch their tiny feet.
In the spring, they travel from flower to flower then find
another Hummingbird to love from hour to hour.

She liked this one—to be included with the other prose of her journal.

Her name was called; it was her turn. She selected the mandarin orange facial, the Brazilian body wrap, and manicure. It all came to a total of $90.00. It would have gone well over $300.00 without the discount; she felt lucky. They offered champagne and other drinks but she declined. The plan was to start with the facial, then the body wrap, and finish with the luxurious manicure. Mashé liked this royalty treatment and Neil would be proud to know that the Brazilian Body Wrap was virtually a hands-free service.

The facial was as fragrant and soothing as she expected. The body wrap entailed seaweed and body creams applied all over; then she was wrapped in a fine cloth. They told her to lie quietly for thirty minutes and then she would be led to a heated shallow pool for rinsing. Eila and Rhial came to mind; she imagined how they would love this experience—this was something they had yet to do together. She missed them and wanted to return to their regimen of talking on the phone as a threesome. Later next week she planned to contact Rhial to check on how matters were going with her and Halvan. She wanted to tell her parents about her situation but Rhial's parents might not be aware—she should check on that too. Her thoughts wondered back to the extensive exchange she had with Tia. She had taken to heart what she needed to do, which was to numb Chandler out of her life.

The effects of the body wrap and the power of the aromatherapy relaxed her into a deep sleep, which brought about a dream of her and Chandler. He was in the Spa with her and he proceeded to undo her body wrap. She became anxious and vigorously looked around but saw no one. She tried to speak, but she had no voice. Chandler began to play with her hair and with his strong hands with which she had become all too familiar, he started to caress her; then, Mashé heard her name called.

Spa Attendant: Hello, Mashé. Please wake up!

Mashé: (Drowsy) I…must have been dreaming!

Spa Attendant: You certainly were; forgive me for interrupting, but you are due for your rinse in the pool. Let me help you?

Mashé stood in the middle of her kitchen speculating on what to prepare for dinner. Although normally prepared for two, she decided to do her famous poached salmon recipe. Her spa treatment was unmatched by any other she had experienced. She amused herself hoping that if she had another dream about any man, it would be Neil, because he was her dream come true. She realized that dreaming about Chandler was not surprising—receiving his letter and then hashing out with Tia the particulars of her unresolved feelings. However, she had wanted that dream to go on, but this would always be a secret between her and God. While she was receiving her spa treatment, her phone was turned off; she wondered if Neil had tried to reach her. She noticed one call from him so she did a call back but it went to voice mail; in leaving him a message she made sure she used her sultry voice. Now she had a call from her book agent, Von, she was excited and thought it must have been about her royalty check.

Von: Mashé, it has been a while; I trust you are good? Yes, I am. I have some good news for you. No, not yet, however, we are getting closer. You remember those college students who came to the Book Fair? I received a call from the Chair of the Department of English at York College, one of the eleven schools affiliated with CUNY. You have an official invitation to speak before their seniors' level Romantic Poetry in English Literature course. Wait, there is more. A student from Tulane University purchased your poetry book online and asked her English Literature professor to have you come to their campus and speak.

Mashé: This cannot be happening all at once?! So, what happens next?

Von: I need your official yes, then I can contact them to proceed with their scheduling; expect this to be fairly soon. I have the email address of both academic departments, so you can notify them by email to confirm as well and they can update you on your travel arrangements. There is still one area you are responsible for.

Mashé: A place to stay. (She thinks of Eila) They have a resounding, Yes. For New York, I believe I know where I will stay. For Tulane, this means traveling to Louisiana; I will book one of their finest hotels, maybe. You know, Von, having my royalty check would come in handy right about now.

Von: (Sighs) I understand. You'll be pleased to know that your book agent does not collect commission from speaking engagements or personal appearances. Mashé, you are "living in the moment"; go ahead and put "a feather in your hat." How is that for famous phrases?

Mashé: I already knew you were a savvy book agent. You are right, this is the best news ever, and the timing could not have been better. We will keep in touch, Von.

She ran to the stove to save her poached salmon. What happened to her appetite; her insides were churning. Who should she break the news to first? Her parents, her Best Girls, Tia, and naturally, her Neil. Instantly she wondered whether Chandler had any influence at York College per se. After collecting herself she decided to wait until all details were settled.

Neil called her back.

Neil: How is my woman?

Mashé: I am great. How is my man?

Neil: Doing well. This conference has attracted some prominent speakers and the workshops have encouraged us to be more enterprising. Above all being with my wife would bring it all home for me.

Mashé: Having you here with me would be sublime, so we could say a toast.

Neil: A toast? (Mashé told Neil about her two speaking engagements at York College and Tulane University, and that she could be leaving fairly soon). Mrs. Rollins, we were just talking about this the other night. Congratulations to my wife, the poet. I would like to join you.

Mashé: Neil, do you think that might be possible? It would be during the week when classes are in session. I only plan to stay overnight in both places. While I was talking to you, I sent them an email acceptance to their invitations.

Neil: If the dates work, I should be able to. Now I have a news flash for you. We are staying here two more days; believe me, it was not my idea, however, Jamison (Mashé sighed) wanted us to preview some new systems devices that may impact the way we train our employees. So I wanted to know would you pick me up from the airport Sunday morning instead of Friday?

Mashé: Sunday it is. I will have Saturday night all alone.

Neil: Please do not make me feel guilty. I am honestly ready to come home, but some exciting things are happening…

Mashé: And you should be there. You had better get back to it; I love you too.

She had been looking forward to seeing Neil Friday night; she had a special dinner in mind for them. Because of the three-hour difference in time she had better eat dinner and then contact Eila.

Eila had finished a phone conversation with one of her fundraisers when she noticed the caller ID read M. Boston.

Eila: This is a pleasant surprise, I hope all is well? Good, I have been thinking about you and Rhial. I would like to fly down this weekend and see about her. I think we both should go, You can bring Neil and I'll ask Lowell to come too. That a fact, a conference in Las Vegas, you may not see him for a while, just joking. I was thinking about you because of that last talk we had, I needed to open up to you, Mashé, and you made it so easy for me. A few months ago I thought I had lost you as a friend forever. No man or situation is worth that. Do you know I do not have one female acquaintance in this town? It's because there are no two better friends than you and Rhial. And since you called I am going to have Lowell over tomorrow night and put my cards on the table, to coin a phrase.

Mashé: My goodness, Girl, what do you think his response will be?

Eila: Mashé, this is the second time in my life I have seriously shown an interest in someone. If I may say his name, Chandler was the longest, but then again, there were some inconsistencies with our relationship. But even when we had those "time outs," he was still my man. Mashé, are you all right with what I am saying?

Mashé: It's fine, Eila. However, I need to tell you why I called. I have accepted an invitation to speak before an English Literature class at York College and I need a place to stay for one night.

Eila: What! You, Mashé? I can see you are about to climb that spiraling staircase to greatness. You mean you would rather room with me than stay at The Belvedere Hotel? I am so proud of you; tell me when are you coming?

Mashé: I am working that out with them as we speak. One more thing, Neil may be able to join me.

Eila: Certainly, I can accommodate both of you.

Mashé: (Jubilant) Eila, after I speak at York College I will leave for Tulane University. I am going on my first little speaking tour.

Eila: And I must put my house in order, because a celebrity is coming to visit me. Can you believe it, now that you are a celebrity you are coming to my place.

Mashé: I had a feeling you were going to say that. Let's keep it simple, I am Mashé not a celebrity, and that is for the record. Let's switch to Rhial for a minute. She told me she was considering coming home for a while maybe not indefinitely, but she needed to be in more pleasant surroundings. Rhial is a fighter, and I love her spirit, but as her friends we need to encourage her to leave. She can complete the term of her pregnancy here with people who would care for her well-being and her child's too.

Eila: I am in total agreement. However, the three of us share one major trait, we are determined. I recall when she wanted to buy that funny looking dress for prom night and we pleaded that she go with the other one. She said, "I don't want to look like everyone else." Well, she was right about that. (They both laugh)

Mashé: Since you are a bona fide New Yorker, I going to leave you to your humble abode that you need to put in order. You will hear from me once I make the flight reservations and all.

Eila: Until then. Mashé, I have a personal question for you.

Mashé: How personal?

Eila: It's about Chandler. Has he been in touch with you recently?

Mashé: Why, Eila? Is he all right?

Eila: I suppose he is. We have not spoken since I went to see him in Las Vegas. I was wondering how he was.

Mashé: You knew him longer than me and probably better than me. I am sure he's doing fine. Have you tried to reach him?

Eila: I thought about it and then decided against it.

Mashé: (Surprised) That must have been difficult for you? I am proud of you.

Eila: That experience was a turning point for me. It happened for a reason; maybe the truth of it will be revealed some day.

Mashé: It was a turning point for all of us. Impulsiveness is another trait the three of us share, on different levels, no doubt.

Eila: A good point. I have another personal question. As I told you, I would like to go further with Lowell, like something permanent. Being intimate with Chandler was revering, wouldn't you say?

Mashé: Eila, on or off the record, Chandler was an exceptional person and he made a lasting impression on me in every respect. I am married to a wonderful man and my choice is to move forward. You have my blessings if you want to try and have him back in your life. I will be in touch with you when I have finalized my travel plans. Take care.

For Mashé and Eila there was a uniqueness to their relationship following their shared Chandler experience. To be estranged from her would have made their lives even more complicated. Staying friends was to prove how devoted they were to each other with a little mix of tolerance on Mashé's side, and again it was no secret to Rhial having a hand in it. The uniqueness rendered a humble kind of tone between them—putting forth an effort to be comfortable with one another. Her Aunt Lennie made notice of it

and wanted to intervene. No one elected to tell her the real reason and eventually she gave up. Mashé had much respect for Aunt Lennie because inevitably Eila was like her child. Here is the picture of us on Staten Island; it was a very windy day and it looks like the tides here are rising again. She is not ready to go indoors and the sky has turned to a calming silver-ish blue. Similar to the sky on the day she came for Neil at the airport.

Neil: I see nothing but beauty before me. Mrs. Rollins, tell me how much you missed me?

Mashé: I can show you better than I can tell you.

Neil: Perhaps I should go away more often. I thought about you all the while I was sitting in those cold air conditioned conference rooms. To be honest it was one of the better ones. I kept it to myself about your speaking engagements. I brought you a little somethin' back as a congratulatory gift.

Mashé: Well bashful I ain't—where is it?

Neil: Look on your dashboard.

Mashé saw a small plump envelope; when she opened it, seven one-hundred dollar bills unfolded.

Mashé: (Joyful) Thank you Neil. Wait a minute, did you go gambling?

Neil: Just for a couple of hours. We had a window of free time; I believe it's called opportunity.

Mashé: (Curious) We?!

Neil: The people I traveled with. And this is something I know you will appreciate; about one-third of the participants this year were women.

Mashé: Now that is what I want to hear. I have a distinct feeling that one day women shall rule the world.

Neil: I have a distinct feeling that anything is possible.

Mashé: Playing it safe—a wise move. Now, back to this monetary surprise gift. Does a story come with it?

Neil: Like I said we had some free time so I went next door to the Mandalay Bay Hotel and Casino and played a little blackjack and won $1,500.00. I took $100.00 and played your favorite, the one-armed bandit and it disappeared right before my eyes.

Mashé: What an opportune time this is. I can put this money into my savings account towards the new house you've been dreaming about.

Neil: Are we going home now—I have got ways I want to thank you.

Mashé: I anticipated that reaction. What you said that night made perfect sense. I still want to hold off from raising a family until I am situated.

Neil: (Reserved) Mrs. Rollins, the phrase, "until I am situated" makes me…

Mashé: Hear me out. Meeting one another halfway would be best. You already know I love the house we are living in; however, as soon as we see some property we can afford, we can start packing.

Neil: When I moved in with you, I was meeting you half way. My townhouse was spacious, but as agreed, a homey setting was what we both wanted.

Mashé: (Resigned) Neil, your townhouse would have worked for both of us, I just needed to know…

Neil: (Interjects) That is not the point. We had the choice of going either way.

Mashé: Enlighten me. Would you still have that burning desire to find a new home if we had stayed in your townhouse?

Neil: Absolutely. Even though my place was in proximity to the commercial district, I wanted my bride to be contented. My rationale was you had recently moved in there, the plans you made prior to me went south, and you had purchased new furniture. I was being a considerate husband.

Mashé: No argument from me. Except from now on, I would like you to consider consulting with me, just a tad—more dialog would be appreciated. (This reminded her of the well-kept secret charter jet to their Saint Thomas Shangri-La)

Neil: Of course, you deserve that, maybe I am slightly quixotic?

Mashé: It is possible; still I have been moved by your good intentions. Be mindful, I have a surprise for you too. Since it is a lovely Sunday afternoon with many Open House signs abounding, I wanted us to visit a gorgeous house in Emeryville. I read about it yesterday; we have about an hour remaining, interested?

Neil: Am I madly in love with you? Of course I want to see this palace. (his cell rings and he ignores it)

Mashé: (Curious) Since you just returned from a conference on a Sunday, are you expected to report in tomorrow?

Neil: Bright and early. Don't forget, Engineers rarely speak the word "vacation." I am really fine with this; I like it when you're driving.

Mashé: That so. Do not get used to it. (His cell rings again, he ignores it)

They drove on to Commodore Drive and followed the Open House flags and there it was. Mashé watched as Neil took long strides up the hill to the entrance. It had a high-end residential design with high ceilings, a blend of stone and timber stucco—two stories and Neil was in awe.

Real Estate Agent: You can see it was tailored for a luxurious lifestyle.

Neil: That it was.

Real Estate Agent: A dream house for you and your wife?

Mashé: Perhaps someday. What is the asking price?

Real Estate Agent: It has been reduced to $2.5 million from $4.5 million. The owner has planned to move to Hawaii to a palatial estate twice the square footage of this one.

Neil: So it has been on the market for quite a while.

Real Estate Agent: Indeed it has. (She excused herself to speak to other prospective buyers)

Neil: I would really love to place my stamp on this one. Then again, there are others.

He turned around and saw that his wife had gone upstairs. He followed and found her in the master bedroom.

Mashé: Speaking of spacious, no add-ons needed here.

Neil: One never knows, we could have twins in addition to.

Mashé: In addition to?

Neil: My paternal grandfather was a twin.

Mashé: Now you tell me. These hardwood floors are prime quality. Did you see the high beams on the way up? Those stained glass windows are a rarity in California, so I am told. What year was this house built?

Start here Neil: The price list indicated 1995, by the owner himself.

Mashé: No wonder he wanted so much for it.

Neil: (laughing) Lady, you are priceless. Let's go to the backyard.

When they arrived, they marveled at the granite walkway from the rear door to a small pond. The horticulture encompassed various flowers indigenous to California. There was a cute lane of dwarf palm trees.

Mashé: This house was designed for an artist. There is so much tranquility here. I need to take a few pictures of this landscape, just to view from time to time. It will remind me of where we could be in a few years.

Neil: I know it can happen. It's about good planning and good timing.

Mashé: Are you ready to go? I have dinner prepared. Also, I expect to have an email reply confirming my schedules from York and Tulane. I have been waiting all day for it.

Neil: Yes, regrettably we must leave our dream house. This was the cherry on top, Mrs. Rollins. After dinner let's lay out a preliminary plan, and we could adjust it, or make changes at any time we like.

Mashé: You may want to discuss that topic tomorrow night because remember I must show you my appreciation for those seven hundred bills you gave me and I do not want to rush it.

Unfoldment (14)

York College of Jamaica, New York, was a campus of extensive diversification in student body, campus life, and disciplines. She spoke to a class composed of 350 students. Since her topic was on Romanticism, she reached back to many written samples of several popular poets and writers of this genre. She emphasized that in her view Romanticism and Emotionalism were one and the same, forever connected, with exception to the Greek Tragedies. Her voice had a special quality. Her listeners seemed smitten as she read many passages from her book justifying her points. The classroom overflowed with enthusiasm and Mashé felt as though an accent had been added to her persona, like being released from a cocoon, or having a breakthrough. During the time she spoke about her own work, she had a sudden reflection of unique characteristics she had not realized before. Afterwards, she was welcomed by a book signing reception.

Upon leaving the campus, she asked the taxi driver to cruise around lower Manhattan. She had a day and a half before her speaking engagement at Tulane University. Neil was all set to travel with her when Jamison called him into his office to speak with him and a few other department heads about hiring two of their interns. To her it was an odd request since Neil only worked with Amber. When she called to speak with Tia, her assistant told her she had taken a mini-vacation out of town, and Mashé knew it was well deserved. She and Eila only spoke for two minutes it seemed, because when she arrived at her front door in Brooklyn this morning, Eila was all so excited. She hugged her, and told her, "Me casa su casa," gave Mashé an extra house key, and told her she would be in late as she headed for the subway. Mashé hurriedly asked her where was her car? Eila yelled back, "Lowell needed it; his was being serviced." Mashé played that reply in her head over and over and it was not measuring up. She had only spoken briefly with Lowell at their wedding reception. He appeared to be outgoing and fun. Being old school, she had difficulty accepting the idea of a woman loaning her car to her man; the other way around was the gentleman like thing to do. Here Eila was taking the subway to work; there had to be a loose screw somewhere.

The taxi driver had a peculiar look on his face and Mashé knew why. She then decided to give him the address to Eila's place in Brooklyn. Mashé was feeling very upbeat about her first speaking engagement, and from her very first published book of romantic poems—she looked to the Heavens and said, Hallelujah. As she walked up the steps to the front door she looked up the block and watched three adorable little girls mixing, talking, and giggling. For a moment, she imagined back in the day when she and her Best Girls would spend the afternoon basically having all the joy little girls could have; there were no worries, only homework and music lessons. As she refocused, she uttered to herself, "a time gone by."

Eila lived in a brownstone; it was Mashé's first time to be inside of one. Her friend had impeccable taste. There was a master bedroom and a guest bedroom. The guest bedroom had a bathroom without a shower, so she decided to use the other full bathroom in the master bedroom. Fully undressed she stepped into a steamy like oasis. She began to hum a jazzy tune and covered herself with lavishly scented lather. In the midst of her bathing, she thought she heard a thump, then she believed she heard voices; she concluded that Eila was able to get away earlier than she thought and that Lowell drove up, coincidentally. This made her very chipper, thinking they could go out for dinner or order in and visit since tomorrow she had an early afternoon flight destined for New Orleans. She stepped out of the shower just to have a peek of where Eila might be so she could let her know she was there, but she was startled when she got a glimpse of Lowell and another woman, conversing in the hallway. Immediately she turned off the water and wrapped herself in a towel, wondering how she could inconspicuously maneuver her way out. Her heart was pounding, she braced herself against the tile, and she could not remember where she placed her handbag, as she said to herself over and over to calm down and breathe, breathe. The talking then stopped, and she hoped they went toward the kitchen. She slowly tiptoed toward the door, opening it again, and saw no one, although she did see her handbag lodged in the cushion of Eila's leather lounge chair. She attempted to ease out when the woman said, "let me go to the bathroom first." Mashé quickly backed up, stepped into the shower, and lay down. She heard this woman come in, and within minutes the commode was flushing, so Mashé thought they must be leaving soon. Now it seemed unlikely because Lowell's voice sounded closer than before.

Lowell: Don't keep me waiting, I have been fantasizing about us since we met last week.

Woman: We should have gone to a hotel; she could show up at any time.

Lowell: No way, she's working late tonight and she thinks I am too.

Woman: She is going to know something went down here.

Lowell: Listen, she will have no clue. And why should we go to a hotel; it is possible that someone could recognize us, then run and tell her. C'mon, trust me. I know her goings and comings.

Woman: Better now than later that she knows about us.

Lowell: Listen, when the time is right, she will.

The woman walked out of the bathroom then within seconds she heard the springs of the bed. Mashé covered her mouth because undoubtedly the sounds she heard she should not have heard. Her thoughts were racing on what to do next. She could not lie stretched out in the shower because eventually one or both of them would come in to use it. She had to take a chance so she rose up, stepped out of the shower again, and grabbed her clothes and shoes. Fortunately, it was almost dark outside and the lights were out inside as well. Mashé did an army crawl, and with all of the bustling going on, she managed to crawl to the guest bedroom, close the door, then lock it. She was so cold, since she had not been able to dry off with the bath towel. She then got a jolt through her body because she forgot about her handbag. As she looked at the nightstand she saw a landline phone and rushed over to call Eila.

Eila: Hello, who is this? Yes, Mashé, I saw my home telephone number appear, but then when I recognized your voice I relaxed; I was concerned for a minute there. What do you mean? No, I cannot relax. And why are you whispering? Tell me what is going on, Mashé? All right, I am on my way. Yes, I am leaving right now, bye.

Because Mashé was unable to gauge how long it would take for her friend to come home, she decided to wait about ten minutes, then call the NYPD. In situations like this, who could guess how Eila would react? Mashé tried to imagine how she would behave. How could this be happening, especially when Eila told her that she believed he was the one? She thought it best to call around to different hotels, but not yet. It was hard to listen through the door; she thought maybe they were finished—there was no guessing with a situation like this so she decided to stay locked in the guest room. Now fully dressed, she determined that more than ten minutes had gone by so she walked to the bathroom and proceeded to call the NYPD. Then she put down the receiver, what would she tell them? That her friend's boyfriend was cheating on her? How ridiculous was that? An idea popped into her head.

Mashé: Hello, I would like to report a very loud disturbance in one of the brownstones here. The address is 503 Clarkson Street, Number 2, in Brooklyn, New York; I prefer not to give my name. Please send a car now? Thank you so much.

Within fifteen minutes, Mashé heard a knock at the door. She noticed from underneath the door that a light came on. There were no windows to look through, and Mashé was nervous because once they were inside they would search the entire place. She kept asking herself where Eila was; maybe she had called the police too soon. The police were inside, if she could understand what was being said. Then she could not believe her ears: What a strange excuse, the woman said she thought this was his place. She had difficulty understanding Lowell, but he was definitely speaking at a higher than normal pitched voice. The police asked who lived here? Oh no! Now the police asked was anyone else inside. They told the police No.

Mashé rushed into a narrow closet and just when she was about to close the door, she heard a familiar voice; it was Eila's and she was asking Lowell what happened and the police were insistent that she calm down. Then she told him and the other woman to leave. The police had them wait outside so they could collect their names. Mashé felt so embarrassed for Eila, and she decided she had better unlock the door to go and comfort her friend. When she reached for the door knob she heard Eila scream, "I don't ever want to see you again." The police concluded their questioning and bid her a good night. Eila was sitting in her living room rubbing the palms of her hands when she looked up and saw her best girl.

Mashé: Eila, I hope you are not upset with me, but he brought that woman here and they didn't see me.

Eila: They didn't see you? Were you in the guest bedroom the whole time?

Mashé: No. I was taking a shower in the master instead. When Mashé finished telling Eila every detail of her experience, Eila started to laugh. However, once she collected herself, she told Mashé how stupid she had been. Mashé asked what she could do for her. Eila jumped up and went straight to her bedroom and yanked off the bed linen, telling her friend to pardon her while she did her laundry. Mashé followed her, offering to take her out for dinner. Eila said she was so glad she was there with her.

Eila: Mashé, please don't tell anyone about this? The police asked if I wanted to file a complaint, like for trespassing. I have decided to just forget all about him. It will be hard. Seems like my dealings with the opposite sex are like walking down a dead-end street.

Mashé: You are going to need to give yourself a chance. First of all, you should slow down and allow a man to be a gentleman. You are aggressive, assertive, and impulsive and I love you, Girl. So, please promise me you will just ease up and practice celibacy for a while.

Eila: Seriously?!

Mashé: I mean it, Eila. I am convinced that this episode was a sign for you to change your ways. Twice now I have been subjected to your waywardness, or that of someone you know. Wait, three times, am I right?

Flight Attendant: Ladies and Gentlemen, we are approaching Louis Armstrong New Orleans International Airport, please discontinue using all electronic devices and have your seats returned to an upright position.

While the plane descended, Mashé revisited all of what happened yesterday from the high moment at York College to the low moment at Eila's brownstone and once again entertained the thought that she and Eila should have some distance between them. The word subtlety came to mind. She decided to call her mother when she arrived at the hotel; she hoped she would be home.

The Hotel New Orleans had a certain panache in blending the old with the new characteristics of New Orleans. Her mood had become cheerier. Her room had a vintage decor with gold tassels draped across the bed frame. A perfect room for her and Neil to share. Having reviewed her schedule once more, she had close to three hours before her presentation. When she peered out the window, she saw so many people walking about, and they seemed to be proud people. When she looked across the way she saw Saint Thomas Street; that would have certainly hit home for Neil. She picked up her cell to call her mother; instead her father answered.

Eugene: Mashé. Hello there. This is a surprise. She went out with a friend of hers, having lunch probably, and bragging to everyone about you. Where are you now? New Orleans, my kind of city, I sure wish Neil had gone too. How was York College? You must be on cloud nine, I know I would be. Is there something on your mind? I am your dad, whatever it is. You want to talk about Eila, I think I should pull up a chair; I am listening.

Mashé told her father everything that happened in that brownstone; afterward there was a long pause between them. She wondered if her cell had shut down and then he began to speak.

Eugene: This may seem like a selfish response to you. While I listened, I was so glad you were unharmed, and of course the others. First of all, you were in New York; second of all, you chose to stay with Eila. Why? My guess, you wanted to spare her feelings in lieu of going to a hotel, also to reinforce your tight friendship, and to save some money. You should have stayed at a hotel. Your mother and I appreciated the money you gave to us from your winnings in Saint Thomas. You did not need to do it. We found no fault with you and if we had, we still would have been okay as long as you were okay. I know you are thinking, if you had not been present this guy, Lowell, would have continued misusing her. Would it surprise you if that were her hallmark? There are different reasons why some men stick around. So, you go ahead and give yourself kudos, you acted like a good friend; I sincerely believe she appreciated your role in it. However, look what you subjected yourself to, better yet, what she subjected you to. I have often said to you, "If it looks like a duck, walks like a duck, quacks like a duck, it's a duck." Even though Eila did not knowingly and intentionally date and marry the same man you planned to marry, it still put her in the middle of it all, because of her trickery, in my opinion. I believe the phrase the younger generation uses is,

"She was found out." Mashé, you are gaining considerable recognition for your work. As you know, I keep you in prayer. However, sweetheart, you should sever your ties with her. You are not little girls any more. I dreaded the thought of the police walking in on a situation that could have been worse, and your name dragged through the mud. Your dad cannot predict the future; however, now that you are establishing yourself, avoid anything or anyone who could destroy what you have built.

How serendipitous, of all the times she has called for her mother, her father answered. "He got her told."

The front desk called to tell her that a car was waiting to take her to Tulane University. She did a quick wash down, put on her brand new pantsuit, and took the elevator down. Her room was on the tenth floor and she was hoping there would be no stops, but the elevator did stop on the fifth floor. When the doors opened, the arrestive eyes of a gentleman met hers. He acknowledged her; she smiled and looked away. There was another stop, this time on the third floor. Two people joined them. Mashé amused herself over the fact that to her far left was a man who appeared refined, moreover regal, and she could not wait to hop into the limousine, because he was also unquestionably pretty. When they reached the lobby Mashé walked briskly toward the front desk. While she was so doing someone from behind sought her attention. It was him. Extending his hand to hers he introduced himself as Major Adulante with no connection to the military. Mashé was responsive but curt, indicating she had a car waiting. He continued and asked was she in politics and she said No, she represented the literary world. He begged her indulgence and asked was she to speak at Tulane University this afternoon and before she could respond, he said he was a member of the Black Alumni Alliance and read an email about her. He said he was on his way to a meeting but now having met her, his plans had changed. Finally, he released her hand; she thanked him, then headed straight for the revolving doors.

Upon entering the Tulane University campus, Mashé was directed to look across the street at the famous Audubon Park, a highly recognized recreational area off the campus beautified by aging but lush cypress and oak trees. The Chair of the English Department met her at the school's entrance and she was led to an auditorium that appeared to accommodate at least five hundred people. Mashé's heart was racing as she took deep breaths. The Chair introduced her to two other enthusiastic faculty members and enlightened her on the day's agenda. It was Women's Week on campus; there had been a series of female speakers from different disciplines, and Mashé was selected for the Humanities category. When she learned of this, she felt she had to upgrade her presentation.

The auditorium was gradually filling up and the effects of what had happened twelve or more hours ago in that brownstone had mainly been dismissed. Having been welcomed and introduced by the Chair, Mashé opened with a brief history of her family. She spoke of her maternal grandmother aspiring to be a writer, and even though she had to drop out of college to support her family, she continued to write and left behind many unpublished pieces that would likely spark the interest of any avid reader. Her parents were both retired high school teachers entrenched with an interest in the cultural arts. As she gave credence to becoming a romantic poet, she asked everyone in the audience to picture themselves being void of an imagination, followed with, "imagine that." She painted a picture of how great strides in human history as well as human culture could have straggled as she referenced great inventors, acclaimed musicians, playwrights, philosophers, sculptors, and others. The audience responded to her sentiments. She said she applauded the forthrightness of visionaries and although some were highly criticized, this ability gave them the opportunity to display courage, and they laughed when she said an idealist was actually a real person.

While she read excerpts from her book the tone of her voice and her levity stimulated the audience with an endearing spirit. She once again emphasized that the lack of imagination meant a lack of creativity. Her talk went well over the time allotted, which went unnoticed. When she finished she was given a standing ovation. Mashé spoke so passionately—as a fountain of unwritten words flowed from her lips effortlessly and profoundly. The Chair invited all to a reception and book signing for Mashé in an adjacent library. Some eager students swarmed around her as she tried her best to respond to every question, when a deep and distinct voice asked her to autograph his book. It brought stillness among them. She turned to notice it was Major. The students watched closely as she took his book, autographed it, and then thanked him. Mashé then suggested the students join her in the library.

Major: This was definitely a life changing experience for me. I have yet to be drawn to poetry, particularly the romantic version; it was well worth my while to come here.

Mashé: Thank you, Mr. Adulante. I hope your absence was excused in relationship to the meeting you bypassed?

Major: I am one of the bosses. I oversee the operations for one of the main oil refineries in the state of Louisiana. Forgive me but I have to ask, where is your entourage?

Mashé: That is a project in progress.

Major: May I share a café noisette with you back at the hotel later this evening?

Mashé: (Reserved) Mr. Adulante, I should be in the library as we speak, surely you understand? It has been a pleasure.

Major: Absolutely, this is your day. I shall wait for you, please, take your time.

She walked toward the auditorium exit, then entered the library, which was huge. There before her was a pictorial of herself and numerous copies of her book. A female faculty member asked her about one of her poems, entitled "A Blaze of Passion." Did the poem stem from an actual experience, or her imagination? Mashé answered that none of her poems were connected to an actual event, though it was possible that the poem itself might reflect on someone's actual experience or desire to seek such an experience. The faculty member laughed because as she read it she was reminded of a once upon a time heated romance. Mashé responded that what was one person's imagination was another person's truth or reality. With conversation after conversation, Mashé was having her own "natural high" and somehow it needed to be stressed to Neil to join her the next time to share it with her.

Mashé hurried to the limousine because she wanted to avoid Major. The Louisiana charm he pitched at her could take effect and she did not want to imagine the aftermath. She had been keeping notes in her journal for her next book of romantic poems and decided to create one behalf of Major. She decided the title would be "You are just too pretty for me."

Mashé wanted to have a nice southern meal before her flight out so she asked the chauffeur to recommend an authentic restaurant. He named many and she asked him would he join her—it would be her treat to him. He was modest about her offer, although he did accept it. He introduced her to the Bayona, located in the French Quarter of New Orleans. All of the earlier activity made her ravenous and the chauffeur was amazed with her appetite. Truth be told, Mashé had one meal at the reception and book signing arranged for her at York College. When she boarded the plane for New Orleans in first class they served a better than average light lunch. So practically all the while, her stomach growled, even during her speaking engagement.

She arrived at the airport two hours before her flight time so she decided to call her husband.

Neil: Is this my wife finally calling me?

Mashé: Neil, I am so happy to hear your voice. I really should have you come with me the next time.

Neil: What happened, Mashé, and where are you now?

Mashé: New Orleans is a city reborn—it is wonderful here. I am at the airport coming your way later tonight. I wanted to be certain you are meeting me at the airport.

Neil: I have your return schedule right in front of me, and looking forward to bringing you back home. Now, tell me what happened?

Mashé had semi-promised Eila she was going to keep the incident in New York quiet but she has already told her father, so why not tell her husband. Again, she revealed every detail that took place in that brownstone.

Neil: That was a close call. I am sure you are familiar with the phrase, "Crime of Passion." You will remember I told you on our way to the airport that I preferred that you stay in an upscale hotel. I have to say that while on our honeymoon when I asked about your long-time friendship with her I secretly questioned her stability. I did not want you to become defensive.

Mashé: My father laid the cards on the table, to put it mildly. He strongly advised me to cut it off with her. Since she lives in New York there is not much challenge there. We don't live across the street from one another like when we were children. Neil, I must be honest with you. I really do not know if I could do it. She admitted that she was envious of me from time to time, but she had my back and Rhial's too while we were growing up and vice-versa. I have been toying with how to say it.

Neil: My Mashé, "Actions speak louder than words." Try not to labor over this; don't give yourself a chore. She may act like a fool but she's not a fool. I believe this is the opportune time to start right now. Whenever she comes home to visit you don't actually dodge her—you are just busy. It might be a fib but think of the alternative, Mashé?

Mashé: But what will she think?

Neil: She can think whatever she wants. It will be touch and go for a while. Benefits will come from this, I assure you. She does not need her hand held. Fortunately, I also don't believe that she has been stringing you or Rhial along. Talking with a therapist might help and New York is probably full of them.

Mashé: So I am just supposed to drop her? As far as Rhial is concerned…

Neil: Rhial is having a baby and true she has husband problems so there will be no time for her to be concerned about this minor detail we're discussing.

Mashé: (Sighs) It's not minor to me, Neil, but a rational rebuttal I don't have at the moment.

Neil: May we change the subject then? What about me?

Mashé: (Sultry) Yes, what about you?

Neil: Now, don't you want the comfort of your man?

Mashé: There is no better thought in my head.

Neil: A nice rub down is waiting for you also; I will have some melted dark chocolate and strawberries. Always remember, you are my black cherry; I picked you.

Destined for the Bay Area and seated by the window Mashé attempted to take a nap when an approaching passenger asked, "Is anyone sitting here?" Mashé with her eyes closed mildly replied, "Not to my knowledge." For several minutes, there was silence, and then she heard the following passage: "Since the sun aligns with

Venus, my touch is for you and only you. Since the sky cannot go beyond itself, my lips are for you and only you. Since night and day are married in perfect harmony, my thoughts are of you and only you; it's a universal truth, you are mine and only mine."

Mashé slowly opened her eyes and looked to where the voice came from. She displayed calm but inside she was electrically taken aback. The passenger was Major Adulante.

Mashé: A coincidence, Mr. Adulante.

Major: I am not a stalker, Madame, but yes, it seems to be. After your affair, I looked for you to have café noisette together. So when I could not find you I went back to the hotel and waited until it was time to leave for my flight. I did not want to make you feel uncomfortable and if I have, one thousand pardons. Although, I do marvel at your majestic beauty. And what is most unusual is you are a gifted woman. One does not find beauty and brains a typical match.

Mashé: That sounds a tad condescending, Mr. Adulante.

Major: Oh no, have I done it again? This poem from your book is on top. I love the title: "To be Sure." I should become more familiar with the arts. I mean I love jazz, who doesn't? I enjoy plays and the movies but to be sitting next to an Artist. I liked your talk about imagination; it is true, where would any of us be if we didn't have it?

Mashé: So you were there the entire time.

Major: Yes, did you not take me seriously?

Mashé: There are all kinds of people in the world, Mr. Adulante; some you take seriously, and some you do not.

Major: Well, that was a mouthful. As I said, you are special. Pardon my asking, you seem preoccupied, maybe even pensive.

Mashé: Is it that obvious?

Major: I noticed the lovely diamond ring on your left hand.

Mashé: You notice a lot, Mr. Adulante. And what about you, married?

Major: I am in a bicoastal relationship. She lives in Los Angeles. I have a meeting in Santa Cruz, then I am off to visit with her. It has become very expensive for both of us. I come to see her more than she comes to see me. She is in the real estate business.

Instantly, Mashé thought of Chandler; having a bicoastal relationship with him was adventurous.

Major: Are you happily married, Mashé?

Mashé: Very.

Major: This situation that has you looking so serious, can it be worked out? We just met but when people are traveling on a plane, they strike up a conversation and before you know it…

Mashé: What have we been doing all of this time, Mr. Adulante?

Major: You are too beautiful to be troubled, and I am a friendly stranger, who would like to listen and give my opinion if needed.

Once again Mashé crossed the I-promise- not-to-tell line and gave the highlights of what took place at the brownstone. Without naming them, she said she had already spoken to two men about this incident regarding her childhood friend.

She understood their points of view but still there were not enough pros and cons to reason with.

Major: In listening to you, I was trying to put myself in your shoes. Does your friend have a history of just dating—nothing romantic or serious ever comes about?

Mashé: I believe she wanted to be in a serious relationship with him. Their relationship lasted for several months, longer than any others did. I asked her what would it take for her to just straight out state what her expectations would be of him?

Major: I sensed that you want a woman's point of view as well.

Mashé: At first, I thought that way and understand, I value a man's opinion but there was little empathy for her. A woman usually supports another woman in the situation I have described. It is pointless to search for exactness; it could have been worse and I am glad I handled it the way I did.

Major: I agree your intervention was key. Now it is my turn. As a man, a lot would weigh in on my relationship to this woman in question. I am speaking of family ties such as my sister or my daughter. My emotions would be so keen because a man whom she had interest in just simply took advantage of her. My first thought would be she let it happen. I would sit her down and find out what she really wanted. Should her answers concern me, I would find professional help for her. You mentioned earlier that this was the longest relationship she had thus far. Going by what you have told me, the opinion of either would not matter. What matters is her self-esteem in relating to men. You have it right; she must not have given him the impression that she wanted to be respected. That has to be determined immediately, because when a woman behaves in an unclear manner, a man will probably respond in an unclear manner. Also, it is common knowledge that a decent and upstanding man would distance himself.

Mashé: Very well said. She needs to work it out. I have a question for you. When you saw me for the first time what were your initial intentions or thoughts?

Major: (Prudent) What registered to me when I first saw you was natural. I wanted to know who you were. I observed the wedding ring and I respect the wedding ring. However, there are some unhappily married women in the world, Mashé, and I am happy to know you are not one of them. Nonetheless, I do have a red flag observation.

Mashé: Please, go on.

Major: If you were my wife, I would not allow you to visit New York or New Orleans without me. Even if you boasted about being independent, it would not change a thing.

Flight Attendant: Attention all passengers. We are approaching the San Francisco International Airport…

Mashé: The male perception is unique, Mr. Adulante. Some men have a hidden agenda and some put their cards on the table. It is always a pleasure to be in the company of a southern gentleman.

Their channel of conversation continued until the plane taxied in and Mashé's initial assumptions about Major subsided. Neil was in her sight the moment she walked into the lobby.

Neil: Hello gorgeous. That was the longest four days of my life.

Mashé: Mine too. Neil, somehow, we need to work out a plan with your boss allowing you to travel with me on these speaking engagements.

Neil: You know I wanted to join you this time. What happened with your book agent, Von?

Mashé: Well, I am not his only client and I kinda told him to go ahead with his other plans.

Neil: I see, so this had something to do with Eila.

Mashé: I have been thinking so much of what I have experienced in the last twenty-four hours. You and Daddy were both right. I should have stayed at the Palace or somewhere on that scale. Anyway, I could not see us both staying at her place. Deep down inside I cringed at the thought of sleeping in a place with a revolving door. But, let me tell you about York College and Tulane University: both audiences received me in a way I could not have imagined; I had this iconic feeling the entire time. Neil, I have started my second book and I am going to dedicate it to you.

When he heard that, he brought her to him and bestowed many kisses upon her. As they drove away from the airport, Neil had some news to share.

Neil: I have some breaking news for you. I am scheduled to attend a conference next month in Colorado Springs, Colorado. It will take place the weekend before Palm Sunday. I believe you'll have a Spring Break around that time so you should be able to join me and protect me from scandalous situations.

Mashé: (Pauses) I would never make fun of your friends if they were in a precarious position. I would like to go with you, although the dates for Spring Break this year may be after you return from your conference. I presume Jamison was instrumental in this one as well.

Neil: Not this time. It was Amber. Mashé, I swear this woman probably gets about two hours of sleep a night. When we are in our planning meetings, she brings in all kinds of information on professional workshops and related events taking place around the country. Events that are relevant to our programs too. She is very industrious.

Mashé: Was Amber hired through a friend of a friend or right from the application pool?

Neil: I am not sure, why do you ask?

Mashé: You are married to a woman with a curious mind. (Neil's cell rings and he ignores it)

Neil: Oh no! How could I forget, your mother wants to hear from you sometime this evening.

Mashé: I should call her now since you are taking me out to dinner on this serene Sunday afternoon.

Neil: May we order in so you and I can stay in? Four days is a long time, Mrs. Rollins.

Mashé: Sounds tempting. You lead and I will follow. (She called her mother)

Clover: Hi! Are you home? Good. Your father told me about your plight with Eila Wynston and that boyfriend of hers. First, I would like to hear about your presentations. Did your Book Agent arrange these talks? He must have "a lot on the ball," to coin a phrase. You mentioned your grandmother. That was considerate of you. We need to find her manuscripts. She was an ambitious woman. Mashé, that would be amazing if you could have them posthumously published. I am so proud of you on many levels, Lady. I believe your Aunt Jewel could help us. Leave it to me. I appreciate your modesty; you sound composed, which is great. Second. I was under the impression your husband was going with you. Exactly, Neil explained that part to me. Is he with you now? Fine. Let's talk when you have more time. I am so excited for you. I love you too.

Neil: Are we both in trouble or just you?

Mashé: She must have realized I went on without you when my father told her about my predicament with Eila. My good friend insisted that I keep it to myself. Now I have broken a promise.

Neil: May I ask how many secrets she kept for you? I know how devoted the three of you are to each other.

Mashé: Those secrets are so old and they in no way compare to what just happened.

Neil: Just what I expected you to say. Sweetheart, you are still friends; however as I suggested, handle yourself differently.

Neil and Mashé arrived home and ordered their dinner. She went into their bedroom and plopped her bags on their bed then she went straight for the bathtub, and Neil walked in.

Neil: Our dinner will be delivered in an hour. Before you soak in that bubble bath, could you come to the kitchen; I have something to show you.

When Mashé walked into the kitchen there was a note on the refrigerator, "Open me!" When she looked inside, every shelf, including the shelves on the double doors, was full. He had gone grocery shopping while she was away.

Mashé: There must be a month's worth of food in here. You read my mind; I was about to ask you what you wanted so I could write out our grocery list. Come to me, my darling? (His cell rang and he answered)

Neil: This is Neil. Yes. We can talk about that tomorrow. I know you want a head start, but it's Sunday. We'll meet tomorrow afternoon, because that's as early as I can meet with you. That should work. Fine. Take care.

When Neil returned to the kitchen, his wife was gone. He went to the bedroom and peeked in the bathroom, finding her in the bathtub covered with lather. Her eyes were shut but she was not asleep; he undressed and stepped in and stretched his long legs against her body. She asked him how was work. He laid his head back and said it was a job with benefits and perks. She asked him who called and he said it was Amber. Then his wife asked how many times she called him after working hours on a day-to-day basis. He said he did not count them. She then asked him to "guestimate." Neil began massaging her legs, looked over at her, and said possibly once or twice. Mashé described her as an "eager beaver" and Neil chuckled. Mashé reminded herself to be cool as Tia advised, although she was genuinely curious how they interacted with one another on the job. Neil's eager hands took a voyage over her torso; his pressing and stroking were taking effect, and with her eyes still closed she asked him to listen for the doorbell. He told her he had placed a note on the door to leave their food on their back steps. Mashé replied, "You think of everything." She preferred their bed but he preferred their tub. The water splashed onto the walls and floor. They rolled and extolled, tenfold. There was a full moon and the newlyweds were still full of desire for more. Neil must have filled the tub up at least two more times, all the while tenderly holding his wife close. Shortly thereafter, they did make it to their bedroom and later Mashé uttered that she was hungry.

Neil: Oh, Man! I will be right back.

Mashé: (Giggling) It's fine. I'll meet you in the kitchen.

Mashé thought, how sensational, and wondered would this rendezvous last him for about three or four days because she would be holding a book fair on campus starting next week. She was the appointed chairperson so she and the Head of the English Department planned it for Tuesday, Wednesday, and Thursday afternoons until 6:30 PM, giving the students, faculty, and all others an opportunity to participate. Neil called wondering was she still coming.

Neil: That was a scrumptious meal.

Mashé: Neil, you might have to pull me out of bed tomorrow morning. Look at the time. Also, I meant to tell you that the Head of the English Department and I are hosting a book fair on campus this week and it starts on Tuesday lasting until Thursday. I will be coming home later than usual.

Neil: Is your poetry book featured at this book fair?

Mashé: Yes, along with thousands of other books.

Neil: Congratulations, Lady. I need to bring you up to date too. I have been helping Amber prepare a prototype for her systems engineering project—we are working from our Data Center Operations. In layman's terms, she is charged with illustrating the operational needs toward producing a product or service encompassing configuration baselines and developing solutions to essentially satisfy a customer need, and as a result, she has been working overtime in order to be ready to present her project to us. That is why she has been calling so often…

While he was again justifying all the particulars about Amber Vale, Mashé wondered, "Could someone else help the girl?"

Neil: (Continuing) And of course, she is not the only intern doing this. All projects are to be completed by this Thursday. Therefore, it may seem like I am "burning the candle at both ends" again because of my own ongoing projects.

Mashé: I appreciate these updates and I am hoping you will take many breaks and avoid burning yourself out. By the way, I loved going swimming with you in the bathtub. Did you detect my hesitancy? At first, it seemed somewhat awkward.

Neil: No, I was on a mission. I was with my favorite mermaid.

Mashé: (Baffled) Your favorite?

Neil: (Humorous) Well, my other one has been framed, you understand.

That following morning Neil and Mashé did manage to rise early and prepare for their day. As she entered her classroom a few of her students arrived preceding class time to tell her that they read about her visits to York College and Tulane University on social media, saying that the comments were favorable.

Mashé was pleased to have heard this news and decided to make a note to herself to call Von during her lunch. This morning she opened with a lecture about the beginnings of Literature, Ancient Literature particularly pertaining to Egypt. She discussed poetry, folklore, and stories and songs. Many historians stated that human literature began just before the fourth century BC, during the Pharaoh Dynasties, though she stressed let's not exclude the predynastic time period of Egypt.

Mashé: You will recall in your readings that the hieroglyphics qualify as printed references: telling a story. Also, recall that this historical fact is pre Alexander the Great, commonly known as the Lord of Asia, King of Macedonia, and he reigned from 336 BC to 323 BC. At some point in time with the efforts of sophisticated technology soon, we as a modern society shall be brought up to date about the actual timing of prose that was produced in Africa.

This topic had been a favorite of hers while she was in high school and college and she would have selected this area of study as her primary major though it would have required extensive travel and research. This was one of the reasons she wanted to delay having children due to her yearning to catch up. She was skeptical of Neil ever accepting her stance on raising a family. However, she stood firmly because as she perceived, once a child comes into your life some of your dreams are liable to remain just dreams. As she ended her lecture, she assigned her students to review their syllabi and select an ancient tale that pertained to romance and/or drama; decipher its context, and present it after Spring Break. Mashé was so amused at the expression on their faces. It would be two more weeks before the start of Spring Break so they had plenty of time.

As her next class was about to begin she went to her journal to make more notations and then it hit her. She had for some time wondered about how Amber and her husband interacted at work. So, since he explained to her that he could be burning the candle at both ends she decided to bring him dinner tonight, unannounced. Should his reaction show alarm or disbelief then this could lead her to wonder. Should his reaction be receptive, showing gladness, then she would be relieved. As for Amber's reaction, she would wait until tonight.

Mashé had brought her lunch so she remained in her classroom and called Von.

Von: Hello. So you are back. You received rave reviews from both campuses. Also, you'll be happy to know that your check is on its way to you from the New York Book Fair. How much is it? I did not look. I am not privy to that information because I did not coordinate the event—I see, you were testing me. Listen, it seems like the only way is up for you. I want to explore booking you for some magazine interviews—we should start with some of the well-known Black publications; we need to determine your standing with that targeted audience and the age factor is important too. Why?! Because we need to know. I must admit, I've been wondering why you haven't been considered by any Black colleges. But it's still early in the game and as you said, it is very competitive. Oh, I see, so if you were a Rapper it would be on, with your Rhythms. Mashé, if I had said that you would have been offended. Great, I am happy to hear that. Good enough. Take care.

Her work day was done, she went to her car, pulled out her phone, called a popular Creole restaurant, and placed an order for two of shrimp etouffee, salmon croquettes, jambalaya, creamed spinach, and peach cobbler. She was told the food would be ready in thirty minutes, so she decided to call Rhial.

Rhial: Is this you, my Best Girl? How timely you are. We are definitely telepathic. I just came from my doctor's office and baby and mother-to-be are doing very well. I only work half day now, Girl, you should see me, I am swollen. The bigger the better; well I do not know about that. Halvan is well. The baby is fine. He made an appointment for the paternity test for next Monday. Something about helping his father with this big job around the house. You know, like us he is an only child. Please understand me, he plans to do it because every time we talk he knows the subject will come up. Where are you now, in your car. Oops! The baby is moving, so strong too. I told my Doctor I do not want to know the sex. I am going to bypass having a baby shower because of our circumstance. Yes I am still thinking about coming home. Just to update you, I have some very nice neighbors and they want to help me in any way they can. I agree they are a blessing. My Urban Planning venture is in progress as we speak. What! You just returned from your trips. Where have you been this time? No way! Mashé, you are iconic. What does Neil have to say about it? You are so blessed to have a husband like him. I shall never forget the way he looked at you at the altar. Practically everyone was talking about it at the wedding reception. Look at us, Mashé, we are so independent. Have you spoken with Ms. Wynston? Oh that's right, you went to York College. And you spent the night at her place in Brooklyn. Boy! Were you brave. Was she on her best behavior? Really, that is good news. How is her man doing, Lowell, that's right…you did not see him. Really? I will honor that comment and move on. Like I said. I am still thinking about coming home, though my doctor recommended the Metropolitan Hospital of Miami; so you see things are moving along at a nice pace. My pregnancy has been so pleasant—I can eat anything I want. By the way, Halvan, his father, and I did have that meeting. He patiently listened to everything I said. He told his son that he must bear the responsibility if he is indeed the father, and more importantly, he felt his son should return home with me since I am his wife. Yes, I plan to tell my parents after I learn the results of his paternity test. Bear in mind though if he is not the father, what is there to tell? I am glad you called, I promise to do that. Bye for now.

Mashé was not completely comfortable with Halvan's reason for not taking the test; it would only take about three minutes. Anyway, it was time to pick up their food. Rhial's comment about how much devotion Neil displayed the day of their wedding was memorable and perhaps she should reconsider how to do this. After a few minutes she decided to take his dinner to him, quickly excuse herself, and then leave. She uttered to herself that this needed to look clean—he cannot ever detect that she does not trust him. A funny thought popped up in her mind, could he have filled up the refrigerator to camouflage something? Then she felt silly. She found a parking place a few feet away from the entrance; there still seemed to be someone working the front desk. Her car door swung open; she stepped out with a pep in her step and entered the lobby. The receptionist recognized her immediately and told her he would try to locate her husband for her. Instantly, she leaned to the side and saw an open door to a conference room and then she heard Neil's voice, so she tiptoed over and saw Neil and Amber working on a slide projector, which must have malfunctioned somehow. Then to her astonishment, Amber suggested that he take his shirt off, so it can stay fresh, commenting that he worked too hard. In her mind she thought to stay calm, however, she must make a move; she anxiously waited for his response. Neil said, "It is not jammed; you said you plugged it in, but you did not. Look at the outlet." Mashé had a good sigh of relief but Little Miss Goodie Two Shoes had some issues. She strolled in.

Mashé: (Cheery) Good evening, Neil. I was thinking how hard you have been working—oh hello, Amber, so good to see you again. Anyway, here is your dinner; I was almost sure you hadn't made any plans. So, if you are going to burn the midnight oil, you might as well do it on a full stomach. Don't you think so Amber? You two go right ahead. Please pardon the interruption. I hope it hits the spot.

As she turned to walk out, Neil ran and stopped her and led her to a secluded area. He gently brought his hands to her face and then gave her a luscious kiss. Afterward he took her by the hand and they returned to the conference room. A pink Post-it placed on the projector read: Neil, I just remembered I have an errand to run so I will see you tomorrow, bright and early. Mashé was smiling broadly inside. She was proud of her husband's reaction. Now that Amber had been found out, the next few weeks should reveal even more about her character. She might consider wanting to work in another department or be assigned to another mentor. Mashé knew it was a chancy thing to do but men do not know women like women do.

Neil: Looks like we have the room to ourselves. This smells outrageous, is this Creole?

Mashé: Of course. I brought back a little of the Louisiana brio with me. This is the first time you and I have eaten Creole together. I guessed at what you might like.

Neil: I am not hard to please. I love their jambalaya.

Mashé: Good. It's in there. Sweetheart, you go ahead and serve yourself. I'll take my portion and go home. You eat while you work.

Neil: The work I have is in my office on my computer. In fact, I was making some headway when Amber stopped by earlier needing help with this projector. There was nothing wrong with it, other than to plug it in. I suppose she felt a little silly.

Mashé: (Resigned) I could see that.

Neil: I am loving this meal, woman. Before I forget there is a company picnic following our Colorado Springs event. We should dress casual; it's going to take place at the state park.

Mashé: I have heard of those. The employees bring their family members and they eat, play games, and what have you. Looking forward to it. (Her cell phone rang. It was her mother)

Clover: Please stop by before you head for home? Good. I will be waiting for you

Mashé: My mother asked me to stop by. So, I will leave you with this spread.

It was almost 6:30 PM. They embraced and then she left.

Mashé walked into her parents' house and and found them sitting at the breakfast room table looking pleasant.

Eugene: There is my girl. We had you come over to talk about a certain topic.

Clover: We won't keep you away from your husband too long.

Mashé: You two have the most interesting expressions on your face, a look I have not seen before. What's happening?

Eugene: Neil's parents want to be grandparents. I just finished a phone conversation with Donovan. They have talked to their son and the feedback we were given was you want to wait about five years before starting a family, is this true?

Mashé: (Curious) Yes, Neil and I have already come to an agreement.

Clover: Which is?

Mashé: To wait for about five years, as you were told. He preferred three years and I told him since the woman's body provides the incubation for an unborn child, he needed to recognize that I want to accomplish a few ambitions, for instance, travel, do some more graduate work, things like that. Above all, Neil and I are getting to know each other, Mother, I remember that's what you told me when you and Daddy were newlyweds. I was born about five years later.

Clover: You have not mentioned the deciding factor. What we heard this afternoon was if Neil was able to afford a house that met your satisfaction for spaciousness, location, and I believe you wanted it to be two stories, with a huge backyard where the children can play.

Mashé: (Reserved) Yes, that was his idea. I felt I was being coaxed a little; then again I did say it could work. Listen I never signed a contract. I have heard about marriages that want you to produce three children in five years to benefit from a family trust; who needs that kind of pressure, not me?

Eugene: Good point little girl. Now listen we have been asked to present this suggestion to you. They, his parents, mean well. They explained to us that they can assist in buying a house that meets both of your standards and pay on it for the next five years if you might consider starting a family in two years. As I heard, Neil is doing well and you are successful, so there should not be any monetary concerns, which is a supreme plus. California real estate has some good offerings and we think you should take them up on it.

Clover: They asked your father and me to talk to you. First of all, I support whatever you decide, but I have to say, if my in-laws were willing to buy a house of my choosing just for the sake of having grandchildren, I would have said, "Where do I sign?" figuratively speaking of course.

Mashé: (Pauses) How funny. Neil had not mentioned this to me. I just came from his office.

Clover: You just came from his office? Why?

Mashé: You could say, I was being a good wife. I took a hot-plate to my hard-working husband.

Clover: Out of curiosity, how often are you doing this?

Mashé: This was my first time. He has been given added responsibilities and often works late. I want us to maintain that newlywed spirit.

Eugene: Sounds good to me. To answer your question, all we know is that he told his parents what you two discussed on your honeymoon about starting a family. Now, when you go home tonight, be calm about this and try not to feel like you are being pressured. Frankly, you know I would love to have a little grandson or granddaughter to play catch with and ask me a zillion questions like when you were little.

Clover: And to piggyback on that, holding a brand new life in my arms would be a blessing. Your five-year plan is a sound one. For some reason Donovan and Zora have a plan laid out that includes grandchildren and they are ready now.

Mashé: I have heard of these arrangements made in the best of families, I would have never imagined it happening in our family. Did they offer a list of suggested names?

Clover: (Smiling) Oh my goodness, no. Although that is a good question. When you go home tonight you and your husband share with one another as you have been doing, and see what understanding you can come to. Judging from the look on your face your mind is made up. My daughter, you are talented and you and I have talked about that boat of opportunity sailing your way. Keep in mind there are different types of opportunities, some more attractive than others. Go home and talk with your husband and like your father said, be calm. You have a particular boat of opportunity sailing your way; then again you could let it sail on by.

Mashé: (Subtle) I shall take this under advisement. Is there anything else going on?

Eugene: Have you been in touch with your friend from New York?

Mashé: No, Daddy. And thank you for saying "friend."

Eugene: I told your mother what happened. I have some calls to make, so I will let you young ladies take it from here.

Mashé and Clover talked at length about the havoc that took place in New York and her mother told her she had some genuine concerns for Eila. They both promised to avoid sharing the ordeal with her Aunt Lennie. She told her mother that her father wanted her to sever their ties. She said his tone reminded her of when she broke off her engagement with Chandler, not to have any further contact with him either.

Mashé: Are life's issues supposed to separate you from your best friends? As I told Neil, we bonded as children; she told me she would work on changing.

Clover: With regards to Eila, the glass is either half empty or half full. I admire the friendships you have with Rhial and Eila. The three of you grew up in a time that was emerging and streaming with positive change. I often watched you girls walk to school together and I thought, those three little Black girls are going to make quite a difference in their lives. You three have been determined to go your own ways in life and manage to stay connected, to stay loyal. However, when it comes to one's reputation, it carries a lot of weight. You are a rising star in the literary world and I am just dancing all inside about it. How hurt your father and I would have been had something more serious happened at Eila's home. You know, once the horse is out of the barn, he has gone. Sweetheart, I don't think you should count on her to change. Your pathways have taken different directions for the better, as I see it. I have been meaning to ask about Rhial; have you had a chance to talk with her since you've been back?

Mashé: (Reserved) Yes, we spoke earlier today. She had just come from her doctor's office, and she and baby are doing well. Maybe you haven't heard she developed a housing improvement project with the City of Miami Beach, which is in progress as we speak.

Clover: That is outstanding. I need to call Trista and Tolson and congratulate them for raising a fine and intelligent woman like Rhial. You know, I had some misgivings about her husband like others did. She refused to give him up and now they are married and expecting a baby. Did her husband have any role in that city project?

Mashé: No, only Rhial.

Clover: Probably just as well. They are certainly an interesting pair. Did you two talk about a baby shower for her?

Mashé: I asked her about it. She has so much on her plate; she might need to bypass it or wait until after her baby is born; but then you know Rhial, she could change her mind in mid-stream.

Clover: You are looking so serious. How are things at the college?

Mashé: Things couldn't be better. I am co-chair of our three-day book fair this year. It starts this Tuesday. I will be keeping late hours myself, but like I said, it is only for three days. Some schools do an entire week.

Clover: My Mashé, the Queen of poetry. You know there is a package that came for you yesterday. Look on the dining room table.

Mashé found the package, opened it, and was excited to see their wedding pictures inside. She and her mother took them all out and spread them across the dining room table. There were close-up shots of her and Neil as they exchanged their vows. Eugene came down wondering what all of the hurrah was about. Clover showed him a picture of him and his daughter dancing at the reception. They were so caught up enjoying all of the pictures that they totally lost track of time. Mashé assured her parents she would have some duplicates made of their favorites and bring them by; she bid them a good night.

When Mashé arrived home she sat in her car for a few minutes and wondered how she should bring up his parents' offer delicately. She loved this little house and she could easily live in it for another two or three years. The open house she and Neil visited last week had stayed with her. She wondered now if he had mentioned that house to them. He may have even given them the address to go see it. Then it clicked; that's where this stemmed from, so she reluctantly had to give herself credit—it was her idea, just the same, she never imagined an outcome like this. She walked in the house, placed all of her belongings on the living room coffee table, and turned on the wide-screen TV. She started feeling sleepy and noticed the time, it was 8:50 PM. She hoped all of that heavy food had not made her husband fall asleep at his desk. She took a hair clamp and wrapped her hair in a loose bun. She became amused because her dinner may have begun to take effect on her.

She decided to lie across their bed for a few minutes. Instantly, she went to sleep and the dream of her and Chandler reoccurred. Her once upon a time wizard of love brought his lips to hers, this time she did not resist. His vigorous moves slammed her from every direction; a pool of sweat formed beneath them. She was euphoric, screaming his name, and now she was about to come. All at once, she heard a door shut and she woke up.

Neil: I made it in. I have some news for you (enters their bedroom). Baby, do you have a fever? You look clammy, are you hot?! (He lay down next to her and stroked her forehead)

Mashé: I...I feel fine. So glad you are home. What time is it?

Neil: It's almost nine thirty. Can you get up?

Mashé: Sure I can. I must have dozed off. (She went to the bathroom and Neil spoke to her through the closed door) I need to give you some credit; after you took off I went back to my project, finished my conceptual design update, integration control along with all of my other program activities, and had Jamison take a look at it. He found it worthy enough to be submitted for review at our Philadelphia office. They may adopt it to replace some functions that have been in need of upgrading. I am not the first to produce this; nonetheless, my boss is pleased about what I have done and because my wife showed up and fed me, that was power for the core. I had been interrupted so many times, finally.

Mashé: (Walking out) "Behind every great man is a great woman." Let there be a slight paraphrase, "Beside every great man…"

Neil: I love you, woman. Why are you still in street clothes? Are you working tomorrow?

Mashé: Yes, I went to my parents' house. They summoned me over to discuss an offer or shall I say a proposal your parents made. Also, our wedding pictures are back.

Neil: There must be a million pictures. That photographer was busy. A proposal, interesting!

Mashé: Yes. They want grandchildren and if I agree to start a family with you in the near future, they would like to purchase a larger and more spacious home for us.

Neil: Okay, first of all if you think I put them up to that, I did not. My mother asked me were children in the near future? I told her that you were a career woman and you had dreams you wanted to fulfill. I only mentioned that you would probably be more inclined to start having children earlier if we were in a larger house.

Mashé: There is no shame or blame. I told my parents I would talk with you. So where do we go from here?

Neil: When the time is right, I will go by and see them. You said you wanted to wait five years so, unless something climatic happens we will wait. Are you taking any birth control?

Mashé: Sometimes, I have taken the morning after pill. Strange you would ask me that now.

Neil: It seems to be a delicate subject with you, and I support you. We are both driven and our mindset is to be well-off in life. Bottom-line, I could take care of us. You could stay at home and write your poetry or whatever your choosing.

Mashé: I should feel fortunate to have these different choices. First, a new house without mortgage payments, stay-at-home mom and/or do artistry at home. Maybe I am crazy, I don't mean to be nonchalant, but five years is not a long time.

Neil: You will be well into your thirties, but my darling we are on the same page; as I said, I will talk to my parents and convey a no thank you.

Mashé: No thank you! You said you were going to go see them when the time was right. Essentially, you are walking up to them and saying No thank you, because of me? For matters to go the way you want them to, just spill it out one more time?

Neil: Fine. If I were running the show, we would be packed and moved out of here. Living in a gigantic estate, maybe something like 5000 square feet with a grand backyard; basically a four- or five-bedroom house. There would be top-grade hardwood floors and high ceilings. Subletting this house would work but first we would need to buy it. I believe that was your sentiment. And most importantly, we would be splendidly pregnant. I could live in a house of those proportions once my position is augmented.

Mashé: Let me understand something. You want me "barefoot and pregnant" right now? Meaning our baby is on the way and the gigantic dream house is imminent?

Neil: Like the cliché says, You can't have one without the other.

Mashé: Has Jamison assured you of anything; I mean is there a tangible timeline in place for you?

Neil: We have spoken about it. I feel optimistic. As you know, moving up involves the actions or input of others. Mine alone may raise recognition, but it's kinda like a pinball machine, before you hit that mark or reach that level of achievement, you'll be led this way, then that way. That is the culture of the game. As I mentioned in Saint Thomas, maybe two or three years at best.

Mashé: Aptly put. I love teaching and I love writing as well. If someone was to ask me to choose one over the other, I could not. This may be a naïve statement; however, I believe we will be better parents once we are comfortable with ourselves as individuals, meaning there are fewer distractions and regrets.

Neil: (Awed) Listen to you, the great literate. In essence, you hold the cards and I would never attempt to make a deal with my wife but I am glad that we are clear on our aspirations of "success" as you put it and beginning a family.

Mashé: We have a lucid perspective and I feel better now. Wow! What a day and night this has been.

Neil: Amen. Ah, when I walked in you were mumbling something; I could not make it out, were you dreaming?

Mashé: (Discreet) I guess I was. Maybe I had better avoid Creole cooking; it may be a little too spicy for me.

Showcase (15)

Easter week had come, which meant a one-week break for Mashé. There was no feeling self-conscious about it either. On Monday morning she watched her husband rise and shine and run out the door. He was so skillful in his work. More often after hours he would receive calls or texts from coworkers seeking his advice on different programs related to prototyping, designing, merchandizing, or testing methods. He had received more feedback about his project that was shared with their Philadelphia office also. He planned to fly back there next week to meet with some Vice Presidents in the area of Bio-medical Technology. Her worst fear was that they might have to move to the East Coast. She didn't wish any bad luck for her husband's advancement, but it would bring her immeasurable ease if Jamison were relocated instead. Sometimes she believed Neil was being made out to be the Poster Boy. There was one other Black male engineer who worked with Neil and his name was Arland Gantz. Neil hardly mentioned him, other than he was a dependable coworker.

Seldom did she have the opportunity to lie in bed and just think. Trying to decide what she would do for the next five days turned out to be the fun part. Since she and Neil talked about their plans to move to a larger house and start a family, he seemed to be keeping his nose to the grindstone. Still, she had been the nice wife; his dinner was always ready for him and he behaved like his normal self when he came home. She feared he could be overworking himself, but he liked his job so perhaps she should relax her concerns. More than ever, he had been showing less restraint. They have been married for nearly two and one half months and he had been coming to her in the shower, or just before the alarm sounded in the morning, and on the weekends they would occasionally take in a movie but once they returned he was ready for action again. She concluded he was not taking any energy drinks and mixing them with drugs to enhance his performance and he was "fit as a fiddle," in a manner of speaking. She had an inkling that her husband was trying to get her pregnant even though she told him she was taking the morning after pill but not on a regular basis. The main reason was she detested taking drugs even for a headache. Her thoughts leaned toward him trying condoms. Chandler had used them occasionally but he did not care to, though he was considerate. This was what Mashé wanted to avoid, tossing thoughts around about what to do to avoid getting pregnant. She could be married to a sly little fox; nonetheless, she wanted to please him completely. Tonight she would just come out and ask him to start using condoms from time to time.

She would have liked to go back to sleep; when she looked over at the nightstand, she saw her new membership card for the new fitness center that opened around the corner from them. Weight had not been a problem for her at least so far, but she wanted her body to stay toned also. Convinced that married life could be a juggling act, she believed more than ever to stick to her personal priorities. Immediately she decided that every day this week the fitness center would be her focus and during the weekend, she would practice her exercises by watching the women's cable channel on health and fitness; also, there was an opportunity to review her journal and continue with her poetry writings. In the back of her mind, she wondered if Neil actually told his parents, No thank you? In a matter of minutes, she fell asleep.

Perhaps a half an hour into her slumber her cell phone rang and this meant she had to leave her nice warm bed to pull it from her satchel. It was Eila and she was pleased to hear her friend's voice. Eila is excited because she is planning a trip to Easter Island, an island off the coast of Chile, a well-deserved vacation. She wanted to let her and Rhial know before she boarded the plane. She said she placed a message on Rhial's cell phone. Mashé asked her who she was traveling with and Eila told her a gentleman friend she met when she first moved to New York City. She amused Mashé when she told her not to worry; she and her traveling companion were staying in separate hotel rooms, and she was turning over a new leaf. Then she said, he was White. She said very emphatically, "I think I need a break from brothers." Mashé listened to her friend's voice. She seemed lively and groovy, but who was this man?

Mashé: Eila, you sound good and I would love to jump in your hip pocket and go to Easter Island too. Their Polynesian culture is like that of the Hawaiian Islands, French Polynesia, and New Zealand also. When you can, send some pictures to my phone and include your friend too; I want to see what he looks like. What is his name?

Eila: Paul Desmond and he has the perfect face. He's an accountant for the state and he has never been married. I believe your husband is slightly taller than him and his physique makes me want to run around in circles. Oh, and I know you want to know who is paying for this trip. We are going Dutch, and you should see this necklace he bought for me…

Mashé: (Interjects) Do pray tell, share why I am just now hearing about him—another secret?

Eila: No never. He and I have been eyeing one another but I have never dated a White guy. He asked me out and I continuously refused him; but you know what's strange? If he were Black and looked the same way, Girl, it would have been on. He is so polite…

Mashé: Could you slow down just a tad? Listen, have you told Aunt Lennie?

Eila: I plan to call her. I knew you would ask me that question and I am going to buy her something she will really appreciate from my travels.

Mashé: That would just warm her heart, Eila. Gosh, this White man has certainly made an impact on you. I cannot wait until you return to find out what is next on the agenda or shall I say, itinerary.

Eila: Now hold on. We are taking it one day at a time—I have decided to take that twelve-step program.

Mashé: Well, clue me in.

Eila: No sex for twelve months.

Mashé: (Gasps) Kudos for Eila. Good luck!

Eila: We have been on the phone for a time—where are you?

Mashé: At home in my bed. It is Spring Break and I am going to spring into action at the fitness center all week.

Eila: Is that right. What's going on?

Mashé: I need to stay in shape; although I am not out of shape. I joined this new fitness club and now that I am married…

Eila: Is Neil being a man, Mashé? I know it's none of my business but that's it, isn't it?

Mashé: I am not following you.

Eila: You know the first time I met you I said to myself, now there is a square. She'll probably stay a virgin until she's fifty. Don't take offense.

Mashé: (Unfazed) Believe me I am not. In that department, you and I are like night and day.

Eila: (Undaunted) Very well. Is he wearing you out? Because if so, you are definitely on the right track.

Mashé felt compelled to share with Eila about the "start a family now and get a free house" offer from her in-laws because she desired the opinion of a woman in her age group, and Eila certainly qualified. She revealed that her parents were the ones who broke it to her, not her in-laws, and wondered if she would consider it. They wanted to be grandparents too although they stressed they would support her decision. She told her that she had some goals in mind and would like to start a family in five or so years. Eila asked about her husband's wishes and was told that he planned on being promoted in a couple of years and he presumed that would pave the way toward moving into a larger house and starting a family immediately.

Eila: Well, my goodness, how many children does this man want?

Mashé: I recall him saying three. I want two.

Eila: My, my, decisions, decisions. Rhial is pregnant and her husband got another woman pregnant; you don't want to get pregnant at the present time. Your husband, your in-laws, and your parents want you to get pregnant, and it could all be settled if you accepted a brand new big house, mortgage-free. I love this. I must admit: I am doing better than both of you, with a virtually stress free life. Seriously, now that you have refused his parents' offer he's determined to work twice as hard at his job and get that promotion sooner and twice as hard at home with you hoping you'll conceive sooner; and now you are on your way to the gym, goodness gracious. I do wish you the best of luck, Best Girl. I know what you are thinking, do I have any advice, or what would I do. I admire your determination to pursue your goals; you, Rhial, and I boasted about them all of the time while growing up and look at us—we are doing well. I meant to tell you I was promoted last week to Senior Supervisor. I have fifteen people reporting to me now and I am more involved with public works too.

Mashé: Yes, you should have told me. I am proud of you. Oh, that happened while I was staying with you.

Eila: Yes, and with all of the stupidity going on, we never really had a chance to catch up. Would you believe Mr. Lowell called me the other day to apologize? He said he would have done it sooner, but he was waiting for me to cool off. What was I thinking? Mashé, you just never know.

Mashé: (Clearing her throat) So true. One day I do believe you will forgive him. Now what were you saying about…

Eila: Right, I see two ways of looking at this. Number one, your in-laws have a lot of nerve. They're acting like a monarchy—King and Queen. Number two, a big investment must have paid off and they want to apply the money toward their only child; you and your babies obviously benefit from it too. Either way, I would take it.

Mashé: What?!

Eila: You are very principled. I learned my way around early in life as you already know, and some see it as not for the better; sometimes things that happened or didn't happen are beyond our control, but one could feel victimized. From your perspective, you have pride and it appears that you want to stay in control. From my perspective, I have had a different stack of cards dealt to me. I shall never forget the night you met Neil at that Cuban restaurant. He took one look at you and swung you onto the dance floor; now how often does that happen? Then at your wedding, he looked into your eyes and let the world know you were his.

Mashé: Eila, answer me this? That night at my birthday dinner, the guy that you walked out with, did you know he was with someone? (There is a long pause)

Eila: (Bold) Yes, I did, but I did not coax him. He was willing.

Mashé: (Sighs) Like you said earlier and I quote you, "He was being a man." I know you are familiar with the phrase, "Live by the sword." Please explain why you are traveling with a perfect stranger as though you were married to him. Why do you take on such risks?

Eila: Mr. Desmond is harmless and is a gentleman too. He was the one who suggested the trip.

Mashé: You'll remember that you almost went on an unexpected trip to the Bahamas with strangers. Guess who called NYPD to save you? Just one guess is all you have?!

Eila: Either you or Rhial?

Mashé: (Firmly) Close enough. Our friendship needs to be put on probation.

Eila: Are you serious? Mashé, why?!

Mashé: Because you don't care how you treat those who care about you. Lady, you have broken the code.

Eila: Code!!! Mashé what has set you off like this? I told you I have placed myself on the twelve-step program. I am now celibate. You want me to stay away from just day-to-day living—that is impossible. Now, Paul and I are friendly with each other and he pays for our dining out, going to the theater, and...

Mashé: The theater, you are becoming a little acculturated, Miss Wynston. Enjoy your travels and be very careful. I will miss you very much. I am still peeved at you, but there are worse things. You have an interesting spirit; try to contain it.

Eila: (Laughs) And you try to get pregnant so you can move onto a brand new house, scot free!

After that riveting conversation, Mashé was fully awake, so she washed up, put on her sweats, and rushed off to the fitness center on an empty stomach. When she arrived, the place was packed. Luckily, the stepmill had become available so she climbed on and began building her momentum. If her mother could see her now she would tell her she was shining like a brand new penny; she had worked up a good sweat. She rested for about ten minutes then she grabbed a couple of dumbbells, only five pounds, and pumped for a few minutes. After that, she went for the elevated treadmill. What a challenge that turned out to be. She put in a good hour of working out overall and then noticed some Pilates videos were for sale, and bought a couple. The main thing she loved to watch were those trained in Tai Chi and one day she might add that ancient method to her fitness repertoire. She thought about taking a dip in the pool but there were just too many people; she had to bear in mind that she wasn't the only one on spring break.

Having returned to her car, she briefly revisited her conversation with Eila. Apparently, Eila had been comparing herself to her and Rhial for years. Even though they lived on the same block, her world was distinctly different from theirs.

The bottled water she had brought was now empty and she was hungry too; fortunately at home there was a refrigerator still full of food, so she was about to put the car in reverse when her cell rang—it was Zora.

Zora: It's me. I heard you were on spring break. You must have some special plans?

Mashé: Yes, I am putting them together; what is going on with you?

Zora: I wanted to stop by and speak with you and Neil tonight. What time do you expect him?

Mashé: It's hard to say, he has some major, ongoing projects he has been working on lately. But come by at whatever time you like. I am leaving the fitness center now.

Zora: Fitness center, you work out?

Mashé: Yes, as often as I can. I would love to go to the spa right now but I would not want to over extend myself. Would you like to join me for an early dinner?

Zora: Certainly, I would like that. I wanted to talk to you two about receiving a gift from Donovan and me, a larger house.

Mashé: (Confused) Yes, Zora, my parents relayed your generous offer to me and we may need to decline.

Zora: Well, I still would like to speak with you two about it.

Mashé: I understand. As I said, Neil has been working longer hours recently. I suggest you contact him and find out what time he plans to come home tonight. Isn't Donovan going to come with you?

Zora: He's golfing today, nothing could get in the way of that.

Mashé: I see…I should be going; I am sitting here in these sweats so I had better go home, shower, and change; let me know what you find out from Neil? Also, I want you to see the wedding pictures; there are quite a few good ones of you and Donovan.

Zora: The wedding pictures are ready! Yes, I am anxious to see them. I will call you later on.

What is this little lady up to? she wondered. She hoped Zora reached her son because his presence would be important. It seemed her curiosity of whether or not Neil conveyed the "No thank you" to his parents was clear. With all the activity in planning their wedding, the opportunity to observe Neil's relationship with his parents had been minimal. They were a close-knit family, and as she thought more about it, maybe it would be a good idea to have the four of them meet and discuss it; in fact, her parents should be included. She thought more about Eila's comment of Neil's parents resembling a monarchy and considered it a point well taken.

When she walked into her house, she undressed and stepped into the shower. She could have stayed in there for the remainder of the day. Going to the fitness center was fun and tonight she planned watching the Pilates video. She began feeling some tightness in her thighs, which she expected since she had given her lower body muscles a vigorous workout.

The turkey with avocado and melted cheddar cheese sandwich was filling, but she wanted to make another one. The land phone showed a caller.

Mashé: Neil, are you all right? Yes, I am good. Yes, she called me earlier wanting to meet with us about their gift. Tonight is fine, and since I am off this week, it would be perfect. But I was concerned about you.

Neil: I can manage to leave at a reasonable hour tonight. Also there is some information I need to share with you. So I should be home around five o'clock. You have a dinner surprise planned for me and you'll be the dessert, right? Why are you sore? You…went to the fitness center. Lady, you are in fabulous shape. Fine, that is right, keeping in shape is very important too. How interesting you are. Yes, absolutely your parents should be there as well. Good. See you tonight.

Mashé: Mother, I was hoping you would answer. Is Daddy there also? Excellent. You are being summoned to attend a meeting at our humble abode, tonight at 6:00 PM. Have dinner with us too if you like? Oh yeah, the subject is a new house; Neil's mother called me and wanted to come over tonight and discuss it. I really do not know what she feels a discussion will bring, but I am trying to be polite.

Clover: Good. I am pleased that you are handling it the way you are, but my dear, you have yet to share your answer with your father and me.

Mashé: I said, "No thank you." I spoke to Eila this morning; she told me to go ahead and accept, think of it as a long-term benefit; I swear she amazes me sometimes.

Clover: Your friend has a point. But you know what? This whole situation may have some fascinating undertones. Like I said, if I were in your shoes I would have considered it. But you have a genuine right to your stance. I shall act like a lady and just listen, but please understand that I shall publicly speak up for you if necessary. As you know, our house is willed to you. We have four bedrooms and three bathrooms. So I would say your future looks bright, my dear.

Mashé: (Touched) Mother, you have given this picture a new perspective. I would rather not think about the will part, not now anyway.

Clover: Still, you need to be aware of it. Your parents are looking after you as well. You know it just occurred to me, I wasn't going to tell you this, but when I told Zora that your father and I gave the Wedding Suite at the Ritz Carlton to you and Neil as your wedding gift, she looked crushed. And the next thing I know was your father telling me that he bumped into Donovan at the carwash and was told they rented a Learjet for your honeymoon rendezvous. I thought nothing of it, though I have heard about the parents of the bride and groom competing with one another. I find it less than dignified and I refuse to engage in it.

Mashé: Let the drama unfold. I shall prepare a special dinner for us tonight; it could be a night you could actually share with your grandchildren one day. (They laughed out loud)

She noticed that it is almost 2:30 PM so she decided to take a nap. As she walked down the hall, her hips were feeling tight also; she thought she might have had too good a workout. She lay across the bed and fell asleep instantly. When she awoke, it was nearing 3:30 PM. She jumped up and rushed to the kitchen to look for the cookbooks her mother gave to her when she went off to college. While thumbing through it she thought of her mother's famous deep dish chicken pot pie. She put on her apron and gathered all of the essential ingredients. She took a whiff of the fresh garlic and cilantro and went to work. She started to boil the potatoes and roast the boneless chicken breasts. She chopped her celery and added sweet paprika. An hour went by and the house smelled like a bistro. She made eight individual pot pies and the crust had begun to brown nicely as she peeked through the oven glass. She pondered a while about what to serve for dessert; then it came to her. She made cute little lemon cheesecakes. Then, she made a huge pitcher of wine punch. It was almost 5:30 PM so Mashé hurried and dressed in a skirt and a matching shell top. This time she decided to wear her hair down and since she had the week off she called her stylist and made an appointment for this coming Friday. For some reason Jasmine came to mind. She had promised her she would contact her after they returned from Saint Thomas. She found her phone number and called her.

Mashé: Jasmine, guess who, it is me, Mashé. I wanted to see if you are free this Friday. I have an appointment with my stylist; you could make an appointment for yourself too. I love this woman—she has gifted hands—and what about having lunch afterwards? The honeymoon was over the top and I will explain that one. Neil is fine; his job keeps him busy. How about Gordon, he what?! And you said yes of course. Congratulations, when? Why next year? Right, it is important to have your money matters under control before you walk down that aisle. You work for the school system, so you are off this week too. I am going to savor every day. I just emailed her contact information to you. My appointment is for 10:00 AM. We should have lunch at the Marriott downtown; I cannot wait to see you, Girl. Bye.

Seated at the dining room table she waited patiently for her husband and guests. She found herself randomly writing down different phrases in her journal like working with little pieces to her poetry puzzles. At last the front door opened and they all walked in together.

Neil: This was totally unrehearsed; we all drove up at the same time. It smells delicious in here.

Mashé: Everyone should have a seat. Let's get this party started.

Zora: Chicken pot pie, looks good.

Donovan: Is that wine punch? I am definitely at the right address.

Clover: Mashé, you worked too hard. You are on vacation this week.

Mashé: I wanted to impress upon you that I can cook almost as good as you.

Clover: I'll help you serve.

Eugene: And I will help you eat.

As everyone was becoming situated Zora began by saying she wanted to go into more detail about the gift she wanted to make to her son and his bride. She said that some years ago they wanted to move and decided not to for many reasons. Mainly they loved the neighborhood they lived in so they decided to stay there. Now that they were older, moving into a larger house would be senseless. She said that she and Donovan would like to have grandchildren one day but they understand that Mashé wanted to travel and pursue some personal dreams of her own. She pointed out that she had ambitions too when she stared out. As she reminded Mashé she wanted to be a novelist and she had written some short stories but they had not been published. She pointed out that women have so much more empowerment and the chance to do whatever they want in this new century, which astounded her. She boasted that if her in-laws had offered to buy them a home, she would have jumped for it. Then she said that Donovan made a wonderful life for them. She said she respected Mashé's decision to wait. She said Neil told her five years as opposed to three years. There was only a two-year difference.

Clover: Yes, I told my daughter that I would support her decision and I would love to be a grandmother one day, but I can be patient. (Some grinned at that comment)

Eugene: Neil, what is your mindset about this? Is waiting five years too long for you?

Neil: (Cleared his throat) My parents asked me how soon we would start a family. Mashé and I talked about having children while we were dating, but nothing definite was said at the time. We have already dealt with the three- or five-year choices. I prefer three and she prefers five years (looking directly at his wife). I asked her if I got a promotion allowing us to afford a larger place in less than five years would she then consider starting a family, and she said that was possible.

Donovan: I have been more of a listener because I am just now being brought up to speed about this matter (Clover and Mashé glance at one another). Mashé, you have choices, and whatever they are, that's fine. I agree with your mother; I can be patient, although I love the element of surprise.

Mashé: Can I get anything else for anyone? I made some coffee.

Clover: I would love some and let me do it. You have done enough and it was all so good.

Neil: Absolutely. (Mashé gave her husband an cryptic look)

Eugene: So does this mean the offer is still on the table? (Everyone looked at Zora)

Zora: An amount of $1.5 million is available. Of course, you two may choose to do it on your own. I am just letting you know and Donovan is too since he is the one who did the investing. Neil, sweetheart, upon your promotion you two can apply this amount to your dream house. After all, you just got married and Mashé, I know how fond you are of this house. (Mashé thought to herself, Well, she sure did clean that up. Thank you, Daddy)

Neil: Mother and Dad, I love you. We are so happy to know that there is money there for us to use when we are ready.

Mashé: That is right; it is so generous of you. At this very moment, I feel so gratified. What a wonderful blessing.

Mashé brought out their wedding pictures so everyone could relive that remarkable day. They all exchanged different comments and laughter. It was approaching 10:00 PM, so their parents decided it was time to head home. It was good to see what appeared to be a challenge for Mashé end on a high note; everyone seemed satisfied, even Zora.

🍒   🍒   🍒

Neil: I am extremely glad that is over. What about you, gorgeous?

Mashé: I was beginning to feel like a pressure cooker. I did not want to feel torn between you and your mother.

Neil: Certainly not. You know that 1.5 million dollars added to what we could be approved for at some future date would be a Godsend. As I see it 1.5 million would not be enough for what you and I have in mind; however, we have seen some nice homes that fall in that price range.

Mashé felt so relieved to hear her husband utter those words. When she heard that amount she thought, "Is that all?" Like Neil said, they could use it now but they want their dream house to be even dreamier.

Neil: Mashé, did you hear me?

Mashé: Yes darling, I did. It's my first day off for a week and already I feel as though I went to work. I did have a bone to pick with you. All's well that ends well.

Neil: Let's hear it.

Mashé: There is no point. You have been completely cleared.

Neil: Are you speaking about the money? Listen, I had no idea what the amount was. Even if I had, I would have accepted it. I was taken by surprise. I knew my father had done well in a few of his investments, particularly when he chartered that jet to take us to Saint Thomas. He is not wealthy but he is well off without question, and I want to be like him.

Mashé: That is admirable, except you cannot get pregnant.

Neil: True, but I cannot wait to have a hand at it.

Mashé: Without question. So, what is the latest—you said you had some news for me?

Neil: I suggest you take a seat. There seems to have been a conflict of interest charge brought against our company, and Jamison might be relieved of his responsibilities, but not terminated. Apparently, Jamison has stock in a technology corporation that shall go unnamed and has profited well. This corporation is a sister company to us and there is a policy that states if we (employees) have stocks or are stockholders with a sister and/or parent company, we must report it. Jamison did not.

Mashé: You mean report it to the IRS?

Neil: Them too.

Mashé: Who blew the whistle?

Neil: Amber Vale.

Mashé: I must say, she is a busy girl. How did she learn of it?

Neil: She was in his office working on his laptop per his instructions while he was meeting with his boss and she read a fax that was being generated and recognized the corporate logo and proceeded to read it, plain and simple.

Mashé: "As quiet as it's kept." I knew she was not plain and simple. That is extremely unfortunate for him; as for your company, what happens next?

Neil: "The plot thickens." It is possible that it could go to trial due to the amount he earned. And the court must decide what to do with the money. Jamison has already retained an attorney and so has our company. It was reported that he does not want to release the money because he was unaware of the policy that I just mentioned. All directors and senior engineers are to have a closed meeting tomorrow morning. I am supposed to attend this meeting, and of course, Jamison is excluded. He is presently on administrative leave with pay. Now bear in mind he can still walk onto the premises but he has been locked out of his files, computer accessing, and related services.

Mashé: What about Amber Vale?

Neil: She is the main reason for all of this. She is an "eyewitness," get it?

Mashé: "Oh what a tangled web we weave When first we practice to deceive!" This one is from Sir Walter Scott.

Neil: How insightful of my wife. So, you believe Jamison is unworthy?

Mashé: Maybe I should wait until I learn what the judge believes. I must admit I felt he was calling upon you too much. I would never want to interfere with the details of your job but he seemed to enjoy delegating.

Neil: You hit the nail on the head. Behind his back people were calling him the "Delegator."

Mashé: So who is in charge of your operations now?

Neil: That will be announced at the meeting tomorrow by Jamison's boss, Evin Cole.

Mashé: What is he like?

Neil: He is aloof. Very sharp obviously, a no-nonsense type of person. I am confident that whoever is chosen to lead will be a sound choice. Evin will carefully see this one through.

Mashé: (Optimistic) What if you are the chosen one?

Neil: I thought about it; imagining how I would enforce the programs necessary to go forward. Sweetheart, this is why I chose this field; it is forever evolving and changing. No stagnation allowed. One must pursue progress with precision.

Mashé: You sound like you are in charge already. To me you are the most qualified, so should they call your name, just be cool and rule.

Neil: Listen to you, Girl! Seriously, there are other qualified people as well wanting to hear their names called. I have been checking out your cute outfit; it looks good on you. Now, you say you felt like you went to work today. Tell me about your day?

Mashé: I went to the new fitness center, the one near our house. It is so well equipped with the state of the art merchandise. I worked out for over an hour.

Neil: (Concerned) What did you wear?

Mashé: My sweats, why?

Neil: Some creepy people can show up at these fitness centers and you are a beautiful woman who needs a bodyguard to guard your body.

Mashé: I know and that would be you. Don't worry about me, it was fun on the treadmill. I walked four miles; although I am a little sore so I am walking very carefully now. I plan to go maybe two or three more times this week. I also bought some Pilates videos.

Neil: How many times in your life have you been to a fitness center?

Mashé: While I attended U Miami, I went to the school's fitness center. What is the matter, feeling a little challenged?

Neil: Who, by you, no way! You already know how fit I am. However, Mashé, please, you need to be careful.

Mashé: The plus is it's twelve minutes away by car. Neil, if Evin decides you should take Jamison's position, how much of a pay increment would that be for you?

Neil: (Smiling) It would inspire me and you to look for a brand new dream house and then we could consider reopening the discussion about starting a family.

Mashé: (Musing) Oh…it would be that much?

Neil: Don't forget my parents' monetary gift. You can calm down, this would be a pro tem appointment, so I honestly don't know—it depends on their qualifications. Keep in mind Jamison has been in the game for quite some time and he may be reappointed; it's anyone's guess. (Mashé's utterance about wanting Jamison to be relocated echoed in her head repeatedly)

Neil: Hello, what are you thinking about?

Mashé: (Fibbing) I saw this dress, it was too cute, and it was only $500.00. I should have bought it. I am going to put these dishes in the dishwasher and you should get some sleep; you have a big day tomorrow.

Neil: You are a woman of expensive taste, more reason to start climbing that corporate ladder. Oh yes, one more thing, my Philadelphia trip might be postponed, otherwise pushed to another date this month; and the sister company's attorney they hired is going to come and canvass our entire operations, and interview some senior employees, which would include me. This guy has an impeccable reputation; I heard he's won all of his cases—his name is Chandler Tollare.

Mashé felt tingling throughout her body; of all the astute attorneys around, they had to go and hire him. She kept moving; at some point, she must tell Neil that Chandler was her fiancée before him. She thought, this has got to be a nightmare; I need to wake up. Neil told her goodnight and she told him she would be in there soon. She then reasoned that it might not be necessary: he was going to be there for just one day and then will probably not need to do a repeat visit. She would play it by ear. The next morning, Neil woke up earlier than usual and gave a quick kiss on her cheek before leaving. She pretended she was asleep, but she hardly slept at all. She reached for her cell phone, the time was 7:15 AM, and she wondered if her mother was up. She decided to wait another hour. She rose and looked in the mirror; her eyes were slightly red and tired looking too. She went to the bathroom and filled the bathtub to the rim. While bathing, her thoughts were scampering about. She wanted to disguise herself and go to Neil's job today, now that was just silly, or she could call Chandler and tell him her husband is one of the employees at Applied Systems, Inc., so he should recuse himself. She began feeling drowsy and fell asleep. When she woke up it was 11:00 AM. She stepped from the bathtub, dried off, and rushed to the kitchen to make a quick breakfast. While the blender was making a smoothie, she called her mother.

Clover: Good morning. I was just about to call you to say what a piece of work your mother-in-law is. Donovan didn't even know about that gift. I really like the way you graciously handled everything too. Your dinner was perfect. As we were driving home last night your father and I thought how interestingly it all played out. You were going to be given the money anyway; interesting how she had to throw in grandchildren. I feel I owe you an apology, well, because she had come across so unassuming to me and your father. Looks like I will have to go back on my word. What I mean is, when you do become pregnant I am throwing you the biggest, slam-dunk baby shower on earth; do I have your approval? Thank you! So you said you want my advice on something, yes of course, yes I am sitting down. I am sorry to hear about your husband's boss. Why is it a conflict of interest case, but that's his money? Oh I see it's against company policy; who did you say is representing Applied Systems, Inc. Mashé, no! First of all, I would wait until your husband comes home tonight and listen to what he has to share. I would not if I were you. Why should Chandler recuse himself? But your husband will not be on trial; he's just one of the employees there. Besides, it would be to Neil's benefit to be totally unaware of who Chandler is, particularly in this instance. Now, by just using common sense, I presumed they would meet one day, because my dear, it is a small world and you should calm yourself. Even when you two dated, Chandler was coming this way often for various cases he was trying. Very well, if you come to that bridge then you will cross it; do not bring the bridge to you. Are you feeling better, sure? Good. Take care.

Mashé had not banked on her mother taking a nonchalant position with her concern about Chandler meeting her husband. In the long run, it was an uncontrollable situation and she needed to ease her mind. She wanted to call Tia about her intimate dream with Chandler; then again she had already shared so many personal experiences with her and Tia was a forthright trustworthy person, but she'd better save it. For any new developments occurring, she would handle them herself. Moreover, she could always confide in her parents; they were the salt of the earth. Years ago, she bought a book about dreams; she would take some time to find it. The peach smoothie and hot oatmeal hit the spot and her soreness was gone so she headed back to the fitness center.

Once inside she decided to go for the punching bag; it was her first time. If Neil were here, he would probably try to talk her out of it. A fine looking man by the name of Gian approached advising her not to go for the granddaddy punching bag and directed her to the electronic punching bag.

Gian: Forgive me for intruding but you could seriously strain your biceps and triceps if this is your first time with the granddaddy. My name is Gian Luca, I am the Senior Trainer here. (Mashé found herself starring at his biceps and triceps)

Mashé: Y…Yes, I am Mrs. Rollins. Do I need to warm up first?

Gian: Mrs. Rollins, it is a pleasure. Well, you could warm up with this electronic punching bag and do kick boxing too. Let me show you how it works.

Mashé felt like a child. She was glad Gian came to her rescue because she would have punched the granddaddy too hard and she would have ended up looking and feeling like blubber. She didn't notice him before; his courteous manners made all of the women feel comfortable. He would ask permission to touch your shoulder or hand to demonstrate a movement or exercise.

From the punching bag, she went to the pool. Since she planned to go to her hair stylist on Friday, it would be a good idea to work out in the pool. The water was filtered and sparkling. Mashé had been swimming since she was six. She, Rhial, and Eila would head for the pool at the YWCA every summer until they started high school. While doing her backstrokes she imagined her Best Girls there with her. Looking back had her smiling. She could see Eila going to the deepest end and diving in and then popping up, making it all look so simple, and Rhial would just float; Mashé was so amazed by that she finally learned how to float also. Being in the water relaxed her, while at the same time she was exercising practically every muscle in her body. After she went to the showers and dried off, Rhial came to mind, so she decided that she would call her the moment she returned home. Having had a light breakfast made her want to have a good lunch. Opening a box of angel hair pasta, she decided to make a cold pasta salad, so while the pasta boiled she called Rhial.

Rhial: Mashé, I have been thinking about you so much. Yes, forgive me, I know I said I would call you but there is nothing to tell. Halvan prefers to wait until our child is born; he said that it's best. Okay, though, hear me out. I shall be there next week and I have decided to stay with my parents until the baby is born. I have told my doctor and he has referred me to an obstetrician there in the Bay Area who is highly recommended. I sent him an email and once I arrive, I am going to connect with him. Yes, I know I sound content because I have made up my mind that I need to be with family. I cannot change him and he cannot change me. No, I have not told him yet. I have it all planned and please do not tell anyone, not even Eila. The day I am to leave I will send him a voicemail, a nice long one telling him what I feel is best for our unborn child and me. My plane leaves this coming Sunday at 1:05 PM Eastern Time. I have a couple of trunks I am sending ahead to my parents' house. I have told them; my father was incensed, to put it mildly, and he said he wanted to have a heart to heart talk with Halvan once I come home. Listen, Mashé, this is what I predict. He has some misgivings or hesitations and if I am not there he may come to terms with the obvious. I don't know what the obvious is; he has not taken the test. I realize my mistake with our relationship. I have been a human sponge; whatever goes down, I have just soaked it up instead of challenging or questioning. I have to stop settling (she began crying). I cannot wait to see you, Mashé. How is Neil doing? It must be nice to have a hard-working husband. I promise to do that and the moment I arrive, I will call you. Do you think I should? All she is going to say is, I told you so. That a fact? Where is she going? To Easter Island, the South Pacific, with a White man. I still wonder what happened with Mr. Hero Sandwich. (They laugh)

Mashé: I support what you are doing. You are so brave, Rhial, and I trust that all is going to work out fine. Also, if you want a mini–baby shower with just a few friends and family, consider it done. I respect that. I love you too. See you soon.

Neil walked in pumped up, looking for his wife.

Neil: Where are you?

Mashé was in the backyard working on a new flower garden, and rushed back into the house.

Mashé: Hi. I was in the backyard. So tell me how did it go?

Neil: There were two people selected—one to handle the supervisory side and the operations side. Guess who is in charge of operations.

Mashé: My talented husband. Congratulations.

Neil: I was not surprised because it appeared Jamison was placing me under his wing. No doubt, he is a knowledgeable man.

Mashé: Yes and he brought with that other qualities.

Neil: One more thing: I met with Chandler Tollare. He's pretty straight up. He said that he might need to decline from taking on the responsibilities of this case because he's getting married.

This news impacted Mashé in a way that was hard to process. She liked hearing about Chandler possibly removing himself from the case; however, the reason had a effect.

Mashé: Talking about expecting the unexpected…so what is next?

Neil: Well, for the present time he is their legal counsel, but he had to obligate himself to let all concerned know. There should not be a problem finding another reputable attorney; it's this man's track record that could put the fear in any opponent.

Mashé: (Pauses) All of this serious talk has made me hungry; let's have dinner.

Neil: As our meeting was adjourning, he mentioned that when he told Evin about his pending nuptials, Evin told him I was a newlywed and he wished me the best. It was interesting; he asked if my wife was an engineer too and I told him you were in education, and I definitely was not going to tell him about my wife, the poet.

Mashé: (Relieved) Definitely not.

It was Wednesday morning and she was still in bed. She found slumbering late very appealing. She grabbed her cell phone and called her mother to share the latest about Chandler and about Rhial.

Clover: It seems things worked out for the better. Sometimes we must practice keeping our lips closed. I called Trista yesterday, and we talked about her daughter's dilemma. Then again, she was so proud of Rhial's work with the City of Miami Beach; she said sometimes it felt like being on a seesaw, and she had some kind words for you.

Mashé: Did she?

Clover: Yes. She admired your decision to continue with your career plans. Even though she will welcome her first grandchild with open arms, she wished Rhial had done the same because she has so much potential.

Mashé: I appreciate her support more than she could realize. I told Rhial that she had to do what is best for her and her baby, and her due date is getting closer. Oh, but I have some news about Eila and please, keep this under your hat? Eila has been promoted to Senior Supervisor; did you know she worked for the State of New York? However, the secretive part is, she and a newfound gentleman friend are going on vacation to Easter Island, and to add a little twist, he is White.

Clover: To be honest sweetheart, a White man may be just what she needs. Your friend likes to take risks, be adventurous, so keep me posted. I wonder if Aunt Lennie knows of her promotion, I am happy for Eila and when I have a moment I will call and congratulate her aunt; she deserves credit for those positive points, whenever they happen.

Mashé: Eila told me she was going to tell her. Mother, I appreciate your tolerance with me about Chandler; this new development did make me edgy.

Clover: That's what mothers are for. I have prayed over your circumstances, from wedding to another. You are a strong woman, but of course, it runs in this family. When I think about us moving out here from Kershaw, South Carolina, I knew we were making the right decision for ourselves and for you. Do not get me wrong, I am proud of where I am from, but we wanted more and we felt we were entitled to it. I know your grandparents felt the same way. Circumstances are what they are.

Mashé: Mother, was teaching your first choice or were you interested in other fields?

Clover: I wanted to be a sculptor, and I was good at it too. Then again, I also wanted to eat, so teaching became my aspiration, and I taught myself to love teaching.

Mashé: This is the first time I am hearing this. I have to see your work; where…

Clover: At your aunt's house in her attic. She promised to preserve my work for me. I preferred to keep it to myself; however, your father knows.

Mashé: That explains the artwork collection in your office. Do you have a famous Black sculptor?

Clover: Yes. James Washington, Jr. He was born in Mississippi at the turn of the 20th century. I would now like to return to the topic of Chandler. I cannot believe I am doing this. He is still in your system; once you flush him out, his goings and comings should not matter to you. Mashé, I know he was your first love. Sometimes matters may begin but not end with the first one; take it from me.

Amplified (16)

Easter Sunday service was packed with colorful hats. It took a little effort but Mashé managed to encourage her husband to attend the service with her. She was dressed in a pastel blue silk chiffon two-piece suit with a matching spring hat, and Neil was looking fine in his dark suit, a soft blend of camel and angora mohair. The sunny day created a setting of newness; it was springtime and tomorrow she must return to her working routine. Rhial went with them. She wore a pink tiered maternity dress with pink accessories and instead of Mashé cooking, they decided to have brunch at the Berkeley Marina. Neil was fine with it as long as he arrived home in time to see the NBA game. The brunch had started, the crowd was there, and again the place was packed with colorful hats. Mashé told Neil that since he was a good sport she would prepare a plate for him. He thanked her but he still wanted to be home in time for the game. It was an amazing spread and Mashé just piled Neil's plate with practically everything that was available.

Rhial: He's not going to eat all of that.

Mashé: True, though I expect him to do well. Tall people have an advantage, and he works out, so to splurge once in a while is good. What about you, Mommy? What are you eating?

Rhial: I am going to splurge too. I have been meaning to ask. Let's see, it's been over two months—when can we project Mashé and Neil to be pregnant?

Mashé: You know that had been a hot topic until recently.

Rhial: (Curious) I see. Care to share the details with a friend?

Mashé: Oh I intend to. Please allow me to determine when it is best. What I have to tell you will blow your mind.

Rhial: Any word from Eila? I received her voicemail message about her trip. That woman is out of this world.

Mashé: To say the least. How are you feeling since you have been home?

Rhial: Physically I feel blessed and wonderful. Emotionally, my morale teeters. When I looked into my parents' eyes, I felt like a child and they just embraced me and made me feel normal.

Mashé: You are normal. You have an experience that happened near you but not to you. Your parents are proud of you and soon they are going to be holding a beautiful child in their arms to spoil rotten. (They return to their table)

Neil: Rhial, I think this is your plate. It looks like a meal for two. (They laugh)

Rhial: No way, here is mine. Your wife wants you to stay buff, so eat up. I have a request to make of you two. It seems appropriate; it's Easter Sunday so I would like for you, Neil and Mashé, to be my child's godparents. Do not be surprised. I have admired the two of you since that night at the Cuban Fantasía Restaurant where you first met; everyone near felt your connection. I would like for my baby to be exposed to two people who are so real with their love.

Mashé and Neil looked at one another and told her unanimously that they would be honored.

Neil: Rhial, what did Halvan say when you told him you decided to come home?

Rhial: To be exact, I placed a long voicemail on his cell phone indicating my distrust of him. I told him I deserve respect. As his wife, I said he is only to have children with me. I told him that I still loved him, however, I could not be with him right now. I insisted that he take the paternity test immediately and that our child should come to a home that is blessed and filled with love, not innuendoes, and confusion. To answer your question, I have a message from him but I have not listened to it; I plan to later tonight.

Neil: I was trying to imagine as a man, how a responsible person winds up like this. Rhial, the man has to grow up. I am sure you are aware that in the Black community the ratio is seven women to one eligible man and when people get divorced it becomes wider. I would not be surprised if he were here to be with you within a week. I am certain he is concerned how receptive his in-laws might be.

Rhial: True. My father cannot wait to have a chat with him. But you know, I don't need any more tension, no more.

Mashé: Your father knows that and he will keep a cool head; you have to believe that. So are you still determined not to know whether it's a boy or a girl?

Rhial: Yes. When that day comes, I want to have that newness experience. Still, I have been shopping for essentials, like a bassinette, baby blankets, and I bought this stroller; it reminds me of a little space ship; it is very compartmentalized.

Neil: It sounds like you are going to have a space age baby. Whether it's a boy or a girl, it won't matter to me because he or she will sit on my lap and watch the games with me. Which reminds me, ladies, it is about that time. I am going back for one more breakfast sausage; pardon me, ladies.

Rhial: It is very clear your husband wants to be a daddy. Tell me again how long you want to wait?

Mashé: About five years. Rhial, I am not going to be made to feel guilty. I want things to be perfect, as perfect as they can be for our children.

Rhial: Then plan on my baby bouncing on your husband's knee for a while; I can see him enjoying every minute of it.

After taking Rhial home, Neil took Mashé to an open house he saw publicized on the Web located in San Jose on Tierra Bella Ave. As they parked in front of the property, she asked what the asking price was and he said about $4,500,000.00. He said the objective was to gather information about the types of homes they would like to consider when they became serious about buying. Mashé was struck by his comment, "when they become serious," knowing he had been serious from the very beginning.

Mashé: We are going to require something like $3,000,000.00 after we use the gift from your parents should we want a house of this size, and it is magnificent without question. Just so we understand each other, there will be no pool.

Neil: Yes, your majesty. What is possible now is to take that money and buy a home within that price range; we could add on later.

When they entered, there were two staircases. The realtor explained that the house was once owned by some local entertainers and they had it designed for the purposes of privacy. Neil immediately said that that's a good idea when you are planning to raise a family. The realtor looked over at Mashé for some kind of reaction; she maintained her countenance. Mashé suggested that they take turns with the two staircases and then switch. When she reached the second story she saw what must have been the studio for one of the artists. She walked through, looking out of one of the picturesque windows, and was taken in by the scenery. She recalled a phrase she heard her father say once, "Being poor has so many inconveniences." She stepped into the master bedroom and there were so many different directions to go in decorating. She was hip to Neil's subtlety, so she went along with it, showing no resistance in looking. However, tonight she intended to ask him to start using condoms. Neil walked in behind her.

Neil: Are you ready to switch? What do you think of it?

Mashé: I think that anyone who is fortunate enough to buy this property is going to be very happy. I am curious as to why the previous owners moved away.

Neil: The agent said they were looking for a similar house in Southern California; they wanted to be closer to Hollywood.

Mashé: That should not be a problem for them. So let's switch. (When Mashé turned to leave, a couple of women recognized her).

First Woman: Pardon my staring but are you Mashé Boston, the poet?

Mashé: Indeed I am.

First Woman: See, I told you I recognized her.

Second Woman: I have your book here; would you autograph it for me? One of my favorites is "Wizard of Love." Was he fictitious or…

Mashé: (Interjects) Ladies, meet my husband, Neil Rollins.

They conversed with him for a minute or two. She had to side-step that question. When they returned to the car, they were both stirred by the likes of that house, particularly Neil.

April was Neil's birth month so Mashé decided to throw a surprise birthday party for him and since he liked the painting of the sensual mermaid she gave to him from Saint Thomas, she came up with a rich creation of her own to present to him at his party.

Mashé: Do you think you'll have room for dinner tonight?

Neil: What a question, how about you?

Mashé: No, I have dined sufficiently. What do you have a taste for?

Neil: You promised me some chicken enchiladas some time ago.

Mashé: Si, Señor.

Neil: I owe you an apology. I have yet to pick up your book and read your work. It seems like women are drawn to it; maybe that's the reason why I have taken so long.

Mashé: An apology is not necessary. I was planning to ask you had you read any of my poems? I want you to keep in mind that they are romantic poems, poems for lovers, so you would qualify. By the way, what about your NBA game you wanted to rush home to watch?

Neil: Right, I meant to tell you—I checked the schedule online again, the game is tonight. We're good.

Mashé: So where to now?

Neil: I have homework now that I oversee Systems Operations. I have an outline I started working on. It complements some of the applications Jamison implemented and I would like to make some changes to our technology solutions efforts to benefit the operational performances essential to customer expectations and satisfaction. This is a major objective Evin wants to see happen, so now it is up to me.

Mashé: I am the luckiest woman on this planet. I have a husband who is a genius, and cute too. Is the pay what you expected?

Neil: Since Jamison's position was divided in half, that changed my expectations, but I will bring home an impressive amount, enough to motivate me even more, and I have calculated on the net side that I'll bring home an extra $3000.00 a month that I can put aside for our dream house.

Mashé: Good things happen to good people. Congratulations! Have you told your father? He is going to walk around with his chest out, I can see him. I have been meaning to ask you, what do you want for your birthday?

Neil: I plan to call him and my mother tonight. It would be nice to have another engineer in the family—to keep that legacy going—as well as an artist or a novelist. To answer your question, whatever you want to give me and then double it.

Mashé: I…see. Consider it done.

Neil: Happy birthday to me! And you need to know this about me too; I love to accept early birthday gifts. (She glanced at him, smiling) Those fans of yours back at the open house, I spoke about not yet reading your material, and they have sparked my interest, "Wizard of Love," break that down for me?

Mashé: (Cautious) Break it down…let's see. When a man's sincere and indisputable love is completely enthroned and received by a woman, her mind, body, and soul have been impacted infinitely.

Neil: Basically, the brother blew her mind.

Mashé: In poetic terms, my darling, in poetic terms. If you find yourself unconnected to my material, it's fine. Poetry is to render another realm of thinking and perceiving and once you are there, it becomes an artful experience, for certain. I am convinced it is not for everyone.

Neil: Pardon me…but did you just get me told?

Mashé: (Defensive) I answered your question. Whenever you talk about your job, systems engineering, I do not always follow or understand the terms you use; still, you make it all sound so interesting because the words come from your lips.

Neil: Lady, you just aroused me—that was moving, now when you talk like that, we need to be at home. Which reminds me, we need to get back on schedule.

Mashé chose silence to that last comment. This past week had given her new insight on how to conduct herself around her in-laws and her husband. She would prepare herself for any and all comments referenced to childbearing and be gracious, as her mother stressed. It was exciting to plan on having children; however, her maternal thoughts and feelings were not at the forefront at this time. When she was putting on her Easter outfit this morning, she noticed that her workouts had begun taking effect. Even when she and Jasmine met at the salon on Friday, Jasmine commented on how healthy she looked. Most importantly, she wanted Neil to notice. They arrived home just in time for him to change clothes, grab a lite beer, and park himself in front of the flat screen. She motioned her way to the kitchen to start his dinner and thought of timing him on when he was going to resume working on his outline for his systems engineering plans.

🍒   🍒   🍒

Mashé sat in bed with her flat screen muted working on her college lesson plans for the week. She imagined what tomorrow would be like. They would be a little fidgety, though once the lesson began they would become calm and focused. She began revisiting the time when she, Rhial, and Eila went to summer camp at Yosemite National Park. They were thirteen years old and they shared a cabin together. On this one particular day while on a nature walk they separated from their group to watch this humungous waterfall. It was so loud and it seemingly had a hypnotic effect on them. In an instant, they heard a growling sound. It was coming from behind them, and it was a California Black Bear cub. They froze, knowing that when they saw a bear cub or baby fox, the mother was nearby. Mashé recalled saying, "Let's walk softly," and Eila said, "In order to do that we'll have to pass by the bear cub, see the ledge, there is only one way to go." She tried to convince her friends to move anyway. So she just started on her own when the mother appeared. That was a big bear. Mashé thought if they did not seem like a threat to her cub, then maybe they could make a run for it. Rhial called out to her, "Don't move any more, Mashé." The threesome and the mother bear stood a few short yards from one another, and then she started to roar and growl louder and louder, when without warning she and her cub backed off. Their Camp Counselor had come looking for them and she had a technique that distracted the mother and her cub away. What she did they would never know. That was a time when Mashé came to terms with surviving, as did her friends. Rhial and Eila kept telling her to be still, as she was trying to figure a way out. Neil joined her in bed.

Neil: That was a very good game; you missed it.

Mashé: I was doing my homework, how about you?

Neil: After I ate my delicious chicken enchiladas, I went right to work. I can continue tomorrow. I just needed to have something to put on the board for tomorrow's staff meeting. Are you done with yours?

Mashé: Almost, you look and sound anxious.

Neil: Exactly, and you get all of the credit for it.

Mashé: I have a request and I want you to still be madly in love with me after I ask it?

Neil: Mrs. Rollins, I am listening, why all the suspense?

Mashé: I want you to wear condoms from time to time because I don't want to be dependent on contraceptives like the morning after pill.

Neil rested his head against their mahogany wood headboard and closed his eyes. Mashé was expecting a response; she looked away, thinking what else she could say.

Neil: I have The Night Light Glow in the Dark, the pleasure pleaser, the strawberry, sugarplum, or chocolate scented; all of the above are latex rubber condoms. I would not recommend lambskin.

Mashé: You are serious, Glow in the Dark? I want to see that one.

Neil: Then you'll need to turn the lights out. And once the seal is removed you know what that means.

Mashé: Why were you holding back? Never mind, do not answer that. Do you have just the traditional ones?

Neil: Yes. And I confess, I prefer not to use them, but anything to please my beautiful wife.

🍒   🍒   🍒

The next morning they awoke to a spring shower. Neil grabbed his cinnamon toast and off he went, with Mashé right behind him. Before going to work, she stopped by an art supplies specialty store and purchased some oil based paints, a painter's caddy, acrylics, a linen canvas, and paintbrushes for her husband's surprise birthday gift. She rushed back to her car and made it just in time for class. As she predicted, her first hour class was restless so after welcoming everyone back she opened up with a few of William Shakespeare's famous quotes. She began with, "The course of true love never did run smooth," "Love is a wonderful, terrible thing," and "this above all: to thy own self be true." She asked them to divide into groups and share their interpretations. Afterwards, she asked had they done their Spring Break Assignment of selecting an ancient tale that pertained to romance and/or drama. They unanimously said, "Yes." She told them she had been anticipating their readings, so following the group interpretations of the Shakespeare quotes each student would present before the class and give his or her perceptions. As Mashé always knew, the instructor was not the only teacher in the classroom; students were informative as well. She had many advanced thinkers in her classes. Their analysis of various works from centuries past to the present made for a stimulating academic experience, and now with the semester half done, she observed how so many of them had become more polished and a little character development had taken place too. This was why she chose English Literature because it undeniably transcends one's ability to grasp the meaning of creative writing; and this applied to any culture or society.

Staying in for lunch again meant working through lunch. While grading papers she logged onto her email account and sent an email announcement to a few people inviting them to Neil's birthday party. Luckily this year it was on a Saturday. She called the same restaurant that catered their wedding reception and placed a very healthy order. She had a brainstorm and called Applied Systems, Inc., and the receptionist recognized her voice immediately. Mashé asked him to name those closest to her husband in his unit, she was throwing him a surprise birthday party, and she also extended an invitation to him. The receptionist, whose name was Amel Lyons, said he would send a special email announcement only to those specific people, and promised to keep her posted on who would come. She had already invited their parents. She was feeling great about this. She then thought about her friends Rhial and Eila, and could not leave out Jasmine and Gordon. Her cell phone rang and without looking she answered, thinking it was Amel.

Chandler: (Laughing) Who is Amel? It's me. Are you at lunch now?

Mashé: (Reserved) Chandler, you took me by surprise, are you in town?

Chandler: Yes. There is a case that has summoned me. Applied Systems, Inc., a highly recognized engineering group. I have been interviewing for the past two days. I thought of you of course, so I called to hear your titillating voice and for another reason.

Mashé: I am listening.

Chandler: I am getting married to a kind and gracious woman named Poeme Ettles.

Mashé: Congratulations. Love is in bloom.

Chandler: So it seems.

Mashé: Her name is special; Poeme, it means poem in French.

Chandler: Yes it does. I was taken aback by that, Mashé. You are a poet, whom I was to marry. Something happened and then I met her. You have never told me your husband's name.

Mashé: It is probably best. It has been a stiff adjustment for me, Chandler. The experience you, Eila, and I endured made a sizable impact and we are overcoming it…

Chandler: (Interjects) Speak for yourself, Mashé. I had to explain to my fiancée the events that preceded her. She and I are working to go forward.

Mashé: As you should and I strongly feel, we are the better for it. My afternoon class is about to start. I can imagine your parents are excited?

Chandler: Very much, when did you last talk to Eila?

Mashé: It has been a week now…she and a friend are vacationing on Easter Island.

Chandler: Grass does not grow under her feet. I hope you don't mind my asking you about her?

Mashé: Not at all. She is still my Best Girl, the one with the drama. It seems some of us carry tags.

Chandler: One of the many things I lo…I like about you, your perception about life is so healthy. You are inspiring. I suppose I should say I will not ever call or write you again. That I cannot promise. I have a request to make of you.

Mashé: (Poised) What kind of request?

Chandler: I am going to be near your campus later this afternoon. I want to see you one more time, Mashé. I will not attempt to make any contact with you. I am prepared to sit in my car and enjoy the sight of you.

Mashé: Are you going to be alone?

Chandler: Scout's honor!

A few students stayed after her last class. They had some follow-up questions regarding her long lecture. They were so determined and she found herself pulling out references and reviewing her notes for clarity. They were there for nearly two hours. Her wall clock read 5:50 PM. She cleared off her desk and turned out all the lights. Walking to the parking lot took about three minutes from where she taught class. It had drizzled some earlier and she was glad it had stopped. In locating her car, she used her remote to unlock it; in so doing, she noticed a car unfamiliar to her parked two rows down. Mashé uttered, "He was serious." She stood there and looked directly at the driver's side window. The windows were tinted so even his silhouette was camouflaged. Although her disposition may have been unwarranted, she firmly gazed in his direction for close to five minutes. Afterward, she opened her car door, took a seat, started her engine, and slowly drove onto the boulevard. In so doing, she intermittently glanced in her rear view mirror. The car was still there, no activity of any kind, and it was like that until it was no longer in her sight.

She beat Neil home; her fingers and toes were crossed hoping to be the first to arrive. She had quite a few bags and they were heavy too but she managed. There was a message on their land phone; it was from Neil saying he would be working later than he expected—there were more details to handle and he would have dinner in his office. After hearing that she wondered was this the beginning: the late nights, early rises, rushing here and rushing there. Anyway, she definitely had dinner on her mind, so she quickly changed and planned on spending most or all of her waking hours alone. Moreover, she envisioned when that golden opportunity did come and they moved into their dream house, he probably would still maintain late hours and she would be there in that big house, barefoot and pregnant; then she uttered, there are worse things.

The closing of the door woke her up. It was 10:45 PM by her cell phone. She could hear him tiptoeing into their bedroom; he put pressure on the bed leaning over her to check if she was really asleep and then kissed her cheek.

🍒   🍒   🍒

On a Saturday afternoon, a week before Neil's surprise birthday party Mashé sat at her computer checking her email from time to time for those planning to come. Amel gave her the names of eight people and that worked because their house could only hold about thirty or so people comfortably, and his parents gave her names and contact information of some old friends from high school, people he had not seen in years. She was excited and Rhial promised to take his picture the moment he entered the house. She had not heard from Eila and would be surprised if she did make it; either way, she expected to hear from her. Her portrait was almost finished. She was painting again and she had no other thoughts on her mind while doing it, her great escape. During her mixing of colors, she decided to add more definition to the eyes. The portrait was of him and her embracing under a waterfall. His pronounced physique was well emphasized and she painted herself proud too; he did say, whatever she planned to give him for his birthday to double it. For years, only her parents and Rhial knew she was an amateur painter. When she saw that the mail had come, she looked to the heavens praying for her royalty check and there it was. She tore into it, the amount was $2,300.00 and as Von pointed out, with most of the sales going to e-books, the payment would reflect a lesser amount, but like everyone else she had adapted to the digital age.

Neil had gone to visit with his parents; his father had some work he needed help with; he would be away most of the day. Her husband still brought to her attention houses that were on the market. There was an adorable two-story house for 1.5 million dollars he shared with her by email the other day. The slight differences were it was a two story with one additional (third) bedroom and full bathroom. Her (their) house had two bedrooms and two full bathrooms, and her house had an attic and a basement that house only had an attic. She had to get accustomed to him doing this because she knew he sincerely wanted to live somewhere else. She hoped he would not be self-conscious when his colleagues saw where they live. Her cell phone rang; it was Eila.

Eila: Mashé, thank you for the invitation, we will be there, Paul and I. No I did not scare him off. So, I am allowed to bring a date? Great. Yes, Easter Island is magnificent. Did you receive the pictures I sent to you? Well, I am not surprised, because the connection for service there was poor. Listen, Paul said he was crazy about me. Mashé, I told you I promised myself I would stay celibate for a while, my twelve-step program. Your girl is determined and I owe much credit to you. Who did you say called you? Chandler! What did he want with you? He's getting married, really, to whom? Poeme, a pretty name. Are we invited to the wedding? I supposed you're right; that was crass. He asked about me.

Oh good, you told him I went to Easter Island. I am going to hold my tongue; there is nothing further I will say. I am proud of me too. When we come home, Paul and I are going to stay at a hotel. You know Aunt Lennie is not going to allow my boyfriend to stay in her home and I respect that. Do you think that is better, but I am not concerned about what others think. So you're saying I should stay with her and he should stay in a hotel. I cannot believe I am hearing this. I could consider it. You know what, since I am going to be there for a week following Neil's party, can you take a day off, play hooky, and spend the day with Rhial and me? I know she does not want a baby shower, which is dumb to me. I would love to put my hands around Halvan's throat. You know, we could have a surprise baby shower for her, just the three of us. She would love it. I am a thoughtful person from time to time, Mashé. I love looking out for my girls. It will be fine because Paul has to return to New York the day after. I have told him all about us. Do I love him? I will admit the only person I have loved so far has been Chandler. Mashé, I know you would not discuss it with me before and you don't now, but I must say this to you— you and I shared the same man unknowingly. He was handsome, confident, smart, passionate, and slightly arrogant. He was sexually infectious, a habit I found hard to break. Again, you do not need to comment, however, I am willing to bet, you would totally agree with me. I can see us in the far-off future as little old ladies talking about him; maybe you'll open up with me then. I have to go too. I am looking forward to this shindig, I know, 6:00 PM sharp. Take care.

Lately every time she finished a conversation with Eila, she wanted to run around the block a few times. It brought tears to her eyes when she spoke about him and of him. She was exact in her descriptions; nevertheless, she cannot and will not share what she and Chandler had with anyone. She contended that some promises were never to be broken and some secrets were never to be shared.

She was taking a nap when Neil came home. He leaped onto the bed telling her that his mother made a chocolate cake, one of her favorites, and it was in the refrigerator. She thanked him and tried to go back to sleep. He would not let her.

Neil: (Curious) Why do you smell like paint? What did you do today?

Mashé: (Drowsy) I cleaned the house with a new cleaner. It was the industrial strength kind.

Neil: You ain't never lied. C'mon, let's take a shower together. It has almost been a week, Lady.

Mashé: That's because you work so hard and come home so late. I hope that tapers down for you, for us.

Neil: Sweetheart, relax, it will. Mashé, wake up!!!

🍒   🍒   🍒

Their house was full of anticipating guests. The caterer was pulling up in their driveway; for some reason they were running late. Mashé asked that they arrive before the guests did, which would have been around 5:30 PM. Still, she was calm. Rhial and Eila helped serve everyone hors d'oeuvres to keep them from unsettling. Paul let the caterer in and he and Clifton, who was Neil's cousin and Best Man, helped bring the food in. The initial plan was that Neil's father was to have car trouble and wanted to have Neil's opinion; all the while, Mashé had told Neil she was treating him to dinner at the Cuban Fantasía Restaurant later in the evening and had invited his parents to join them, which she thought was clever. Since Donovan was to express misgivings about driving his car, they would return with their son, pick up Mashé, and then go to dinner. Mashé was in the kitchen, adding more decorations to Neil's birthday cake, when Eila walked in).

Eila: I love your little house and the decor is you in every way. You have become the little homemaker. The cake is perfect and the food smells so good. Mashé, some of those men your husband works with are fine. They are all engineers?

Mashé: (halfway listening) Of course, and they are all married; did you see their wives too?

Eila: Pardon me, I meant no disrespect, just making an observation. You haven't said anything about him.

Mashé: My opinion should not matter. If you like him I am happy for you; keep in mind we had very little to say to each other because I have been the little hostess, remember? By the way, where are you and Paul staying?

Eila: We're staying with Aunt Lennie, she was uncomfortable at first but she likes Paul and he offered to help her with the things that needed a man's touch around the house, can you believe that?

Mashé: That sounds good and I know just having you home for a while makes all the difference in the world. You and Rhial have kept it together for me around here. I am so grateful; it's kinda funny, when you plan an event in your head, you clearly see what you need to do and you expect it to flow the way you thought it through. The caterer was late; now, what if Neil had driven up? I hope I have ordered enough food.

Eila: Neil is going to be so surprised. There are a lot of people here so if we run low I can send Paul and one other guy to pick up more food. Hang loose, Mashé, it's a Saturday night.

Mashé: True. Eila...I am glad you are here.

There was a whimper here and there when Rhial walked in and became curious as to what the matter was, and the threesome then hugged each other.

Rhial: Are we all doing okay in here? Your house is live, girl, and I love the music, "old school." I have been keeping a look-out.

Eila: Not if you are in here.

Mashé: Ladies. I am supposed to receive a one-time ring from Donovan…and there it is. Let's close the drapes and have everyone huddle in the living room.

Rhial with the camera was in position. Everyone was quiet and they could hear Neil and his parents about to reach the front door. They walked in and everyone said, "Surprise!" Rhial took his picture at the moment of entry. Neil stood in place trying to collect himself. Mashé stayed out of his sight on purpose. His parents told him to keep walking—they had done their job and now they wanted to eat. Mashé's parents walked over to him and had everyone sing happy birthday to him.

Neil: Something smells good, Mashé did you cook all of this food? And where are you?

Mashé walked out holding his homemade birthday cake. He told everyone how he was definitely unaware of this and it was good to work with people who knew how to keep a secret, which got a good laugh. When he saw his classmates from high school, he asked how they knew about his party and they told him to ask his parents, and his parents said to ask Mashé. He turned to Mashé and gave her a staggering kiss, and Rhial took a picture of that too. The music was amplified again and everyone partied. Clover asked Mashé to meet her in their bedroom.

Clover: The gentleman that came with Eila seems nice. Is he the one she went to Easter Island with?

Mashé: Yes, he's an accountant where she works.

Clover: I have to hand it to your friend; she attracts some interesting men. I gather you two have talked.

Mashé: Yes we have. She said she was upgrading herself in more ways than one; as you can tell.

Clover: Did I tell you I dated a White man once?

Mashé: What?! You. So who was he? What happened?

Clover: We met in college. It was the early sixties so inter-racial couples appeared in spurts; nonetheless, we were still in the South. His name was Gavyn McDaniel and he was a White man—Fine. We dated close to a year.

Mashé: Yes, but what happened?

Clover: Your grandfather was very concerned for me and insisted that I break up with him. You might remember how stern he was. Your grandmother, the writer, the artist, took a neutral position.

Mashé: Mother, that almost sounds like a sad story, but wait, you and Daddy met in college too.

Clover: Your father came later; I was in my junior year then.

Mashé: It sounds like you were in love.

Clover: We were and I will let you in on a little secret, I took a mound of clay in my hands one day and sculpted a bust of him, one of my best jobs too. It's with the others at your aunt's house.

Mashé: Mother did you two ever…

Clover: A lady never tells, and keep in mind that when I met your father I fell in love again and I am still in love.

Mashé: It is hard for me to picture you back then with someone other than Daddy who was… Would you mind if I wrote a poem about it—no one need not ever know it will be about you and Gavyn.

Clover: You have my permission. Also, I wanted you to know that this party is swingin', a term from my generation, but your father and I are going home now and let you young people do it up right. I hope he likes the gift we bought him. Let's talk soon.

She finds that poem she had written tucked in an envelope of a sleeve in her photo album. The paper had yellowed considerably but she could still read it:

We met in our prime at a very tumultuous time. White vs. Black, Black vs White
How were we to go forward when they did not see us in "a good light"?
There was no shame in loving you or your loving me
My arms longed to reach for you like the branches of a mighty oak tree
I can see us now making sweet honey like a honeybee
The flowers around us were in full bloom, they were
of many different colors that anyone could clearly see
My being and your being were the same, Two people
from the South; you had the courage to love me and love me well
this should have been a story for our grandchildren to tell.

The party was going at a steady pace. Neil and his classmates were revisiting memory lane and one of them mentioned prom night as the night he became a man. The Best Girls were in the next room about to explode with laughter; maybe he had too much to drink. At this point, Mashé went over to Neil and asked if he would like to open his gifts. He agreed; he looked like he had had one too many but he was still behaving in a cool manner for a thirty-three-year-old man. Everyone was called over to watch him open his gifts. His parents asked that he open theirs first so they could leave. He found it and lifted the lid, it was a high definition camcorder, state of the art, just marketed, and he loved it. Since Clifton offered to take them home, Neil had just offered to walk them out when the doorbell rang. Mashé thought how strange—it was almost 10: 30 PM. Neal opened the door and it was Halvan. Eila and Mashé looked at Rhial, who seemed cool. Mashé remembered that Neil believed he would show up, but not necessarily at their house. Mashé stepped forward and invited him in. Neil said he would he back in a second.

Halvan: I normally do not crash parties, Mashé, but I understand my wife is here.

Mashé had him follow her to the kitchen and in so doing she casually introduced him to a few guests. Having made eye contact with his wife, Halvan paused, and Mashé motioned for him and Rhial to meet in their guest bedroom. Mashé looked back at Eila, who seemed to be controlling herself. What was to happen next, she wondered? When Neil returned he excused himself from their guests and found Mashé in the hallway. She whispered to him that he was right about Halvan and that they were meeting in their guest bedroom. They reluctantly asked Eila to watch the fort so to speak while they returned to their company.

Neil proceeded to open his gifts and time went swiftly. Paul asked where Eila was and Mashé pointed him in the direction of the hallway, near their guest bedroom. They were on pins and needles waiting for something; the quietness made them feel awkward. Mashé thought this would be a good time to present her gift to Neil. She thought of doing so in private, due to the slight nudity, but it was artwork and it was done in good taste. She announced that she did an oil painting in honor of their union. Just then Rhial and Halvan walked out hand in hand with Eila and Paul behind them. Rhial wanted to serve Halvan a plate, and she gestured to go ahead. She whispered to Eila asking what happened; Eila just threw up her hands. Neil went ahead and removed the wrapping and there it was a 5' X 6' portrait of the two of them. The colors she used were blue, silver, white, sienna, and gold. They stood face to face embracing—a three-dimensional depiction softly showered by a private waterfall. Her hands grasped his muscular arms and her head was cradled in his hands. Neil was speechless and then he said looking at this painting made him want to return to Saint Thomas. He and two others took it and hung it on the wall in their den. Mashé asked Eila to serve birthday cake to everyone and to change the CD selections. The momentum continued with more food, dancing, and singing. Rhial and Halvan walked into the kitchen to speak to Mashé. Eila was with Paul in the living room dancing.

Halvan: Mashé, again pardon my intrusion but I had to find my wife and speak with her. She has agreed to return with me to Miami Beach. We are going to leave this coming Wednesday.

Mashé: There was no intrusion on your part, Halvan. I certainly hope everything is working out for you two. May I suggest that she not leave so soon? Rhial, you said you wanted to hang with us. Can you put it off until next weekend—you are pregnant. You really should take it slow.

Rhial seemed anxious to agree.

Mashé: Great. I know you probably want to rest; maybe you had better take her home. Halvan, where are staying?

Halvan: Hopefully with my wife and my in-laws.

Mashé: (Concerned) Yes, hopefully.

Rhial told her Best Girl she would call her and Eila tomorrow night so the threesome could plan a day together. Then in came Eila and Paul.

Halvan: Eila, good to see you again. Hello. My name is Halvan Sanders.

Paul: Halvan, I'm Paul Desmond, Eila's boyfriend.

Mashé: Eila, I was just telling Halvan that Rhial, you and I will be planning something soon so he is going to postpone taking her back to Florida on Wednesday.

Eila: (Pretentious) Rhial, you just got here. Thank you, Halvan, we haven't been able to catch up on anything for some time.

Shortly thereafter, the guests were asking for more birthday cake and drinks. Eila, Rhial, and Mashé went to the den for privacy.

Eila: Please understand me given your condition, but Rhial, you cannot be serious. You just got here. You need to stay in California period. Your husband cannot expect you to bow down to his every whim. No woman should do that. It is so difficult to be in the same room with him.

Rhial: I appreciate the points you and Mashé have made and as you can see he made up his mind to come for me.

Mashé: (Sighs) Rhial, I am speaking for myself. You need to be secure in one location right now. Are your parents actually going to allow him to stay in their house? Let's take it to another level. I am glad they had a prior engagement because otherwise, they would have been here and I could just imagine your father's reaction upon seeing his face at my door.

Eila: Right, let alone my reaction.

Mashé: Thank you, Eila, for not showing out. I wanted this to be a pleasant celebration for my husband. So much is happening on his job and he needed this.

Rhial: What is going on at his job?

Mashé: I should not share too much because many of his colleagues are here, as you know, but he has taken over some of the responsibilities of his boss's job. An investigation is going on. It has nothing to do with Neil, but things are just upside down at the moment. Please keep this to yourselves. (Rhial and Eila both promised) Rhial, you should call your parents now and tell them that Halvan flew in to see you and ask if he could stay the night?

Eila: The decision is yours, Rhial—send him back home!

Rhial: I have already called them. I am waiting for a response. I let him do all of the talking while we were in your guest room. I respect your household and anyway, arguing won't solve this situation. The baby has been very active tonight so we should go home and wait there for my parents. Eila, when do you leave for New York?

Eila: This coming Friday morning early and I am going right into work when I arrive; my desk is full of work to do. Let's try to do something this Wednesday for our outing and have some fun for a change.

People gradually began leaving around 1:00 AM and Mashé was so happy that it was about over. She had been hyped up all week planning and coordinating without him knowing and she gave Amel a generous helping of food for coordinating the contacts from his job. She waved good night as they walked out one by one, and she was so relieved because there were so many directions it could have taken. She vowed to herself to wait many years before planning another one of these.

Paul and Eila were the last two remaining guests. They stayed about an hour and the four of them talked about several things in relation to work and politics, and Eila and Paul had nothing but good things to say about Easter Island and recommended that Neil and Mashé make a point of going since they were not having children in the immediate future. Neil wondered where that came from; nonetheless, his comeback was that he wanted to start a family within three years and that his wife wanted to wait five years from now. He told Paul that somewhere in that two year difference—that window—there may be a breakthrough. Eila glanced at Mashé with roused curiosity.

Then the conversation unsurprisingly shifted to race relations. Mashé and Neil said living in a state like California gave them exposure to people from all over and they imagined it was the same for him being from New York. Paul agreed and said when he met Eila for the first time, her color was not the main attraction, but her personality and boldness were. He had told his parents about her; he said they believed it was just a passing phase, but he pointed out to them that there was no experimentation going on—he enjoyed her company. Eila looked to him and smiled and Mashé noticed how relaxed and poised she was; she perceived something new on the horizon, couldn't put her finger on it, and despite all that had happened recently, this relationship could be an upswing in progress. Paul and Neil got along well, acting so cool. As he and Eila were leaving, they were given some birthday cake since Eila claimed she was never given a piece. Both were looking forward to Wednesday. Neil closed the front door and locked it, then walked over to his wife.

Neil: How did I deserve you?

Mashé: I think the same about you.

Neil: Everything was outrageous—bangin'. Did you make that cake from scratch or did you get some help from Barbara, Betty, whomever?

Mashé: Very funny! I was the only woman in my kitchen, got that!

Neil: Thank you, Lady. I loved everything you did. Now tell me this, when did you have time to paint us? It took me some time to process it—you are a gifted woman. We need to open up a gallery somewhere and show you off, I'm serious. We may need to take that mermaid down. And you are kinda naughty too. That I like. Come to think of it, we did not have the time to experience that private waterfall.

Mashé: That's why I chose that particular theme. However, it may have been a blessing because Saint Thomas had us living on the edge.

Neil: Definitely.

Mashé: I wanted to ask…your fellow engineers—you weren't too self-conscious about our little house, were you? Everyone seemed comfortable, this place was rockin'.

Neil: It was a flawless experience—it could not have been better. Sweetheart, I know that when the money becomes available you'll be ready to leave. Don't let thoughts like that enter your mind. It could have been a wigwam or a hut, so what, if you are in it, then it's home.

Mashé: Also, apologies on behalf of my friend Rhial and her husband.

Neil: Again, it's not your problem; Mashé let them deal with whatever they need to deal with. She looked well, cute and pregnant.

Mashé: You are cute too! Eila seemed tranquil this evening. I hope she puts her "fork in the road." He has her acting like a lady.

Neil: I am still on the fence about her. But tonight she was behaving like you said.

Mashé: You and Paul were acting like homeboys.

Neil: His vibes were good and you seemed to like him too.

Mashé: For her sake, yes. (Yawning) I am going to bed.

Neil: And I am going with you. I will help you clean up tomorrow.

Mashé: I have a cleaning service coming in tomorrow at noon, but thank you anyway.

Neil: Don't get me wrong, but I wanted to make a wager.

Mashé: I am in—what about? Or who?

Neil: It's who. You and your Best Girls as you say will not be seeing each other on Wednesday because she does not want to be here—she wants to be with him in Florida. If I'm right, my wife gives me her famous scented oil back massage and a shredded pork sandwich all in the same day.

Mashé: And if my husband is wrong, he is going to take me shopping for a new pair of black leather boots.

Neil: (Pondering) Very well then.

🍒　　🍒　　🍒

Neil obviously had a sixth sense. On Monday night Rhial called Eila and her on three-way to tell them she was going back to Florida with Halvan. Eila was livid; she could not believe her ears, but after a few minutes, she settled down and offered her friend blessings and the best of luck. Telling her it was a mistake. But then she said she'd made a few of those herself. Immediately she said I am taking the next red-eye out too. Paul had departed earlier that morning. Mashé asked Rhial how her parents reacted. Rhial said that when they realized she had made up her mind to leave with him, they decided to join her. Eila started to laugh hysterically and Mashé had to join in.

Mashé: Why didn't you just come out and say your parents were going back too?

Rhial: They caught me by surprise. I had to pinch myself. My father is very disgusted about our situation; however, my parents are very spiritual as you know and they said we're going to get through this.

Mashé: I believe that too. So are they staying until the baby is born?

Rhial: They said they will go week to week. My father will only have a few weeks to use, he said he's calling in for a "Family Leave." My mother has not worked in years so she might. It will be good to have them there, but under these conditions I am a little embarrassed.

Eila: Halvan should be a little embarrassed. I am more at ease now knowing they are going to stay with you—it makes perfect sense. Oh wait a minute, is he back in the house?!

Rhial: No, I told him to go and take the test, tell me the results, and then we'll talk.

Eila: Good, Rhial…you are starting to make more sense.

Mashé: (Interjects before Rhial) Eila! You are talking to a pregnant woman. Rhial, ignore her. I am hoping you will have someone with you when you start to go into labor. I am serious. If they need to leave for whatever reason, I will fly down and help in some way.

Eila: Me too—there is going to be a happy ending, you'll see.

Rhial: I know you mean well, Eila. I have been meaning to ask. Are you and Paul an item for real? He introduced himself as your boyfriend. What happened to Lowell? You said he was so attentive and…

Eila: I was not the only one he was attentive to. He is history.

Rhial: Too bad. How is it with Paul? I am just so stunned to see you with him, but if you are happy, so be it.

Eila: Like I told Mashé, I am taking this relationship slowly. We enjoy one another's company. He's intelligent, we eat out at some of the swankiest restaurants in New York, and he said he loved my Aunt Lennie. (Mashé expected to hear he loved her)

Rhial: Taking it slowly sounds like a good idea.

Tuesday morning, a very significant morning—the arraignment for the conflict of interest case involving Neil's boss. Mashé wanted to know every detail of the case moment to moment and Neil promised to call her whenever decisions or actions came down. The proceeding took place downtown at the Superior Court House.

Mashé had given her students an assignment in class to act out amongst themselves the roles in William Shakespeare's *The Tempest*. This was her first time experimenting with their ability to appreciate this work while acting. She professed that while her expertise was unequal to teaching Drama, her objective was to engage them in the plot using their imagination and visual perceptions. Allowing them the free will to compare one another's characterizations of Prospero (the protagonist) and Ariel (his helper), for example, promoted them to interact and share critical thinking.

Her students liked her unique teaching approaches and for the past several years, her student evaluations had been exceptional; she was sometimes considered a non-traditional instructor. All at once, her cell phone vibrated, so she stepped out into the hallway. Neil said that he heard that Jamison entered a not-guilty plea and because his defense attorney stated that this was the defendant's first offense, that he did not have a previous criminal record, he asked the judge to release him on his own recognizance as well as reduce the charge. Then the judge responded by reducing it to a misdemeanor charge, and Chandler Tollare passionately objected due to the seriousness of the crime. He said this involved an amount of 2.5 million dollars and he asked that the judge review the "code of ethics," respectfully saying upon the defendant's date of hire he signed a company agreement to reveal any and all personal activity relevant to company stock activity. Neil quoted Chandler as saying, "Basically your honor, he put the money in his pocket." Then Neil said, to everyone's amazement, the judge set his bail at 1 million dollars and within minutes, he had someone post his bail. Neil told her he had to go and would see her tonight.

Mashé returned to her classroom and they were in the midst of finishing. It seemed Chandler had put on quite a performance in court today. He used his persuasive prowess on the judge and landed points for the prosecution side. She mused when they were together of the times he had been very persuasive. On considering the fate of Jamison, she began feeling very concerned for him; aside from the fact that he had her husband burning the candle at both ends, his plight gave her an ill at ease sensation. In thinking about the morale of the company, she hoped that the reputation of Applied Systems, Inc., would not become a slippery slope situation. For some reason, her concerns continued to snowball; she thought how the local press would treat this case and she concluded that whether he was found guilty or not, the company had become seriously wounded, and how could they seek redemption? There was a faculty luncheon about to start, so she gathered her belongings and headed for the door. Just as she was about to lock her classroom door, she paused, uttering, I must talk to Chandler.

Contemplating what could happen as a result of the conflict of interest case had her pacing back and forth. She wanted to speak with Neil on what rebound plans his company was putting in place. In taking a seat, she reminded herself to calm down. She admired Neil's composed behavior through all of this yet, she was sure he was concerned for his company, his job, and the jobs of those he worked with. She read in the papers about companies much larger than Applied Systems, Inc., with similar cases undergoing lingering ripple effects. As she rubbed her palms together and stared at her cell phone, she squinched her eyes and called him.

Mashé: Chandler. Hello, are you able to talk? I don't mind waiting.

Chandler: Mashé, is everything good with you? You know when I recognized your number I was thinking, she's calling to ask me how long did I wait for her in that parking lot, well it was a long time. You looked well, very well.

Mashé: Chandler, as proficient as you are in the legal arena, please pardon my layman perceptions of the legal process, but I need to talk with you.

Chandler: Are you in a situation, in trouble?

Mashé: No but someone I know is and you are at the center of it.

Chandler: Me? How so?

Mashé: It is regarding the conflict of interest case against Jamison Leigh. (She heard papers being shuffled and a door closing)

Chandler: Mashé…What is his relationship to you?

Mashé: None. Although I know someone who is. Chandler, I understand you are the prosecutor for this case and I humbly and politely ask that you work something out with the defense, please?

Chandler: Would you like to meet and talk about it? Talking on the phone is ill advised. I am on my way out the door. You know, I would like nothing better than to be in your company, with all due respect to your husband and my fiancée. But I should not interface with you at all.

Mashé: Yes, I am aware and I could not forgive myself if I were to put you in a precarious position. I realize attorneys have a strict code of ethics that must be adhered to, as with any noble profession. I have tried to look the other way and all day I have been so tensed up…

Chandler: I have to admit, you didn't sound this troubled when you quit on me. What is your worst fear? Yes, I am the prosecutor, and I represent his employer pure and simple. The case cannot be thrown out, Mashé. Bear in mind, I am not the judge; do not forget about him.

Mashé: Oh he'll listen to you like he did today (oops!).

Chandler: What did you say? Mashé, the arraignment was today; were you there?

Mashé: No.

Chandler: I know you teach, so what time in the evening should we meet?

She heard Neil walking up the driveway.

Mashé: Chandler, I promise to call you tomorrow around noon. I want to collect my thoughts on why he needs to be vindicated.

Chandler: Vindicated! Call me and tell me where you want to meet. Oh, wait! I have an idea. I can drive to your school again and when you come out, I could follow you unless one of us drives the other? Let me know. Good night. (Neil entered)

Neil: Good evening, Mrs. Rollins. Baby…are you all right? You look tired—and I probably look tired too but it is very seldom for you.

Mashé: I am concerned for Jamison and you too. What about the reputation of your company, Has there been any press coverage yet?

Neil: I believe the press is very much interested in this. Thus far according to my sources, if you will, they have not appeared at the court house so far and probably won't until a verdict has been reached. What fascinates me is, the judge is the jury, and like I told you earlier today, this prosecutor tossed a wrench in the middle of the defense attorney's plea. I have the impression that when he reduced it to a misdemeanor, Chandler must have then interrupted stressing the seriousness of the crime and that's when the judge set bail.

Mashé: One thing you have to admit to, he appeased both sides.

Neil: Leave it to you to make sense out of a mess like this one.

Mashé: Your dinner is still in the oven; are you hungry?

Neil: What a question. You did notice I came home earlier this time.

Mashé: (Concerned) Why?

Neil: Since this legal issue developed Evin wants most engineering managers to hold off on some of the roll-outs that were slated. Luckily, my current projects are going forward, because we are the largest division, and Jamison the delegator had us spinning our wheels, but in the weeks to come, it's anybody's guess.

Mashé: I was concerned about those ripple effects. It seems that they have already started.

Neil: My hours are the same, but my coming home late as I have recently will lessen slightly. But you are reacting too early, if that makes any sense to you. One man's mistake does not reflect the good character of Applied Systems, Inc.

Mashé: Do you think this incident could uncover the antics of others?

Neil: A good question. That has crossed my mind too. There could be some extenuating circumstances though. Like I heard, Amber just happened to be there when the fax came in so, if she had not been there…

Mashé: Or had not revealed it.

Neil: Exactly. All things being equal, either way it was bound to surface. We have a bureau that is supposed to monitor that kind of activity. Did I tell you that it was configured to look like his 401K? You can count on the Prosecution calling them in.

Mashé: Jamison is fairly new, right? I remember you told me when we were dating that there were some unit heads battling for power.

Neil: You are right and they were removed. Jamison was one of the replacements for my former boss.

Mashé: Was Evin the one who hired Jamison?

Neil: I believe so, but not sure. He may have been recommended. Another good question. Mrs. Rollins, let's have you apply to Law School, poetry is too soft for you. What say you?!

Mashé: Perhaps in my next life. You seem content in spite of this predicament.

Neil: Well, I am not the one on trial and like I said, it is too early to speculate. Maybe I am a good actor, but to be honest this might be an incentive to start looking, but not right now.

Mashé: The ones from your unit who were here for your party—how are they taking it?

Neil: They seem fine. Actually, there is too much work to focus on. May I eat now?

Mashé: Of course.

Arriving an hour early was a good idea. She pulled out her legal pad and prepared a pros and cons list on the benefits of meeting with Chandler. After two minutes, she then tossed it in the wastebasket. Through the course of the morning she conducted her classes routinely and when the noon hour came she sat at her desk wondering if she had over-reacted; then she went ahead and called Chandler.

Mashé: Chandler, how are you? Yes, I am well. Listen, the last thing I want to do is waste your time. Well you know what I mean…Right. I'm savvy at what I do and you are savvy at what you do. It was an inappropriate demand. Yes, I am somewhat unsettled. This is Thursday, my shortest day. How long are going to be there? Fine—this is what we can do. My last class ends at 2:30 PM. You have an official invitation to my classroom. Come after 2:30 PM and I will meet with you because actually I need to understand the process of the court system. Then I will see you between 2:30 and 3:00 PM. Take care.

She was glad she choose her classroom as their meeting place; it was a neutral location as opposed to a restaurant or to siting in his car or vice versa. Since their break-up she had had trust issues with regards to herself and him. The resonance of his voice and his persuasive mannerisms still made an impression. She was pleased with herself because she did not succumb to his suggestions and then there might have been more suggestions to come. Although she appreciated him, she duly recognized that they were both in serious relationships. So her classroom would be her safe haven.

Inputting test scores on her database, she took a moment to stretch, and a familiar voice said:

Chandler: I need to re-take English Literature; I understand you are the best and I deserve the best.

Mashé: (Reserved) Mr. Tollare, welcome, take a seat anywhere.

Chandler: My mother told me to always sit at the head of the class, right next to the teacher.

Mashé: (Reserved) Good. You were obedient and it paid off.

Chandler: Mashé, in essence you have asked me to finesse the judge. I would be insincere if I told you that you were the first with this panicked approach. Usually, it involves a relative, a close friend, or something similar to a possible or developing relationship. Basically, you have denied all of the above. So, I resolved that you are trying to help someone unbeknownst to them because indirectly it will impact you. That is as far as my analytical skills will take me. I need your help with the rest of the pieces to the puzzle.

Mashé: Chandler…my husband works for Applied Systems, Inc. He is one of the lead engineers. I am fearful of the negative publicity that could plague the company due to the mistake of one person, and granted it could be more than one person, they just have not been found out.

Chandler: (Refined) Would you have done the same for me, I wonder. He is a very lucky man, however, that's a given. I won't ask you his name, although at some point it will be revealed. We have already crossed the forbidden waters of legal sanctity and I believe there are no active electronic devices in our midst. Since I am getting married, I may not be able to continue with this case. I will have to notify the court soon. Due to the delicateness of our past, Mashé, I cannot think of a reason to say I decline to help you and your husband. How did we come to this? Look at our story, your life and mine. I don't think we shall ever separate from one another. Sure, we are going forward, but I have to admit and you do too that we will be with each other always; if only with our thoughts and dreams. (She briefly closed her eyes with that last statement) I sit here now reliving how we loved and we loved hard, Mashé. I must know this, when you walked down the aisle on your wedding day, I was there too, wasn't I? When I marry Poeme, you'll be the other bride.

Mashé: Yes, Chandler, you were, it was as though you were trespassing the ceremony, but by the same token, I left the gate open. Please, I would like to return to the matter at hand.

Chandler: Certainly…we must never expose what is about to be said. I have enough evidence to convict him. This is a felony case that has not been reduced to a misdemeanor; the burden of proof is with the Prosecution and I can prove he is guilty beyond a reasonable doubt. My work is essentially done. Now, his attorney wants to plea bargain because the defendant claimed that an offer was initiated and he was misled, or he misunderstood; be mindful that there is an opportunity to make a motion to reduce his sentence providing he "turns state's evidence." Are you following me?

Mashé: I believe so; by Jamison sharing the name of an accomplice he would then be required to testify as your witness against the accomplice, and if this pans out the court could exonerate Jamison.

Chandler: "Perfect deducement." This would be a high-end crapshoot and essentially nothing has transpired out of order of the court except the request you made of me earlier to have him vindicated. For the future, for always, never ask a lawyer to manipulate a case.

Mashé: But Chandler, I was not requesting this favor of any lawyer, I was asking you.

Chandler: (Moved) I love your spirit. I also love practicing law.

Mashé: (Cautious) I have some information that might stick. On or off the record, I suppose that is up to you.

Chandler: Fine. I am listening, nothing illegal about doing so, but if I process it and apply it, that is another story and if it were found out, I would be required to name you, you understand?

Mashé: I do. A reliable source said that the fax in question, the evidence was configured to look like a 401K plan.

Chandler: How interesting. All I can say is, this is news to me, and I will clarify by indicating that tomorrow when we have our pre-trial conference the defense is expected to detail how they want to go forward with their plea bargaining. Rest assured, I have made a mental note of it.

Mashé: Time is ticking away. Shall we adjourn our meeting now?

Chandler: I have a request to make of you. I would like a dinner date with you, whether it goes to your liking or not; I believe I am entitled to this request, right?

Mashé: We have both been walking a tightrope this afternoon. Yes, Chandler, but it must take place at a time that is suitable for a married woman and a man who is betrothed to dine together.

Chandler: Of course, before dusk, agreed without question. So, our understanding is to await the verdict and to set a date to dine for the last time.

Mashé: Yes, but what if you notify the court that you plan to remove yourself from the case because of your...

Chandler: Not to worry. Good night.

Mashé waited until Chandler drove out of sight, and she was taken aback when she saw him in the same car that was parked on the campus parking lot . She presumed that part of being a stellar lawyer was to be shrewd in thought, literacy, and action. When she sat in her car and started the engine, she felt as though a heavy weight had been removed. As she drove home, she repeated to herself that this was the secret of all secrets. The entire time they sat before one another, she was aroused and her heart rate elevated too. To be in a room with the person she once intended to marry was nostalgic and it was not over, with their agreeing to meet one more time regardless of the court's decision. She had to hand it to him; he was the master of the "power of persuasion." Moving her thoughts back to the present, she decided to cook an unforgettable meal for her Neil tonight. When Neil arrived home and walked into the kitchen, she had made a seafood gumbo and was serving herself.

Neil: What is the special occasion? It smells good and it is only a Thursday night.

Mashé: (White lie) After our talk last night, it was obvious that I was over-reacting. I was concerned for our livelihood and I admit observing your demeanor helped me calm down. Like you indicated, it is too early to make assumptions.

Neil: Does this also mean that we can turn in early tonight?

Mashé: (Smiling) I love that idea, although this morning you indicated your team was playing tonight.

Neil: They won't miss me and I won't miss them.

Mashé: (Curious) What happened at work today, Neil?

Neil: I am going to meet with the VPs at the Philadelphia office next week. Evin received a call from them and they want to further explore the program I prepared. I leave this coming Monday. What's going on?

Mashé: (Mystified) I don't want to move to Pennsylvania! Just the same, I am very proud of you. I really have mixed feelings about this, Neil. Is Evin getting nervous?

Neil: If so, he's a very good actor, though that is a good question. Sweetheart, trust me, it is going to be fine. I know that you are a California Girl.

Mashé: I also know that if you are offered a job with a better salary you will go for it.

Neil: Like anyone would. May I eat now?

Mashé had been drifting off when she began experiencing a gentle warmth up and down her thighs. It was not a dream. She turned over to face him. He kissed her practically everywhere. She loved the sensations of his touch. In the midst of their making love, she imagined they were on that Learjet, elevating, going higher in more ways than one.

The sun was up and when she turned to reach for him he was in the shower, so she rose and went to the other bathroom. She relished the thought of it being Friday; subsequently her thoughts turned to the pre-trial conference that was to take place this morning. She imagined the worst outcome; then she imagined the best outcome. She heard her man call out, "See you tonight." She was excited for him and when he went back east she would find things to do. Working out with her Pilates video had paid off. Since she had been working out more often, her drowsiness had diminished and she had more pep in the mornings.

She had come extra early because she had prepared a quiz for her morning class and it required more editing. When she opened her door and placed her belongings down, her cell phone rang. It was Eila calling.

Eila: Mashé. How are you; can you talk?

Mashé: Yes for a few minutes. Where are you?

Eila: I am in Jacksonville, Florida, and guess who I just saw?

Mashé: I cannot guess, and why are you there anyway?

Eila: We are having a retreat. It is what many state employees do around this time every year. It is only for about three days; then we head back for New York. When Rhial decided to return with Halvan, I decided to join my co-workers. The weather is a little warmer and nicer down this way also. Anyway, remember you told me about Poeme Ettles, Chandler's fiancée? I saw the woman. Oh my goodness. She is almost six feet tall, not bad looking either. Her father owns a chain of restaurants here; I suppose that may have caught his interest.

Mashé: That is none of our business…and…

Eila: She drives a Maserati Ghibli S Q4. Girl, you should see this car.

Mashé: Well, good for her, Eila. Where is this retreat? You sound like you are in a vacuum.

Eila: I am in my rental car. Mashé, I did some checking up on her. She is a graduate of Jacksonville University. She was an English major. Now that is a coincidence, wouldn't you agree?

Mashé: Ms. Wynston, go back to your retreat and mind your own business.

Eila: Hold on, I see her coming out of this fashion boutique. You know the kind that sell only the finest designer apparel. I would love to go in there and "shop till I drop." Her figure is nowhere as nice as yours or mine, but I suppose she would pass in that department. And one more thing, she is flouncing that store bought hair; it's streaming down her back. Please don't get me wrong, that is her choice. However, I remembered how Chandler used to play with my hair, and he probably did with you too. It's hard to imagine him tolerating a weave. Ever since you told me he was engaged, I confess I had this burning desire to have a glimpse of her. I had no idea this would happen; this was purely coincidental. All right… now she has put her purchases in the trunk and she is walking over to this cute little bourgeoisie type of café; it looks like she is only going to order coffee.

I am going to drive a little closer so I can have a better look. Hold on…I have parked right next to her car; Mashé, seriously you should see this car. Hello, pardon me I was admiring your automobile; I have a friend in New York who just loves his. Does it perform as well as advertised, that a fact. I see…well as I was saying, only wanted to stop by and say how I admired your choice of motor coaches. My name, I am Ms. Wynston from up north and you are, Ms. Ettles, and what a lovely diamond too. Please pardon me but I must return to my retreat. I love Florida this time of year. Oh yes I graduated from U Miami, right, great school. Really! Did you like Jacksonville University? Well it certainly is a small world. Ms. Ettles, good to meet you and perhaps we will see one another in passing, perhaps New York, or even Paris, Oh, I love Paris—now that would be something. You too. Take care. Mashé, are you still there? She is an ordinary looking woman. Mashé, she is not Chandler's type, believe me. Wait, I saw her engagement ring; it is a flawless marquis, white diamond. It could be around, I would say, three carats at best. Also, she had that gel manicure. Have you ever tried it, me neither.

Mashé: Eila. What are you doing imposing yourself like that? Are you back in the rental car yet? Well, hurry up.

Eila: She doesn't suspect anything. It just occurred to me that she was wearing an Albert Nipon two-piece knit suit. I know that cost some money. I have to hand it to Mr. Tollare. He hit the jackpot. His in-laws have probably booked the Four Seasons in Boca Raton. I heard that is the place for upscale weddings, Mashé. I also heard that her mother visits Monte Carlo at least once a year. Forgive me for holding you up like this but I wanted you to know that his third attempt in heading for the altar will be quite an experience. You know I just realized, he probably does not even need to buy them a place to live. Of course, I know he is doing very well on his own. You know what; I bet she has this big fat trust fund. That's what this is all about and I figured it all out by talking to you. Well, I hope the money is going to last because when you marry into families like hers, if the money-well goes dry, so does the marriage. Mashé, are you still there? Of course, I am in the car. I am driving toward the hotel where they have us staying. How I wish you were here with me now, Best Girl. No not yet, I will call her just before we leave for New York. Yes Ma'am, I promise. Take care.

Mashé sat at her desk almost numb. All the while she had been under the impression Eila was making improvements in her behavior, it seemed she still had an emotional attachment to Chandler. After her morning sessions were done, Rhial was going to receive a call from her. As she took her last swallow of homemade potato salad, she reached for her cell phone to call Rhial.

Rhial: Hello. What a surprise, is everything good? What do you mean, maybe? Of course you are fine. My mother and I are combing through a favorite recipe book of hers. Mother, Mashé sends her best. Sure, Mother, I will be back shortly. I am in my bedroom now, tell me about Ms. Wynston. I see your point of view, but Mashé, she is acting normal to me. It would be abnormal if you or I behaved that way, but not for Eila, that is her normal. She has gotten along in life thus far. Mashé, let me say this to you. You have invested too much time in trying to help her as well as understand her. You mean she followed her and watched her shop? Jacksonville University is a great school. You know I was in need of a laugh, so all I can say is, Thank you. Mashé, she is grown. We shall not ever forget our New York private club experience, right? I put my fork in the road right then and there, and you should have too. I am glad I was here to listen to you. She actually did that; she introduced herself to the woman, that was rich. I am here to testify, that was rich. No, I have not heard from her yet. What she will probably do is when she returns to New York she will call and say, "Hi Rhee, I was in your neighborhood, but things got busy for me so I just wanted to say hello anyway, because that is so like her. Yes, Dad is going to stay another two weeks hopefully. Having them both here has been a Godsend. I have been a little self-conscious about this situation I am in, or we are in. You know, while

I was listening to you talking about our girl, I always knew you were the one with the most sense, Eila was the one with the least amount of sense, and me somewhere in-between. You know I like to joke with you, well because while we were growing up you told me I was so serious, and business-like. True, it does go with my profession. Thank you for asking; yes we have had the groundbreaking ceremony and prayerfully this summer, the structures will be completed and then an open-house will be the next step. It shall be a double excitement because my baby will then be in my arms. Of course, Godmother, you will have your turn. Forgive me for asking you again; your five-year plan to start a family, is that definite with you two? I respect your preference and we'll just wait and see, because I believe your husband is going to, how do you say, "shake you down." What about him, he is still staying with his father. As far as I know, her baby is doing fine. I have not observed him buying the baby anything; we share the same banking account, it's hard to say. I am maintaining a low profile for obvious reasons. I would rather not know, Mashé. True, godparents have special privileges. Very well, I will think about it. Once again, don't let her antics get under your skin. Stay busy with your poetry and become famous, promise me. Good. So long for now.

Mashé valued her relationship with Rhial more than she realized. After talking with her she felt better. She returned to her desk and started perusing the materials for her final examinations, because the month of May was on the way. She opened her notebook and began surfing the school's intranet for various forms of literature with references when a news flash popped up. The report was brief, indicating that an engineering executive who was charged with conflict of interest by his former employer, Applied Systems, Inc., was exonerated of the charges by reason that he "turned state's evidence." The lead prosecuting attorney, Chandler Tollare, confirmed that the court's decision stemmed from an actual inside job whereby an unnamed former stockbroker who worked within their retirement plan programs manipulated the stock earnings by doubling their value and depositing that given amount into the defendant's 401K plan. The value was doubled was so that the defendant could pocket the manufactured funds, if you will, and avoid paying federal taxes with the assumption that, these funds would forgo documentation. The exact amount originally estimated was 2.5 million dollars, though further investigation revealed that the amount could likely double. He concluded in reporting that the defendant awarded the individual a certain percentage from the manufactured funds at every payment cycle.

She was astonished and relieved. All the same, her thoughts were spinning with what-ifs. She wanted to call her husband, and then decided not to, and to just wait until they were both warm and cozy in their own little house by nightfall. Humming a favorite tune and referencing her materials online, she received a call on her cell phone.

Mashé: Hello. Good afternoon to you as well. It seems congratulations are in order for you.

Chandler: Thank you very much. It seems that the trapeze act is over. Let me seize the moment since we are on a phone line. This is Chandler Tollare seeking the company of you. Therefore, apprise me of what date and time for our farewell meal?

Mashé: Why so formal? (since Neil will be back east) Next Wednesday night? The restaurant you took me to at the pier.

Chandler: Good choice, and?

Mashé: Let's say, 6:00 PM. Does this suit you?

Chandler: Perfect, I have to head out. There shall be more to share when we meet over dinner. Lastly, a monumental appreciation to you. What great partners we might have been. Until Wednesday, good night.

Mashé: Good night.

Mashé drove her husband to the airport. He looked so regal in his new pinstriped charcoal and blue suit. He was dressed and prepared because once he stepped off the plane he was going directly into the meeting to make his presentation. She was so proud of him. He promised to call her the moment he arrived in Philadelphia. Evin told him that if his material was accepted, it would be an automatic increase in position and salary for him. After the company's legal embarrassment was settled, the ripple effects subdued some. Still, everyone seemed to be looking over their shoulders. It brought a sigh of relief for Mashé because she initially hoped Chandler was going to remove himself from that case but then it became apparent that this presence was warranted, and he came to the rescue.

On her way, she wished it were already Wednesday. Having dinner with an old friend should be her mindset; this was a date she was not looking forward to. She imagined sitting across from him trying to talk on a topic they both liked, as they used to. What was so peculiar about this dinner date was he seemed to have had an edge on the outcome of the case. As soon as she asked for his assistance, he was composed and in control. He actually gambled with his profession on her behalf. One thing she was certain of, he and she both liked to take risks, not the stupid kind, but the kind that put your skills to the test. There were several reasons to be in love with him, and here she was driving on the freeway sorting through them again.

Walking into her classroom she placed several print-out copies on her desk of the works of the famed American poet Langston Hughes. She wanted her to students to consume the originality of his skill for creative writing. One by one they took a copy and she asked one of her students to read a poem, one student selected "Dream." As the student read aloud, Mashé looked out of the window feeling as though the words about missing a lover had been written for her and Chandler.

The week hurried to Wednesday night. She stood in her walk-in closet, considering a smart-looking silk blend suit or to just go basic black, with a three-piece pantsuit. She went with the black pantsuit; it made her look hip. For some, seeing her in this kind of outfit could give them the impression she had dressed out of character. She wore her hair to her shoulders and chose to wear the sterling silver earrings given to her by Neil. So should he ask about them, she could say Neil gave them to her. She grabbed her tiny handbag and keys.

When she arrived at the restaurant, she announced her arrival to the hostess and was immediately told to follow her. She was taken to a private room and there he was looking the way he always looked, Fine!

Chandler: Good evening, you look like a female version of 007.

Mashé: Good evening. I see you do have your wits about you. Why are we here in a private dining room?

Chandler: Mashé, remember, you had your way, now it is time to have my way.

Mashé: It definitely smells good in here. Are we to go Dutch?

Chandler: That's no way to treat a lady. You are my guest. Have a seat and order from the menu, whatever you like. Do you still like sparkling wine?

Mashé: Yes.

Chandler: Mashé, you seem uptight, have I offended you?

Mashé: No, not at all. This is a bizarre event happening here, and I am trying to grasp it. I am fine.

Chandler: I agree. I turned my cell phone off; did you?

Mashé: Mine is in my car.

Chandler: What kind of car are you driving now?

Mashé: A Range Rover Sport. It handles beautifully. One day, my husband and I are going to drive it to Yosemite National Park. I have wanted one for so long. Oh yes, finally, I must thank you for my invitation to York College. I will cherish that experience for the rest of my life.

Chandler: That was your doing; all I did was encourage those students to meet with you at the book fair in New York. You just happen to be very good, short and sweet. Shall we order?

Throughout the evening they started from the very beginning of how they met and what struck them most about one another. Chandler spoke freely and candidly. While she sat there looking at him he looked at her and asked if she would like to dance with him for the last time.

Mashé: Chandler, we rarely danced, why now?

Chandler: Truth be told, it is the only way I can touch you again without being in violation. Now just think about that, being in violation; this would not be our first.

They slow danced to the song, "You're My Angel," recorded by Anita Baker.

Mashé: Chandler, how much did I subject you to, in meeting and talking about this case?

Chandler: Maybe not disbarment but a definite meeting with a legal professional conduct committee, or the equivalent. There are ethical issues they may want to review with me.

Mashé: I apologize, Chandler. I debated with myself several times before calling you. It was a perplexing feeling and I hope I never have that feeling again.

Chandler: From my point of view, it would be beneficial, actually, there are two-fold reasons: as a lawyer to get you out of trouble and then to get you into trouble with me. You see, Mashé, we lawyers can be self-serving. On that last point, getting into trouble with me, I was being facetious.

Mashé: I gathered that earlier, believe me. If the circumstances were reversed, I would do what I could for you, I realized that more than ever now.

Chandler: Shall we form a pact, unbeknownst to anyone else in the world, that when you need me you will call upon me and vice versa, no matter what?

Mashé: I am feeling a little apprehensive about those terms—they are too broad. We need to define the word "need."

Chandler: Here is a hypothetical. It is the future, I have a son or daughter needing help with an English composition assignment, or a letter of intent for a college application. I am too busy, so may they call upon you?

Mashé: They could ask their Mother (oops!). (Chandler stepped back with his hands still around her waist, looking curious) I have to tell you something. We should sit down. Yesterday, I was minding my own business when I received a call from Eila. She was on a professional retreat in Jacksonville, Florida. (Chandler's eyebrows twitched) She told me she happened to meet up briefly with your fiancée, Poeme. She described her as tall and attractive, and that she had been an English major at Jacksonville University, pardon my Freudian slip comment—that story has been with my subconscious, I was concerned about your reaction if I mentioned this to you. We both are very familiar with Eila's ways. Just so you are aware, I told her she was out of order. Your intended may bring their encounter up. All the while, I pondered on how to give you advance notice, and now you know.

Normally his eyes rarely blinked although in this instance, there was quite a bit of blinking. They sat there looking at one another, then looking away. The nuances she felt were odd; his expression was stoic, but Chandler was difficult to read anyway.

Chandler: I have never quite met anyone like Poeme, then again of course no one is comparable to you. Your story got us off course for a minute and your reasoning made sense to me, I bet in the back of your mind, you may not have wanted to tell me ever. Mashé, I appreciate you on so many levels. "What might have been."

Mashé: I know that poem: "When the tides of life turn against you and the current upsets your boat, don't waste those tears on what might have been, just lie on your back and float. Surrender…"—Anonymous.

Unfinished (17)

In the middle of the month of May, students were preparing for finals and some were preparing for graduation. Neil had hit the "ball out of the park" with the Philadelphia office and plans to implement his recommendations were on the table for consideration. It was a Monday night and Mashé was in bed grading papers. She was in her element in a way because her students for the most part had bloomed in grasping the fundamentals of storytelling, particularly in the Romantic Period. To her, integrating the works of popular writers and poets, past and present, allowed them to experience the development of literature from the French Revolution, to human slavery, women's rights, and even the political values of the present. She amused herself as she traditionally began each new semester looking at her students as undeveloped in their perception of literature; they reminded her of unhatched eggs throughout and towards the semester they reached their peak, and they had fully developed (hatched) and displayed their wings of knowledge on paper, classroom presentations, and their finals.

Neil walked in whistling and came straight to their bedroom.

Neil: There she is, my Black Cherry. Whoa! Look at our bed, how will I get to you?

Mashé: Please hold on, finals week is upon us. Hallelujah! I trust you had a good day?

Neil: My day was full with meetings. Here is an update for you. It seems that the ripples have stopped. Evin wants me to maintain my interim status until the end of the fiscal year. Next year we'll know whether or not I am confirmed.

Mashé: Excellent! My husband the Manager. What became of Jamison Leigh?

Neil: I heard he found a job in Atlanta. The person he was supposedly consorting with got the book thrown at him. You know, considering the seriousness of his crime, it is remarkable how when Jamison turned state's evidence, he was able to walk out of court as though nothing happened except for resigning as a part of the deal. No jail time at all. In high profile cases like that, attorneys must know what bottoms to push.

Mashé: Good point. They must keep their eyes on the ball. My wonderment is how do they sleep at night?

Neil: Theirs is a different mindset from you and me. I know it's late, but is my dinner on a plate?

Mashé: The corny poet. Yes. Go look in the oven.

Revisiting that episode, she and Chandler were surely of the same mindset. After she graded her last paper, she began opening her mail. While sorting bills from junk mail, she came across an envelope with the return address of the University of California, Berkeley–English Department and she tore into it. It was a letter from their academic affairs office informing her of a lectureship opening in nineteenth and twentieth century English Literature. She almost rolled off the bed. Years ago she had applied for a post there and was denied, undeterred, she was told to establish herself, interface with others of her profession, and gain notoriety. Mashé had not thought of herself as a bashful person but if she was interested in moving on in higher education, she had better get busy. She ran to the kitchen to tell Neil.

Mashé: I received a letter from UC Berkeley. They have invited me to apply for a lecture post with their English Department. I want to apply.

Neil: That is great news—your published book and speaking engagements are paying off. It looks like your five-year plan remains in effect.

Mashé: (Puzzled) Neil, tell me exactly what you are thinking; we promised to stay open with one another.

Neil: Going to the UC system will increase your activities; you will need to stay above board. Of course, this does not take anything away from the community colleges; however, you know you'll have more expectations placed upon you. You are certainly capable; I was just wondering how far you want to go?

Mashé: Neil, I do not see that far ahead. How far do you want go in the engineering profession?

Neil: Let's not compare ourselves to each other. I asked a sincere question. If you cannot say at this time, I'll accept that.

Mashé: This is a climactic moment for us, isn't it? What I know for certain is that when two people want to conceive, one impregnates the other, they should be in the right mood.

Neil: My mood is receptive and clear. Like you said before, you have plans. I would like to be a father before I am forty.

Mashé: Neil! In five years, you will not be forty.

Neil: (Candid) Close enough to it. Your dinner as always was delicious. I am turning in early, I have to lead a meeting tomorrow, and Evin plans to sit in.

Mashé: Neil…I love the way you put your hands on me.

Neil: I do too. Good night!

🍒 🍒 🍒

During her lunch hour, Mashé went online and applied for the Lecturer position. She was certain she was not the only one who received the announcement but if she was invited in for an interview, she would be ready this time. Her spirits were up about it and if she was offered the post, she would gladly accept. The community college system paid nicely, even though lecturing at a major university paid more, it would not necessarily be about the money but her stature and her exposure. There were women who teach at all levels and they manage to have babies and keep going in their careers. Then it just occurred to her, Neil's mother Zora might be responsible for urging him along. Before she went home tonight, she would call Zora from her cell phone. Reliving their discussion last night periodically interrupted her train of thought while working. She might need to call Tia again, though she would rather not. She paused to justify that Tia did not have children and she wondered what she and her husband had agreed to. On top of it all, Neil, for the first time in their young marriage, refused to make love.

Her last class ended early, so she reached for her cell phone to call Zora.

Zora: Hello, yes, Mashé, how are you? Are you still at the college? I see. Please go right ahead. Yes, Neil and I talked last weekend. Actually, he brought it up, Mashé. It was not me, though we dwelled on the subject for quite some time. He behaved like his normal self. As you have discovered by this time in your relationship as husband and wife, it would take an overwhelming amount of drama or static to rile him up. Though I must say like his father if that happens, you'll need to step back, my dear. I understand, and I am glad you called.

Mashé thought, That was short and sweet, and Zora was very receptive to admitting they discussed it at length, and there is no harm in talking, in a calm manner of course. Even though it was the dinner hour in New York, she decided to call Tia.

Tia: Mashé, I recognized your voice immediately. I am well and you? How was your big lecture tour? Well, you go for it, my sister. No, my husband and I prepare our own meals and it's always been that way. I am always glad to speak with you, let's talk. What is on your mind? Very well…that makes sense. Let me ask you this. Before your wedding day did you two talk about having children? About once or twice is not good enough. Believe it or not, my husband is indifferent about it. We wanted to establish our careers. Langley is a CPA, remember? I thought you knew that? Bear in mind, he came from a large family and living in a quiet house for a time is music to his ears, seriously. Before Langley and I met at the altar, we talked about our expectations and of course there were disagreements, but through our course of discussion we laid out a plan and, I must say, so far so good. Yes, I want children at some point, I love children, and Langley would welcome being a father, just not at this point in time; our professions are at center stage for now. Mashé, all you need to do is make yourself clear. Neil does not look like the argumentative type; then again my association with him has been minimum. You set the plan for five years from now; then that is the plan. All right, so you might shave off two years in case your monetary situation improved, that is good. It sounds to me like you have been very open and flexible. I have to say this to you directly; it's either him or his parents. You called her before you called me, today? Well, you are a direct person, Mashé, you may have put her on the defensive. In my opinion in-laws need to be kept at bay anyway (they laugh). All kidding aside, do not lose any sleep over this. The ball is in his court, and let it stay in his court. You are establishing yourself and now UC Berkeley has notified you of a position opening. I have always been ambitious. Some people are late bloomers, and you know that. I understand that, but being a woman, nature selected or designated you to give birth; the decision has already been made. You and I will look back on this and laugh ourselves silly. People need to leave drama to Broadway, and the movie house, seriously not in everyday life. Furthermore, you are aware that nothing and no one is permanent. Let me know what happens with Cal Berkeley, please do. Good night.

Mashé felt like a shooting star after that conversation. If Neil preferred to deliberate over this topic, that would be his choice, yet inconsistency would not be hers.

There was a note waiting for her when she arrived home, indicating he had gone around the block to check out the new fitness center. She was surprised because he had cautioned her not to make a habit of going there alone and now he had chosen to try it out. If he liked the place then they could go there together. Reconnecting to her conversation with Tia, she scoffed when Tia told her that she and her husband prepared their own dinners. They both worked long hours, and their work hours could flip-flop; nonetheless, Mashé believed a woman should cook for her husband. Maybe in time with a growing family she could encourage him to cook as well. Then again, she could test his skills now, in fact when he comes home, she would pose the question.

After eating her dinner, she went to her studio and began experimenting with her paintbrushes. She started to dabble with various colors and she entitled her creation "Flared Emotions." Just then the front door opened, it was 9:00 PM. and she calculated that it had been maybe three hours since she had arrived home. Neil knocked on her door and entered, pulled up a chair, and sat close to her.

Neil: So you saw my note?

Mashé: Yes, how do you like the fitness center?

Neil: You were right, it has everything. I could become a regular there.

Mashé: What prompted you to go?

Neil: My job. Our division may undergo some changes, all the managers are expected to bring, and I quote, "their innovative ideas." Evin is reminding me of Jamison in a way.

Mashé: So is that a good thing, or…?

Neil: It could be, but I just returned from Philadelphia and my ideas are to be considered and implemented there hopefully. There are some recent unexpected developments and so this should stimulate the pace for us all. There is no doubt that I can keep up. It's all connected to what I call "Jamison-gate." We have to prove that the finagling of one or two has not hampered our quality of production and service—Evin shared the phrase "credibility deficit," which signals we must work diligently to offset any loss of clientele trust.

Mashé: So in essence you went to the fitness center to work off your stress.

Neil: Right, also, I decided to take you up on your recommendation. It's nice and we should go together sometime. (Mashé smiled) What a surprise, I find you in here painting; another project in progress? It looks abstract; can you give me a hint?

Mashé: Yes, I am in here for the same reason you went to the fitness center. I will give you more than a hint. I am calling it "Flared Emotions."

Neil: My baby's stressed! What happened, could this have something to do with last night?

Mashé: Good guess. I was concerned about how we spoke to each other last night, but I am much better now after doing some pros and cons of our situation.

Neil: First of all forgive me for my tone, I meant only to point out that when we do have children, I know they are going to be beautiful, but I want to still be fairly young when it happens—and true, I may have exaggerated just a tad. What were the results of your pros and cons?

Mashé: That we accept the fact that we are both ambitious and we have some goals to reach. When I become a mother, I want to be able to stay at home with our children when they are very young. The hustle and bustle of working and finding suitable day care before they begin regular school is what I would like to avoid. My mother has already assured me that she would be glad to assist in this area. However, I did point out to her that she and my father love to travel, so what happens then? Her response was we will "cross that bridge if and when we come to it." I had to laugh, because I can tell how much she is looking forward to being a grandmother, and enjoying her retirement. We should also ask your mother about day to day babysitting. Actually, I think you should ask her. Trust is uppermost in my mind. I am thinking long-term planning and not short-term planning. I have often thought about lecturing or teaching at a major university in northern California and there is an ample supply of them to choose from. And who's to say that we are destined to stay here? You mentioned that you might be attracted to a position back east. I must confess that it looks like we are not so much competing with each other but that you feel your goals are more significant than mine, since you are a man. On my end, I want both of us to be happy at what we do, now and for the future.

Neil: (Rises from his seat to face her) It's good that you are thinking long term, because once a parent, life will change forever. I have spoken with a few of those at work who have kids and they describe it as going up and down—you just have to be ready for whatever. We both have a healthy outlook about it and that is power for the core. But! I have in no way implied that my career is more important than yours is. I am an "equal opportunity" type of brotha'. However, Mrs. Rollins, I reserve the right to wear the pants in this house and the next house we live in too. (Mashé seemed to appreciate his viewpoints and smiled)

Mashé: All I want is peace between us. We obviously want the same thing, just in different time periods.

Neil: Yes, it looks that way. To comment on your points about moving back east; there is a slim chance of that happening. Do I want the opportunity? Absolutely, yet and still, I prefer to stay in California. I like that smile on your face. Did you eat?

Mashé: I did and yours is in the oven. Neil, how do feel about cooking occasionally?

Neil: Cooking! It is possible. I like to make breakfast, but judging from the look on your face you are referring to dinner. Allow me to practice some and we'll see. I should let you return to your "Flared Emotions" project.

Mashé: Fine. I will be in here for a while.

Neil: I wanted to say one last thing. One day, I will get to the end zone. (He dashed out)

Mashé shook her head and uttered, men like to have the last word.

The next day Neil called Mashé at work and told her that there was an engineers' convention to take place in Chicago and he was asked to attend with a couple of other engineering managers. His flight out was for tomorrow night and he would be there for three days. Since it was finals week, Mashé instantly thought about Rhial and came up with the idea to pay her a visit this coming weekend and maybe into the following week since the semester was essentially done. She wanted to call Eila to suggest that she come too, but quickly withdrew that thought.

When she arrived home, she went straight to the kitchen to prepare their dinner. With one hand she stirred and the other she called Rhial.

Mashé: Rhial, it's me. How are things? The same...I see. We're both doing well and you know what month this is? Yes, which means school is out soon. Neil is going to attend a conference in Chicago this week for three days so I had a brainstorm; I want to visit with you for a few days. Will there be room for me? That is nice, so you do have an extra bedroom. I hope not to crowd you and your parents. I will make flight arrangements for Friday afternoon. Not to worry, a cab ride is fine. It will be like a home away from home vacation. I am excited already. I cannot wait to see you. So long.

Mashé made lemon chicken soup from her mother's recipe; it should hit the spot. Neil came home earlier than usual. He gave his wife a walloping kiss on the lips and asked her what smelled so good. She told him she made some lemon chicken soup. He said he had a phone call to make and would come back. When he did he asked her why her suitcase was sprawled across their bed. After she told him of her plans to visit Rhial, he expressed mixed feelings due to her friend's marital drama and wished she had consulted with him first.

Mashé: I understand your concerns but I am only going to be there for maybe four to five days. What could happen? My obligations with the college are just about completed. You and I are going to keep in touch anyway; you'll know where I am and I'll know where you are.

Neil: That may very well be, but when I come back, you will still be in Florida. That's the other issue I have with this.

Mashé: Neil, only for two days at best. True, which includes that weekend, but time will fly you will see. This is interesting to me because I have been alone in this house when you are away and you can't accept the fact that I am only to be gone for a short while. This scenario never occurred to you?

Neil: I have been away on business trips, only job-related travels. This has nothing to do with your occupation.

Mashé: Neil, you are right it has nothing to do with my occupation but it has everything to do with friendship. Rhial is my friend, not an acquaintance, or a fair weather friend, but a genuine friend. As we agreed, good friends are hard to find and hard to keep. I want to visit with her, that is all.

Neil: Aren't her parents still with her?

Mashé: Yes they are. Her father can only stay a couple of more weeks. Her mother may plan to make back and forth visits as her delivery date approaches.

Neil: Apparently, your mind is made up; though while you are there remember your husband who is also your friend will be here. I am ready for my soup.

They sat across from one another at the table eating without a conversation; this was not normal for them, then Neil made a request.

Neil: (Sober) Would you buy an NBA T-shirt for me while you are there, please? Miami Heat or Orlando Magic, no preference?

Mashé: Of course. I am done here. I will clean up all of this later.

Neil: Where are you headed?

Mashé: To the shower, would you join me?

There was no hesitation on his part. She made sure the water was very warm. They undressed one another, then got wet. It had been nearly a week since the last time they were intimate. Overtaken by his willful caress of her bosom, she was passionately swallowed by his reels and sways. In working their way to the bedroom, Neil's charismatic affection was enduring; by morning they had maneuvered themselves near their media center, clear across the room. As they suddenly woke up, they scrambled to prepare to go to work and laughed almost to a point of hysteria. Mashé applied hair wax and made a suitable bun. Neil was trying to match his shoes with the outfit he selected. It seemed they could be late for work and fortunately for Neil his plane was scheduled to depart later in the evening.

🍒   🍒   🍒

Mashé and Elliot worked past their normal hours to carefully assess and properly grade every final examination. Having accepted an additional course this year meant more students and thus more papers and examinations to grade. At first, she was uncertain as to whether she could handle more of this responsibility; as a result, it proved to be very fulfilling. However, if the offer were made again she would probably decline. As Elliot was leaving she wished him a great summer vacation and then her cell phone rang; it was Neil.

Neil: I want to speak to my wife, the one I was with last night.

Mashé: You are speaking to her. Were you late this morning?

Neil: Would you believe our meeting was cancelled because Evin needed to have an emergency conference call with one of the sister companies in New Mexico. Therefore, I was right on time. How about you?

Mashé: Elliot and I walked in together; all went well here too. Are you at the airport?

Neil: Yes and I am about to board. I love you and I miss you already. Oh and do not forget to take out the trash.

Mashé: Someone thinks he is funny. Have a safe flight and let me know when you land? I love you so much. Bye.

After she cleared her desk and put away her reading materials, she called the airlines and scheduled an overnight flight departure that evening. A second thought came to mind about letting Eila know she was going to visit Rhial and once again she decided against it. Her father's forewarnings convinced her to maintain a good distance and the echoes of her mother's and husband's admonishments were resonating in her mind as well. How could a situation like theirs become any more perplexing? Eila being unaware of this made her feel uncomfortable, but it would pass, it had to. She rather admired Rhial's attitude. In so much as them being best friends, she wasn't going to question or analyze Eila, as if to imply, why?

She has always wanted to help Eila and as a rule, they helped each other; nonetheless, as the cliché stated, "You can't be all things to all people," which clearly included one's friends.

After she spoke with her mother, the guilty cloud formed over her again. Clover agreed with her husband, which was she should be home when he returned from Chicago. Even the explanation she gave her mother made no impression, though she did hit a high note when she told her of the application invitation from UC Berkeley. Eugene picked up on the other phone line also expressing how proud he was of her and stressed that she and Neil were still newlyweds and admonished her to put the world's concerns on hold—that meant friends too. While growing up her parents had instilled their "Southern ways" of rearing her and she definitely planned to do the same with her children.

The flight was completely sold out—a non-stop to Miami Beach, Florida. She actually felt very lucky since she had booked at the last minute. She brought her journal too so she could continue working on her second book of romantic poems; and because it was a five-hour flight, she was encouraged to try for a nap as well. When she finally did doze off, she had a dream of herself, Neil, and Chandler. This time it was not at the spa, but on a secluded island. They seemed to have been lodged in a beachfront house. She was indoors and Neil and Chandler were sitting out front interacting with each other like old friends. There was a beach party going on and the people were boisterous and having a good time of it. Being totally confused as to why they were so friendly, she attempted to speak to them and they did not respond—as though she were invisible. In an instant she awoke to the voice of the flight attendant asking her would she care for refreshments; she declined. She felt flustered because she wanted the dream to continue. She looked out the window and could tell they were nearing their destination because the sun was rising and the sky was reddish in color.

Mashé picked up her baggage and found a taxi. When she arrived at Rhial's home it was close to 8:45 AM. Rhial was at the door.

Rhial: I cannot believe my best girl is here. Come in, my parents are just waking up; they could not believe their ears when I told them you were coming to visit.

Mashé: Your house is you, Rhial, everything is in its place. Rhial, forgive my saying, you are huge; are you sure you are due in June?

Rhial: Yes and I am feeling good too. Something has to go well, right?

Mashé: Listen to me, we are going to talk freely and let the words flow without reservation.

Rhial: I would like that. My parents might want to say a word or two.

Mashé: Why not. Tell me where my room is?

The room was nicely decorated in blue and white. Mashé asked Rhial where the baby's room would be and she said in the master bedroom for a few months. Rhial told her while she was visiting she wanted her to see the neighborhood project under way that she contracted with the city; then Trista walked in.

Trista: Look at you. I heard you are staying with us for a few days. Are you still working at the college?

Mashé: Yes. We just finished with finals week. You could say that "I am free as a bird."

Trista: Time waits for no one, does it? Come downstairs and let's all have some breakfast. Rhial, once again I asked that you avoid unnecessarily taking those stairs; you are in your third trimester. Mashé, help me with her?

Mashé: Absolutely, we are going to be in the living room until it is time to eat.

Rhial brought Mashé up to date. She said that Halvan was working for the city in Community Relations. She knew someone who was hiring in that area. She said they talked by phone at least once a day and they agreed not to quarrel. He maintained his premise that it was better to take the paternity test after their baby was born, and she was leaning in the direction of that mindset.

Mashé: I am not here to judge. I am here as your friend; seriously, it is good to be away for a bit.

Rhial: Is everything good at home?

Mashé: (Sighs) Yes, more or less. The topic of raising a family, it still comes up from time to time, though I believe I have made myself clearer, not only with him but with his mother too.

Rhial: (Emphatic) The man is determined, Mrs. Rollins. How fortunate you are. He wants to be a family man. I admire that so much and you know I respect your preferences, but Mashé, you cannot look the other way and act like you are unaware. "There is an elephant in the room."

Mashé: Rhial, I appreciate his desire to be a father and we are fine on the subject now.

Rhial: I was just thinking, your children are going to be so blessed. All of that love just waiting for them.

Mashé: (Clearing her throat) I want to plan a nice outing for us. Where shall we go?

Rhial: Let's go to Ocean Drive and have lunch, then go from there. Hold on, my cell phone is ringing and guess who it is?

Mashé: No way, Eila? (They laugh)

Rhial: Eila. How is the Big Apple? I am good. Your best friend and I are about to have some breakfast. You can ask her yourself, it's Eila.

Eila: Is this supposed to be a secret? You go to Miami Beach and not give me a clue of what's going on?

Mashé: (Reserved) Hello, Eila. Best Girls do not keep secrets from one another. This is a little visit to check on our pregnant friend.

Eila: How interesting, I asked if she needed me to come and stay with her and I was told not to bother. What type of answer is that?

Mashé: Eila, how did you know I was here, just being curious?

Eila: I called Aunt Lennie. She made me promise to call her more often. So this morning I had a free moment and I called and while we were chatting she asked did I know you were in Florida visiting with Rhial? I was speechless, believe it or not, so I had to call to check up on you two. Are you going shopping or something today?

Mashé: Believe it or not, we were just talking about it when you called. Are you working today?

Eila: Yes, but you know what? There is really nothing significant happening in the office, so I can come down and join you two. What do you think? There is a plane leaving for Miami Beach every hour.

Mashé: (Guarded) It is your call. How is Paul doing? Won't he miss you?

Rhial: My Paul? He is fine. Did I tell you that we are an item, it is official? I just love his spirit, I believe he is the one, ladies, mark my word. He will not mind if I tell him I going to be with my Best Girls. He knows how tight we are. (Rhial and Mashé glanced at one another) Are you still there?

Mashé: Yes, Rhial and I are right here. (Trista announced their breakfast was ready) Listen, we are about to eat breakfast, and I am ravenous.

Eila: Sounds good. I am online now, and I just booked a flight for today at noon. This is going to be exciting. We tried to do this at home but Rhial and Halvan had to leave right away; we can make up for lost time. I should be there by 3:30 PM. Take care.

(Tolson joined them. Trista prepared waffles, Spanish omelets, breakfast sausages, southern potatoes, a beautiful fruit compote, and hot beverages).

Tolson: Mashé, your timing is perfect. Rhial told me you threw an amazing surprise birthday party for your husband, so sorry we missed it. Are you still writing poems?

Mashé: Yes, I am working on my second book now. It will take a while, still, it is my labor of love, it brings me balance.

Tolson: That is phenomenal, Mashé. How is your husband doing? I find it strange him letting you come all this way without him.

Mashé: It seems you men think all alike. He is on a business trip as we speak. He went to Chicago for a conference—it was the perfect excuse for me to come this way and see how Rhial is doing, and I find that she is doing beautifully.

Tolson: How long is his trip?

Mashé: He's supposed to return by Friday evening and I return Sunday morning.

Trista: I guess he knows by now that he married a woman with a mind of her own.

Rhial: (Interjects) He wants kids too. (Mashé looked up at the ceiling)

Trista: My goodness! It appears you married a man who is straightforward.

Mashé: So true. Once we accomplish a few goals we will be well on our way to parenthood.

Tolson: I am happy to hear that you two have a pattern or plan in place. It seemed that Trista and I always knew we would have only one child, and she has become a very industrious young woman.

Tolson went on to express his dissatisfaction with Halvan as a husband and as a man period. Rhial was complacent for much of the time and as Mashé listened, she made a keen perception of Rhial's delicate situation. As a child, Mashé recalled how Rhial was the model child as far as her parents were concerned, particularly her father. Both of Rhial's parents were Civil Service employees for the State of California and they did well. They were one of the few Black families that lived in Berkeley Hills during the early 1980's. When they were little girls, Rhial told Mashé and Eila that she always thought her father would have preferred a son. He had a strict side to himself and her mother seemed to follow suit. Now that Mashé thought back on it that could have been why Rhial's cousin Madison was her escort to the high school prom. Madison had been accepted to Yale University around the same time. He probably scared the neighborhood boys or classmates away who might have been genuinely interested in Rhial because they were not worthy, or good enough in her father's opinion. Tolson spoke about how when he was growing up there was a time for everything and that upstanding men and women knew how to conduct themselves. He continued with his argument for several more minutes and then Trista asked Mashé and Rhial what were their plans for the day. Mashé was so grateful.

Mashé: We want to take it slow. Rhial suggested Ocean Drive to start. We will not make a full day of it. I will keep a watchful eye on her for you.

Trista: Mashé, I have been trying to coax her to come home with us. It does not have to be indefinite, but she and the baby would be surrounded by caring people.

Rhial: Mother, Halvan's parents are caring people too. Perhaps not as caring as you two, but they have called me and asked if I needed any assistance with anything and I told them I would let them know.

Trista: Rhial, that kind of reply was wrong. You should say yes, please stop by.

Tolson: They need to talk some sense into their son, the prince. (There was a giggle here and there)

Rhial: Oh yes, we forgot to mention that Ms. Wynston shall be joining us later this afternoon.

Trista: Was this at the last minute? You only said Mashé was coming here.

Mashé: Mrs. Curry, earlier this morning Aunt Lennie told her that I had flown in to see Rhial, so she wants to make it a threesome.

Tolson: Is she staying here, Rhial? If so, I suppose she could sleep in your den.

Rhial: That should work but, I did not get the indication that she was planning on spending the night; once she arrives we'll find out.

Mashé helped Trista clear away the dishes while Rhial went to her room to lie down. Tolson went to the computer store to buy some new software. This gave Trista the opportunity to convey some details about Rhial and Halvan, which related to her father. She expressed that Rhial wanted an avenue to escape to; she sought freedom from the house she grew up in. She revealed that her father's strict behavior may have affected her self-esteem. There were only certain people allowed in the house, and he disallowed most of those she wanted to connect with.

Mashé: Mrs. Curry, are you saying that Rhial married Halvan as a means to be away from her own father? That is deep. I had the impression that he was very serious while we were children, but I concluded he was acting like an adult. My father was the man of his house too, but nothing close to the way you are describing Mr. Curry. Are you also saying that she is being spiteful too?

Trista: That is my belief. She has spent all of her life trying to live up to his expectations as though she were his little soldier. Now that he is displeased with her current circumstances, she is really not that apologetic, although I have the distinct observation she never meant for things to go this far, involving another women with a baby and all. I also admit that Halvan is not worthy of her, but she married him anyway.

Mashé: Mrs. Curry, would Rhial admit to your impressions?

Trista: I am not sure she would. However, Mashé, I am telling you this because you are close friends, I probably should have been stronger. I feel like I was the ostrich with her head in the sand to some degree. She is smart and independent, a quality like you and Eila have. I am glad you three still stay in touch. It brings me peace of mind.

Mashé: You did not fail your daughter. She loves you and her father very much. There is no way for me to challenge your beliefs and I respect them. I too wondered about her involvement with him but then again any of us can hit a bump in the road. They talked a little while longer revisiting certain events of the past when they heard the doorbell. It was Eila.

Eila: (Calling through the front window) Guess who's here?!

Rhial woke up and rushed to the front. Trista and Mashé walked over to the foyer and Rhial opened the door. The four of them repeatedly shared emotional hugs. Trista, wiping away tears, told them she would let them visit with each other.

Mashé: Are you staying over?

Eila: You know, I pondered on that possibility and it's too soon to say. Let's see how the day goes. Rhial, you are expanding; I am amazed that you can even walk.

Rhial: That is a good one—expanding. Well my baby is growing, Hallelujah. Have you had something to eat?

Eila: Yes I have. Thank you. Let's have a seat and plan our big day together. You two know this was meant to be, us being together right here and right now.

Mashé: There must have been something telepathic going on for sure.

Eila: To let you know how smart I am, I rented a car, because I know at this point in time, Rhial you are probably not driving.

Rhial: Actually, I still do, my doctor is quite liberal. She said that whatever my routine was before I was expecting, I could still do in moderation while I am expecting.

Mashé: That makes sense.

Rhial: Yes, Mashé, you keep that in mind for when your time comes.

They agreed that for the sake of time to take Eila up on her offer to drive them around. They went to Ocean Drive and found a popular café to have a late lunch. Although it was crowded, they still managed to have a table to themselves outside. After an hour of talking about random things, Eila being Eila had to bring Halvan up.

Eila: Please forgive me. I am not trying to upset you. However, are you still insisting that Halvan take that paternity test?

Rhial: Of course and as I said he wants to wait until our baby is born.

Eila: Have you listened to yourself talk? Rhial you need to go from passive to assertive. He knows you won't rock the boat. Sweetheart, it is time to tip that boat over, I am so serious right now.

Mashé: (Concerned) I am in slight agreement with you; then again there should not be any outside intervention between husband and wife—they have to work it at their pace.

Eila: Rhial, do you agree with her?

Rhial: I agree with both of you, but I am in no position to exert force.

Eila: Well it is your lucky day, my Best Girl. I want to help you.

Mashé: (Stern)) Eila, please do not contact Halvan, leave him alone.

Eila: I am. I want to contact her.

Mashé and Rhial in unison: Her!

Eila: Remember you said you did not know her name but you knew of her. I think we should go find her and ask her politely to tell the truth, be honest, and bring all of this drama to closure.

Rhial: He has been very protective of her.

Eila: Exactly, and why is that, we should find out. Rhial, do you know where she lives?

Rhial: Yes, Halvan finally revealed that much information to me.

Eila: Do you have the address with you?

Rhial: I should have it in my purse somewhere. I remember I wrote it on my note pad. I found it.

Eila: Good. Let's go pay her a visit. You can stay in the car, I shall represent you, leave it to me.

Mashé was beginning to feel suspicious. The woman lived close to Little Havana. Eila parked the car and walked straight to the front door. A young woman answered and Mashé and Rhial were poking their heads out of the car window to observe as much as they could. Then Eila went inside with the door closed. Rhial and Mashé were so concerned for Eila, how could they allow this to happen, they said to one another. They heard some loud voices and then a baby crying and then it was silent again. Moments later Eila walked out with an interesting smile on her face, the kind of smile one could not remove even with dynamite. She got into the car and gave a sheet of paper to Rhial to read. As she read it Rhial suddenly began crying. The letter was essentially an affidavit affirming that the baby she gave birth to was mistakenly referenced as Halvan Sanders' biological child. She promised to avoid any further contact with him or any persons related or associated with him. Then Eila quickly started the engine and they took off. Mashé was in awe. She asked Eila what she told that woman and did she threaten her. Eila simply replied that she indicated that she represented Mrs. Halvan Sanders and wanted to clear things up once and for all. She said the interpretation the woman made was of her own choosing. She never said she was her legal counsel, the word used was "represented." That was really all she needed to say in order to put a little fear in her. Mashé replied that she obviously did that. Eila added that they needed to have the affidavit notarized as soon as possible. Rhial was highly emotional and was very appreciative of what just happened; then without warning she began having contractions.

Mashé: Rhial, are you in labor?! My goodness, Eila, look what you did!

Eila: What should we do?

Mashé: Find the nearest hospital and keep your eyes on the road. Rhial, come on, breathe slowly; it's going to be fine, we're here for you, your Best Girls.

It wasn't long before Rhial had given birth to a seven pound, twelve ounce boy. Rhial named him Halvan Sanders, Jr. He was a healthy baby with a very strong voice. Eila did find the hospital but it was after Rhial delivered. Mashé had involuntarily appointed herself as mid-wife, an experience she would never forget.

When she returned home she was called in for an interview at University of California Berkeley for the Lectureship post; she was offered the job and she accepted it. Neil was offered Evin's position as head of the entire Division and he accepted it. Since both of them received promotions, they gladly accepted the monetary offer from his parents as a down payment on their dream house located in Emeryville, California. It had four bedrooms and a great looking backyard for kids and pets to play in. In less than two years Mashé found herself barefoot and pregnant. Rhial and Halvan were once again living under the same roof with their son, Halvan, Jr. Eila Wynston married Paul Desmond and they remained residents of New York City, though this time, in a luxury Upper Manhattan condominium that his family owned.

Epiphany (18)

As dusk was making its way in, she had dozed off a few more times. The wind subsided and that was good. She had reached the end of this particular photo album. How she was able to relive all of those special situations and events with her Best Girls was an exceptional gift. Perhaps she should hire a ghostwriter to help her tell the stories; it would probably sell well, because all of those events were real and she has the pictures to prove it. She has to give them credit for ushering her into every chapter of her long life.

Here it is the year 2055. She looks up and it registers that she is 84 years old today. She says, "That's right, it is June now." Neil lived to be 89, and how she missed him. There are still a few family members that come in and out of her life. Whenever she thinks of someone but cannot call out their name she refers back to her chronicle of pictures; then when she locates that person's picture she is able to make the connection. Since it is her birthday, she wonders if she was going to have any cake. Given that her beachfront house is eerily quiet she will just use her vivid imagination, which she is hanging onto so dearly. She always liked strawberries with rich whipped cream; now that would be sweet enough for her.

Many of those she has come to know over the years are rarely heard from anymore, and that's the way life is, she reasons. She somehow lost contact with Eila and Rhial a few short years ago. However, she imagines them still living somewhere on God's green earth. Just then, she hears a door open from the inside. Lou is barking and twirling, so it must be someone he knows. It is Mashé's grandchildren, two girls, Nela and Doria. Mashé gave Neil twin boys, and they each have one daughter.

Nela: Grandma, Happy Birthday. Did you forget we were coming?

Doria: I have your favorite cake. You are here all alone now and it's time for you to come and live with one of us.

Mashé: But I enjoy the ocean. It makes everything out here so fresh.

Doria: We have a birthday surprise for you. Now, close your eyes and no peeking, okay?

She could hear slow moving footsteps. Whatever is going on, Lou is barking so loudly it is beginning to hurt her 84-year-old ears.

Nela: Now open your eyes, Grandma.

There stands before her a face she recognizes immediately; searching through the photo album would not be necessary. It is Chandler Tollare. He was significantly older though still handsome. They pull up a chair for him and seat him right next to her. She is in overjoyed amazement. She asks Nela and Doria where they found him and they say he found them. He and his son, Chandler, Jr., also an attorney, came across an old gallery exhibiting some of her oil paintings and he asked the proprietor where she could be reached. They called her and here he is. Mashé asked her granddaughter Nela to take a picture of them sitting on her deck.

Chandler asked her was she living alone, she said yes, and then he said, you were.

CPSIA information can be obtained
at www.ICGtesting.com
Printed in the USA
FSHW02n1939180918
52388FS